LANKA'S PRINCESS

Kavita Kané is the best-selling author of *Karna's Wife: The Outcast's Queen*, *Sita's Sister* and *Menaka's Choice*. She started her career as a journalist and is now a full-time novelist. She is a post-graduate in English literature and mass-communications and a self-confessed aficionado of theatre and cinema. Married to a mariner, she is a mother to two daughters and currently lives in Pune with Chic, the friendly Spaniel and Cotton, the unfriendly cat.

LANKA'S PRINCESS

KAVITA KANÉ

RUPA

Published by
Rupa Publications India Pvt. Ltd 2017
7/16, Ansari Road, Daryaganj
New Delhi 110002

Sales Centres:

Allahabad Bengaluru Chennai
Hyderabad Jaipur Kathmandu
Kolkata Mumbai

ISBN: 978-81-291-4451-5

Thirteenth impression 2022

15 14 13

Printed at Yash Printographics, Noida

To my Aaji

Loved by all as Kaki aaji.
And the one who first introduced me to Surpanakha
and the later stories to follow.

Miss you.

Contents

Prologue:
Kubja

He spotted her immediately. He could not tear his eyes away from her distant figure. Leaning against a roadside tree, she stood out in the thronging crowd on the streets of Mathura. Krishna stared at her for a long, thoughtful minute before he started to move towards her.

'Where are you going?' asked Balram, perplexed. He looked at his younger brother, a darker version of himself. 'We will be late. King Kamsa is waiting to meet us at his palace.'

'Just a moment...' replied Krishna, his eyes still seeking the woman. She was still standing near the tree, watching the bustling crowd around her, as if enjoying the street scene. She ignored the young street urchins giggling at her. One attempted to throw a stone at her.

She looked distinctly surprised as she saw a young, dark, handsome boy approach her. He could not be more than seventeen, his face boyish, with a wide, warm smile but there was a quaint air of maturity about him. It was his eyes—smiling yet mocking in their solemnity. He looked eerily familiar but she could not place him. Not that she could have forgotten such a good-looking face, she reflected, feeling a strange emotion rise within her.

'Do you live here?' asked Krishna politely, smiling.

She was taken aback at the unabashed familiarity of his question.

'Do I know you?' she asked coldly instead, but not looking away. The boy had an immediate amiability about him: you could not help but like him.

'No, I am a stranger here,' he replied cheerfully. 'I have just arrived from Gokul and am on my way to the king's palace.'

She gave a start at the mention of King Kamsa.

'You are to meet the king?' she asked curiously.

'Yes,' he said briefly, almost cryptic. 'I am Krishna,' he flashed his deep smile again.

'I am Trivakra,' she said. 'But I am known as Kubja, the hunchback,' she added tonelessly.

'So I noticed,' smiled Krishna looking long at the young girl— bent almost double, her hands and feet gnarled, her face looked aged, stamped with a lifelong pain.

Kubja would have otherwise bristled. But she again felt a faint stirring of...what? Why did this young man make her feel like a woman and not an ugly hunchback which she was cursed to be? She turned her face away, as if to end their conversation.

'You seem to have the most fragrant sandalwood in the city!' he commented, looking at the array of sandalwood pastes around her.

Her eyes flared with animation. She nodded brightly.

'Can I have some, please?' he said.

'How much do you want to buy?'

'No, could you apply that paste on me. Please?' he asked, his smile reaching his eyes, which softened them with a certain tenderness.

Kubja swallowed, staring at him blankly. 'That paste out there in the bowl,' he urged, pointing to the brass container. 'Could you please apply some on my forehead? It's really very hot. Some sandal paste would be cooling!'

He lowered his head so that she could follow his request.

'It's meant for the king!' she snapped. 'I have to take it to him now.'

'Just a little?' he begged, his winning smile not slackening.

Kubja hesitated. 'I am a maidservant,' she said in a low tone. 'A hunchback. A pariah.'

'Never mind, but your sandalwood is heavenly!' he dismissed airily, thrusting his face closer.

She quickly dipped her hand in the paste and raised it to his face, gazing straight into his twinkling eyes, smearing his forehead tentatively, her hands shaking.

She heard him sigh in satisfaction.

'It *is* cool!' he exclaimed, swiftly stretching out his well-muscled arms in front of him so that she could apply some of the paste there as well. She was surprised that she obliged him, not unwillingly. She felt a cold shiver of pleasure run through her as her calloused fingers touched his skin. She could not refuse him, and she was strangely drawn to this handsome stranger.

'Gratitude!' grinned the man. 'I feel like a new man now!'

Kubja blushed. 'Yes, my sandalwood is the best in town.'

'I'll come back to you once I am done with the king,' he said. 'Where do you stay?'

Overwhelmed, she pointed a shaking, twisted finger at the house across the road.

'I'll meet you soon. I promise!' he smiled, waving at her.

She watched him walk down the street, away from her, not believing his words which were still floating back in her mind.

She sighed. She knew she would not see him ever again.

It was almost a fortnight later, the sky had dusked to a deep purple, when she heard a knock on the door. Kubja frowned. *Who could it be? Certainly not some call from the palace. After all, King Kamsa is dead now.* The city was rife with rumours and jubilation that he had been killed by his nephew, Krishna. The name sent a shiver through her again. Was he that young man she had met on the street some days back?

She heard the knock again. It was louder and more persistent.

Kubja hobbled to the door, opening it impatiently. She was greeted with an unexpected sight and a jovial voice.

'I said I would come back!' said the young, handsome man,

standing with his arms akimbo.

Krishna!

Before she could recover her breath and senses, he had stepped inside her small room.

'What do you want?' she spluttered.

'You.'

Kubja gasped, her face drained of colour. 'I have heard you are a kind man, sir. Don't make fun of me so cruelly!' she said angrily, tears of hurt shining in her sullen eyes. 'You are a prince, a hero. A handsome young man. What does he want with a poor, ugly hunchback like me? Why are you here?'

'To make you happy. You have suffered enough, my dear,' he said.

The gentleness in his voice hurt her. Kubja winced, her eyes filling with sudden tears, recalling each moment of her wretched life—the taunts, the stones pelted at her, the wicked sniggers, the contempt on peoples' faces. Her very sight made them loathe her.

'Even the name given to you is cruel—Trivakra, disjointed at three places,' he murmured touching her lightly under her chin and raising her tear-streaked face to his. She felt a tremor at his touch.

'Please don't mock me,' she whispered.

'How many saw the beauty behind this ugliness?' he asked gently.

'Beauty?' she drew back, her face confused.

'Yes, you are supposed to be kind and selfless, and that's what I have heard,' said Krishna.

'None!' she whimpered. 'I have been living a life of hell. Even the dogs and kids bark at me whenever I pass them... What did I do to lead such a cursed life?'

'No more,' he assured her, pressing her chin and touching her feet with his toes. She felt a crackle of heat flash through her, from toe to head, the heaviness of the hump suddenly easing, the spine slowly straightening, pulling her up to make her stand tall and willowy. She stared at her arms, her skin was creamy and glowing. She caught her reflection in the mirror. She was lovely. She looked down at her body. It was not twisted, but buxom in its beauty with full, firm breasts, a slender waist and flaring hips over slim, long legs.

'What did you do?' she cried hoarsely.

'You made me a new man with your sandal paste, remember? I made you a new woman!' he smiled.

'You are laughing at me!' she cried, her lips trembling. '*Who* are you?'

'Don't you remember?' he asked softly. 'I am the one who turned you down once. I am that same man. Ram then, now Krishna.'

Kubja shook her head frantically. 'Ram?'

'Yes. I come for you Kubja, for the grave misdeed I committed in my last life, where you were Surpanakha in your previous birth. And I was Ram.'

She stared at him transfixed, speechless. 'You were born a beautiful princess Meenakshi, the sister of the asura king Ravan, but your wickedness turned you into a monster—Surpanakha, the woman as hard as nails...' he explained. 'Do you remember me? The man who rejected you and in your wrath you took a terrible revenge on me, my wife Sita and my brother Lakshman...?'

'What did I do so terrible then that I had to lead this life in misery?' cried Kubja, terrified.

Krishna smiled, taking her trembling hand in his. Kubja felt a strange sense of fulfilment.

'Well, allow me to tell you your story...'

She

'*I*t's a girl!'

Kaikesi heard the words as the last wave of pain and relief. *It was a daughter, not a son,* her heart sank, her aspirations drowning in a flood of disappointment and easy tears.

Her husband frowned.

'Why are you crying?' he chided. 'We have three sons; a daughter is what we needed!' he smiled encouragingly, wiping his tears.

Vishravas would not understand. She needed sons to consolidate what she had dreamt of: an asura empire with her sons as the rulers of the three worlds; and Lanka, their lost golden city as their capital. She sighed, shutting her eyes to remember the golden glory of her former home. Tall and imperious, the golden towers piercing the sky in all its arrogance. So lavish and luxurious and powerful, the grandest palace, the loveliest, the richest city the world had ever seen. Even the gods in Heaven had been envious.... *Lanka, my lost home,* Kaikesi grimaced. Her father had been forced to surrender to Vishnu to give up his crown, throne and the kingdom. *Vishnu had cleverly installed Kuber, the God of Wealth as its new king,* she suppressed an angry sigh. Kuber, the son of Rishi Vishravas, grandson of the famous Rishi Pulastya and the great-grandson of Brahma himself. *That is why I married Vishravas,* reminisced Kaikesi grimly, *so that I could beget the best progeny, the most powerful and the most wise to win back what we have lost.*

But her husband, that gullible Rishi that he was, remained blissfully ignorant of her intent; he was an uxorious man, too much in love with her to ever doubt her of ill-intents. He would never know that her parents, the erstwhile asura king, Sumali and mother Taraka had conspired on a chance meeting of their beautiful daughter Kaikesi with him. Rishi, who although was married to Ilavida and the father of a young Kuber, had fallen in love so deeply with her that he left his family and married her, facing opposition from his father, his grandfather Brahma and his father-in-law Rishi Bharadwaj. Kaikesi had had three sons from him and was hoping for a fourth, but it turned out to be a daughter... Kaikesi looked down at the baby and could not help cringing or quench the well of bitterness. *This girl has cheated me of my plans*, she thought angrily, a faint stirring of unease making her more restless.

'And she's as pretty as you, though a shade darker!' mentioned Vishravas, wistfully. She did not miss that hesitance, as he gently placed the bawling baby in her arms. Kaikesi's thin, dusky face was classically beautiful, her big, lustrous eyes looking directly at him, as she took the baby hesitantly. The infant girl cried louder.

'Why is she crying so much?' she sighed with rising exasperation.

'Hold her closer. She needs your warmth,' said Vishravas.

Kaikesi tried to steady her, but the baby wriggled harder, stiffening in rigid discomfort.

'Is she unwell?' asked Kaikesi worriedly.

'No,' frowned Vishravas. 'She seems perfectly healthy.'

'But then why is she so crabby? Her face is red with the crying...' she frowned, suddenly feeling spent. 'Take her, Vishravas, I can't handle her. I need to rest.'

'But she has to be with you. Make her sleep by your side,' he suggested. The baby suddenly quietened, the eyes tightly shut, the tears squeezing out. 'And nurse her if she cries again.'

'She hardly looks beautiful or like me. In fact, she's quite ugly!' said Kaikesi, staring at the sleeping child, a frown deepening on her lovely face. 'She's scrawny and much darker than me!'

'Yes, she's dark,' smiled Vishravas, and again she heard the doubt in his voice. 'But she's a newborn and all babies can't be as bonny as Kumbha or fair as Ravan or Vibhishan!'

Kaikesi flushed guiltily. 'Yes, because of me!' she said bitterly. 'You had said that each of our children will be remarkable, that each shall change the future of our race, our family. How is this dark monkey going to bring us good fortune? No one will ever marry her!' *There were more chances that this little girl would not get married because of her asura blood*, thought Vishravas dryly, *and not her looks. But then, I dared and deigned to fall in love and marry an asura girl*, he sighed. His decision had prompted a lot of unpleasantness: a married rishi marrying the rakshas princess, almost triggering a new war—in his family and amongst the devas as well. None had been pleased, all were furious at his temerity—some called it his stupidity—and worse, the of the consequences.

'Your children from her will be asuras, never Brahmans, remember that!' his angry father had warned him. 'But I don't need to say that—you will be reminded of it each and every day from now on, as your children grow!'

He looked down at his sleeping daughter, the tears having dried on her soft, dusky cheeks. He suddenly felt sorry for the little bundle with her closed, swollen eyes and tiny, long fingers with sharp nails, feisty and fierce, born fighting against the expectations of the world. 'She's our only daughter. This little girl of ours shall wrought what our sons will never be able to do!' he predicted softly.

'What? Be the only ugly spinster in the asura kingdom or the rishi community?' scoffed Kaikesi.

'I married you, didn't I?' he retorted, annoyed and unable to resist the barb.

'I *made* you marry me!' she snorted dismissively. 'You were so in love with me that you left your first wife and your son for me!' she riposted, with two bright spots forming on her high, delicate cheekbones. 'Not that your son does not forget to remind both of us of that deed!'

Vishravas floundered, at a loss with words when it came to his eldest son Kuber. Kaikesi hated him and Kuber did not hide his contempt for her either, even after so many years. Kaikesi shrugged and turned her attention to the doorway of her chamber. 'Why are we quarrelling because of this child? Let the boys in. They must be waiting to see their little sister.'

As on cue, three boys noisily rushed into the room, surrounding the cradle to have a glimpse of the baby. But the sleeping girl remained unfazed and did not wake from her ill-sought slumber.

'She's tiny!!!' boomed Kumbhakarna, his voice and size defying his age of six.

'She cannot be as fat as you, Kumbha! Though she is as dark!' laughed his brother Ravan, two years older than him, but his trim litheness made him seem the younger one. His fair, handsome face was screwed in genuine amusement.

'But yes, she's as tiny as our little dwarf here,' he added, nudging his youngest brother

Vibhishan, whose round, fair face remained unfazed by the nasty remark; he was very fascinated by the small, sleeping form of his baby sister.

'He might be small, but at the age of four he has more brains than the two of you put together!' snapped Vishravas, casting a quelling glance at his eldest son.

'Ravan's just teasing!' piped in Kaikesi. 'And he's a clever boy too!' she said defensively.

'Yes, way too clever! He's more interested in weapons than the Vedas!' her husband remarked disparagingly.

As if susceptible to the mounting tension in the room, the baby's eyes flew open, her stare sharp and steady, looking at each one of her brothers carefully.

'Ma, what lovely eyes—just like Ravan's—like golden drops!' lisped Vibhishan, clutching his mother's hand excitedly. 'And see how she's staring at me!!'

Kaikesi glanced at her daughter a little longer. She was

looking up at her, unblinking and unsmiling, her eyes huge and honeyed, like twin golden orbs shining against her deep mahogany skin.

'Meenakshi,' breathed Vishravas. 'Her eyes are as golden and graceful as a fish's. That would be a lovely name for her, don't you think, Kaikesi?'

Kaikesi was staring at the baby's abnormally long nails. They were almost like claws, curved and somewhat curling, with a prominent moon-shaped crescent. *Needs to be clipped and quick*, she thought. All she could think of was the name Chandranakha for her daughter.

✍

'The neighbours have been complaining bitterly. Why did you pick up a fight again, Meenakshi?'

Kaikesi did not wait for her daughter to answer, she knew it. The five-year-old stood belligerently, her hazel eyes glittering a vicious gold, her thick, frizzy hair unkempt, tangled in unruly locks, her knees bleeding, and her arms scratched.

'I saved Vibhishan!!' was all that the girl muttered mutinously, for she knew her mother would not understand or believe whatever explanation she provided.

'Vibhishan is a boy, and he's older to you. He doesn't need your protection!' snapped Kaikesi, checking the bruises on her son's arms and legs. She turned to the snivelling, nine-year-old boy, with his round face and big ears, the fair, delicate skin broken and bruised all over his skinny frame.

'You wimp, can't you fight for yourself? You allow your younger sister to come to your help each time? Where was Ravan?' she demanded, glaring at Meenakshi.

'He's never with us. He and Kumbha were duelling with maces....'

Kaikesi's face brightened. 'They were, were they? Then why didn't you join them, you sissy, instead of tagging round with your baby sister?!' she gave the tearful Vibhishan a hard shake.

Vishravas decided to intervene.

'Stop it, Kaikesi! He was studying the first chapters of the Upanishads while the other two boys scampered away to play the fool!' he interrupted.

Vishravas usually looked benign but now his face was mottled red with annoyance. Rotund, balding, with grey wisps of hair which softened his florid complexion, he looked older than his fifty years.

He looked at Meenakshi, frowning. 'Why did you interrupt Vibhishan while he was studying?' he barked. 'You don't like to study yourself and don't allow him to study either, you vagabond!'

Meenakshi's eyes smarted with tears. She could suffer her mother's severest beatings but strangely, she could never endure her father's smallest reprimand. He had stood up for Vibhishan again, almost indifferent to her bleeding bruises.

'Why do you pick on everyone except your precious Vibhishan?' Kaikesi broke in furiously. 'Practicing the mace is not fooling around! You always cover up for Vibhishan—that's why he's still such a baby!'

Vishravas shook his head, his lips pursed angrily. 'As do you with Ravan! That boy is thirteen and still irresponsible, more interested in picking fights or brandishing spear and sword rather than sitting down and mastering the Vedas.'

Kaikesi straightened her shoulders indignantly.

'He's so bright, he has already mastered all the Vedas and the Upanishads, but you are too myopic to recognize the true potential of your child. He's bored, and he needs to vent out his energy...'

'He needs to practice, yes, and he knows his Vedas but is too smug to glean the real knowledge from it. He doesn't register what he has learnt because he's so full of himself!'

Meenakshi looked from one angry parent to another. They were fighting again over their respective favourites—Ravan and Vibhishan. She touched her swollen arm tenderly. It still hurt. But what hurt her more was that neither of them had noticed the angry welt where she had been hit by Som, the big bully who had teased Vibhishan. Her eyes reddened with checked tears. She stomped away, running outside, away from the angry voices inside the house and the loud, angry voice screaming in her own mind.

She stopped in her tracks. What she saw made her blood freeze. Maya, her pet lamb was lying on the ground, her neck twisted at an odd angle, the small pink tongue sticking out, thick and swollen, the eyes vacant and bulging. Meenakshi screamed, rushing to her side, the tears now flowing unrestrained and uncomprehending. *What had happened to Maya*, she thought urgently. She gently lifted her. Maya looked limp and through the thick haze of her coursing tears, it dawned on Meenakshi that Maya was dead. She broke down, violent whimpers shaking her slight body.

'Ravan killed your pet!' announced Som, with devilish glee.

Meenakshi stiffened, her sobs abruptly stemmed, her tearful eyes looked accusingly at her eldest brother. Right then, he looked neither contrite nor uncomfortable. He stared back at her defiantly from his golden, beady eyes, his fair skin stained with a flush at her protracted glare.

'You should have trained your pet, Meenu,' Ravan growled. 'She ambled in and chomped away all the medicinal plants I had planted for the rishis in the ashram. Can't you look after your silly goat?'

Kumbhakarna looked visibly horrified at his brother's uncalled for violence.

'But you didn't have to kill Meenu's lamb. She was her pet!' he intervened, his fat face ashen. 'Why can't you rein in your temper, brother? You go crazy when you get angry! Even I could not wrestle you away from the poor animal, you had gone berserk!'

'She ruined months of effort and patience, that dumb animal!' shouted Ravan, flushed, his amber eyes blazing golden.

Meenakshi felt her throat going dry, feeling the heat of fury coiling slowly inside her. Grief was forgotten, replaced swiftly by a blazing rage. Her brother had killed her pet. She stared unseeingly at the listless body. *He had strangled Maya with his bare hands.* Meenakashi felt her own hand twitch and like a cat sprang on the unsuspecting Ravan, digging her nails into the tender flesh of his neck, her teeth bared in apoplectic frenzy. Ravan gave a cry of surprise, curdling into a scream of pain, one arm protecting his face against her clawing fingers, the other trying to wrench her off. But she clung on, ripping her sharp nails unto any exposed flesh, tearing the skin, sinking deeper to gouge. Vibhishan was too scared to move, shocked speechless. The heavy but nimble-footed Kumbhakarna was quicker. He caught hold of his sister's wrists and pulled her off Ravan, now bleeding profusely, shaken but as furious as his little sister.

'You ugly wretch!' he snarled raising his arm to hit her, but Kumbhakarna stopped him, forcing himself between his warring siblings.

'Ravan, stop, she's a kid! Let her go…! Vibhishan, take your sister inside!!'

'Surpanakha, that's what she is. Not Chandranakha as Mother calls her, but a witch with long, sharp claws. Next time I'll break your bloody arm, Surpanakha!!'

The word echoed in her ears. Surpanakha. Meenakashi looked down at her bloodied nails, some of her brother's skin still hanging loose on them. *If this could protect me, then well, I am Surpanakha*, she thought with perverse pleasure.

'No, you won't hurt her or anyone else!!' cracked a soft voice, yet hard and brittle. It was Vishravas, his eyes furious.

'How dare you??' he shouted, his face mottled red with fury.

He did not wait for the answer, slapping his son hard across the face. There was a short, ringing sound, settling the bloody ruckus in sudden silence.

'How dare you resort to violence in my ashram? You are my son, you are supposed to be the propagator of peace but all you are capable of is senseless squabbles! Get out and don't show your face till you are remorseful of your actions.'

Ravan turned on his heel but not before throwing his sister a last, glowering look. Kaikesi tried to intervene but a scathing look from her incensed husband, cut off any word of protest. Vishravas threw his wife a look of open disgust and walked off. Kaikesi fumed silently, glaring at the cause of the friction. Meenakshi was looking defiant, almost triumphant that her father had reprimanded her brother in public. If she knew her brother well, the words must have hurt him more than the slap. Ravan could never endure humiliation and his father had insulted him in front of everyone in the ashram. Her small smile was quickly wiped off and the happy thought dashed down with the hard slap she saw coming from her mother's raised arm.

'You dared to attack your elder brother, you wildcat!' she heard her mother scream, slapping her hard again. 'Which sister does that?'

Her cheeks burned with anger, the pain smarting, livid, red welts appearing quickly on her bruised face.

Kumbhakarna tried to intervene. 'Mother, please, Meenu is already bleeding badly. Let me tend to her wounds...'

'You fat oaf, go after Ravan and bring him back!' cried Kaikesi, holding Meenakshi tight by her wrist, the fingers digging into her flesh. But Meenakshi did not utter a single whimper, the shooting pain giving her sudden strength to battle again.

'Why can you not behave like a girl? Always fighting and squabbling, hitting boys and throwing stones and scratching the eyes out of anyone who provokes you. Surpanakha, that's the right name for you, you monster!'

'Yes, I am a monster!' screeched Meenakshi, her eyes flashing, baring her claws at her mother. 'See them? If anyone hurts me, I shall hurt them with these!! I am Surpanakha!' Her high-pitched voice was filled with rage. Her nails glinted in the sunlight. A new sensation crawled up Kaikesi's spine—icy cold fear. She stepped back in alarm at the pure hate on the little girl's puckered face, the words dying in her throat. Was her daughter a monster?

Asuras

✣

$\mathcal{M}$eenakshi shifted uneasily. She was sitting cross-legged for more than an hour and her feet were painfully cramped.

'You are fiddling again!' scolded Vishravas sharply. 'And you are distracting Vibhishan as well. Go and stand under that tree, and next time there's no need for you to attend these classes. You have no head or heart for it! You are nine but I am afraid, you won't get through even a five-year-old's level!'

Meenakshi felt her eyes sting, blinking hard, but her heart burst into ready tears. She had disappointed her father again. He was teaching them Vedic math but she had soon got bored, her mind too boggled with the intricate calculation. Vibhishan had been quick on the uptake, solving all the problems with swift aplomb. He displayed an astonishing talent for figures at an early age. He threw her a slightly superior look and scribbled away victoriously, his big ears cocked in concentration. Lips quavering, Meenakshi slunk away in the hot noon sunshine, feeling miserable all over again.

The news that her grandparents Sumali and Taraka were coming to visit them brightened up Meenakshi considerably. *It would make up for the past bad week*, she thought, perking up. It had been a hard week as usual: her mother had scolded her all through the days; and each time, her father had not checked his wife's tirade, but instead had thrown her a look of acute disappointment, sighing and shaking his head. He did not rush to her defence nor did he draw her close to comfort her, which he often did with Vibhishan, although he was older. Her brother would grin at her surreptitiously, his smile sugary, and there was always in his plump figure, always bowing to his father, something of a child-like obsequiousness which used to incense her further.

It had been Kumbhakarna who had comforted her with a sympathetic look. The tall, lumbering, overweight Kumbha was too kind-hearted: he could not hurt anyone. For his huge bulk and big girth and mighty arms, he was a gentle giant, always kind to her, the only one who saw her as the youngest member of the family, his kid sister that she was, protecting her from Ravan's moody tantrums or their mother's sharp tongue. As usual, he was shabbily dressed in a limp, rough dhoti and there were food stains on his mouth and angavastra for he was a gross eater. But he was her saviour.

Ravan, as always, ignored her, barely aware that she existed, busy with either his studies or his adventurous exploits. He barely tolerated her, sweeping her with an impatient look whenever she was near. He had rechristened her Surpanakha after that fateful assault and that name had stuck. Everyone teased her with that hateful name and she knew Ravan derived a vicarious glee each time he saw how the name affected her when it was uttered. But she did catch a grudging, swift look of appreciation each time she handled a fight or returned home bruised, but her ego intact.

'You are one hellcat!' he would comment. 'As always. Don't let it go.'

Or was it plain wariness of her violent temper? He was now more careful with her, if not far more kindly. It was as if they now shared a new bond in blood and gore.

Vibhishan conveniently wrapped himself in his cocoon of knowledge and thoughts, oblivious to what was happening around him. Kumbha called it daydreaming: Meenaskhi considered him weird and silly, though he was five years older to her. But for Kumbha, she found both her other brothers annoyingly supercilious and superior. Strangely, though Vibhishan and Ravan were so different, they were unusually alike: both submerged in their world of self-absorption.

Meenakshi glimpsed the approaching chariot with her grandparents and her uncles Subahu and Mareech. She saw the chariot stop and her uncles helping their parents climb down. Meenakshi forgot her punishment and rushed towards the gate. Her uncles were both so tall, dark and handsome. *And kind*, she thought, as Mareech gifted her a huge basket of sweetmeats, ruffling her hair affectionately. Subahu promptly swung her high on his broad shoulders. She broke into a burst of giggles—tinkling the staid air of the ashram and taking the people by surprise; they had rarely seen Meenakshi smile, forget laugh. Her scowl was a permanent feature pasted on her small, grim face. Meenakshi was oblivious of their reaction. She was happy: she would be wonderfully pampered, she was certain, swinging her thin legs merrily from her perched height. She soon wriggled down from her uncle's shoulders and hurried into her grandmother Taraka's waiting arms.

'Oh my! How has the little girl grown!' smiled Taraka, soundly planting loud kisses on each of her granddaughter's soft cheek.

Kaikesi gave a snort.

'Has she? She's nine but looks as if she's still five—she has neither grown in brains, height or even looks for that matter!' Meenakshi was aware of her mother's critical eyes moving minutely over her slight, dark, skinny frame and flushed unconsciously, trying to disengage herself from her grandmother's snug arms. 'She's a stunted dwarf, in every sense! I had hoped that my daughter would take after me, just as I took after you, Ma.'

Meenakshi promptly glanced at the two ladies. Kaikesi had Taraka's dusky beauty, slimness, long legs and beautiful hands, and thick raven hair. She had her mother's high cheek bones and sharp, straight nose but while Taraka eyes were warm with humour and good spirit, Kaikesi's were flinty, burning with an intensity difficult to gauge, as they alternated between anger and resentment. Taraka now found that same fire blazing often in Meenakshi, though they glowed golden when provoked, embers of a stoking anger burning in them.

Unlike us—and most Asuras—Meenakshi is petite, but does Kaikesi not recognize that she has inherited our sharp, regular features with that uncompromising, decided chin? Kaikesi is too biased, too disappointed about Meenakshi, Taraka concluded, glancing at the little girl in her arms: her hair and clothes were dishevelled, her face streaked with dirt, her hands and feet grubby. Her habits and habiliments were as neglected as the poor girl herself was in this family. Taraka felt a rush of emotions for the child.

'Don't be nasty, Kaikesi. You always had a mean tongue that didn't go with your looks!' frowned Taraka.

Meenakshi felt suddenly good, soaked with a warm, quenching feeling whenever her grandmother scolded her mother, which she did bluntly enough, irrespective of the audience. Ma used to flare up and a war of words was a common feature whenever her grandparents paid them a visit. It seemed it would start again, surmised Meenakshi watching Kaikesi's face darken.

'You mean I had the brains and beauty,' remarked Kaikesi tartly.

'Yes, you have,' admitted Taraka. 'that's how you managed to make Vishravas marry you. But I wish you had the heart too. You could be more kind to Meenakshi.'

'Don't discuss her when she's around, I have told you several times! She throws your words at me later!'

'Then why do you disparage her in front of everyone all the time, Kaikesi, openly ridiculing, humiliating, and wounding her?'

She did not wait for her daughter to answer: Kaikesi would not correct her ways. She drew Meenakshi closer to her, hugging the forlorn girl. 'And now, my dearest, what are your plans for us this time? You want to learn cooking, painting or...'

'Magic, Nani!!' exclaimed Meenakshi, her eyes shining with the prospect. And the fact that her mother had been soundly reprimanded by Taraka. They often differed because of her and each time Meenakshi felt a sense of victory, a vindictive glee as Kaikesi was censured volubly by Taraka. It made her mother angry and Meenakshi secretly revelled in the knowledge that her mother suffered the same ignominy, the same burning resentment that Meenakshi had to daily live with. Her smile widened, her Nani was here and she would be safe from her mother's cutting remarks, for a while.

They had not heard Vishravas enter the hut with Sumali, Kaikesi's father. Vishravas made a movement.

'No, you are not to study magic!' he ordered. 'It's unnecessary and unhealthy! How is that you pick up these things faster than your studies, Meenu?'

He looked at Taraka warily. 'Kindly refrain from teaching her any new tricks. She gets distracted. And I clearly disapprove of magic, it is dangerous and evil,' he said shortly.

Vishravas respected his mother-in-law, she was an exceptional woman. She had been born as a boon by Lord Brahma to the Yaksha king, Suketu, blessed with a mind as brilliant as her bewitching beauty. Born a Yakshini, she had a natural affinity towards the woods and the mountains as a benevolent forest nymph would. But Vishravas suspected Taraka more to be a tutelary spirit, more involved in the supernatural and sorcery to haunt and control the wilderness she ruled over. He admitted that he was wary of her. She might have been born a Yaksha princess, the natural protectors of the woods and its sylvan treasures of trees and vegetation but he had heard her fascination for nature extended to the supernatural and astral connections, stretching into the realm of sorcery.

'It's an art that invokes the supernatural powers,' retorted Taraka. 'Is that why you are so afraid—that it shows your God is not an invincible as you presume him to be? And my magic proves it!'

Meenakshi was aware of the tightening tension in the air: there was going to be another argument. Her father was always coldly civil to her grandparents. For Meenakshi, this was particularly distressing as it involved her two favourite people— her father and her grandmother. Why didn't they like each other?

'Do you believe in God, Taraka?' asked Vishravas thoughtfully.

'Yes, in our God, who is fair, not differentiating between

rishis and kshatriyas, daityas and devas, asuras and adityas, caste and colour, creed and country. Your God did that and created a division not with all people but amongst Gods too!' Taraka appeared bilious, a scowl marring her lovely, lined face.

'Mother!' intervened Kaikesi warningly.

'Where's Ravan?' said Sumali, hoping to change the topic.

He was a tall, thin man with a mop of jet black hair that emphasized his dark, cadaverous complexion. His black eyes were sunk deep and burned feverishly in his skull-like face. His eyes searched for the person whom he had come all the way for. Ravan was like his Kaikesi, he acknowledged with a secret smile, ambitious, slaked by a thirst for success and achievement.

Sumali was the erstwhile Asura king of Lanka. He could never forget it nor did he allow Kaikesi to forget it all her growing years. And now it was Ravan's turn: he had to win back what they had lost. He had to reconquer Lanka and restore the universal glory they once commanded...

The subject of his thoughts appeared in person. Sumali's face lit up with smile and pride. Ravan was a handsome boy, tall, already strapping with his powerful, muscled arms and shoulders and the way he swung his arms and jerked his head in an unmistakable arrogant manner. A faint trace of a moustache was an attempt to announce to the world that he was no longer a boy. Light-skinned and light-eyed, Ravan seemed to resemble his father because of the obvious fairness but it was Kaikesi's striking good looks that gave him that stamp of individuality—her decisive, square jaw, her proud nose flaring with temper more than often, her flashing, unsmiling eyes. He had wide set, amber-gold, alert eyes that often had a jeering light in them, a strong, well-shaped nose and a wide, thin-upper lipped, humorous mouth, which could charm anyone. He was a teenaged boy but he mastered attention as easily as he had the four Vedas and the six shastras; his mother now proudly called him Dasamukh—the ten-headed one. Kaikesi, on the occasion of his thread ceremony on his eighth birthday, had presented him with a rare necklace made of nine pearls, in which she could see his face reflected ninefold. Ravan wore it immediately, much to his mother's delight. He is his mother's boy, the worthy son of a worthy mother, Sumali beamed proudly.

And he was as articulate as he was erudite, again a perfect, although rare mix. But since he was five years old, Ravan had made it his keenest weapon. *He had always had a way with words, be it verbal or scripted. His avid passion for politics was natural, thanks to the asura blood in him*, thought Sumali proudly, *but his interest in esoteric subjects like astrology and ayurveda made him something like a wizard.* Ravan was surprisingly well versed in music as well, with the Samaveda being his most favoured liturgical text. Leisure and relaxation for him meant stringing the Rudra Veena: that complex plucked stringed musical instrument, which he cherished most besides the sword. As the name represented, 'the veena dear to Lord Shiva', it was through it that Ravan revealed his deep devotion to Lord Shiva. Sumali was pleased: *Ravan being a Lord Shiva devotee was good. Lord Shiva had always helped the asura and daityas. And the fact that he was Brahma's great-grandson was also a calculated advantage. Our only enemy now in the Triumvirate was Vishnu who had usurped our Lanka from us and handed it to Kuber. Vishnu could never be our friend.*

Ravan seems detached to the effervescent family reunion, his face studied and impassive not showing any emotion but he was ready with a quick smile to charm the most hostile. That was another trick Sumali had taught him: never let anyone know what is running in one's mind. Mask the emotions and he was doing it very well, but Sumali knew he was secretly pleased to meet him again. He was fond of his grandfather, who was also his secret guru in war and weaponry.

But for all his stolid, impassive demeanour, Ravan had inherited his mother's sullen temper. Sumali gauged the same in little Meenakshi as well, as if they were angry with the world at large. Sumali felt a momentary twinge. *Was this my legacy to them; this restless resentment, the impatient urge to retrieve their lost glory, that naked ambition?*

Sumali sighed. Theirs was a violent history and they were

violent people. It had all started once upon a long time when he was barely a teenager. He with his two brothers—his elder brother Malyavan and younger brother Mali, had together performed a severe *tapasya* to Brahma and asked for two boons: first, that their fraternal love would be forever strong and unbreakable and second, that they were in-vanquishable, so that no one would be able to defeat them. Pleased with their sibling love, Brahma blessed them with the twin boons and consequently the three brothers conquered every deva and daitya, ruling the three worlds, spreading terror everywhere and among all, the Heavens and Earth, the devas, the manavs, and even the asuras, daityas and danavas—their different clans. After having defeated the devas, they were the sole rulers of the world. With these new powers they asked Vishvakarma, the celestial architect to build a city for them. Lanka was duly created for the three brothers, residing with their respective families in love and luxury. But not for long. The devas retaliated and in the ensuing battle, Mali was killed by Vishnu. That single, individual death broke them. Defeated and dejected, Malyavan and Sumali were forced to flee for their lives and take refuge in the netherworld: that hated, dreaded place called Patalok. Meanwhile, the devas reigned supreme again in Lanka under the newly appointed king—Kuber, the young son of Vishravas.

Those were the worst days but Sumali's sole consolation was his family. His beautiful wife Taraka, the unusual and powerful Yaksha princess, who bore him two sons, Subahu and Maricha, and a daughter, Kaikesi who grew up to be as exquisite as her mother. Call it cunning or circumstances, but Sumali could see his beautiful daughter as his only salvation, their saviour. He wished her to marry the most powerful being in the world, so as to produce an exceptional heir. His choice was Rishi Vishravas, the most brilliant mind of those times. And more importantly, he was Kuber's father. He had to make Rishi Vishravas meet Kaikesi and make him fall so strongly in love that he would give up his wife and son to live with Kaikesi. Sumali was surprised that Kaikesi agreed readily to his plan. She was fed up with their life in patalok as well. She had to get out from the hell. Her escape would save her and her family. She was sure her beauty would seduce Vishravas, she would marry him and have his children: ones with the best of the rishi brain and the asura blood to make the most formidable warriors–the *brahmarakhsas*—which the world would witness and fear. And so were born Ravan, Kumbhakarna, Vibhishan and the little surprise, Meenakshi. Kaikesi had been sorely disappointed after having a daughter and she demonstrated it amply, often cruelly. But Sumali disagreed. There must be a reason why a girl had been born. *Would she be like Kaikesi, changing the fortunes of the asuras and the daityas to vanquish the devas? Or was she meant for more grand designs*, wondered Sumali staring long at his granddaughter. Right now, she looked innocuous with her wild, dark looks and her slight form, more likely to be dismissed as Ravan invariably did in his arrogance but Sumali staunchly believed Meenakshi would change the fate of all of them. Just like Ravan would—they were strangely similar, these two brother-sister siblings, tempered with violent restlessness. But what worried Sumali was that there seemed to be no love lost between them. Or was he over-reacting and the tension between them was merely because the two were startlingly alike in manner and mood?

He was disturbed by a rude noise. The door burst open and what appeared to be an elephant stamped into the room. This was how Kumbhakarna normally made an appearance. In spite of his heavy lumbering frame, he moved always with a quick rushing charge, surprisingly light on his large feet. Before Sumali could avoid the rush, he was engulfed in enormous fat arms and hugged to be buried in a flabby chest, beaten on the back with hands that felt like scaffold, then pushed back while Kumbha beamed at him, with his enormous, jovial fat face, creased and delighted.

Meenakshi noticed how Ravan's golden eyes too lit up at the sight of his grandfather: just as hers when she had met Taraka. Ravan was everyone's favourite, including her grandfather and uncles. Watching them hugging, all of them looked like giants— tall and strapping. Even her grandmother was exceptionally tall, taller than even her father who looked diminutive in front of that asura family. She too felt especially dwarfed by them. No wonder her mother called her stunted. Now she knew why she was short: possibly because of her father, a fair, short man with a serene plumpness about him. Their half-brother Kuber looked exactly like him, even that soft voice was remarkably similar.

But we siblings have distinctly taken after our asura grandparents, Meenakshi grinned radiantly, clutching at Taraka's hand and taking her father's in the other. *My two best people,* she thought contently. She was so happy, she declared to herself, looking forward to better days.

Taraka

✧

$\mathcal{M}$eenakshi grimaced at her reflection in the mirror. What she saw never pleased her. It did not today too. There was a change in her physical appearance, but not a pleasant one. She was now twelve years old—yet she was still dark, skinny, gangly chit of a girl with a burgeoning bosom, too large for her tiny waist and slight, short figure. She scowled and instinctively pulled her bodice tighter as if trying to hide a deformity. She closed her eyes in frustrated prayer. Her lack of charm and her plainness had never been so pronounced. She had been praying, waiting, hoping for a miracle, but this wasn't the year of miracles, she realized. It was a sign that she would always remain an oddity, an outcast; she would never be a part of her family of good lookers.

'You would look a lot better if you replaced the scowl with a smile!' remarked her grandmother casually, stirring the herbal mix she was preparing. 'And why are you frowning anyway? What are you so angry about, child?'

'There's nothing to be proud of that I can see here!' whined the girl, giving a last glimpse at her reflection and sitting down forlornly next to her. 'Can you make me beautiful with one of your potions, Nani?' she asked abruptly, throwing her grandmother an almost-pleading look.

Taraka felt a stab of sympathy for the girl. She looked so vulnerable with her huge honey-golden eyes, framed by impossibly long, dark lashes which she batted more angrily than coyly as girls of her age would. But Meenkashi was guileless in the art of seduction. She was not even aware of the budding beauty that she was. And that rankled Taraka: both the parents were to blame she thought. They shamelessly neglected her and worse, disparaged her endlessly. She patted the girl's hair affectionately.

'I do have potions to change beauty, form and figure and I shall soon teach you how to go about it. But you shan't need it to use it on yourself, my pretty! You are beautiful with the most exquisite eyes—that's why you were named so!'

Meenakshi pouted, evoking a laugh from her grandmother.

'Oh dear, you do that prettily! I know you seem to be unhappy about the colour of your skin, but aren't your mother and I not dark as well? Are we not beautiful?' she asked softly.

The girl nodded vigorously. 'But I am not like either of you. I am darker, like the night sky!!' she said miserably, staring earnestly at her grandmother's refined, dusky face. Nani might be old, but she was so elegantly lovely that people could not take their eyes off her. Her mother was more voluptuous with a fuller face, but undeniably attractive. Meenakshi knew what beauty meant and what it implied. She had grown up amongst it. Except Kumbha who ran abominably to fat, her brothers were very good looking. So were her uncles. And her grandparents. Her father was instantly likable because of his open, friendly face which Kumbha had inherited. It shone with good humour and good nature, his wide grin and twinkling eyes that made people immediately like him. Although her father and Kumbha were plump, which heightened their jolliness, they certainly were not as ugly as her. He was a hulk but a popular one. *Unlike me*, she thought a little sad again. No one noticed her, especially not the boys in the ashram. She glanced down self-consciously, hunching her shoulders.

'Don't, you'll develop a slouch!' said Taraka sharply. 'Or is it your attempt to hide your breasts! They are blooming beautifully!'

Meenakshi's face flamed red with embarrassment. Her grandmother could be delightfully blunt and frightfully coarse at times. 'Breasts are symbolic of a woman's power and yours promise to grow into nicely rounded, big ones—you'll have men chasing you in no time,' she chortled amused at the mortified expression on her granddaughter's pinched face. She sobered, saying softly, 'Never be ashamed of your body, your femininity, Meenu,' said Taraka, giving her a meaningful smile. 'Beauty should be flaunted, and don't start off that you aren't one! Beauty lies in your head and heart, you have to believe it. But for that first you have to love yourself. Love is magic; it has the mysterious, supernatural power of influencing your heart and mind and the soul and change the course of events in your life. You'll fall in love one day and that will be magic too. You do believe in magic, don't you? Then, first start loving yourself. Love that smooth dusky skin, love the petite, fragile figure of yours, those big, honey-drop eyes...'

'Oh, you sure have a sweet way of describing the most mundane! That's also called lying!' Meenakshi burst into a giggle, amused at Nani's sanguinity. *She is always optimistically cheerful and confident about me.*

Her unexpected laugh took Taraka's breath away and the old lady could not help but be mesmerized by what she had just witnessed, a rare smile from her granddaughter. It transformed her beautifully—the smile erasing the perpetual frown lines on her forehead to show a clear, wide one marked with a pair of dark, shapely eyebrows, over thick-lashed cat eyes, sparkling in incandescent vivacity, the smile reaching her high cheekbones and adding a soft colour to her glowing cheeks. It was a breathtaking sight. She gave the girl a spontaneous hug. 'My dearest Meenu, when will you know you are lovely?!'

'I am dark and a dolt!' snapped the girl, the smile again buried in the folds of her frown.

'Stop putting yourself down!' sighed Taraka. 'Would you believe it if I called you Menaka?' asked Taraka.

Meenakshi sniggered, bursting into a fit of giggles. 'Really??' she gurgled.

'Then why is it that you believe those people who call you dark? You are dark like me—be proud of it. Have you done any wrong? Then why should you be ashamed of yourself? If you don't believe you are a Menaka, then you shouldn't believe that you are a monster either.'

Meenakshi did not reply. The word monster was echoed to her so often and each time it brought a rush of memories...her mother flinging that word at her, her eyes spitting venom and dislike. Meenakshi shivered. She could not forget that day, nor could she forget those words. *Monster. Surpanakha.*

Meenakshi pursed her lips, clenching a retort. She did not want to hurt Nani's feelings by complaining about her mother. *That was not done; it was unforgivable. It was a private matter, between the family. Snitching about one's family meant the person lacked in family pride. It was betrayal,* she thought. But she could not resist painting her mother black in her Nani's eyes.

'I am the monster of the family, and I am never made to forget that!' she said slyly, without letting out her mother's identity.

'Those words are said in anger, don't take them so seriously,' said Taraka as if reading the girl's troubled thoughts. 'Kaikesi's bark is worse than her bite. She is impatient with you because...'

'I am slow?' Meenakshi finished the sentence promptly.

'You are smart and sweet, and there shall be no more argument on this. Say it, Meenu and believe it, and not what the world thinks of you!' retorted her grandmother. 'You make the world believe what you are, not believe what the world believes of you. But for now, you could look a lot sweeter if you tied your hair neatly into either a bun or a plait. Come, I shall oil it for you!'

She pulled the mutinous girl down to make her sit at her feet and pulled out a bottle of scented sesame oil. She poured some onto the cupped palm and slowly massaged into the girl's long, length of flowing hair.

'Saying it won't make it come true!' snorted the girl.

'You have a way with words but stop huffing like a wild boar in the forest, it's indelicate!' grinned Taraka, unmoved.

'...and now you compare me to a boar—dark and ugly!'

Taraka gave a sharp tap on the girl's head. 'You are over-reacting , if not being over-sensitive,' Taraka sighed. 'When will you see sense?'

'See, even you think I am a fool!' muttered Meenakshi.

Taraka sighed again. She would have to work on this child just as Sumali had handled Ravan so beautifully. She had to be made aware of the hidden weapons she possessed—her beauty and her brains. Meenakshi was aware of neither, and Taraka blamed Kaikesi. Kaikesi should have brought up her daughter the same way she had been brought up, not just with the power of knowledge but with the knowledge of power. Kaikesi knew how to charm and seduce. That had been her power. Meenakshi would need the same and more, to brave the war that they would soon start. Her beauty would be her arsenal, her wit and her words will be her weapons.

'You are smarter than you and everyone else thinks!' continued Taraka. 'See how quickly you picked up the rudiments of magic and witchcraft! It took Mareech ages and he's honing to be the best!'

'That's probably because I am being told not to study it by Father,' said Meenakshi dryly. 'I like the forbidden!'

She sounded defiant which Taraka knew was part of her intrinsic nature. Meenakshi was anything but meek and timid, though her petite-ness denoted otherwise. And she was sharp as the long nails she brandished and the poor girl was stuck with that ghastly name—Surpanakha—Ravan had dumped her with. She was as brilliant as him, with a razor sharp, quick mind. Not the laboured studiousness of Vibhishan but the crafty cunningness that was swift to observe, absorb and assimilate.

'But why am I not allowed to study the Vedas like my brothers, Nani? I know I am not as fast in my calculations as Vibhishan or clever as Ravan...'

'You are! You are as mentally resourceful as them, it's just that you have not been given a chance to prove it!' assured Taraka.

'But why?' cried the girl. 'Am I not Rishi Vishravas' child too? Then why am I not studying the shastras and the Upanishads like my brothers? Why am I not with my brothers right now who are performing austerities and invoking Lord Shiva's blessings near River Narmada? Am I daft?'

'You are far more clever, dear girl, than you allow yourself to believe and the others consider. I know as I have seen it. The others have not seen that, yet!' smiled Taraka. 'But I shall teach you all about sorcery!' her eyes gleamed.

'Father will never allow it!'

Taraka shook her head. 'He will never know of it! We shan't tell him!' she added in a conspiratorial whisper.

Meenakshi's eyes got rounder, her mouth agape. 'But...' she spluttered.

'You don't want to deceive your father?' guessed Taraka astutely.

Meenakshi nodded meekly.

The girl is very loyal. Taraka wondered how she could prise the child away from Vishravas; the girl was devoted to him and he was no good to her.

Meenakshi felt a momentary qualm of uneasiness. She hated lying to her father whom she could not bear hurting in any way. She would never disappoint him; that was a vow she had promised herself a long time ago. But he barely bothered about her. He lathered his attention solely on Vibhishan, the brightest of all his children whom he believed will be the only one to follow his dream. Meenakshi felt a stab of red hot jealousy as it always did where it concerned her father. But he was oblivious of both—her jealous fury and her zealous adoration.

But she wanted to show him she was good at something. But that something which she was good at, was disapproved of by her father, she well knew. *But why? Why was studying about the supernatural considered evil? If education was a means of guidance so was witchery,* she thought. She wanted to discover the mystery of the magical spells that had the power to rein in occult forces and evil spirits to produce a magic of its own. Father termed it as an evil, unnatural force in the world. Witchcraft had the power to harness even the unknown: Meenkashi felt a prickle of excitement. Would she have the courage to defy her father?

But father need not know, Nani is sure about it.

'Does Ma need to know about this?' asked Meenakshi.

Taraka hesitated just for a moment. 'Yes' she said truthfully. Kaikesi had been part of each plan of theirs. Sumali and she had groomed their daughter accordingly. Without her, their scheme—contrived romantic encounter between Vishravas and Kaikesi in the forest where she had pretended to be lost—could not have succeeded. By the time, Vishravas had helped her find her way home, he had lost her heart to her. The wedding was attended by none but the new asura family. The children were soon born and while Sumali trained the boys, Taraka had wanted to groom Meenakshi but Vishravas had been openly displeased, wary of any asura leanings. But Sumali had proved smarter; he cleverly managed to teach his grandsons the art of war by stationing himself at the ashram of Vishravas on the pretext that he was happier staying with his daughter than his wife. Taraka smiled. What a rascal Sumali was! Vishravas could not refuse or throw out his old father-in-law.

With Meenakshi it had been difficult. Taraka had somehow managed to get her here for barely a month but what she had to teach Meenakshi would take longer. At least a full six months, but how was she to lengthen the stay? The girl answered the question herself.

'If Mother knows then it shouldn't be a problem,' said Meenakshi shrewdly, knowing she had no reason to feel guilty now. Her mother knew, she had her sanction and the permission of one parent was enough to pursue her dream—she wanted to be a beautiful sorceress like her famous grandmother.

'I shall stay on,' she said quietly. 'And learn everything I need to learn.'

'Good. You will need to stay back now. I will think of an excuse to tell your father. How about me falling very sick and needing you to nurse me back to health?' questioned the elderly lady with a wicked glint. The girl nodded happily.

'But be warned, not a word to your father.'

The girl held her lips between her two fingers tightly and

nodded silently.

'So are you prepared for longer hours and longer days from now on?'

Taraka was greeted with an enthusiastic nod from the child.

Defeated

❧

Ravan claimed to be amongst the most powerful warriors in the country having invoked Lord Shiva's blessings: he looked visibly jubilant. But the good news was short-lived. Meenakshi woke up one day, to a pall of gloom that blanketed the house and the family. She had never seen her mother in tears and watching her burying her face in her hands, the tears dripping though the pleated fingers, made Meenakshi sure something was very amiss. It had to be about Ravan: only he could make her mother crumble in grief. Vibhishan was pale and quiet than he usually was, his face as taut with restrained emotion as was her father's.

She turned questioning eyes towards Kumbha. He looked equally devastated, his round, friendly face puckered in worry and fear. 'Tell me, what has happened?' she asked.

He looked despairingly at her. 'Ravan's been captured and imprisoned in a cage—in chains!' he blurted incoherently.

The idea was so preposterous that she let out a tiny giggle. She saw Kumbha's eyes flare in sudden fury and her irreverent amusement subsided immediately. She sounded contrite in her next words. 'That cannot be, but how?'

Ravan, she got to know through Kumbha's garbled, disjointed explanation, had been unexpectedly captured by Kartaviryarjun, the powerful Haihaya king. It seems Kartaviryarjun was having a bath in the River Narmada with his wives, disturbing Ravan, who was praying to Lord Shiva nearby. An incensed Ravan challenged the king but was soon trounced. And to add to his humiliation, he was captured and confined like a beast in a cage in his capital city Mahishmati to be displayed as a trophy to a crowing public.

Ravan would have wished that the king had him killed, thought Meenakshi, *rather than endure such disgrace.* She would have done the same as death was more dignified than disgrace. For the first time she felt a deep emotion for her brother. Was it sympathy, worry or sorrow? Or all of it? It was over-riding love: that gushing emotion that drowned the jealous anger she reserved for him, resenting him for being their mother's favourite, the golden boy who excelled at everything, loved and lauded by all. An overwhelming worry, a lingering anxiety gnawed at her scared heart. How would they be able to rescue Ravan?

Ravan's ignominous capture meant negotiations with Kartaviryarjun who would dismiss all their efforts of peace. Sumali was grief-stricken but ready to wage a war against Kartaviryarjun. Vishravas had restrained him, reminding that he did not own as huge an army as his opponent. This argument incensed Kaikesi further, tipping her to frenzied fury.

'Don't you care??' she screamed at her husband, tears of rage glittering in her eyes. 'You brush off my father claiming he has no army to boast of. Well, you don't have an army either to help your son, so what do you intend to do? Nothing? How about your powerful relatives whom you flaunt so often at me? Where is Kuber? Will he fight for his brother now?' she taunted. 'Where is your father the mightiest rishi, Pulastya? Does he not wish to save his grandson? And yes, the great Brahma himself, he can intercede and resolve the matter peacefully. But will he?' she said scornfully, anxiety making her more querulous than usual.

'I cannot call in Brahmadev to solve my problems each time!' started Vishravas. 'Or my father...'

'The last time he visited, he was open in his contempt for both me and my parents,' Kaikesi cut in angrily. 'But this time will he help or just pontificate? That is, if you swallow your hollow pride and ask him for help? Vishravas, I shan't allow or forgive you if you take this threat lightly. If it was your beloved

Vibhishan, you would have scoured Hell and Heaven to seek him out. I want my Ravan back safe and sound, and you will see to it that it happens!!' she screamed.

Even Meenakshi could see that Kaikesi was being unnecessarily harsh on Vishravas. And as she always did, Meenakshi unconsciously sided with her father, not because her mother could be annoyingly unreasonable, but that blindly and unquestioningly, she loved her father. Right then, he seemed as worried as her mother but without her frantic frenzy. Ravan was her favoured son and even the mere thought that he might be hurt or harmed, made Kaikesi hysterical. He was in real danger now and the thought struck her with terror, spinning her into a state of violent mental agitation. Taraka tried to console her distraught daughter but to no avail.

'I shan't have a drop of water till you get Ravan back!' she wept, bitter, angry tears ravaging her beautiful face. Suddenly, to Meenakshi, her mother looked aged, with her face drawn, the eyes bleak, and her body shrunken in grief.

Vishravas was worried as he knew that he could never dare, defy or even request the mighty Kartaviryarjun. He was too powerful a king to listen to a rishi and held no particular regard for him. *But maybe he will agree to my father's request*, he thought. Vishravas was born through Muni Pulastya's blessings. *I would have to approach my estranged father*, Vishravas decided. *I will have to put aside my pride, for my son. That is my sole resort, my only option.*

Expectedly, Rishi Pulastya did not take this incident too kindly.

'Kartaviryarjun is the fulfilment of the Supreme Lord,' he warned, greeting his son with a laconic nod of his head. 'No one can vanquish him—no mortal, demon or deva but only the Lord himself. Not even your mighty son Ravan. Ravan was foolish and arrogant to challenge him. But he's young and hot-blooded!' sighed the old man, his eyes solemn. 'This is the last time I shall help you out with Ravan, Vishravas. Rein him in. He is brilliant, an exemplary scholar. But don't ever forget besides his extraordinary intelligence, he is a fiery warrior as well—thirsting for more, so fevered and formidable. As I warned you before, he has stronger Asura blood in him than that of a rishi's; you know it but don't want to acknowledge it. Nip it at the bud or it might be too late. He is too much under the influence of Sumali. He and Kaikesi, as I had apprised you much before, are simply using you to gather more power and prominence. That's why she married you,' he added scornfully. 'Not because she was in love with you! She fooled you, and so will this son of yours!'

Vishravas flushed, more embarrassed than angry at his father's jibe.

His father continued, 'He is an example of how the Asura has already defeated the rishi! In fact, all your other children but for Vibhishan, are more Asura than rishis, even that daughter of yours!'

'Meenakshi?' repeated Vishravas incredulously. 'She's but a child!'

'She's no child—neither small nor inferior in strength or significance,' retorted his father. 'I have seen in her the same mad passion that fires Ravan, they are alike. Fiery and resentful, marked by an indignant ill-will. Both will start a terrible war...'

Vishravas stifled a gasp of horror. *Meenakshi? That scraggy girl with her unkempt hair and wild eyes who loved to play than study?*

'She will be responsible for unseen turn of events. She is the one fated to bring about Ravan's destruction just as he is hers...' Pulastya paused before continuing. 'But yes, she is a boon for us rishis, mark my words!' he continued enigmatically.

His two children were to be siblings and rivals, dreaded Vishravas. He had witnessed snippets of their animosity, often bloody, but had dismissed them as childish pranks. *They were destined to be each other's nemesis?* It sent a rush of cold blood down his spine.

'And Vibhishan?' asked Vishravas anxiously.

Pulastya smiled. 'You worry about Ravan right now. Go home. I shall go to Kartaviryarjun to release Ravan. He won't refuse me.'

The aged rishi turned out to be right about Kartaviryarjun.

The powerful king bowed down to the rishi's request. *Kaikesi knew this would happen. That is why she had sent me to my father,* thought Vishravas. For the first time, he saw Kaikesi in a new light. Her beauty had distracted him from her ruthless cunningness all these years. He had been blinded in love: not been able to see her for what she was. He now feared for Ravan and Meenakshi. Did he, the great Rishi Vishravas, not know his family at all? Did he have a family or was it a trick Taraka had played on him using her daughter and now his children? His heart thudded with sickening dismay. *Meenakshi had been with Taraka for over a year recently. Had her long illness been a pretext to keep the little girl with her to groom her into sorcery?* Fear gripped him; had he lost Ravan to Sumali and possibly Meenakshi to Taraka? His children were suddenly not his own. Neither was his wife. She never was; Kaikesi had always been her parents' daughter, never his wife. And now his children were theirs too.

The thoughts raced through his head as he headed home, fearing he had almost lost his family now. He wanted to see them all again, keep them safe, away from war and violence. But in his heart, he knew he was losing this battle.

◠

Her father had got Ravan back home. Meenakshi felt proud that her father stripped his pride and ego, to seek help from his estranged father and beg for his son's life. Meenakshi felt varied emotions at once—relief, joy and certain apprehensiveness due to the sudden course of events disrupting their lives. This was what family was all about; a crisis had surely brought them closer. Or so she thought.

Ravan had returned but he was like a crazed, wounded animal, responding excessively and violently to anything and everything around him. His wounds might have healed but the scars festered, his pride broken, his fury fermenting. He wanted to kill Kartaviryarjun but what incensed him was that he could not. Meenakshi knew he was roiling in helpless rage, hating his apparent weakness.

'I shall not get my revenge till I kill him!' he shouted as he often did when he flew into an apoplectic fury. When in one of his fearsome black moods, he ranted and raged, like dispelling out molten lava inside him. Strangely it never frightened her; she knew exactly how he felt. She did it often in the privacy of the thick forests, as she snarled her fury, digging her nails in the soft ground, clawing and scratching, whenever she knew she needed to vent her anger—which was often—each time frightening the birds away from the tall trees. None knew about it but Kumbha who had been horrified seeing her in that paroxysm of fury.

'You cannot kill him!' replied Vishravas calmly, secretly repulsed at the display of unmitigated rage. It was a vulgar, conspicuously inelegant behaviour, often appropriated with the asuras, more prone to such explosive temper tantrums, he silently disparaged. 'He is too powerful for you. He has been born out of a divine benediction. No one can defeat him—but the weapon of Vishnu that can kill him—none of yours!! That is why he could vanquish you so easily; he is the king of the three worlds. He could have killed you. You were saved only because my father requested him to do so. And he was honourable enough to listen to his entreaty and release you. Be thankful, Ravan and stop your tantrums!'

'This is not tantrum, father!' exploded Ravan, his fair face flushed a deep red, his beady eyes flashing a dangerous gold. 'Can you not see what he did to me? I would have rather died than live with the indignity inflicted upon me; he bound me in a cage and spared my life because my grandfather entreated so! What sort of a man does it make me? A coward!'

'No, a young fool!' retorted his father. 'Realize you weakness and know his strength, Ravan. Your ego refuses to make you accept your defeat. Learn to take failure in your stride as well. It is through failure that you get your success; it is through failure you should get to know where you went wrong. That is, if you want to introspect and interrogate yourself and not others!'

'There has to be some way I can defeat him!' argued Ravan, almost desperately. 'I am younger, stronger...'

'...and hot-headed and impulsive!' said his father. 'Ravan, let this go and focus on your work instead...'

Ravan shook his head violently. 'I shall not seek peace till I vanquish that man! There has to be a way to become more powerful than him,' he repeated. He stared unseeingly at the distance. The sun outside was blazing as harshly as was the rage within her brother.

Ravan broke the prolonged silence. 'He sought a boon of immortality and it was granted to him. I shall seek one too!' he said softly, the quiet purr resounding more loudly than a shout.

Meenakshi could hear the menace in his whisper, feel the rustle of violence in the deceptively low tone.

Vishravas stiffened. 'What do you mean?'

'Kartviryarjun sought immortality by virtue of his birth,' said Ravan distinctly, his tone slow and soft. 'I shall do so through worth. He was blessed by Dattatreya with a thousand arms and a golden chariot, invincible to his enemies. I too shall seek the blessing of my great-grandfather Lord Brahma for immortality.'

In his sinking heart, Vishravas knew what the words of his son portended. Doom. His son wanted immortality which he could never acquire.

'Kartaviryarjun will die one day. This wish of immortality is a mere illusion. Don't succumb to it,' he pleaded but one look at his son's determined face told him his warning was futile. Ravan had always been obstinate, his tenacious unwillingness to yield often risking him to untold danger, but he remained stubbornly persistent in wrongdoing. 'Kartaviryarun will meet his nemesis, his death. It is not you but it will be someone else. So why do you rant? Don't make the same mistake he is doing. He is the king of the three worlds but still unsatisfied...'

'When I am blessed an immortal, I too shall become the king of the three worlds!' said Ravan.

'Are you mad?' shouted Vishravas, losing his temper. 'You are a rishi's son, not a warrior, not a king of even a village! You are just a teenager with this crazy lust for revenge. What silly ambition are you aspiring for now? You have been roundly trounced by Kartaviryarun and you hope to be him one day. What can I call this but madness?'

'I have made up my mind, father. If I don't do it, I shall go mad!' scowled Ravan. 'I am proud to be your son and it hurts me that I as the son of Rishi Vishravas had to taste defeat because I was unarmed with the arsenal Kartaviryarjun boasts of. I shall not rest in peace till I get what he has, father. I would rather die than come home defeated again. I promise myself that I shall have it, or die in the process!'

Each word was infused with the burning flame of hope and determination. The heat of his words inflamed Meenakshi, consuming her in a blaze of dream, desire and drive. She felt inspired: she wanted to be like her brother—invincible and strong. She looked around the room. Her other brothers looked equally instigated, their eyes glittering with the flicker of new excitement. Her mother looked radiant, glowing with malicious satisfaction, her smile triumphant. But her father had a lost, vacant look in his old, weary eyes as if he was witnessing death. She froze, and then felt a cold stab of pain in her heart. Her father looked crushed. Devastated. Her feeling of euphoria evaporated, filling her with anxiety.

The silence in the room was thick and hard, stifling each in a new emotion. Kumbha's face lost its innocence and was tense with determination. 'I want to go with you, brother,' he announced.

'You would!' Meenakshi interrupted viciously. 'You are his pet dog, following him everywhere!'

Kumbha's fat face wrinkled in astonishment at her virulence. So did Ravan, his eyes narrowing.

'Don't interfere, sister,' he looked down at his massive hands, frowning. 'It is between us—the father and the sons. It does not concern you.'

Vishravas nodded. 'Meenu, stay silent. It is bad manners to interfere and what you just said to your brother was downright disrespectful, if not rude!'

Meenakshi glared at her father. 'Why did you always take their side?' she demanded. 'Because they are boys!? They are the ones who are leaving you, against your wishes. And I am here always by your side, but you prefer them to me each time!'

'This is not about you, it's about Ravan,' said Kaikesi curtly. Meenakshi had become more assertive since her return from her grandmother's, more confident, less wild but still fearless. 'Either stay quiet or leave the room right now!'

Taraka threw her a warning glance. Meenakshi bit her lip, stilling the angry retort, trying to contain her fit of temper. That would be unwise; she wanted to know what was going on, what was going to happen.

'I too want to join Ravan in his quest for the ultimate knowledge and enlightenment,' repeated Kumbha, his voice soft but stubborn. 'We should seek our great-grandfather's Brahma's blessings.'

Ravan nodded, his smile grim and assured.

'And so will I!!' interjected Vibhishan.

Meenakshi turned to him in shock. He rarely could do what Ravan did, though he desperately aspired for it. He often could not, as their father forbade him. But not today. Ravan's words had kindled an ember of a new hope in Vibhishan that she too had experienced. He was flared with the same purpose as his brother: to endeavour to achieve the impossible. She again glanced at her father.

He was a man devastated man. Vibhishan was his sole hope, on whom all his expectations were centred. His unexpected decision was the final betrayal. She saw her father suddenly aged and ancient, distraught and destroyed.

She looked around the room: it was her father against all of them. And all because of Ravan's one stubborn wish. Her brother had brought that haunted look into their father's eyes. He had made him a broken man. Just moments ago, she too had been intoxicated with Ravan's seducing words but now witnessing her father's anguish, she felt a gush of resentment for her brother. He had wounded her father, tearing apart the last few remnants of a tattered relationship. He was his oldest son, his hope, his succour and it was he who had driven the knife in him. A swirl of mist blurred her eyes: was she crying or was she seeing her brother through new eyes? Was he so selfish that he could destroy his father with his mere words, the axe of his actions yet to befall on them? She felt the bitter taste of bile in her mouth. It was that emotion of dislike so intense that it demanded action. She felt like flying at him and clawing his eyes out with her nails as she had done years ago as a child. She wanted to scream at Ravan to stop his madness, which was breaking the family, shattering the man whom she loved so devotedly. She wished Ravan had died, she prayed fiercely, and had been killed by Kartviryarjun. They would not have to see this day: this open, ugly confrontation of father and son that was shattering the family. She saw Vishravas' haggard face, lined with defeat and disappointment. He was Ravan's father too, so why was he hurting him so cruelly?

But Vibhishan was quick to notice his father's abject disappointment.

'I do not wish for power or want immortality, Father,' announced Vibhishan, in his soft voice. 'I will go with Ravan to seek the best in knowledge and enlightenment from Lord Brahma. I want no weapon, no celestial warhead but the divine blessings and love of my great-grandfather.'

Ravan flicked his younger brother a contemptuous glance. 'Knowledge is power, Vibhishan. It is a double edged sword: a possession of controlling influence and exercising authority. Make it a weapon, an instrument for fighting not persuasion,' he smirked. 'Kumbha has been blessed with mind and muscle. He is physically so powerful that even Indra is scared of him these days and will find ways to undermine him. That, Father, shows that even the Gods fear us brothers! We are considered a threat and I intend to make our position more strong.'

'Unconquerable—that's what you aspire to achieve,' corrected Vishravas. 'So that none can overcome or subdue you. Will you be able to handle the responsibility that comes with this power?'

Kaikesi had not spoken a word till now. She was about to intervene but Ravan shook his head. He did not need his mother to defend him any longer. He looked squarely at his aggrieved father, standing almost a foot taller than him. Vishravas was forced to look up at his son.

'You have coached me with all the knowledge that man can obtain,' smiled Ravan disarmingly. 'I sought your guidance, your advice, now I seek your blessings.'

Vishravas shoulders had sagged, his heart sinking at every word his son had uttered. Never had he felt so powerless, he wanted to shake his son from his stupor of revenge, to hug his son and protect him from his ambition and greed. He did neither, standing helpless and bereft.

'Use wisely your knowledge which you have amassed,' advised Vishravas simply with a sigh. 'You will always have my blessings. And come home victorious.'

Kuber

Meenakshi dreaded Kuber's visit each time he came to meet his father: it invariably threw her mother into a nasty temper, the brunt of which she had to often face. Yet she silently admitted that she could not help but be fascinated with this exotic man however fat, suety-faced and nondescript-looking. He was a fair, thick-set man with jet black hair, short like his father, and, like Vishravas, prone to plumpness. His corpulent waist thickened perceptibly each time she saw him on his biannual visits. His rotund frame shimmered in gems and gold—from the elaborately heavy ruby and sapphire-studded crown on his head to the thick anklets on his feet which resembled gold fetters. His florid fatness was almost sickening, lacking refinement.

Kuber reminded Kaikesi of her childhood days and it rankled. But Meenakshi knew it was more than resentment her mother nursed for Kuber. She loathed him. He was the son of her husband's first wife Ilavida. Meenakshi had never seen her; Ilavida had left Vishravas when he had married her mother and Kuber had taken her away to Lanka, but not without mincing his words at his father's new bride. Kaikesi could not forget those unkind words but she hated him more that he was the King of Lanka—her erstwhile home. He was living in her palace, lording over her land.

Kuber was well aware of her animosity for him and it was mutual. Yet, he had not broken contact with his father; his each visit was a reminder to his father that there existed another family which Vishravas had forsaken for Kaikesi. This open contempt riled Kaikesi.

'Why does he come here?' she complained bitterly. 'To remind you and the ashram that he is your son, the great King of Lanka?'

'What annoys you more Kaikesi that he is my son or that he is the King of Lanka, the kingdom your father lost?' asked Vishravas quietly.

'He was always your son and will always be but that throne was never his nor does he deserve it!' she said waspishly.

Meenakshi wearily turned away from the usual argument and stared at Kuber's flashy chariot standing outside, visibly mesmerized, her eyes widening in open wonder—the Pushpak Viman. It was the first flying viman of its kind, distinct from the devas' flying horse-drawn chariots, the most flamboyant being those of Surya and Indra. But this was an aerial chariot, resembling a bright cloud as it floated in the sky, shimmering more than the stars. It was said to be originally made by the celestial architect Vishwakarma for Brahma, her great-grandfather. Brahma had no interest in it and neither had any of his sons—Vishravas, Agastya or Narad. But later Brahma gifted it to Kuber, his great-grandson who had an avid fondness for all things bright and beautiful. *If Ravan ever did win Lanka back, he would own this splendid vehicle too*, Meenakshi wished with growing excitement. She wanted to touch it, step inside and travel in it. But Kaikesi would not allow her or any of her children to venture anywhere close to it.

'It is his!' she hissed. 'You need the *laghima*, that supreme ego to propel that aircraft which Kuber has in plenty to make it work!' she disparaged. 'He floats on it so does his aircraft, both strong enough to counteract forces of resistance!'

Her sarcasm was not wasted on her or her father.

'Stop feeding Meenu with poisonous nonsense!' he snapped. 'It is only through the very force of levitation that the chariot can rise, Meenu, not ego or pride as your mother claims. It is a power often displayed by learned rishis and Kuber learnt it from me as have your three brothers.'

But not me, she thought woefully, peeking longingly at the flower-domed chariot.

'I don't want you to even glance at it!' warned her mother.

But Meenaskhi could not tear her eyes away from the magnificent chariot.

'Would you like a ride?' a voice tempted her.

Meenakshi swivelled to see her half-brother, standing and looking as resplendent as his chariot. He looked older than he was, his red fleshy face, jutting chin and thin hard mouth gave an immediate impression of ruthlessness. He had had his usual siesta and looked fresh and his hazel eyes shone as brightly as the gold on his body. With a start she realized he had hers and Ravan's golden eyes. Just like their father's.

Meenakshi wanted to nod badly but a baleful glare from her mother, quelled her instinctive agreement. She kept silent, biting her lip in quiet frustration. *Why do adults fight so bitterly? Unlike the kids who soon forget their quarrels and are back to their game in no time?*

He glanced around. His small, piercing beady eyes were frosty as they took in the tension in the room.

'Where are the boys?' he asked perfunctorily.

There was no love lost between them either.

Kaikesi threw her husband a warning look but Vishravas ignored it. 'They are seeking the blessings of Lord Brahma.'

'For what?' asked Kuber nastily. 'To usurp my throne in Lanka?'

'Kuber!' Vishravas looked shocked.

'So the rumours are true that the three brothers have sought more divine powers through our great-grandfather!' he smiled unpleasantly. 'I am confirming what I heard. That Ravan is eyeing my throne. He believes it to be his as his grandfather Sumali ruled Lanka once,' emphasized Kuber, giving Kaikesi a meaningful look.

'Ravan would never hurt you!' argued Vishravas. 'He is your brother.'

'Half-brother,' smoothly corrected Kuber, still looking at Kaikesi. 'All of us cannot allow ourselves to forget that. Father, either you are naive or you are feigning ignorance. Ravan wants Lanka!'

'No, he hopes to defeat Kartaviryarjun!' protested his father. 'Ravan wants to get revenge from him, not you. You are his older brother, he holds no grudge against you.'

'Father, once he is back with his brothers, all-powerful and mighty, the first person they will attack is me, not Kartaviryarun! You have got to see that, it is evident. He has been whetted for this since his childhood. Neither Sumali nor my mother Kaikesi,' he paused, his lips curling, 'have ever reconciled to the fact that they were defeated and I was presented the throne by Lord Vishnu. They have been training the three brothers—and your three sons—to reconquer what they had lost: Lanka, that City of Gold. And they will, Father, they will.'

'You had delusions of grandeur now you have delusions of persecution!' reprimanded Vishravas, a sharp sting in his voice. 'Jealousy has jaundiced your judgement!'

Meenakshi had never seen her father use that tone with Kuber before. In fact, she had never seen him angry with her half-brother. He adored him as he adored Vibhishan. But her father was essentially a fair man, never thinking ill of anyone, and disapproving of those who displayed or were affected by prejudice or envy. That was why he had frequent arguments with her mother; he found her ill-feelings distasteful.

Kuber gave an arrogant shake of his head. 'No, love for them has jaundiced *your* judgement! You can neither see through them nor your wife's schemes!' he fumed, flushed a dull red. 'She stole you away from us and now she and her sons shall steal my Lanka away! And all you will do is watch silently, as you did the last time!'

Vishravas went pale, amazed at Kuber's unexpected impertinence robbing him of speech. For once Kaikesi kept silent, enjoying the new, unusual display of hostility between the father and son.

'You are insulting your father!' muttered Vishravas, through stiff lips.

'I am being frank and trying to make you see the truth,' replied Kuber. 'I have guessed your sons' motives, you still have not. My doubts have been sufficiently validated and I shall do everything in my power and purpose to protect my throne...'

'Yes, that is your right and duty,' agreed his father blandly. 'But I won't have you casting aspersions on your mother and brothers.'

His words, though softly uttered, flared up the hostility further.

Kuber raised his voice. 'I don't care what you believe, and I shan't try to convince you otherwise. But no one gets my Lanka!! Do remember, Father, when your sons—my brothers as you say—come back, your wife shall instruct them to attack Lanka and hold me prisoner or force me to flee...' he held up his plump arm as if to stop further argument. 'But I shall avoid such a situation. I have a bargaining weapon,' he smiled suddenly, his cold, beady eyes traveling slowly across the room to Meenakshi. She looked up at him uncomprehendingly. For his size, he moved quickly to step towards her, his fat paws snaking out to clamp on her thin wrists.

Meenkakshi felt a shiver of chilly fear crawl up her spine. She knew what he meant. He was going to use her as his leverage, a concession to be used in his negotiations with her brothers to favour his position. Kuber meant to take her with him to Lanka so that they never dare attack the golden city.

Her father gathered his implication quickly enough and so did her mother.

'Don't you dare touch my daughter!' she spat, almost lunging at him.

But Kuber for all his heavy rotundness ducked and was quick on his feet. He tightened his hold on her wrist and started dragging her out of the room.

Vishravas was too stupefied to react swiftly. But Kaikesi stepped in front of Kuber, almost towering over the short, plump figure. He didn't cower. He threw her roughly aside. Kaikesi reeled under the impact.

'Kuber!!' What are you doing?' roared Vishravas.

'Safeguarding my Lanka and my interests!' retorted Kuber. 'This girl stays with me till I get an assurance that Ravan will not attack Lanka.'

'Isn't my word assurance enough??' shouted his father.

Kaikesi was back on her feet and the only weapon she had found was Vishravas' walking stick. 'I shall thrash you if you don't let go of my daughter!' she hissed venomously.

Kuber sneered and raised his arm to take hold of the brandishing staff. As he tackled her mother, Meenakshi took her opportunity and buried her nails into the soft flesh of Kuber's finger, gripping at her wrist. He flinched, the grip slackening slightly. Swiftly, with her other free arm, she raked her nails all down his bare arm, scouring deep into the flesh. Kuber yelped more in surprise than in pain. He had not expected the young girl to retaliate. He looked at her in startled consternation: she was thin and small, her wrists so frail that he could have easily crushed them between his gripping fingers but in her eyes he saw a flood of fire, gushing forth to scorch him. What raked him instead was a quick flash of her nails as he felt them tearing down his face, ripping his skin, the blood spurting through the deep gash. He instinctively clutched at his face, letting go of her.

'Hellcat!' he spluttered.

'Yes, that and more!' she sibilated. 'I am known as Surpanakha!!' She spoke in a glacial, featureless voice that did not quite conceal a frightened anxiety.

And she lunged at him again, clawing viciously at his bare back and shoulders. Kuber retreated, covering his face with his pudgy hands as the girl attacked with renewed vigour. He could feel her nails scouring out his skin and felt the warm gush of blood on his face. He screamed in agony, his hands trying to get hold of the wretched girl with her flying hair and flaming eyes. She scratched at his wrists, kicking strongly at his legs, making him lose his balance. He staggered and almost fell. His father fortunately came to the rescue, prising the flailing girl from him, holding her forcibly by her shoulders in a protective hug. The girl struggled to break free, glowering with murderous eyes and intent.

Kuber looked at her fearfully, retracing his steps hastily.

'I think you should leave, Kuber,' Vishravas said quietly. 'Meenakshi has amply shown she can protect herself! She is no weakling to be dragged down and held as ransom—she's my daughter!' Vishravas looked grim. 'And you had the temerity to touch her! Or did you forget she's your sister too?'

'Your devilish family!' growled Kuber, wiping the trickle of blood, still oozing out.

'....and you are no saint!' retorted his father. 'That you were going to kidnap my daughter to teach my sons a lesson is beyond my comprehension! Power may have made you stronger but your throne has made you weak and insecure!!'

'....for it was never his!' interjected Kaikesi contemptuously. 'And yes, after what you did today, I shall see to it that Ravan does do what you so fear the most!'

'Kaikesi!!'

'No,' she rounded on her husband. 'Ravan shall get back what my father lost. Lanka is Ravan's right, his inheritance. He is entitled to it.'

'Are you talking about Sumali, dear mother Kaikesi?' asked Kuber silkily. 'You are still trying to fulfil your dead father's dying dream??' he added cruelly.

The colour drained from Kaikesi's flushed face, her eyes widening in horrified grief.

'What are you talking about?' asked Vishravas sharply.

'Actually I had meant to let you know sooner of this tragic piece of news. Your brother, dear father, the great rishi Agastya got rid of Sumali and his father Suketu as they kept troubling him in his yagna. Both are dead. Agastya spared Taraka and the sons Subahu and Mareecha, cursing them to turn to monsters and drove them away to the Dandak forest so that they never trouble him or any other rishis again!'

'Monsters?' repeated Kaikesi through white, parched lips.

'Yes they are rakshasas, aren't they? My uncle cursed them to their true form in all their ugliness—from within and outside!' chortled Kuber, with malicious triumph.

Meenakshi shivered a slight shudder. *My beautiful Nani transformed into an ogre. And my handsome uncles with their warm eyes and warm smiles who had taught me the trickiest of spells. All turned to monsters?* A jolt of pain pierced her, doubling her in pain. She turned to her father.

'Is this Agastya your brother, Father?' she asked tremulously, her eyes dimmed with convulsive anguish.

Vishravas nodded absently, stunned at the news.

'Didn't he know they were my grandparents and my uncles? We are family. Then why did he harm them?' she choked.

'Because they are evil!' spat Kubera. 'Greedy, vicious and wicked.'

'They are not!' she shouted back, the rage drying away the tears in her voice. 'They are good and nice and kind. You are mean!'

Vishravas gently held her by her shaking shoulders. 'No, dear, you won't understand...' he sighed. 'Your uncle Agastya did that for a reason.'

'He is NOT my uncle. My only uncles are Subahu and Mareech, and they have been turned to monsters because of your brother! And Nani...' she stifled a sob, recalling the soft, kind eyes of Taraka, her warm hug, her hearty laugh...where was she? In what state was she?

For the first time she felt a mounting anger against her father. 'Your brother destroyed them!' she said in a hoarse whisper, her eyes blazing with accusation.

'They deserved it!' interrupted Kuber with relish. 'As I said they were bent on causing trouble and they had it coming...'

'Our turn will come too!' Kaikesi's icy voice whipped like a cold lash, sharp and stinging. She stood dry-eyed, recovering her composure and her grief, refusing to allow Kuber to witness her state of devastation.

Her ominous ultimatum was like fuel on burning embers. Kuber went red, his cheeks an ugly florid and eyes bulging in glittering dislike.

'My Ravan shall take revenge on all of you!' she proclaimed portentously.

Vishravas sharply cut in. 'Stop it, Kaikesi. Your parents made the same mistake...!'

'What mistakes?' snarled Kaikesi. 'Reconquering our lost land is a mistake? What were we supposed to do but sit back and suffer copiously? The devas had confined us to the netherworld and you wished us to endure in hell forever! That won't be for long, we shall strike back!'

'Your father is dead and your brothers and mother are wandering ogres in the forest,' said Kuber with malignant glee. 'You fought for them but who will fight for you? Your sons?' he asked softly.

'Yes.'

Kaikes's single word of agreement was a confirmation of the bloody past and all what was to come.

'Hear, hear her, Father! She admits to use my so-called brothers to war with me,' stated Kuber, a small smile playing unpleasantly on his thick lips. 'And yet you refuse to believe me!'

Vishravas fell silent, holding Meenakshi close. He felt her shaking, quivering with dry sobs, the tears refusing to well out, her eyes burning into Kubers. He felt a shiver of fear, recounting Pulastya's words: she would be as deadly as Ravan. Vishravas still could not fathom how this trembling girl could prove to be a bane to anyone, least of all his family.

'That was no reason for you to attempt to kidnap my daughter in my presence!' he said grimly. 'You can leave now, Kuber. You have done enough.'

Kuber had the grace to look a trifle ashamed and could not meet his father's eyes. His fat face contorted, his breath wheezing through his larded lungs, he left as quietly as he had arrived, the Pushpak Viman taking off smoothly without even a swish of a breeze.

Kaikesi collapsed in a flood of tears, sobbing inconsolably. Meenakshi was rooted to the ground, numb with shock. She heard her mother weeping, her heart wretched, wringing out for her. She shook her nerveless fingers from Vishravas' restraining hold and moved slowly towards Kaikesi, hugging her tightly. Kaikesi clung to her, and in that moment of shared grief, the tears seeped out slowly, as they rolled down her pale face, thickening fast as a new wave of pain and fury swept over her. Mother and daughter embraced each other, coming together for the first time in their moment of mourning.

Vishravas looked at them, feeling bereft.

He was about to leave the room when Kaikesi stopped him with a single question. 'What would you have done if Kuber had taken Meenu away just now?' she asked, throwing him a contemptuous look through her falling tears.

'He wouldn't have,' he said weakly.

'He well would have had not Meenu defended herself!' said Kaikesi scornfully.

Kaikesi held her daughter close, having almost lost her. She suddenly realized with a shock that she reached her shoulders. Meenakshi had grown up. But it was within this last one defining hour when she must have swiftly grown up from a young girl to a woman.

'I am so proud of you, my dear.' she patted her daughter's smooth cheek. Meenakshi felt a soaring joy fill her heart; her mother was gazing at her with pride. It was an unfamiliar feeling, suffusing with a warmth she had not experienced before.

Her mother continued, 'I am sorry I could not protect you; there's not even a knife in this damned hut to fend for oneself! But I am sorry that your father could not come to your rescue.'

The sting was silent but sharp. Vishravas paled.

'Now do you realize the difference between a sage and a warrior?' she jeered. 'My daughter, barely fourteen, knows how to defend herself unlike you, you great, learned scholar! Even your mighty words could not stop him from snatching your daughter right in front of your eyes!! Fie your brilliance, I call it cowardliness!'

The words rang menacingly in the tiny hut. For once, Meenakshi found herself agreeing, albeit grudgingly, with her mother. Her father's helplessness fired a sliver of red hot anger in her, sizzling with shame and hurt. He had not rushed to her aid, as she had anticipated. As any child would expect from her father. He had stood silently, shocked but passive as his son had dragged her by her wrist and seized her. This was the same father who, laying aside pride, dignity and differences, had begged for Ravan's release from Kartiviryarun, she recalled with sudden animosity, the acrid taste of disappointment filling her mouth. She hated to admit to herself: her father had failed her. And she was swamped by another wave of hopelessness—that he did not love her. If he had, would he not have fought for her safety? The realization reverberated dully in her weeping mind: her father did not love her, as a father should, or as much as she loved him—so unquestioningly, so faithfully. He had let her down. She felt a dry sob gurgle in her throat but she swallowed hard as the harsh voices of her parents broke through the haze of her anguish. They were arguing again.

Vishravas said, through stiff lips, 'Yes, she is a brave child. Meenu saved herself wonderfully and now I know I need not worry about her. She knows how to look after herself. '

'That is because of my mother!' exploded Kaikesi, her face twisted in grief.

Meenakshi's heart contracted at the mention of her beloved Nani. She could never teach her new tricks now, the spells she made her memorize, the potions she learnt to prepare, the resounding kiss she used to plant on her cheek each time she self-disparaged...her throat welled with tears, her eyes suddenly wet. She felt the hot tears coursing down her cheeks, unchecked and profuse, racking her body. She looked at her parents, but they were still disputing contentiously.

Her father's tone was placating. 'But why are you hell bent on distorting everything, Kaikesi? I was never against self-defence or using arms to defend oneself.'

Kaikesi was quick to twist his words. 'Ravan is defending himself too—he is defending his rights,' she refuted hotly. 'Lanka is his to take!'

'Kaikesi, don't!'

'After what Kuber did today, I shall see to it Ravan gets back what is rightfully his, even if his grandfather is not alive to witness the great day,' announced Kaikesi, her voice as brittle as her eyes.

'Your father is dead, Kaikesi,' he said quietly. 'He used you all his life to fulfil his unrequited dream. Now you are doing the same. Why are you pushing your children to that uncertain, violent fate? Don't use them to fight your battles!'

'You will do the same—try to make them saints, pontificating and poor! I don't want my Ravan to be like you! He is more my father's grandson than will he be ever your son!!'

Meenakshi looked at her parents, glaring at each other in mutual hostility. Her shoulders slumping in saddened acceptance, but she straightened them immediately, stiff with resentment.

They were fighting again: over Ravan. *Why did it always have to be about Ravan?*

Invincible

(H)er brothers were home at last. She had missed them, even Ravan's black humour and Vibhishan's sanctimonious sermons, but it was Kumbha's camaraderie Meenakshi had missed the most; he was the older brother she looked up to. *Hopefully, we will stay together like this*, she wished wistfully, quickly dismissing her parents' current mood of antagonism , bitterly palpable after her grandfather's death. Kaikesi had taken Sumali's death badly, blaming Vishravas viciously for it.

She had greeted Ravan with that news the moment he entered the ashram with his brothers, flinging herself on him as she sobbed out the tragic event.

Ravan was now a tall, powerfully-built young man in his twenties with his unmistakable swinging gait, the quick jerk of his head and the deep gravelly sound of his voice. He was handsome in a rugged way, with humorous amber eyes, but which could go a cold golden when angry as they were now when he heard his mother weeping. He had a ruthless, jutting jaw and his mouth could laugh easily or tighten to a dangerous thinness as she had always known. As he sat on the broken coir bed, dressed, in white rough cotton, his long narrow feet bare, he looked regal, every inch a king. Which he was not. But there was an air about him that reduced the people around him to the size of dwarfs. He looked awe-inspiring, tough and ruthless, but somehow he made her feel secure. He was her brother.

Ravan, as Meenakshi had expected, absorbed the news badly. He adored his grandfather and was one of the few, rare people Ravan respected deeply; a sentiment he did not reserve either for his father or his rishi family. The scorn curdled quickly to viscous anger.

'He did not deserve such a disgraceful death!' he kept repeating in shocked grief.

His anguished whisper held a trace of menace, making it sound like a dangerous purr. 'If Agastya had been provoked, why was he not man enough to challenge Nana in an open battle? Curses and condemnation, is that all that the rishis can pronounce?' he struggled, his voice unsteady. 'But I shall give Nana back the honour he craved for all his life. I am what I am because of him!'

He was not shouting as he usually did when he was enraged. Had the long *tapas* mollified her brother? Or was he beyond that; mad with grief? Just as she had been inordinately close to Taraka, Ravan had been greatly attached to Sumali. Ravan had considered Nana as his father-figure, never their father, and even he was aware of this.

Vishravas found himself helpless, torn between placating his grief-stricken son and secretly relieved by the turn of events. Sumali was finally done away with: Agastya had killed him, his patience worn thin. All these years, Agastya had refrained from confronting Suketu and Sumali, respecting them as his brother's family. But Sumali had taken advantage of Agastya's silence, mistaking it for meek acquiescence. Now Agastya had struck back, his last vestige of family loyalty giving away to bloodshed.

But Ravan would never understand: his mind had been poisoned a long time ago by his grandfather. The venom would remain forever, surely and steadily it will spread and create havoc, soon...very soon. Vishravas knew he had been defeated by his dead father-in-law. He had taken his son forever from him, in his death, Sumali had achieved his final triumph.

'Nana would have been the happiest person today at me having finally received the blessing of immortality from Brahma—

it was his plan and he's no longer here to reap the fruit of his patience and perseverance over the years,' continued Ravan dully. 'I am now ready to do all what he had wanted me to do, but where is he when I need him most? I did it for him and he is not here to give me his blessings!!'

Meenakshi found herself swiftly identifying with her brothers' pain; she could fathom his sorrow. Inadvertently, she felt close to this brother as never before.

Vishravas decided to remain silent: he seemed to be no longer needed. He felt like an intruder in his own house, a stranger who was unwelcome. His family seemed to have driven far away from him, all huddled together in their common grief. Only Vibhishan was by his side, and had touched his feet the moment he had entered the hut. Meenakshi noticed that he had changed too. His tawny eyes no longer looked tiny for his plump face which was rotund no longer, but seemed trimmed down, his face now quite lean. His beaky nose like their mother's seemed pronounced over a weak chin and a full, rather feminine mouth. His ears still stuck out accentuating the studious, intelligent air to his dreamy, forgetful eyes. His smooth, fair face was not sun-tanned like Ravan's but pale and limpid, and the thick fringe of glossy dark hair made him good-looking in a pallid, colourless way. There was the same soft fidelity in the eyes and vulnerability in the protruding ears as a shy student. He lacked the main essence of both his brothers: Ravan's smouldering fire and Kumbha's blustering bulk.

'I have been blessed with infinite knowledge of dharma and all the shastras, father,' he said briefly. 'I hope I can carry the torch of our family.'

'That torch which burned down my family, you mean!' glowered Kaikesi. 'How can you be loyal to this man, Vibhishan? And you, Meenu, forever following him like a faithful sheep!' she rounded on Meenakshi, who was lurking in the shadows.

Meenakshi was as taken aback as Vibhishan. 'He's our father, Ma!' he cried. '*He* didn't kill grandfather!'

He had not, but his family had and for once, Meenakshi could not erase the gnawing grudge against her father she was nursing since her grandfather's death, swamped by an irrelevant rage against her father and his family. They had taken her grandmother and her uncles away from her forever. In her mind, her father had been in some way responsible for the calamity.

She was as inconsolable as Kaikesi, but she refused to cry furthermore, the simmer of anger drying out her tears.

'Mother, it was Uncle Agastya who did it, not him! Why are you blaming him?' asked Vibhishan, his voice mild as always. But there was a trace of mounting apprehensiveness, expanded by the strong sense of alienation which suddenly seemed to have engulfed their family. They were now drastically divided.

Meenakshi glanced at Kumbha who looked distinctly uncomfortable, his earnest face suffused with distress. He had grown more huge, with his tall, beefy, ungainly figure. His complexion was sallow and his eyes were big, black and rather sad in their gentleness. In spite of his size, he could not entirely hide his timidity and shyness. If someone spoke to him suddenly, he would become flustered and turn red, looking anywhere but at the person addressing him. It used to amuse her as a kid; and he was doing it now.

She felt sympathy for him, all of them were going to be torn in this conflict of wills between their father and mother. Ravan would always champion for his mother, Vibhishan would be with their father. Kumbha, being blindly loyal to Ravan, would have to support his mother. That left her: what was she to do? But no one seem to be concerned about her. Or her opinion.

'Agastya wouldn't have dared to touch my family without his brother's commendation!' cried Kaikesi.

Vishravas looked stunned. 'Kaikesi you are accusing me of the unimaginable! I had nothing to do with this—I did not even know of it until Kuber broke it to us.'

Kaikesi remained unmoved, distraught in her pain and fury. 'Your family have always hated me and my clan, you knew it and yet you did nothing to convince them otherwise! We were the despicable Asuras who needed to be annihilated, that is what this is all about!!'

'I understand your grief, my dear, but please don't hold me responsible for your father's death! You know I was not, then why are you bent on destroying our family because of what happened to yours?' said Vishravas. Meenakshi could hear the pleading tone in his voice—he was trying to salvage his family.

'Because they are part of the family you and your brother and father despise—they hate our children too!' she said scathingly. 'Now is the moment of decision—it is either your family or mine, dear husband!' her voice suddenly cooled down, almost glacial, yet sharp and pointed.

'For you, it's always been a moment of confrontation, of strife and conflict!' responded Vishravas quietly. 'You are forcing your children to choose between the parents? Which mother does that?'

'A provoked daughter whose parents have been killed by her husbands' family—and you are partisan to it, in mind if not in person,' she said coolly, her face as calm as her voice, sure and confident. 'I want my revenge—and I am proud my son Ravan will oblige, without me having to prompt him. I am sure he feels the same.'

Ravan looked at Vishravas, his gaze long and hard. The father threw his son a last, hopeless look, begging him to see reason.

'Shall vengeance turn our family against each other? Ravan, with your newly acquired knowledge from Brahma's blessings, you are not just the most powerful person in this world today but the most knowing and knowledgeable,' started Vishravas, desperately. 'Use your knowledge, not the power of force.'

'But knowledge itself is power,' argued Ravan, walking towards his father. 'You said that once.'

'Yes, only if employed wisely,' nodded his father. 'I understand your grief, but this is not the time or reason for vendetta. It will ruin you! You are armed with the best—courage and knowledge. Use them for bettering the world, not for pointlessly fighting for rights or revenge.'

'I *shall* better the world,' agreed Ravan with a soft laugh.

Meenakshi shivered, it sounded ominous.

'I shall better the world,' he repeated. 'I shall give it a new leader—not the devas or Indra or Vishnu. It shall be me.'

It was calmly uttered, but with a shattering conviction. Vishravas clutched at his son's hand, holding it in a strong grip.

'No! No! Don't start a war with them! You were born for a better life than a marauding warrior...'

'Aren't warriors supposed to be brave?' retorted Ravan sardonically. 'And rishis wise? I am both—the best leader the world deserves. I have mastered the Vedas and the holy books, and all the martial arts of warfare and weaponry. And I have been blessed by both Lord Shiva and Brahma. No one can defeat me—not Kartviryarjun, not Kuber, not any deva or daitya, not even Indra or Vishnu. My new boon makes me invincible!' announced Ravan, shrugging himself with his usual cloak of arrogance. He was his old self again.

He continued grandly, 'I was trained by you Father, in the *shastras*, the Vedas and the Upanishads, philosophy and science, literature and art. But politics was taught by Nana. He trained me in war and strategy and how to cleverly battle. But this was not enough. I had to appease and please Lord Shiva: I am his most devoted follower. I had to have his blessings. And after years of penance, he did bless me but I got interrupted by that Kartaviryarjun!' Ravan's brow darkened for a moment. 'It was meant to be a lesson for me. The defeat from his hands proved that I was still weak, not yet powerful enough to vanquish a king. I had to have more! And, who better than my own great-grandfather Brahma himself to bless me with more knowledge and power?' he chuckled softly. 'And so, along with my brothers, we performed intense *tapasya* lasting for all these years. My brothers soon were blessed with their boons...'

'Did Kumbha get his blessing of everlasting strength and courage?' broke in Kaikesi eagerly.

Kumbha shifted uneasily on his heavy feet.

'No, he did not!' answered Ravan grimly. 'Instead of asking for *Indraasan*, the word which came out was *Nidraasan*!'

Kaikesi hissed a gasp of horror, speechless in dismay.

'Instead of the high seat of Indra, Kumbha gets a bed to sleep!' raged Ravan, a muscle twitching at his lean, square jaw. 'I am sure it was a trick! Kumbha realized the slip and intended to ask for *Nirdevatvam*—the annihilation of the Devas but instead again which came out of his mouth was *Nidravatvam*—sleep!! Later, I got to know that this was Indra's doing. He had beseeched Saraswati, the Lady of Knowledge, to make Kumbha utter the wrong words. That powerful Indra was so insecure about our Kumbha that he had to beg for Saraswati's intervention. Aghast at what had happened and what the consequences would spell, I pleaded with Brahma to undo this boon as it was worse than a curse. Brahma agreed but said he was helpless as words once uttered could not be undone. But he promised to mitigate the effect—but now, from henceforth Kumbha shall sleep for six months, and stay awake only for the remaining six!'

'This is outrageous!' cried Kaikesi. 'And wicked and unfair...' she sought to struggle with her disappointment. 'But then, what do you expect from the devas and the rishis?' her scorn was vituperative. 'They are infamously known to cheat when cornered, rather than battle it out!'

Vishravas felt sick with apprehension. The gods were already wary, if not perturbed, and were taking the necessary measures to restrain his sons. The battle had started. Soon there would be war...

Ravan seemed to be reading his thoughts. 'This is the prelude to the war!' he proclaimed. 'I have my boon of immortality but for which I had to prove myself ten times! For this penance, I had to chop off my head ten times as a sacrifice to appease Brahma—otherwise he would not have believed my sincerity. Each time I sliced my head off, a new head erupted, thanks to the blessings of Lord Shiva which helped me to continue with my tapasya. Finally, Brahma was convinced and was sufficiently pleased with the austerity. He, at last, appeared in his form after my tenth decapitation and offered me a boon. I asked for immortality, which Brahma refused to give, but instead gave me a celestial nectar of immortality. It was to be stored just below my navel and pronounced that I could not be vanquished for as long as it lasted.'

'Lasted?' Kaikesi looked puzzled. 'Will it vanish?'

'No, it remains in me till my last breath!' smiled Ravan. 'And since there is no last breath meant for me, the nectar is safe inside me. I am an immortal, Ma, and I can never die!' he laughed jubilantly. 'I cannot be killed by any deva, heavenly spirits, rakshas, serpents, and wild beasts. No one can touch me now!'

'You didn't mention mortals,' noted his father, his eyes narrowing. 'Why? If you could list animals and beasts, why not Man?'

'Man is fleeting!' Ravan argued with an exaggerated shrug of his broad shoulders. 'They are lesser beings—mere mortals! Weak, mean and avaricious, who bring upon their own downfall,' dismissed Ravan contemptuously, his disdain evident. 'Brahma granted me these boons in addition to my ten severed heads—each of them made stronger with the knowledge of divine weapons and magic. Now I am no longer Ravan but Dashaanan!'

'Dashaanan,' snorted his father. 'Your mother nicknamed you Dashmukh a long time ago when she gave you that pearl necklace you are wearing!' He underlined the new moniker in embittered denigration.

'Ten heads?' said Meenakshi wonderingly.

For the first time, Ravan noticed his sister, startled at the transformation. She was no longer a saucy chit, who had almost gouged his eyes out. He touched the scar on his neck. He could never forget what she was capable of. She had grown, not as tall as their mother but no longer diminutive but a sultry girl with a full figure. She was attractive with her large, hazel eyes and the wavy cascade of a thick mane, dusky and sensuous—and Ravan immediately felt protective towards his little sister. But she seemed to know how to protect herself. Her flat, golden eyes were windows revealing a cold and ferocious ruthlessness that made most people flinch from her.

'Figuratively, silly!' he said fondly. 'I don't have ten heads!'

Meenakshi smiled in return, suddenly feeling shy in front of her brothers. It had been years since they had left; they were taller and bulkier since she had last seen them. And divinely influential.

She nodded knowingly. 'You now have the ten heads for the six shastras and the four Vedas.'

'And she's not silly either!' interjected Kaikesi, still looking grim. 'She saved herself from Kuber when he tried to forcibly take her away from this very ashram so that you would not dare attack Lanka or his throne.'

A look of disbelief flickered on Ravan's face, darkening to a furious frown. The incredulity was swiftly replaced with a mask of rage and surging hate; their half-brother had insulted them all through their growing years but that he had the audacity to physically harm her, ripped open a raw, unhealed wound.

'He dared do that!!' he whispered shakily, in black fury.

'Yes, he dared more than that!' countered his mother. 'He would have taken her away had she not defended herself and scratched him bloody with her nails, my Surpanakha!'

Ravan touched the scar lightly again, staring thoughtfully at his sister. 'Our Surpanakha saved herself and the day, but Kuber needs to answer for his unwarranted belligerence,' he remarked, unusually calm. 'He is afraid that I shall attack Lanka and usurp his throne, does he? Let me remove that fear once and for all!'

Vishravas made a vain movement of his hands. 'Please, Ravan, don't! Kuber is an arrogant fool, but you don't have to be! You have greatness in you. But not for the bloodshed you intend to start...'

'I did not start it, Father, Kuber did,' Ravan corrected, his face now impassive, unmoved by his father's pleadings.

He seems cold, his stolid façade is unnerving and he could get hard-hearted, Meenakshi thought, her heart going out to her father. But she agreed more with Ravan than her father, whom she loved to a fault. Ravan was fighting for her, for her grandparents, for her uncles—all whom had been destroyed by the devas and the rishis. Did her father not understand or was he so different from them, as her mother and Ravan always insisted. *Was he the rishi and we the savage asuras*, Meenakshi felt her stomach clench. *Am I not my father's daughter as much as my mother's?*

'But you do not have to pursue this hostility, Ravan,' Vishravas beseeched. 'It will be the beginning of a certain end for all of us.'

'No, it will be the end of them and our new start. There will be no end—I shan't die and shall see to it that my family never comes to harm,' Ravan shot back, his lips tightening. 'Your son had the temerity to enter this hut and snatch my sister in your presence. It is not just outrageous but shameful for us. Can't we even defend ourselves especially from those who claim to be family?'

The sarcasm was not lost on Vishravas. 'Kuber will never come here. I have warned him never to step here ever again,' he assured.

'No he won't, I shall go to him and teach him some manners,' agreed Ravan mildly. 'Guess I am old enough to teach my older brother some rules of conduct and courtesy. I shall protect my family from now on. I have got the impossible, and now I shall do the impossible!'

Her act of self-defence had been blown up as an act of bravery, a reason to war. It had been desperation, not courage for there had been none to save her but herself. She had fought like a tigress and now her brother, prowling and provoked, had caught the scent of blood. Meenakshi watched her father's look of growing despair. Violence would be the answer; there would be war now, Meenakshi was certain of it. She was the legitimate pretext.

'Beware brother, one step forward might take all of us back to chaos!' warned Vibhishan. His earlier diffidence had gone, replaced by a gentle firmness. He was neither mild nor inattentive in disposition any more, but focussed on his older brother with an intent expression in his eyes.

Ravan swept him a look of impatience. 'As pious as our dear father! Vibhishan, you have always had a pure mind and a virtuous heart,' he said making his younger brother's qualities sound like weakness.

Meenakshi smiled wryly, *Vibhishan's piousness leaned more towards self-righteousness.*

'Even as a kid, you spent all your energy and time meditating on Vishnu. It angered me—it still does because Vishnu drove our family away from Lanka. Yet you pray to him, with our father's blessings,' Ravan mocked, his tone laconic. 'When Brahma appeared and offered you any boon you wanted, what did our dear, kind, Vibhishan ask for?' Ravan said scornfully. 'Pure and profound knowledge, which he could use for the welfare of the world and ultimately lay at the feet of Vishnu! He prayed that he should be given the strength to be always loyal to him and serve him and hope for that one day, when he received his blessings and darshan!' he finished, disparagingly.

Each word was laced with dripping disdain, but was it more for Vishnu or Vibhishan, Meenakshi wondered. Or both. But Meenakshi found herself holding the same contempt Ravan had for Vibhishan. Both were her brothers but she could not agree with Vibhishan's strange devotion for Vishnu. It had been Lord Shiva who had always helped them, it was always Lord Shiva who had been their saviour. Why this undue fascination for Vishnu? Why was he so different from them? *Because he was more his father's son,* decided Meenakshi than his mother's, an Asura. *Of all the boons he could have asked for, could he not have asked for something more significant?*

'Your brother Kuber came home and tried to abduct your sister. I, much to my consternation, have been accused of being the offender here instead of Kuber. Dear brother, how would *you* react?' Ravan spoke to Vibhishan opprobriously, with exaggerated politeness.

Vibhishan refused to be snubbed by his elder brother. 'Kuber is scared of you—it was an act, not of defiance, but of cowardice. Ignore him, he won't dare confront you ever again!'

'It was an act of defiance and cowardice!' scoffed Ravan. 'That is why he was going to seize Meenakshi against her will.

Does it not bother you that he dared to harm your sister?'

'Yes, it does,' agreed Vibhishan worriedly. 'But as I said, he's a coward...'

'And does Lanka deserve to be ruled by a coward?' growled Ravan.

Vibhishan was now trapped. 'No,' he conceded unwillingly.

Vishravas got up, agitated. 'Who are you, Ravan, to decide who should rule Lanka? Lanka is Kuber's now, not your mothers' family's. Your grandfather was defeated in a fair battle—his throne was not usurped.'

'So shall it be ours again. I shall not usurp, but wage a fair war against him, challenge Kuber for the throne he is not fit to sit on. Would that be fair, father, a warrior's honourable intention?' he mocked.

The pleased, satisfied expression in his eyes jarred her father into a burst of temper.

'You are attacking your brother!' accused Vishravas furiously.

'He did the same to my home, my daughter,' interposed Kaikesi.

Vishravas was stung at the malice still simmering in his wife long after discretion had died.

He rounded on her fiercely. 'You are the culprit! You have indoctrinated my children with all these ideas of war and violence. You have lost your family to it, don't you realize you will lose ours as well to this senseless violence?'

'I would rather die fighting the devas than live under their subjugation,' said Kaikesi bitterly. 'I have lived it and I shan't allow my children to live in disgrace, shame and fear. They shall be feared, and the devas will tremble!' she spouted with renewed venom. 'Lanka was ours, and we shall win it back!'

Meenakshi knew those were not the last words. This was the beginning.

Lost

*T*hey drove up a winded, dusty road, edged on either side by dense trees. Meenakshi began to feel strangely anxious. She could not explain this uneasiness to herself, but the darkness of the towering trees, shutting out the sunlight and the startlingly high walls gave her an overpowering feeling of being trapped, like a prisoner walking into a cave. She told herself this was foolish nonsense: she was driving into a palace where she would be the princess—the princess of Lanka. But the feeling persisted. Suddenly the gloomy forest was gone and on either side of the road were wide, immaculate lawns and banks of bright flower beds with a huge ornamental fountain at the centre. The colours and congruency was impressive. Meenakshi could see the palace now. It was magnificent: sheathed in gold, with studded, flashing gems in delicate filigree, it glimmered in the bright sunlight, its halo of splendour dazzling for miles around. Meenakshi was awe-struck: it was truly the envy of gods. Shimmering in its golden glory, it was structured as a high built massive castle with looming towers and turrets on a steep sea-facing cliff with a series of columned passageway running all around the orbicular, stepped marbled terraces against a backdrop of clear blue sky and the sea merging in the distance. It was a breath taking vision. She had never seen the sea before and had been instantly attracted to its magic: the sight, the sound, it was as if it had a soul, deep and drowning, the waves moving in constant flux of emotions. She dragged her eyes away from its mesmerizing pull, and turned to glance at the golden palace. It looked what it was: the imposing residence of one of the richest men in the world—the king of Lanka.

Tall and handsome as always, Ravan had ambled into the court of Kuber with his family of brothers, a proud sister, a vindicated mother and a crestfallen father.

Kuber sat on his throne, with a chin beard covering his weak double chin, his enormous bald dome of a head hidden by a gaudy, gem-encrusted crown, his ferrety golden eyes suddenly fearful, and his thick, blunt nose twitching with anger. He had been too shocked to respond, eyeing his distraught father sceptically. Ravan had taken over easily, the situation and the assembly hall, his ostentatious display of arrogance matching the lurid opulence of the royal court. Meenakshi could never forget the look of incredulity etched on Kuber's face as Ravan walked up to the throne which suddenly seemed too huge for him.

'I am Ravan!' he announced.

'I come here to ask for the crown Vishnu took away from my grandfather and placed it on you. He did it through war and it was a fair defeat,' continued Ravan, his tone mocking. 'Should I do the same with my army of asuras, under my grand-uncle Malyavan, which is waiting across the high walls of this wondrous city, Kuber?'

Kuber knew he had lost even before uttering the next words.

'There will be no bloodshed, brother,' pronounced Kuber, with difficulty. 'I don't want Lanka plundered and pillaged.'

'I can never hurt my city, my people,' agreed Ravan solemnly. 'But I take your request as your magnanimity and not cowardice, as most would quickly assume,' he taunted. 'We are sons of the same father and with full respect for him, I shall not lay a finger on you,' he continued disdainfully, his amber eyes hard as topaz, gleaming in silent triumph. '...as you did on my helpless sister. That she was not as helpless as you presumed her to be, is another story.'

It was a fatal master stroke of the bloodless blade of the sword: in one swish he had shorn Kuber of all his pretence, without his crown, his throne, his pride and the last shred of respect. Kuber struggled to get up from his throne, slowly and sorrowfully, relinquishing his crown to Ravan. His hands trembled slightly as he gave the crown to his half-brother. The exchange of the flashy crown was, ironically, without pomp or grandeur, befitting its owner. His bare head made him look almost comical in its nakedness. Without it, he looked inelegant and ugly, just an ordinary, plump, pot-bellied man. Vishravas squirmed: Ravan was leeching him white, sparing Kuber his life but one without dignity or respect.

It was a defining metaphorical moment: the time to vacate his throne had arrived. Kuber had known it since the day Ravan was born, because the younger man had been born for this very purpose. To take back what he thought was rightfully his. He glanced at the slight, voluptuous girl standing near Ravan as they approached him, and Kuber found, to his shame, he could not meet her eye. She stood small and defiant, as deadly as her brother, in no way overawed at the enormity of the situation. It was her moment, and she was celebrating it. He had made a dastardly attempt to abduct her, hoping it would stop the brother from usurping his throne. She looked back at him steadily with her cat eyes, her stare hard and unblinking as if to say, *the day of reckoning has come and I shall decide your fate.*

Recalling those moments of terror as Kuber had gripped her by her wrist and dragged her half-across the room, Meenakshi felt no fear, anger or vicarious pleasure; it was a benign calm that settled in her heart as she watched the look of naked mortification in Kuber's eyes. There was a dejected finality: he had lost his throne to Ravan. And worse, now he was at his mercy:, and his future and his pride were at stake. She had got what she wanted—Kuber's disgrace. *Here was a man without his power and pomposity*, Meenakshi flicked him a scornful gaze.

Vishravas noticed it, flaring immediately. 'Gloating over someone's grief does not become you, Meenu,' he whispered angrily. 'A lack of false pride is the disposition of being humble, not conceited.'

Meenakshi felt a swift stab of hurt. He was still defending his son, not her. She felt betrayed, disbelief at her father's words. 'It is not false pride or fury, Father. It is justice,' she said tersely. 'Had the situation been the other way, the way your son had wanted, Father, I might have been imprisoned in these very walls of this beautiful palace. But would you have ever come to rescue me?' she asked painfully.

The anger was momentarily doused, not the dull ache of hurt. Vishravas pursed his lips, his eyes oddly vacant.

'Your brothers would have, sister!' Ravan's loud, assuring voice lashed across the high-domed hall, shattering the silence.

He turned grandly towards the white-faced Kuber with his fat paws clenched in his lap.

'But who will rescue Kuber now?' he laughed scornfully.

Lanka was won bloodlessly; Ravan had disposed Kuber without spilling a drop of blood, sweat or tear. She had expected a bloody war but the bloodless coup was as satisfying. She had revelled: she wanted to see Kuber in the throes of defeat and humiliation. She did not wish him dead, killed in the battlefield, a martyr but as a dethroned king, forced to submit and surrender. Thrown out from his own land. But Ravan had gone a step ahead and done something better—more grand, more meaningful yet so devastating.

She heard Ravan declare, in his deceptively soft, sonorous voice.

'I know your great love for the beautiful and the wonderful— we share it as brothers,' continued Ravan in mock-kindliness, gesturing at the gems-blazing golden throne, the glaring opulence of the thickly carpeted floor, the exquisitely lit chandeliers scattered across the carved roof of the assembly hall. 'I promise to make one such for you wherever you wish to settle. Where would it be, dear brother?'

Kuber went pallid, his face abnormally deficient in colour. Ravan was seeing to it that he was well on his way out, escorting him out like a polite host. But the exiled Kuber had nowhere to go.

'Go to Indralok , Kuber, I shall speak to Brahma. You shall

be given your rightful place and respect,' intervened Vishravas, his eyes as flinty as his voice.

'Yes, our dear father is always so helpful. He shall discuss with our great-grandfather Brahma. For what is family if it does not help one in need?' sneered Ravan. 'You shall have a similar, beautiful palace in Indralok, Kuber, so you don't miss Lanka much. That is my promise to you,' he added generously to Kuber's retreating figure as he slowly walked down the aisle of the assembly hall. His courtiers bowed, looking irresolute. The victorious asuras openly mocked them, by bursting into a thundering applause. The elaborate, arched doorway seemed no longer beautiful but far, far away. It was a slow, agonizing march for Kuber as he made his ignominious exit. Meenakshi marvelled at Ravan's suave viciousness; he struck hard but with a smooth, agreeable courteousness.

Vishravas stood immobile, a vague, distant look on his face.

Meenakshi slipped a hand in his and whispered, 'It was inevitable, Father. Lanka could not have been his for long. It is Ravan's now, please don't be unhappy about it.'

She knew her father's love and loyalty was been sundered apart; it was a battle between his two sons and he could do nothing but watch their hostility destroy his family. Her father did not reply but the grimness in his eyes no longer had a bleak hopelessness to it, but a glint of finality. He seemed to have come to a decision. But he waited politely for the coronation ceremony to get over, which was as quick and grand as their entry into the walled golden city.

Ravan courteously offered the throne to his grand-uncle, Malyavan, still tall and upright despite his advanced years. Tears of happiness flowed freely down his raddled cheeks.

'Sumali should have been here, this was his dream, his life's sole ambition—to win back Lanka,' he sighed. 'I have lost both my younger brothers now—Mali and Sumali—to the devas and the rishis. I, as the elder brother along with my two brothers had performed tapasya to Brahma, just like you did Ravan, with Kumbha and Vibhishan. But we asked for just one boon—that our brotherly love would hold fast and thick and remain unbreakable and no one would be able to defeat us. We were so blessed and consequently, we conquered every asura, deva, aditya and daitya, and thus, were un-vanquishable. To coronate our victories, we asked Vishvakarma to build a special city for us. This is that beautiful Lanka, the envy of Gods! We three brothers lived here in the lap of every conceivable luxury till we were attacked and defeated and Mali was killed by Vishnu,' said the old king shortly, his face twisted in remembered pain. 'But we are back here today, living Sumali's dream to reconquer Lanka. You fulfilled his dream, Ravan, and that makes you fit to be a king to rule this land. It's your time now, and your brothers'. You have my blessings and my loyalty. I shall serve you and this land till the last breath in my body.'

His words had moved everyone in the hall, followed by a deep silence of reverence. Meenakshi looked around at her family. They were all one large family—her brothers, mother, cousins, grand-uncles—but for once her father was not one of them. He seemed an outsider, a rishi amongst the asuras, a scholar amongst the warriors—unwanted and unwelcome. Meenakshi felt tearful in deep compassion, he was a stranger in his family. It was quickly replaced with an uneasy apprehension that filled her heavy heart.

The celebration feast was impeccable, hosted in an enormous high-ceilinged banquet-hall that could house upto five hundred people. Meenakshi had never witnessed such grandeur before. In the ashram, on festivals and days of special yagna, all of them would eat together—a prudent meal with lentils and sparing vegetables and a dash of solemnity—unlike here. There were footmen and maids bustling serving food and wine to all the guests. The grand meal began with gastronomic gusto with a variety of fish and meat and curried vegetables, followed by an assortment of flavoured rice with the desserts, served in gold bowls and delicately engraved spoons.

'Why aren't you rejoicing with us?' asked Kumbha, guzzling down a goblet as he noticed her standing quietly watching the revelry.

'All of us are celebrating, except for Father,' she said, her eyes searching for him. He was not in the hall. *Had he left*, her heart lurched miserably.

'Don't mope about it. Enjoy Lanka, it is a land of the sensuous and sensuality. We are asuras after all!' grinned Kumbha. 'And you are more of one of us than you would like yourself to believe, Meenu! Not like Vibhishan, who poor fellow is revolted at this vulgar display, as he calls it. He has retired for the day; must be praying somewhere!' he chuckled, more from the effect of wine than humour. 'I am here, with Ravan, not that I mind. He is the one who is going to look after us now. And as his brother, I have promised myself I shall look after him. But you, Meenu, you are more like Ravan and Ma, even though you hate admitting it. Both of you are a pair, too subtle to show your true emotions, yet fierce when it comes to displaying it. You are now worried about Father. But dear girl, the time will come soon enough when you shall have to choose between Father and Ma, between a life at the ashram or here at the palace,' he paused, suddenly serious. 'Between being an asura or a rishi-kanya. You are not like Vibhishan. Nor am I. Saintly and spiritual. He's more of a rishi and there's nothing of the asura in him...'

She shook her hand adamantly. 'You are good, and gentle and kind too, Kumbha, but you are proud to be an asura,' she reasoned. 'Yet the two of you are so different in your kindliness. Being a rishi or an asura is just a matter of attitude involving beliefs and feelings and values and dispositions to act in certain ways, is it not?'

'Don't go so cerebral on me, Meenu. I can barely think straight!!' grinned Kumbha oafishly. 'All I do know is that you are an asura girl all right—all fight and fire—so don't worry. Ravan once got a taste of it, and then Kuber!' he chortled loudly.

Meenakshi smiled, but it did not reach her flinty, feline eyes. 'You know me well, brother,' she said. 'But have you been grabbed by your arm viciously while you struggled, overcome with fear and uncertainty at what would happen next and lived the terror of being snatched away? Looking out frantically as you were dragged out of your own home whilst your parents are watching helplessly?' she hissed, her thin nose flaring. 'I had no one to call for help but myself and it was that brute Kuber who did that to me!' Her eyes were blazing, her voice glacial.

'I know,' said Kumbha, his voice sober. 'We weren't there, but always remember that we brothers won't let you ever get hurt. We are not like Father,' he said shortly. 'Kuber's audacity at what he did to you, prompted Ravan to teach him a lesson and throw him out of his own kingdom!'

Meenakshi shook her head. 'Yes, so all believe. But did Ravan really do this for me? Do you honestly believe that? I was an excuse; Ravan would have taken Lanka from Kuber anyway, one day. He was simply waiting for the right time and opportunity. I seem to have given him that.'

An inexplicable emotion flitted in the jet black eyes of Kumbha making Meenakshi suddenly feel uneasy. 'You are quite thankless aren't you, little sister?' said Kumbha, ruefully. 'Ravan staked his everything for you, for the way Kuber treated you. And you coolly turn around and claim Ravan did it selfishly, because he would have anyways...'

'Wouldn't he?' she challenged.

'He would have. But you, Meenu, you kept recounting to him about what Kuber did, milking his sympathy and goaded him into taking this action, didn't you? You know you were the reason why he did it. You made him do it, but sooner. That is how you manipulate,' he added thoughtfully, scratching his chin. 'You know how and when to unsheathe your claws!'

There was a grimness in his small smile. Meenakshi looked down at her hands, rubbing her thumb over the nails of her weaving fingers. Kumbha was not as foolish as he looked. He had as sharp a brain as she and Ravan but it was hidden beneath his mask of ruddy friendliness. She had forgotten that it was Kumbha's extraordinary intellect which had made Indra insecure, prompting him into tricking her brother. Indra had feared his widsom. So should she. She would have to be careful with him.

Kumbha's eyes grew hard. 'You started two wars here, my

dear—one against Kuber and the other will be soon against Father. You think Father will take this silently?' he smiled humourlessly. 'You started it, Meenu, but you can't end it. And you won't like the end. Father will leave us.'

His words had a harsh finality. Meenakshi's heart sank. She would lose her father because she had instigated Ravan to overthrow Kuber? That had been her retaliation against Kuber. What Kumbha had accused her of was true. She had whipped Ravan into a frenzy. Even Ravan had not realized that he had been used to avenge her.

'As I said you are a true blue asura, there's nothing of our Father in you though you love him absolutely!' smirked Kumbha. 'But be prepared to suffer what you started—you will have to choose soon between our parents. Make your choice wisely.'

Kumbha's words were not garbled in a drunken stupor: they were stark and serious, which soon came true the very next morning. The day was unusually bright, the sun fierce in a winter sky and the same mood lingered within the palace inside.

If Meenakshi thought that she could savour their day of triumph, she was wrong. Kuber left Lanka, amidst much jubilation in the family and the asura army streamed into the citadel city, amidst hollers of victory. But, within the golden walls of the palace, he left a deluge of fury in his wake. The sight of a silently weeping Ilavida, Vishravas estranged wife did what Kuber could not do. It made Vishravas turn against Ravan, fatally and finally.

'Ilavida, don't leave the palace, it's your home,' said Vishravas desperately. 'I am back. I have come home.'

Her face lined with age and anguish, Ilavdia shook her head emphatically.

'It is no longer my home, my lord. I have been evicted from my home for the second time,' sobbed Ilavida.

Kaikesi sensibly kept silent, but her eyes spoke volumes, glittering with dislike and triumph. She looked every inch the Queen Mother, in manner, movement and mood with all the jewels shimmering on her tall, elegant frame. She looked as if she had stepped out of a treasury—splendidly dressed in the best silks and gems—she was extremely conscious that she was now the Queen Mother. Meenakshi gaped at her; she was flaunting unabashedly. She had always known her mother to be a shrewd and calculating woman with a burning ambition for her sons and herself. Yet she also had a cold, magnetic charm, she used well on people, pretending to have an irresistible interest in them and in turn, who felt, when they met her, that their cares were her cares—it was a trick that had served beautifully even at the ashram as it would do now in the palace of intrigue and politics.

'It was never your home, in the first place, mother Ilavida,' interjected Ravan.

Meenakshi was taken aback at his sudden irreverence. Ravan was never offensively impolite, despite his latent arrogance.

The tension thickened perceptibly in the royal chamber. 'This was the palace built for my grandfather by no one less than Vishwakarma. For us,' he said empathically. 'This was the palace where my mother was born and thrown out with her family to suffer in hell for so many years. She has come back home. But that does not mean you need to leave. Please stay, be our guest, and continue to consider this is your home,' he added, bowing. 'Just as the ashram once was.'

Ilavida bit her trembling lips, recognizing the stealth in his smooth words.

'Fie you, Ravan! You turned out your brother and now you are throwing away an old, helpless woman too?' exploded Vishravas, his kind eyes kindled in fury.

'I am not,' said Ravan suavely. 'It is entirely her wish to stay back or leave,' he shrugged eloquently. 'But yes, this is my mother's home from now on.'

'But not mine,' said Vishravas quietly, his voice suddenly sad and defeated.

Ravan's handsome face was impassive.

Meenakshi gasped. 'No!' she emitted a hoarse cry.

Her father looked at her, nodding his head slowly. 'My home is my ashram, not here.'

'But we are family!' she cried. 'You can't leave us!' She turned fiercely on Ilavida. 'For her!'

She saw her father's face harden, his eyes suddenly cold. She clutched his hand in desperation, as if to physically stop him from leaving the room, their lives and them. He placed a soft hand on hers.

'I am always there for you, my dearest,' he said shortly.

She searched for some tenderness in his amber eyes but found none, just a gleam of decisiveness. 'But I am a rishi, I can't stay here in a palace. My place and identity is the ashram.'

'Is it your way of showing your disapproval of Ravan?' Kaikesi looked inquiringly at her husband with those dark, impersonal eyes.

The snub administered, Kaikesi went on, 'You are running away from confrontation, as usual.'

Meenakshi threw her mother a pleading look: she did not want them to quarrel any more. 'I opted to remain in the ashram even when Kuber left for Lanka. Or, even when he took Ilavida to stay with him, in deference to her changed status,' replied Vishravas, his tone laconic, his plump shoulders stooped. 'I choose my ashram again. And what I think, frankly, makes no difference to either you or Ravan,' he supplied pointedly. 'So, I bid farewell now. You all have my blessings!'

'But not your presence, father!' pleaded Meenakshi, looking around her, at her stone-faced brothers: Ravan looked grim, Kumbha's round face had calm neutrality, and Vibhishan was too stunned to react. She felt like shaking each one of them. They had to stop their father from leaving and the only one who was not helping the situation was her mother with her stubborn, bitter hostility.

'Let him go, Meenu. His ashram is his home where he wants to take Ilavida,' said Kaikesi calmly. 'He wants to leave us to go back to them.'

'Trust you to twist the situation the way you prefer it,' sighed Vishravas. 'I am a defeated man, Kaikesi. I lost: I could neither gain love nor respect from you and Ravan. I am tired of fighting both of you.'

Meenakshi looked frantic. 'Ravan, please don't make him leave us!' she cried.

Ravan stood still and silent, unmoved at her pleas.

She turned to Vibhishan. 'Tell him, Vibhishan, he'll listen to you!'

Vibhishan was weeping openly, visibly distressed as he always was during family quarells. 'I'll come with you, Father,' he said instead.

'That's not the answer!' Meenakshi shouted at him.

They were taking sides, creating camps instead of persuading their father to stay back: no one wanted him.

Ravan looked perceptibly shocked at his brother's decision but he controlled his temper and tone. 'Father has his own life at the ashram, Vibhishan,' he said evenly. 'He is a rishi. You are a rishi but also a warrior. We have got the kingdom of Lanka and I need you here to help me look after it. Is that not your brotherly duty?' he questioned over-politely.

Vibhishan floundered, but before he could protest, Vishravas intervened. 'The choice, of course, is yours to refuse, Vibhishan,' he agreed. 'I am a rishi who will spend the rest of my days in my ashram. You have a future, you have a duty to be with your brother—to help and guide and counsel him.'

Meenakshi did not miss the irony of his words. He continued, 'I have done my duty, been your guru and I hope I have been able to teach all what a father is supposed to imbue in his children. All of you are on the threshold of a new life: I have only my love and blessings to give you.'

There was a dejected finality in his voice, which wrenched at her heart. Her father was leaving and she might never see him again.

'I'll come with you, Father!' she burst out and in that moment she knew her choice: she would choose her father over her mother. Her words took him by surprise as obvious from his stunned expression. He stood speechless.

Kaikesi gave a hollow laugh. 'My dearest girl, did you ask your father whether he wants you to come with him or not?'

Meenakshi looked confused, *why would Father not take me with him? I will look after him.* She looked at her father expectantly. Vishravas tightened his lips.

'He is leaving us for Ilavida,' murmured Kumbha gently, putting his arms around his sister.

Meenakshi went rigid with shock.

'He does not want you with him, dear,' insinuated Kaikesi, her smile wry. 'You love your father, but does your father love you enough to take you with him, now that he has his first wife. Do you want to be a princess here at the palace or a slave at the ashram, serving your father and stepmother?' she added waspishly.

Would she be reduced to that, in her own home? The doubt filled Meenaskhi with dread and she could only gaze at her father in hopeful query.

Vishravas took her hand and patted it. 'I cannot take you, dear, I shan't allow you to choose between us...'

'But I have! I choose you!' she said fiercely.

Vishravas shook his head. 'You have to be with your family— your brothers and your mother are your family. I am not,' he said sadly.

What was her father saying? 'You are my father!' she cried. 'You are our family.'

'Not anymore, I cannot stay here nor can you with me. Our worlds have drifted apart.' *That world of the rishis versus the asura, peace versus war, them versus us,* she thought faintly, *that had driven a wedge between us all.* She had lost him.

'You are abandoning me,' she muttered accusingly and saw her father look away. She regretted her harsh words the moment she uttered them. She snatched at his hands, holding them tightly.

'Don't leave me, please!' she cried, the tears clogging her throat.

Vishravas shook his head and with straightened shoulders, and a straight face, made a move to go. She held on to his hand, desperate and defeated. Her father was leaving her.

'You will come and meet us, won't you?' she asked

tremulously. But she knew his answer—he would never come back. An anguished cry tore from her throat but only she could hear it, not her father, brothers, or mother. Each one of them was insentient to her despair. Her face frozen, she stood rooted as she saw her father extricate himself from her clinging grasp, and slowly walk away down the columned hallway.

She saw him pause and her heart leaped in hope. But he had stopped to take Ilavida's hand and take her with him. The double wooden doors swung open and he was gone.

He has gone out of our life, forever. She wept silently, the tears drying within her, not allowed to spurt out. Meenakshi shivered convulsively. She no longer would feel her father's warm embrace, his hearty laugh, his reassuring smile as he wiped her tears away. First her Nani, now her father: both had gone far away. She felt ruthlessly bereft: forlorn and alone, her loneliness weaving a cocoon around her including and involving none other.

Her eyes burned, her heart was tearing, her mind drowning in a cauldron of thoughts and emotions: love, despair, pain. And loathing. She turned to the person who had evoked that familiar feeling in her again—Ravan. Meenakshi stared at his tall, stolid frame with unseeing eyes, blinded by a film of tears and hate. Her resentment was centered around this one person. It was him who had sacrificed his father for his ambition, the person responsible for splintering their family, the man who had separated her from her father. He had not made a single move to stop him from leaving them. Her brother, Ravan.

Lanka

$\mathcal{M}$eenakshi wiped the sweat off her forehead, loosening the angavastra to breathe easier. The sword fighting session with her granduncle Malyavan had been particularly exerting. The man was a veteran and old—yet quick on his feet. She found herself panting, and her arms were aching. But it was a good exercise, she admitted, glancing at her body. *Well-endowed and well-toned*, she smiled archly. She recalled her Nani's words: 'love yourself, love your body, love your mind and love with your heart. Love is magic.' She had followed her advice, except the last bit. There was no one to fall in love with. Life at Lanka was lonely.

Meenakshi stared down from the lofty height of her palace window, scrutinizing the magnificent scenery, the hills, the forests and the rich spring meadows with her quick, topaz cat eyes.

Her bedchamber was vast, with a large, long window that ran the length of the view side of the massive room, commanding a fine, interrupted view of the foaming sea, overlooking a cliff. The other wall was filled with paintings and portraits, most of them of her family and ancestors, all good-looking faces with dark, smooth skin and fine, astonished-looking eyes. She sat down at the elaborate veena and began absently strumming the strings, staring at those very portraits. There was a lot of wealth but little sign of culture; the luxury in the chamber was senseless, haphazard, and ill fitting. The marble floor shone with brilliant polish and the sparkle of the chandelier irritated her. She was reminded for some reason of the frugal oil lamp burning low in the hut at her father's ashram. The memory unfurled feelings she didn't want to feel. She got up impatiently.

Below, the city sprawled in neat clusters along clean, narrow streets, each house with fresh paint and trees and a tiny garden. The people living in them looked as happy, reflected Meenakshi: Lanka *was* a paradise.

The citadel city was more like an island fortress, strategically situated on a high, flat plateau between three protective mountain peaks of the Trikuta mountains with a vantage location. It was on these mountains that Lankapuri, Ravan's capital was located, with this stately palace towering like a golden epicentre and the swirling sea in the distance, surrounding by all sides, forming a natural protection for the island city against nature's agents as well as Man and the devas.

The sea: that was what she loved most of this new country. The sound of the sea was always mesmerizing, almost soothing as the waves ebbed on the sandy shores, drawing her into a hypnotic lull. It reflected her moods: sometimes calm, often angry, the tides churning an unsteady upheaval in her mind. Yet, she felt an innate peace within its foaming turbulence.

The palace, essentially a fortress, established architecture as an art form. Its central palace had a cluster of smaller royal mansions, each unique in beauty and splendour. Built on a main citadel, the grand palace rose high and imposing dominating the land and seascape, rising about a mile from the ground and sprawled across another one in length, and a half-mile in breadth, framed by a series of tiny lakes and ponds melding in the royal gardens dotted with garden huts and gazebos; all constructed under the personal supervision of Vishwakarma. The most beautiful was said to be the Ashok Vatika and the Pramdavan, where she was walking down now amongst the lissom Ashok trees, which lined the avenue with the misty Trikuta Mountain as the majestic backdrop.

How Ravan had managed to infiltrate Lanka and taken over

from Kuber was his military genius. Even Lankini, the fierce rakshasi who guarded the fortress had quietly made way for Ravan, a knowing look in her dark eyes. Meenakshi had looked at her curiously, a massive figure with a grim, unsmiling face, her face set in stern lines. Rumor had it that she had once been a guard of Brahma but her arrogance had driven her out from his abode to be made to guard the citadel of Lanka now. *So that she would learn a lesson in humility*, Meenakshi reflected with a slight smile. *With Kuber and now Ravan as the King of Lanka, she may have instead mastered the art of conceit.*

Kuber was said to be residing at Alaka now, near Lord Shiva's abode, Mount Kailash, and it was supposed to be as lavish a city as Lanka. As Ravan had promised, he had presented Kuber with a fabulous palace; a replica of Lanka's fortress, possibly, to remind him cruelly of the Lanka he had lost.

Ravan had declared himself as the 'Emperor of the Three Worlds'.

He knew he was invincible, not just because of the nectar of immortality he nursed in his navel, but the new sword Chandrahas, which he had recently acquired from Lord Shiva. He carried it with him everywhere, slung trimly at his waist even when he went on his aerial tours in the Pushpak Viman. He was as passionate about flying his Pushpak as was he stringing his veena. He was out again, probably touring some back country he wished to invade.

Meenakshi gave a lazy shrug. She was bored and restless. She had everything here but she enjoyed nothing. She found the opulence of the palace stifling. She missed the rustic peace of the ashram. Something in the scene—the fragrance of the early morning mist on dew-petalled buds, waking her up to the characteristic deep vocal moos of the cow, the lingering scent of sandalwood, the humming chants of the Vedic hymns floating in the air all through the day—was lodged in the young girl's mind as a symbol of unaccustomed peace.

She missed her father and grandmother: the two people whom she loved dearly. All she had of them were memories and a legacy each one of them had bequeathed to her: the magic of sorcery and the passion for reading both of which she could leisurely pursue here. Her mother had generously given her a wing of the palace where she could keep her books and practice her sorcery. Her father could no longer stop her and she no longer needed to be furtive about her practice. In Lanka, sorcery was given the respect of art and was recognized as a skilled science. Taraka and Mareech had taught her well, but Meenakshi would have wanted to glean more from them, had they been here. Where and how were they, the thought troubled her daily.

She got up impatiently, the view outside annoying her now— it was like a beautiful painting, perfect but that perfection was a lie. She needed to do something but she had used up her entire morning first horse-riding, then working on some new spells of enchantment and then at the practice session with her granduncle. Her fingers ached from the powders she had pounded, her muscles of her legs and arms still stiff from the sword swinging. She decided she would take a swim.

She flexed her fingers absently, wishing she had a friend with whom she could have indulged in a mindless chatter. She was the sister of an emperor, a princess, cloistered in her golden palace. Besides her maids, she barely conversed with anyone. Not that she liked mingling at formal occasions either. Their conversations stifled her. The words and topics were so ordinary, so boring that they moved Meenakshi either to irritation or indignation. *What savage manners, what louts, all these people. What senseless nights, what uninteresting, uneventful days all of them indulge in—raucous card-playing, the gluttony, the drunkenness, the ceaseless chatter about the same, over and over again. The men talk of war, victory and wealth and the women seem to enjoy the benefits of each. Such useless pursuits and conversations always about the same subjects,* she thought warily.. The inane talks riled her. There was no escaping or getting away from it—just as though one were in a prison. This was her life in Lanka. She wished she could do something more worthwhile, but for this maddening boredom...

Her brothers and her mother were all she had, all busy,

often leaving her alone by herself. Since her father's leaving, she had distanced herself farther from them, singularly aloof and detached. And like her father had been before—she too was an outsider in the family, bearing no particular affection or affinity.

Ravan was the fond, indulgent oldest brother, struggling to reunite his fragile family, and trying to make up for the loss of their father's absence. *He would never replace Father*, she thought fiercely, *however much he showers me with his kind words or all those expensive gifts and precious gems.* She knew why he was doing this: he was extra protective, shielding herself and himself from imagined danger. He could not overcome that one fear that still made him break in cold sweat—of her attempted abduction. He could not rid himself of that guilt: it had made him more possessive and strict, and he kept a sharp vigil on her. He saw to it that he did not stay absent too long from Lanka or didn't allow her to move outside the palace. That was one of the reasons why he had forbidden her to visit their Father, she rued, not without resentment.

Kumbha was there but as good as absent. He was sleeping out his six month curse at the Charyagopura hills. She wished she could find a spell to nullify it, but Meenakshi knew it was futile. Words once spoken could not be redeemed, they were like inflicted wounds, the imminent scars lingering long. A curse could not be renegaded: not even the mightiest spell could allay the power of the uttered word.

Vibhishan was engaged in the court affairs as the Minister of Defence and Security. For a man of essentially a gentle disposition, his royal designation, was somewhat ironic but Vibhishan soon proved to be an efficient administrator, organized and methodical in his ways. He was content with his job and Ravan was pleased with him as well, banking heavily on him now that his right hand man, Kumbha, was missing most of the time of the year. It had made them come close. They were essentially antithetical, so unlike in nature, virtue and values. Ravan was his mother's son, Vibhishan was his father's. Their parents had parted ways and their legacy lay heavily between them. But Vibhishan doted on his brother, and she hoped their peace would last long.

And Lanka was thriving too, the people supremely happy with their new king. There was no poverty in Lanka, even the humblest had a pot of gold in his house. Ravan had truly made Lanka the golden city, percolating the wealth to all its subjects. Another reason for Ravan's popularity was that he had done what others before him had never attempted before: he had changed the social life of the city where earlier there had been no contact between the classes. Now the poorest could meet with the King any time and the vice versa. The King now streamed through the narrowest lane to meet his subjects. She had not yet attempted to mingle with the public but Ravan did with his customary elan, all pomp and show, and each time he received a rousing welcome. Besides in Lanka, they had a strong sense of history and they loved him for being Sumali's grandson.

His military abilities were as awe-inspiring, giving him enough reason to be more arrogant. He had started a series of campaigns against the devas, manavs and the other asuras, defeating all, even Indra, Surya and Yama. He had conquered the netherworld, appointing their cousin Ahiravan as its ruler, and himself becoming the undisputed overlord of all the asuras. Except for the stubborn Nivatakavachas and Kalakeyas, the two clans he had yet been unable to subdue; especially King Vidyujiva, who was as stubborn as Kartaviryarjun. Fortunately for Ravan, Kartaviryarjun had been killed by the warrior-rishi Parshuram, in revenge for having murdered his father Rishi Jamadagni. The only thorn in the flesh was this young King Vidyujiva. Meenakshi frowned, her brows puckering delicately. *Who was this man who could still challenge my mighty brother? Must be arrogant or a fool, or both*, she assumed with a small smile as she strolled towards the palm-fringed landscaped pond for a swim.

The still, sultry air was shattered by raised voices. She stopped short, surprised. It sounded like her mother and Ravan. Was he back? When had he returned? She proceeded quickly towards the source of the disturbance. It seemed to be coming from her mother's inner chamber, but the windows were open and she could hear each word distinctly.

'Do you realize what you have done?!!' her mother was not shouting as she often did, but something in her voice made Meenakshi instantly alert and more than curious. Her mother had never said an unkind word to Ravan ever, not even a gentle reprimand. But right now, she sounded clearly incensed and worried.

'Yes, but all I could do was watch the girl in horror!' replied Ravan, sounding mortified. 'I lost her!!'

Ravan had never sounded so contrite. Never, she thought.

'What exactly did happen? Tell me again, in detail. ' ordered Kaikesi, more calmly.

Meenakshi held her breath. *A girl. Is Ravan in love with some girl? He is quite a charmer, and with his fair good looks and laughing eyes and witty words, he can make any girl fall for him.* Meenakshi stole a long, furtive look around her, the garden grounds were empty, the guards far away, closer to the citadel walls. She heard Ravan's voice floating through the window,

'It was by perchance. I was flying in my viman near Pushkar and all around the smooth greenery, I spotted a tiny ashram...and her,' he paused perceptibly. 'This girl was in the open courtyard, worshipping the tulsi plant and even from that height I could she was lovely. I drew closer, mesmerized and found her voice was as sweet as her face, as she chanted the mantra. She looked up at me—and at that moment I knew I fell in love with her! She stood there looking so exquisite, so elegant and so simple that she took my breath away! I could not take my eyes off her and she nodded politely and welcomed me to her little hut after reciting her prayers.'

'"You are a guest at my humble hermitage," she said, her voice soft and clear, offering me some water. I drank thirstily, more out of nervousness at seeing her so close and beautiful, next to me.'

Kaikesi made a sound and Meenakshi was not sure if it was out of dismay or doubt. Meenakshi inched closer, peeking cautiously into the room, catching sight of the two figures a little away from where she was standing outside the window. Ravan was sitting in the chair, running his fingers anxiously in his hair. Kaikesi was drumming her thumbs, nervously.

'Why did you go there, when you knew the girl was all alone?' Meenakshi heard the exasperation in Kaikesi's rebuke. 'All are not as permissive as we are asuras!'

'I had to catch a glimpse of her, I had to—and I did!' replied Ravan shakily. 'Burning with curiosity, I asked her who she was. She replied that she was Vedavati, the daughter of King Kushadwaj. I was genuinely astonished and asked her what she was doing in an ashram.

'"I am doing penance so that I can marry Vishnu one day," she said simply, her smile as gentle as the soft breeze. And that was when things started going bad. The mention of the name Vishnu, threw me off balance and I flew into a temper,' said Ravan, shaking his head.

'I laughed derisively and said, "You are a beautiful woman, a princess. Why should you observe penance for Vishnu? You should marry a powerful king instead!"'

'"I shall pray for Narayan for my husband if not in this life, then in my next!" she replied. Her blunt words annoyed me further. "Vishnu!" I mocked. "Who is he? Is he as wealthy as me? As powerful as me? I am Ravan, the King of Lanka, the emperor of the three worlds. Marry me and I promise you, we shall be happy!" I said.'

'She looked at me, amused, and gave me her sweet smile again. "Ravan, you don't mean what you say! Narayan for me is the king of the universe, the king of my heart, my only love. I can only think of him," she said, politely.'

'She stood slim and lovely, but her words rang strongly, punctuated with unswerving love for Vishnu. I was aghast. She had just turned me down! My hate for Vishnu mingled with fury at this girl who had the temerity to refuse me. But I could not give up. Was it my ego or my passion for this girl, I don't know, Ma, but I could not let go of her so easily.'

Kaikesi shook her head disbelievingly. 'You met Vedavati!' she gasped. 'She is supposed to be an incarnation of Lakshmi, Vishnu's consort, you fool! Haven't you heard of her? She was born to Rishi Brihaspati's son, the rajrishi King Kushadhwaj and Queen Malavati as a fulfilment of a boon granted by Lakshmi. Lakshmi is said to have been born as their daughter. It is said that at the time of birth, the infant was reciting the Vedic verses so clearly that her parents named her Vedavati—the embodiment of the Veda and a fruit of his tapasya and bhakti. She grew up to be a beauty and a scholar as well and both the devas and the asuras came forward to wed her. She refused to marry anyone, explaining that she wished for Vishnu alone. She retreated to Pushkar, the place of pilgrimage and spent her days in prayers and worship of her lord. And then you arrived there! Ravan, what did you do!!'

Ravan looked pale, his eyes haunted. 'I begged her, I pleaded, professed my love for her...' he recounted bleakly. 'But each time she refused, reprimanding me for abusing Vishnu. She claimed I was a fool and could not see beyond my arrogance and asked me to leave her ashram.'

'Realizing that I was fast losing her to my most hated enemy, Vishnu, I saw red. I grabbed her by her hair, pulled her close, attempting...'

'What??' asked Kaikesi, fearfully.

'I wanted her to be mine! Mine alone so that she would not dare to think of any man or Vishnu.'

'You forced yourself on her!' cried Kaikesi, her face ashen, sinking into the chair.

'I didn't rape her,' refuted Ravan strongly. 'She fled from me and jumped into the yagna fire!'

Kaikesi sank her face into her hands. 'Oh, no! No!! She killed herself to get away from you...!!'

'Yes, she killed herself rather than be mine!' whispered Ravan hoarsely, and Meenakshi could hear the torment in his voice, see it in his eyes. He looked devastated. 'Before jumping into the fire, she turned to me and declared, "You have tainted me with your touch, and your evil thoughts. I shall never be yours and I shall give up this body which you have dared to desire! I am Vishnu's and shall be reborn as his wife and the reason for your death, Ravan!'"

There was a dead silence, pulsating heavily with Ravan's quick, hard breathing and Kaikesi's horrified gasp.

'But you can't die, can you, Ravan?' she whispered. 'Then how could she portend your death?!'

Ravan nodded, the shake of his head displaying his defeat, his surrender to the eventuality he had tried to hold in his control. 'She will be the death of me!'

'A mortal, a princess, she will undo all what you have achieved,' moaned Kaikesi in terror.

Yes, Meenakshi agreed grimly, resting her reeling head against the cool marble wall, *this woman would be his nemesis. Vedavati was a woman wronged and it was her vengeance which would be his doom. The wrath of the victim on her perpetrator.*

'I loved her and I lost her!' wept Ravan brokenly. 'And all I earned was her curse instead that will haunt me forever!'

Kaikesi saw her son, the emperor of the world, crying like a lost soul, broken and hopeless.

'It's done. She's gone. Don't think too much on this,' consoled Kaikesi, patting his heaving shoulders. 'I shall find you a better girl!'

Her mother's brusqueness was an attempt to sanguinity. She was as always, efficiently brisk, brushing off irrelevancies without subtlety or evasiveness.

Meenakshi stared through the window at the mother and the son holding the other in grief and comfort. *They had not been so affected even when Father had left us*, her lips curled bitterly. Seeing her brother, weeping like a lamb, made her smile. Seeing him indefensible, made her feel strong, but not sorry. And there was another thing—she had now a sense of power over him. She knew his little secret.

Brides

$\mathcal{K}$aikesi took her own words to heart—she had to find a bride for Ravan. *He is rich, handsome and powerful makes him sufficiently eligible with impeccable matrimonial prospects*, Meenakshi thought with some malice. Her other two brothers had been flooded with good marriage proposals as well and her mother preened, brushing away Kumbha and Vibhishan for Ravan as always. Strangely, there were no offers of marriage for her. Meenakshi was now eighteen, but girls younger than her were getting married. The proposals had oddly dried out, and she knew the reason—Ravan and his fearsome might. No king or prince—be it a mortal, a deva or a daitya—was ready to marry her in fear of antagonizing the most powerful man, the supreme emperor. Her brother's influence was felt all over the world.

But a doubt snaked in, digging in its venomous fang. *Could it be because I am not fair and attractive?* The old fear heaved up, leaving a bitter taste in her mouth and mind. *I am not fair, but I am attractive*, she reasserted fiercely. She stared at herself in the mirror, critical but she liked what she saw. A dark, smooth-skinned girl with huge hazel eyes dominating an ordinary face— broad forehead over a regular thin nose, a strong almost masculine jawline narrowing into a determined chin with plump lips above it. They did not smile but puckered in a sulk, Meenakshi grimaced, opening her lips into a forced, tight smile. It was an effort.

She recalled her grandmother's words, those assurances of

encouragement. That she was beautiful and unique. But those had been words from a person who had loved her unconditionally. *Nani had been blinded, not allowing herself to see the ugliness I am born with*, Meenakshi gave a twisted smile as she stared down at her dark hands and her long, curling talons. *Those who love you, always find you beautiful.*

Meenakshi shrugged and slowly strung the diamond spangled ruby necklace against her slender throat. She had gotten used to wearing such chunky, expensive jewellery now. Ravan piled her with gems and gold to befit a princess that she was. A select princess: exclusive but elusive, she said sadly to herself, whom none wished to marry.

'Hurry up, the guests will arrive soon,' remonstrated her mother. 'And you could look a lot more enthusiastic than you feel! Seriously, Surpanakha, you are looking ahem, so...alluring,' she admitted grudgingly. 'Except for that sneer plastered on your face!'

Meenakshi winced; her mother always called her by that detestable name when she was particularly displeased with her.

Kaikesi continued irately, 'You are supposed to help out, not mope around. What are you scowling for anyway?' she snapped, wondering why the girl did not smile.

The cosmetic transformation in her daughter had completely taken her by surprise. She had blossomed from being the short, skinny, shabby urchin to a sultry voluptuous woman, with a generous bosom and pleasing curves, that men could never be able to resist. Kaiskesi smiled to herself. *If only she would wipe that sulk from her face*, she sighed.

Meenakshi's scowl deepened: her mother was more worried about Ravan's wedding and not hers, but she could not well say that aloud. *Getting Ravan married was a priority and not me*, she fumed as she draped the deep emerald silk more vigorously around her opulent curves. Kaikesi needed a bride for Ravan, and urgently. She had singled out a powerful princess—Mandodari—an exceptional choice, whose unusual blend of beauty and brilliance made her the most desirable bride in the kingdom.

Her mother had invited the Danava king, Mayasura and Mandodari for that purpose. Mayasura was an extraordinary architect of the asuras and as prolific as his rival, the more esteemed Vishwakarma. Maya was said to melt even stones for his magnificent architectural wonders and was supposed to have constructed the three flying cities, the Tripuras, made out of gold, silver and iron, for the sons of the powerful King Tarkasura. This was just one fabulous example of his engineering feats among several other architectural wonders. He had authored an astronomical treatise—the *Surya Sidhant*—and that was how Ravan had met him through their common interest of astronomy.

Meenakshi had a suspicion that Ravan must have had a glimpse of his beautiful daughter during one of those visits, for soon after, Ravan had openly divulged his desire to marry Mandodari to his mother. Kaikesi had immediately agreed, eager to formalize his intention into marriage vows. On the pretext of renovating and expanding the palace, Kaikesi had invited them over to Lanka for Mayasura's expert suggestions, hoping to forge a new friendship which Meenakshi knew would translate into kinship soon.

Maya and Mandodari had arrived grandly in Ravan's Pushpak viman, which was rumoured to have been designed by Maya himself. Meenakshi was as fascinated with this flying contraption as she had been of the Pushpak. It was large, almost twelve cubits in circumference itself with four enormous wheels to support it but so designed and crafted of a certain material that allowed it to be light yet strong as it pulled into the atmosphere and sailed in the clouds. She regarded the approaching thin, elderly man with renewed respect. He was as brilliant as he was powerful. His kingdom traded with foreign countries as distant as Baria, Masra and Eran, the exotic desert countries she had often heard of, with a culture as rich and lavish as theirs. Ravan well valued the might and influence of the family he was marrying into.

Her mother had shrewdly called the entire family so that all of them would get to know each other, especially Ravan and Mandodari. Meenakshi was curious. *Will she be as beautiful as the world declares her to be? She will be, after all Mandodari is the daughter of Hema, an apsara and apsaras were famous for their ethereal beauty.* Her certainty was doubly confirmed when she met the girl face to face.

Meenakshi drew in a sharp breath; Mandodari was exquisite. She had shining, raven black hair, which was parted at the centre and fell to her slight shoulders in a carefully careless manner. Her face was heart shaped and her complexion a translucently milky. She could be any age from sixteen to twenty-five, for in her dark, deep eyes hid a depth of wisdom and a maturity belying her age. Her mother had chosen right. Her beauty would drive any man senseless and make him forget all. Like all asuras, she was tall, but she held herself with a quiet elegance that was arresting. It showed in the way she spoke, the way she glanced around, the way she smiled with her pink, soft lips. She was refined, glowing with a sedate dignity that was as exclusive as a precious stone. *Ravan has acquired a rare gem*, Meenakshi acknowledged with a twisted grin. *Another beauty in the family*. Mandodari made her seem like a dark monster, against her fair loveliness.

Meenakshi forced herself to be cordial, welcoming Mandodari with a stiff smile.

'Welcome to Lanka,' she murmured inadequately.

Mandodari responded with a gentle smile. It made her look more lovely. 'This palace is more beautiful than any of my father's creations!'

She graciously fell in step with her, with a graceful stride, as they ambled together. Meenakshi immediately felt dwarfed by Mandodari's height and beauty. She felt awkward, falling a step behind, to keep distance between her and this fair maiden. She was secretly relieved when her mother joined in with Ravan and her other brothers.

Mandodari's brothers were present too. Meenakshi gazed at them openly. They were both tall, fair with good looks. She felt their eyes constantly on her, especially the shadowy cleavage she did not bother to hide. Her sultry sensuality was mesmerizing to many. It was ironic, for all her latent insecurities, Meenakshi was just realising the unusual sway she held over men. She basked in the warm glow: she knew her power over them...

Through the entire morning, Meenakshi had noticed their frankly admiring glances. She looked back at them, questioningly, almost brazen in her direct gaze. She felt a warm flush of desire wash over her: something that often happened when she saw masculine men, but her expressionless face revealed nothing of the feeling that was moving through her body. They were momentarily taken aback and she gave a small smile, friendly yet inviting. She had piqued their interest further, she was sure. She admitted she found them attractive as well, drawn to their sheer physical beauty. But the pleasure was in that power, the hold she swayed: she delighted more in the fact that she had aroused them than they had affected her. Having conquered the moment and the men, she turned away from them and looked at her brother and his bride-to-be instead. They were more interesting to her now.

Mandodari was clearly smitten with Ravan: it shone in her sparkling, lotus-shaped eyes. Ravan seemed more restrained, polite but charming, with his winsome smile and ready wit. He put out his hand and she took his hand with shallow obedience and followed him across the marbled hall. He gave her his long, warm gaze through his liquid amber eyes, which so often sent tingles up the spines of so many girls. It was not just his insanely good looks, but also his warmly assured and ingratiating charm that women found irresistible. That and the robust sensuality he flaunted. No woman could elude him; and he knew it and exulted in it. He reeked of power which women found exciting. He had chased a lot of women after Vedavati's violent death and each liaison had been more torrid than the previous. He was a beguiler, a heartbreaker, and Meenakshi suddenly felt sorry for the beautiful girl by his side. He would break her heart someday, later if not sooner.

The wedding was fixed quickly at an early date as if Kaikesi was worried the bride would change her mind. But Mandodari was too deep in love with Ravan and nothing and no one could have changed her mind. Meenakshi saw that though Mandodari seemed a quiet, mild-mannered girl, she was tenaciously obstinate and not as agreeably submissive as she seemed. People often mistook mildness for docility, an oft erroneous assumption.

Mandodari had just turned sixteen but she was getting married. Meenakshi again felt a pang of envy. Mandodari's brothers were older than her, yet unmarried, wishing to marry their younger sister before them. *Such is the kind of regard a brother has to have for his sister*, sneered Meenakshi, *unlike her brothers. That caring, careful thought for others seem to be absent in my family*, she seethed.

Kumbha's wedding had been fixed too, a month after Ravan's and talks on Vibhishan's were on. Hers was nowhere in the plans.

No one wants to marry me off, she frowned as she stared at the bride and the groom sitting by the holy yagna. Ravan and Mandodari made a handsome couple, both tall and fair and beautiful, smiling. She found herself glancing at Mandodari's brothers, standing right behind the bride as she was behind Ravan. She got to know their names, Mayavi and Dundhubi, both now ready for marriage as well. Again, she felt envious of the bride, as she had doting brothers. She wished she had brothers like them. And she had also fervently hoped one of them would have asked for her hand in marriage. But Ravan had curtly vetoed Kaikesi's suggestion when she had voiced the proposal.

'We have already tied up relations with King Mayasura. Marrying another member of the same family shall serve us no good, no purpose,' he explained impatiently. 'We need another powerful family with whom we can forge an alliance. We should wait and watch and not hurry over Meenu's wedding.'

However, the two brothers displayed an avid interest, and were openly friendly and eager to strike a conversation with her. Meenakshi found herself enjoying the wedding and their undivided attention. She threw them winning smiles whilst the seven pheras were going on, demurely holding the gold pooja thali.

Her mother looked elegant in white and an exotic red. Kaikesi had made her wear the yellow silk to match her eyes and bedecked in all the gold her generous figure could take. The flowing lines of the long antariya amply showed off her flaring hips, the slim line of her legs and her bare, delicate ankles.

'Dark colours look better on dark skin,' Kaikesi had said pointedly, tying the girdle around her trim waist. 'And a girl without jewellery is like a rose without fragrance.'

Meenakshi snorted. 'The girls at the ashram were prettier than the mannequins we see at the palace!' as she rimmed a deft dash of kohl, burnishing her hazel eyes to molten gold.

Through the celebratory cacophony and the lavish feasts, Meenakshi oddly yearned for the tranquillity of the ashram. Of her father. He had not turned up, as she had known yet hoped. None of the others in the family seemed to miss him, and were almost glad of his absence.

'It would be better if he did not come,' Kumbha had said wisely. 'It would avoid arguments. Why re-open healing wounds?'

His words were meant to console her but Meenakshi felt more wretched. *Would I never meet my father ever again? Because of Ma and Ravan, Father will not be attending the wedding. They did not want him here even when a new member was being welcomed into the family. What a family we are, welcoming the new and disposing off the old. The head of the family was not there to bless the couple and never would be. He was a forgotten figure, despised and disowned. All because of the unforgiving obduracy of one person—Ravan.* But her father's absence was conspicuous and many of the guests had, with evident glee, pointed it out. More upset than annoyed, she had rushed away from the intruding queries to seek shelter in the confines of one of long verandahs running all along the palace. She felt lonely amidst the clamour and celebrations, the ringing cymbals echoing through the numb mind. But the sound of the sea calmed her, as always, as she stared unseeingly into the azure distance where the sea met the sky...

'It is unusual for the sister of the groom to be sitting all by herself,' said a voice from behind, interrupting her thoughts. It was a deep, male voice. She whirled around, annoyed. She was confronted with the tall, hulking figure of a young man, blocking her way and too close enough for comfort. His deeply-tanned face was long and narrow and his alert eyes a mysterious black. *Like an abyss*, she thought. With thick, raven dark hair over a narrow forehead, his lean, dark face was attractive, yet not handsome, in an animal kind of way. He was lean and tall and like a beautiful young horse. The width of his shoulders was impressive and his long hair, curling to his strong, bronzed neck, excited her.

She looked up at him, straight into his merry eyes. They were laughing: at her. Her eyes glinted, flashing a hazel fire. *He clearly mistook impertinence for charm*, she frowned.

'It does not concern you,' she said icily.

'No, but you cut an unusual sight,' he smiled.

His thin, swarthy face had a humorous, slightly jeering expression, gazing at her sceptically and thinking she had the largest eyes he had ever seen and that her long, silky eyelashes with the kohl lining made them appear like liquid gold. She was looking him up too, raking him from top to toe, the way a man often did to a woman, but it was she who was flicking her smouldering cat eyes all over him. In the few seconds of silence that followed they sized each other up with frank curiosity and an undercurrent of sensuous tension.

'You must be either bored or unhappy to get away from all that merriment,' he said. 'It's your family wedding after all!'

The temerity of the man, her lips thinning in evident displeasure. He was a guest, she reminded herself, refraining from being rude to him; though she did not know who he was yet. She wanted to know, but did not wish to ask him.

'Please enjoy the wedding,' she said shortly, trying to move past him. But he stood tall and stolid, unmoving. His gaze slithered down her body. Her skin prickled, not out of annoyance but pleasure as if he was running a finger down her.

She looked at him more closely, more out of impatience than curiosity. She wished she had not. The moment she looked straight into his inscrutable eyes, his mocking smile, she felt a hot rush of desire, her blood pounding in her ears, the heat warming her whole body. She shivered. His eyes were still smiling as were his thin, well-shaped lips. She felt an urge to wipe off that smirk with a kiss, quick and hard. She clenched her fingers into a fist, her nails biting hard against her soft flesh, killing the hot flush of pleasure bathing over her. She shut her eyes briefly, blinking hard her mad thoughts.

'I fled from the madding crowd because I am plain bored, but what about you?' he continued irrepressibly, a slight smile in his voice and one stuck firm on his sharp-featured face. 'You are the groom's sister,' he reminded her silkily.

He looks sinister, yet darkly attractive, with his liquid black eyes and a sly, insinuating smile. The random thought assailed her anew, breaking her composure once again, drawn strangely to the raw magnetism he exuded and, worse, evoked in her. *Was it his attractiveness or his audacity that was unnerving?*

'A guest confessing he is bored is bad manners,' she said succinctly but in a very feminine voice: pitched low with a little drawl in it.

'It also means he is not being entertained well,' he retorted swiftly, the smile still intact, revealing white, even teeth, stark against his tanned skin.

The hot, hard light of the sun fell directly on her, and the first thing he had noticed about her was the vulgar amount of jewellery on her. The strings of diamonds that flashed on her long neck and slim wrists and sparkled like fireflies in her hair. The sunlight gave her a sculptured-in-ebony effect. She was not tall but willowy. Her dark curls were piled high up on the top of her beautifully shaped head. She wore a turmeric yellow antariya with a contrasting yellow angavastra and the narrow stanpatta, both of which did not quite hide the full swell of her breasts and the exposed expanse of skin made his heart race. Her enormous eyes were the colour of rich honey, sprinkled with gold when angry—as she was now—and her soot black eyelashes curled upwards enchantingly and seemed to be touching her eyebrows. She looked exactly what she was: the most powerful princess in the world, from the diamonds in her hair to the cold, haughty expression on her rather long but with distinctly attractive, strong face. She looked good, and she knew it.

She glared.

'Clearly you are not a very important guest to be so swiftly sidelined!' she said churlishly, but her crackling eyes were curious.

'Oh, I am the enemy!' he chuckled.

She stared, speechless in momentary shock. 'You are...?' she breathed after a perceptible pause. Again, he seemed to be enjoying her discomfiture.

'I am Ravan's famous enemy—Vidyujiva. In person,' he stated, his tone now openly mocking. She was slightly amused as he bowed with an elaborate flourish.

Meenakshi's head went into a quick spin. She recalled the furore over this particular man being invited to the wedding. Ravan had been vociferously against it but Kumbha and Vibhishan had cajoled him into it as an exercise in diplomacy.

'He is a powerful enemy but he can be made a powerful ally as well,' advised Vibhishan. 'He is the king of the Kalkeyas, the mightiest clan, and we still have not been able to win them. We might as well shake hands and call a truce. Call him for your wedding, it will be the first step. You have invited all the kings and nobles of the country. Not inviting him would be an open insult and worsen matters.'

Kumbha and Malyavan had agreed.

Ravan had acquiesced grudgingly, a thoughtful look on his face. 'I do not wish for unnecessary bloodshed either. We have already had five wars with him. We have not lost but we haven't defeated him either. But *how* does he do it?'

'Because he is a brilliant strategist,' commented Kumbha, the commander-in-chief of Ravan's army. 'He is too much the rebel. He always put himself first. He has no social conscience and he moves so close to dishonesty that I wonder how he is still not been murdered or rotting in some dungeon. He has swindled many out of considerable sums of money from traders to touts, from kings to kingpins. He is tough, ruthless, an expert spear fighter and a first-class archer. He is dangerous, calculating, shrewd and tricky. He has a lot of courage and I am not saying this lightly. He has lived for years in the trouble infested Dandak. He knows Dandak the way I know the back of my hand. He mixes with every kind of crook, swindler, tart and trader. He has shady contacts everywhere. Those who live in the shadows trust him. He has two obsessions—money and women. If there is anyone who can solve your problem, it is Vidyujiva. But he seems to have become your biggest problem. Get him on your side. You hate his guts, Ravan but we should learn a lesson from him. It's not always might and strength of the army that matters. You need a wily fox as a general and he is one!'

'That is because he is a bloody Kalkeya—all of them are rogues!' retorted Ravan heatedly.

Malyavan nodded his silver head in agreement. 'Yes, but he is better as an ally than an enemy. Inviting him for the wedding would be a good pretext to welcome him as one. With him with us, we shall have the entire powerful Kalkeya clan with us.'

'I still don't trust him. Kalkeyas are unscrupulous,' argued Ravan. 'And I cannot get to like him either!'

'That is because he is a challenge to you, he had defied you for too long and hard,' laughed Kumbha. 'Strangely, he is very loyal if he is your friend. In his odd way, he has his standard of ethics. I know him.'

On those terms of agreement, it was decided the hateful Kalkeya king be invited. And he was standing in front of her right now—obnoxious but ingeniously charming. She looked at him suspiciously, gazing at his imposing profile, and again she experienced this devastating pang of desire.

Vidyujiva knew women. He knew all the signs, and realized that he needed more finesse with his seduction at that moment. She was regarding him with her golden eyes: thoughtful, shrewd, calculating eyes that pleased him. This girl knew her way around. She too knew she was making an impression on him.

'The princess has lost her tongue!' he grinned, flashing his rakish smile. She felt sloppily weak as her desire for him mounted, his gravelly voice, his eyes now openly raking her body, arousing her instantly.

Her chin tilted, a jeering light in her eyes. 'And I seem to have lost my wits too. To be speaking with the enemy!' she said, not able to restrain the snap in her voice.

'As long as you don't lose your heart, there is no danger,' he drawled, smiling down at her indignant face.

'You might lose your head for that transgression,' she barked.

'I have lost my head,' he admitted with a pause. '...and my heart as well. All for you,' he whispered his voice suddenly husky, as he stepped closer, his fingers lightly touching her arms. 'A moment of love can have meaning even for a cad like me.'

She looked down at his stroking finger, to hide her heated confusion. He had large hands, large enough to cup her large breasts. The crazy, random thought, almost made her grab his hands, her face flushed with mad desire.

The lumbering figure of Kumbha appeared from the tall trees, interrupting them. She was not sure whether to be relieved or disappointed. To her consternation, she admitted it was the latter. She had not wanted the moment to end, she had wanted to feel his hands on her bare flesh...

Kumbha greeted the king heartily. 'I was searching for you!'

'Your sister was er...entertaining me, wonderfully,' assured their guest, looking composed, the twinkle back in his eyes.

Meenakshi drew in a sharp breath, but his grin widened at her apparent annoyance.

'Come, I want to show you our lovely island,' said Kumbha, his eyes narrowing taking in his sister's frown on an unusually flushed face.

Meenakshi saw Vidyujiva nod politely, not too keen for the palace tour. But he was too gracious to refuse Kumbha, who ignored his obvious reluctance and deliberately led the young king away from her.

Vidyujiva turned around elegantly and bowed, 'Gratitude, princess. Hope we meet again...at *your* wedding presumably, Kumbha?'

Kumbha gave a brief nod, his eyes suddenly serious, the amicability replaced by stern reserve. He walked ahead and

Vidyujiva was about to follow him.

But he waited, as if he knew she wanted to convey something to him; with a small smile on his thin lips, mocking, still playfully vexing. She lifted her arms as if to bid adieu but instead ran her fingers through her hair, her body stretched in feline langour, the sun flitting tantalizingly through her diaphanous uttariya. She was aware that perhaps this was the most provocative gesture a woman could make, if she had the right shape. There was no more telling a move or a look than this and to gaze at a man as she was looking at him now. He nearly fell for it, but not quite: she was like him, a hunter, not the hunted. Both of them were playing the same game. He looked amused, shaking his head and turned to follow Kumbha, very spry and dapper, humming a tune under his breath.

'Sir, don't rush it. You might not be invited for the next wedding!' she whispered saucily.

She gave a throaty laugh as she passed him, her hips in a slow sway, her shoulders lightly brushing his, making him swivel around to eye her again, watching his grin disappear, his eyebrows raised in consternation.

She strolled slowly past both of them but was aware of a pair of keen eyes boring into her, but she did not turn to look back, with her head held high and her heart beating furiously.

Vidyujiva

'All for you...!'

She could not drive away his husky whispering from her mind and her heart, and they kept getting louder than the sea waves lapping the shore outside her room. She hated him yet couldn't deny the pleasure she derived as she lay there, thinking of him with his lean face and his black, curly hair and his strong, beautiful body. He had invaded her thoughts and her hopes, stealing her peace forever. She liked him more than she cared to admit, inflaming emotions and desires she had not experienced before. She lay still, wishing he was right here with her. She wanted him with an ache that tormented her. She wanted him to strip off her clothes and take her with that sudden gentleness he had displayed when he said those words softly to her. *Maybe he has used those tactics on some stupid girls too.* A flash of jealousy coursed through her. *He has to be with me, not some other girl.* She wanted to be bruised, violently used, but she wanted him...Oh! How she wanted him!

She recalled every minute of their encounter—his mocking smile, his teasing voice, his twinkling eyes, his large hands which had barely touched her but which she wanted to feel all over her body; she could feel him, sense him, see him in her eidetic, turbulent mind, making her want him, wishing she could touch him, that he could touch her, kiss her all over, make love to her passionately. Her face flamed hot, the hard knot of desire unfurled deep in her, but she welcomed the dull ache, gladly suffering it, savouring it. *I want him*, she thought savagely. Drunk with aroused excitement, she lay in the middle of her huge bed, her hands cupping her big, firm breasts, feeling the stabbing need for him tormenting her. She imagined how she would have him—him bending and scooping her up effortlessly and carrying her to the bed. The thought of his large hands around her waist and the feel of them on her thighs heated her blood through her body. The faint smell of his body sweat, the hardness of his chest against her face, his thorough maleness sent sensuous waves of desire through her. He would lower her on to the bed...Would she have to be careful, not to be too blatant, not to shock him? Or would he be the forceful lover, tearing at her robes? She would not mind either.

But she would like it more if she could seduce him...when he comes into the room, she would look at him with a long pause and then a smile. Then, he would close the door, she would go to him. He would read the desire in her eyes immediately. He would turn demanding then...or was it was possible that he might be too scared of her or the threat of Ravan looming over him to make a move? She opened her eyes wide, refusing to dream, to think of him anymore. She lay in the semi-darkness, shivering a little. She felt drained and exhausted. *I have to be patient*, she told herself and closed her eyes.

Vidyujiva had been correct: they did meet again very soon at Kumbha's wedding, exactly a month after Ravan's. He had been invited again out of political courtesy but Meenakshi was not shocked at the intensity of her joy at seeing him again, and she had to make an effort to hide her feelings. She would have loved to flaunt it, as she otherwise would have, but decorum of the occasion demanded her to be discreet.

This time, she had prepared to be more comfortable, more confident with him. She had rehearsed the scene often in her mind. But it did not happen the way she had envisioned. He seemed distant, constantly preoccupied, either deep in thought or in conversation with Ravan. He did not cast a single glance at her, only briefly bowing to her in polite greeting. She had stood mutely, dazed with shock. She was hurt, pain pushed suddenly and strongly, thrusting deep into her confused heart. It was unadulterated anguish. She loved him. It just took her a second to realize; and a lifetime to suffer.

But he did not; he had made it clear right away. He never must have, she had assumed his flirtation of a month ago to be the love of a lifetime. Her heart contracted pitifully, shooting a red hot searing pain tearing through her. Was this her heart breaking, each broken shard piercing her with renewed grief, weeping tears of blood? She wanted to flee from the pain, from the wedding, to bury her face in mortification but she could not run away from her cheating heart. Her hopes suddenly sapped, her happiness drained, the wedding felt more like a tired occasion to her.

She watched the wedded couple cynically. Kumbha was looming large over his bride not just in height but in girth. Vajramala, tall, dark, beautifully built and very assured was dwarfed by him. *What had she seen in him? His pure, kind heart probably,* she thought. Kumbha was the gentlest person Meenakshi knew and she was not the only person who believed so. The people of Lanka loved him, he was their favourite, his popularity ratcheted higher than either of his brothers. That was why his father-in-law, the mighty King Bali, renowned for his might as well as kindness and generosity, and whom Vishnu himself had renamed as Mahabali, had approved of Kumbha. Both were kind, just, and generous men. Vajramala possibly must be seeing her father's virtues in her husband too.

But was it love or an arrangement of love? *It did not matter,* she thought dispiritedly as long as the marriage alliance was formalized. *It was a marriage of two powerful kings and kingdoms as well.* Ravan had wanted a family as influential as his, if not more.

King Mahabali was the grandson of King Prahlad, the famous devotee of Vishnu who had come in the form of Narsimha to save him from his asura father Hiranyakashyapu. Bali had inherited his grandfather's devotion to the Lord and generosity of the heart. A wise, extravagant man, he was a scholar as well, had engaged in severe austerities and penance, winning him accolades and respect of all the three worlds. The devas recognized him as a benevolent asura emperor and feared him for his very benevolence. They searched for a chink in the armour and soon found one: a faint pomposity arising from his huge popularity. The high praise from his courtiers, kings, devas and the daityas made him believe he as the greatest king—an affliction. Meenakshi could discern, her brother Ravan shared with him... But Bali's greatness lay in his extreme generosity and he believed that he could help and oblige anyone whatever they asked for. Vishnu decided to teach him a lesson, and in the guise of Vaman, a dwarf Brahmin, approached the powerful king for just three paces of land. Mahabali quickly consented, much to the consternation of the asura guru, Sukracharya who suspected Vaman's identity. Morphing from a dwarf to a giant, Vaman took his three strides over the three worlds: covering Heaven, earth and netherworld in two strides; and for the third, King Mahabali offered his head for him to step on. A pleased Vaman placed his foot on the king's head and blessed him with immortality for his humility, but pushed him into the netherworld. If he had lost his kingdom for his arrogance, he won it back with his deep humility. *Two shades of two extreme emotions that could make or break a man,* she sighed, recalling if Ravan had ever allowed himself a moment of humbleness.

Vajramala must be a remarkable girl too. Kumbha adored her. Unlike her, Meenakshi self-disparaged, who had not been able to win her love, nor can make any man fall in love with her. *Except with some magic spell,* she thought dourly, trying to ignore the hurting tug at her heart which seemed unbearably heavy, filled with unshed tears and wasted hope.

She refused to be unhappy and decided to enjoy the company of Mandodari's brothers. They were friendly and attentive as always, and she found herself laughing, often in an exaggerated manner when she saw Vidyujiva close by. She noticed his lips tightening, his face still impassive. She ignored him, smiling roguishly at the two brothers, who were sufficiently distracting her from the niggling hurt.

'Vidyujiva is a rascal, don't take him seriously,' she recalled Kumbha's warning words when he had confronted her immediately after Ravan's wedding.

She had laughed.

'Don't laugh it off, it's a serious matter,' said Kumbha quietly. 'He has a glad eye like our brother Ravan, so be careful. And like him, has a charm that is more poisonous than winsome.'

'Kumbha, I can look after myself, you know that!' she smiled.

'Yes you can, but you might not be able to handle him. Don't fall in love with the first man that comes along!'

'I am not a fool!' she flared swiftly. 'Or can't you believe he can like me?' she added bitterly.

'He's an outrageous flirt that's what I am saying. A rogue. And you are our sister, Ravan's sister.'

'What is that supposed to mean?' she asked sharply.

'You are the sister of a powerful man. His enemy. He is not a very decent man, dear. He has been nicknamed Dushtabuddhi—the evil mind and it suits him better,' he added deprecatingly.

She was curious now. 'He is *that* wicked?'

'He is supposed to have murdered his mother!' he expostulated.

'And I heard that he killed her because she was a spy, betraying his father...'

'But then that's characteristic of his race—they are barbarians!' Kumbha's amiable face puckered in distaste.

'He is an asura, is he not, like us?' she frowned. The tales about him were more mystifying than the man himself.

'Kalkeyas are part of the Danav clan, but they have their own set of rules and values,' shrugged Kumbha. 'They are a ferocious lot, brutal and boorish and Vidyujiva is their king. Ravan has tried to suppress them several times but Vidyujiva is persistent. He is ambitious and wishes to overthrow Ravan one day.'

Meenakshi smirked. 'As powerful and defiant as our dear brother? Is that why Ravan hates him?'

Kumbha nodded. 'But don't worry your head on their enmity. Be careful. I am more worried about you. He might just be using you as a tool to get at Ravan. Or get closer to him. I suspect both, I don't trust him.'

'You are over-reacting, the typical protective brother! Nothing has happened. It was just a conversation we were having,' she dismissed airily.

She had said those words too easily, she recalled, noticing Kumbha's worried face through the blur of colour and cacophony of the surrounding merriment. It was his day, yet he was troubled about her. His words were a silent reminder, echoing ominously. 'You were warned, little sister. Be careful of him, of yourself and yes, beware of Ravan. Or hell will break loose!'

She had been cautioned, but her heart seemed to have a mind of its own.

'Aha that same frown!' breathed a voice. 'What makes you so angry, always?'

She whirled around, knowing the owner of the voice. He looked exactly like she had dreamed about—the swarthy, narrow face with sharp, high cheekbones, a pair of deep set dark, flashing eyes and a well-chiselled nose over thin lips. She was impressed no longer: she searched for the imperfections to make herself hate him. Not a good-looking face: it lacked amiability and the contours were too harsh and heightened lending it a wild ferocity. She stared up at those burning, smiling eyes but the smile barely reached his eyes, shallow and suspicious as he himself probably was. She felt the smile had dried within her. He moved his leg closer to her on the couch. She stiffened. He laced his fingers at the back of his head, staring up at the exquisitely carved ceiling for some moments, then said, 'You know something, Meena? You are not very subtle.'

That term of endearment! A surge of irritation welled up fanning her face, colouring her face delicately. She was about to get up and walk away. She was shocked when he gripped her by her wrist, hidden from the public-eye within the silken folds of her flowing skirt. It was not the gesture which froze her but his touch. It was as searing as she had imagined, scorching her with the heat of pulsating desire. She felt stupidly excited, her heart thumping rapidly. He pulled her gently to him.

She wrenched her wrist free, enraged.

'Keep your hands to yourself,' she said in a cold, flat voice. 'How dare you?' she breathed, through clenched teeth.

'Why are you so angry?' he whispered, so close that she could sense his hot breath on her neck. 'I should be the angry one, the way you are outrageously flirting with those two pretty boys!'

She opened her mouth in indignation. His face was dangerously close and she suddenly got to her feet, wanting to flee from him. She walked away resolutely taking her steps carefully, not allowing her dignity to be overthrown by the hurt anger roiling inside her. She wanted to get away from him, and the fervid madness of the moment and her eyes sought the refuge of the quiet paved patio upstairs. She rushed up the winding stairs, frantically trying to understand his swinging mood—from frosty politeness to raw passion—as she had just got to witness. Kumbha's warning kept echoing harshly in her muddled mind. She felt the cool sea breeze on her face and she inhaled deeply, calming her immediately.

She felt a movement behind her and she stiffened. He was standing there against the canopy of the jasmine creeper spread over the gazebo, hidden from any prying eye. Her mouth went dry, shock leaving her speechless. *He has followed me upstairs.*

'Why are you angry?' he repeated.

She bridled at his tone. 'I am not angry, just cautious. I don't have a habit of speaking to strangers.'

'But we are not strangers!' he smiled.

'We are. But you seem to be taking too many liberties with our hospitality,' she reminded him tartly, seething silently on the effect he was having on her.

'Are you angry because I ignored you?' he asked softly, walking closer to her.

She wanted to take a step back but held her ground, her

head high, looking straight into his eyes, angry that he had so shrewdly figured out her dilemma.

She drew in an exasperated breath.

'I do not approve of ill-mannered people. And you are no gentleman.'

'I was not being rude, or cold and distant as you may believe. I was being careful. As I am a cautious lover,' he chuckled, but his eyes were sombre.

She swallowed convulsively, but she felt the sudden heat of the passion of his words.

'I couldn't have revealed my feelings in front of your brothers,' he continued, moving nearer, his thigh touching hers. Scorched, she should have taken a step backwards but she felt the urge to press closer to him, cleaving her body to his. She did neither, stilling her restless feet.

She heard his voice close to her ears, his soft breath on her nape. 'Kumbha has had a stern eye on me since I have arrived. It might be his wedding but he seems to have eyes only on me, and not the bride!' he laughed shortly.

Meenakshi was not amused, but she felt herself melting slowly at his words. *Feelings*, she thought desperately, *what did he feel?* Her throat constricted, not daring to speak nor hope. She looked around anxiously; they had their privacy.

He nodded. 'I checked, before coming upstairs,' he said. 'I wouldn't want you to get into trouble. '

'Me?' she croaked. 'You are the one being impertinent! You are the one following me around! You would get into trouble with my brothers. I could get you arrested right now by the guards, but then, you are our guest,' she reminded him. 'And I don't want to create a scene. Why are you chasing me anyway? I thought we were done with our formal talk last time itself.'

This time she took a step back and made a move to walk away but he stopped her not with his touch but a declaration.

'Wait, Meena! I love you.'

She paused, her step faltering, staring at him incredulously. He stood tall and straight, his face bent towards her, earnest yet a little desperate.

'I had to tell you. Let you know about how I have felt about you since we first met,' he started, his eyes serious, but raging with an undecipherable emotion, darkening them with a sudden intensity. 'I am saying it inelegantly, but yes, I am in love with you. These words, the emotions are mine but the decision is all yours.'

His voice and his words washed over her like a wave of joy, sweeping off her feet, leaving her staggering. She did not want to make sense of it, simply delight in the exhilarating feeling of their incredibility which she had yearned long to hear. She could not utter a sound, the ensuing silence was roaring deliriously in her ears. It made her feel light, as if floating, intoxicatingly lulled. She wanted to shut her eyes and slumber in this sweet sleep and not wake to the reality.

But Kumbha's cautious warning cut through her stupor of enchantment, and the beguiling words seem to fast lose effect.

'Decision, what decision do I have to take?' she asked crisply. 'You say you are in love with me. I am honoured,' she continued in a flat tone.

She was looking away from him, remote and thoughtful, her face as expressionless and as smooth as an ebony mask. She knew she sounded clinical and staccato, but she refused to drown in the entrancing whirl of the dream.

'And how does a brief two minute conversation evoke such strong emotions?' She threw him a scornful look, disbelieving in tone and temper.

She saw him flush; was it anger or embarrassment, she wondered cynically.

'Don't laugh at my emotions,' he said huskily. 'I say I love you and I am neither ashamed nor weak nor hesitant to confess it. How could a short talk confirm my feelings you claim? That time was enough for me to decide that you were the girl I wanted—so maddeningly sensuous and smart, so angry and arrogant! And since we last met, all I have thought is about you and the mad power you suddenly seem to have over me. That's when I made my decision. And I am confident that I am not wrong about my feelings,' he added, noticing the scepticism in her wide, hazel eyes.

Words, oh just words, she berated herself, clenching her fists, feeling her hard nails sinking into her palms. She was Surpanakha, hard as nails. Not sensuous, as he falsely claimed with his honeyed words. She flicked him a scathing glare. His sweet lies were bewitching, the smoulder in his eyes was fake.

'But you are wrong about my feelings, Meena,' he asked softly, his eyes astute. 'You don't believe me.' It came out almost like an accusation, laced with hurt, not anger.

No, I don't, she told herself miserably. But the way he syllabled her name was achingly alluring, almost caressing her with its tenderness. She wished he would stop talking and simply go away. She wished she could turn and run but her feet refused to move, her heart declined to disbelieve and her head warned her otherwise.

'I know I am notorious as a dirty cad, a philanderer,' he said without pride or shame, in a matter of fact tone

'Why, Meena? Why don't you believe me?' he insisted strongly, a glitter in his eyes. 'Don't you think *I* can fall for *you*?'

His words hurt excruciatingly.

'Besides being a wolf, you are a Kalkeya,' she lashed crudely. 'You are our guest, but should I forget that you are Ravan's enemy?'

He nodded, throwing her a quick glance. 'That is why I am confessing to you that I love you so that I can proceed with the proposal to your brother,' he stated. 'But I wanted to know how you feel. I cannot go ahead without knowing your response.'

She gaped at his cold logic. He had professed his love and now he was proposing marriage. It was too swift, too incredible for her to assemble her scattered emotions, her tattered thoughts. He was awaiting her response but she had none to give. It was a dilemma: she was certain about her feelings but was unsure about the veracity of his. She was required to make a choice between seemingly favourable options, but how true were they? He had said he wanted to discuss with Ravan, which might mean what he was saying could possibly be genuine but her swelling hope seem to collapse as fast. Ravan. *He would never agree to this.* She did not realize she had worded her doubt aloud.

'Ravan would kill you for this temerity!' she whispered.

'I am prepared for it,' he said evenly.

'You can never defeat him!' she scoffed, the enormity of their situation tumbling down upon her, burying her in a pit of despair. 'Or convince him,' she sighed.

She looked suddenly small and vulnerable, the fight drained from her, surrendering herself to a new reality.

Vidyujiva's heart contracted and stopped himself from sweeping her up in his arms.

'I will fight for you if you let me, if I knew how you felt about me,' he prompted, his earnestness triggering a doubt again in her suspicious heart. She did not want to commit because she did not know him or the honesty of the love he confessed.

'I am not sure,' she admitted. *Not of me, but you*, she repeated to herself. 'It is up to Ravan to decide. It is he who had taken the final decision for this wedding as well and Vibhishan's too. Without his approval, you don't stand a chance.'

'I don't stand a chance until I make you fall in love with me,' smiled Vidyujiva. His smile, disarmed her immediately, warming her indecisive heart. It was neither mocking nor teasing; it was a confession of his emotions, open and frank.

'That is a challenge?' she asked, lifting a defiant chin.

He came closer and held her chin tenderly. She felt the colour rise up her slender neck to her face, making her cheeks flame. *No*, she cried, *this blush is disclosing my deepest secret.*

'No,' he replied softly. 'A request, a mad hope. It is a permit I need, to seek the approval of your brother for our soon-to-be-wedding!'

She wrenched her face away. But she did not want to stop this madness.

'I don't believe you, I don't even know you!' she snapped.

'Then give yourself a chance to know me! The snarl is back in your voice, tigress!' he laughed, taking each finger in turn between his finger and thumb and gently pressing her nails. She liked the feel of his hand in hers. 'To believe me you have to know me and to get to know me, we need to meet. When do we meet next?' he paused. 'And don't say Vibhishan's wedding—that is another three months away!'

'You are crazy. I have agreed to nothing!' she burst out, more amused than apprehensive now.

'You will have to, Meena. Someday. I shall wait.'

He was close, theirs bodies touching, his hips pressing hers, unleashing a hot surge within her. She saw his moving lips inching even closer and if she had slightly moved her head, she could have touched them with her own. She had a crazed impulse to do so. And she did. She leaned and moved against him, licked him lightly between his open lips, pulling at his lower lip, sliding her arms around his strong, bronzed neck, touching the curls at his nape. He recoiled, jerking his head back, his eyes wide with shocked pleasure. She smiled wickedly, her lips parted. He stared, his eyes darkening swiftly, his breath coming out in short, uneven breaths. His hand was unsteady, his fingers touching the cool flesh of her back, clenching in desire. There was that thing in her eyes. His heart was beginning to thump. Just for a brief moment as he was surrendering to the pressure of her body against his, with a conscious effort she deliberately shoved him away.

'Let's see how long you can wait,' she murmured.

He grinned fixedly, his face flushed with desire for her. She deftly moved away, skipping back and quickly walking away from him, one hand went to her hip, and she put on a slight sway as she dawdled away from him.

This time she looked over her shoulder at him, her hazel eyes laughing, swinging her neat hips. He was running a finger over his bruised lips. *Should be a reminder*, she grinned touching her own. Of her, even days after he left for Ashma, his capital city.

Deal

$\mathcal{T}$he sea seemed to beat aloud her hopes; that she would meet him soon. Or was she expecting too much from Vidyujiva as she had done before? That he would react sooner and not later? Or not at all...

The waves rolled lazily in the starlit night, the lull of their movement making her deliciously drowsy as her handmaidens prepared a hot, scented bath. She immersed in it, in her thoughts for long, luxuriating minutes, thinking of him.

Later, as she stretched herself on the vast bed like a relaxing cat, spreading her beautiful legs, she could not help wishing—*If only he would walk into the room and take me...* She closed her eyes, losing herself to an erotic dream when she sensed rather than heard a movement. She sat straight up and a tall figure stepped away from the shadows. Recognition flooded her eyes but stuck in her throat.

He was bigger than she remembered or it could be because he was inside the closed confines of her bedchamber. He was as tall and big-boned but bare chested now, gleaming with running sweat, heaving with heavy breathing, as they stood facing each other, revealing the shadowy heft of his shoulders and the trim outline of his ribs.

'You had wondered how long I could wait, Meena, and I couldn't any longer,' he smiled, almost sheepishly.

'You will get yourself caught by the guards!' she looked

flabbergasted at him, her heart thudding hard, not with fear but aroused excitement. 'How did you manage to get in? It's impossible to scale the palace walls. Did you bribe the guards?' she asked suspiciously. She jumped out of her bed and ran to the window to check the steep fortress wall and the darkened cliff. It was an impossible, terrifying climb but evidently easy for him. He was a man of tremendous strength, fitness and will. He seemed also fearless. *The thought that the rope might break and he could crash to his death meant nothing to him clearly*, she thought with admiration and some exasperation.

'So many questions!' he sighed. 'Are you not happy to see me?'

'Astonished!' she retorted, the shock of seeing him slowly ebbing away but filled by a new trepidation. She glanced furtively at the door, waiting for the guards to rush in any minute, possibly with one of her brothers. She scowled, fear mixing with annoyance at his bold impertinence.

'Why are you always so angry, Meena? I keep asking that,' he laughed softly, ambling towards her. She instinctively inched back, but she could feel the edge of her bed behind her. She had nowhere to run. And she did not want to run away from him now.

'For one, because you are impossible! How dare you get in here?' she frowned.

'Aha, the royal modesty. Or is it hauteur?' he was grinning unabashedly, seemingly unbothered that the guards might rush in. 'Princess, you had complained you did not know me enough to believe that I love you. I decided to rectify that argument. I am here for you to get to know me better. And as you challenged, I could not wait any longer!'

'Please leave. I shall call the guards,' she ordered stiffly.

'Do that,' he challenged, still smiling. 'Are you angry with me because I confessed my love?' he asked, his face serious.

'As I said, I don't believe you!' her cat eyes sparkled gold in chagrin.

'Even when I risked my life coming here? Or that I am ready to speak to Ravan about us?' he quizzed, frowning slightly. 'I don't get it...are you confused, distrustful or fooling with me?

And you kissed me!' he added almost accusingly.

'To teach you a lesson!' she flushed, reminded of that quick kiss. 'I can toy with you as well...'

'Toy?' he looked puzzled. 'What the hell are you talking about?'

'You are playing with me and so can I,' she replied briefly.

'Toy, play—you think this is a game, some fun I am having at your expense?' he looked incredulous.

'I shall put it more bluntly: Is this a new game or a political move?' she could not hide the contempt in her voice.

'That is an unfair accusation,' he said, frowning angrily. 'If that was so, I wouldn't be here in your bedchamber, Meena. I risk being beheaded if caught. As you pointed out, I am still the enemy. Now I have become the interloper, intruding into a lady's room, thwarting the rules of social decency. Just for you.'

'Go away, please,' she said tiredly, every word he uttered disarming her, making her defenceless. 'You flirted with me, I flirted back. It was fun. But not anymore.'

'Are you even listening to me? I am here because I love you not for some damn fun!' he said furiously. 'I can have any woman, I have had many women, but I want *you*!!' his voice thickening with emotion, his face exasperated.

She shook her head. 'Exactly. Women are your playthings and I know you are playing me, you cannot be in love with me...' her voice trailed away uncertainly, confused, bitter, yet hopeful.

He looked at her closely.

'Cannot or shouldn't?' he said quizzically, his brow slowly clearing as a new realization hit him. 'You don't think I am deserving of you...' he stared at her crumpled face, her lowered eyes to hide the flash of pain. 'Or is it that you don't deserve me? Meena, I can keep saying this but you need to believe me some day—once and for all, for us—I don't love you because you are Ravan's sister. Or that you are the princess of Lanka. Or that you believe you are some pawn in this imagined political intrigue, as you just accused me of. Or that you are sexy and intelligent,' he continued, ignoring her raised brow. 'Or haughty and stubborn,' he added, sighing softly. 'I love you because there is *no* reason. I just hopelessly, irrationally did!! That morning at the wedding in this very palace was a torture but for you! I saw you, and I haven't been the same since then...nor do I regret it! Not then, not now—I love you, Meena,' he repeated dully. 'I hope someday you will do the same. I want you to say either a yes or a no. I will never come back. But I need to *know.*'

This man now appeared to be an odd mixture—ruthless, dangerous and clever, but now it seemed there was a sentimental streak in him...or was it pretence?

She could not keep looking at her hands, her curled fingers, her nails hidden from view, trying to evade the questions he was throwing at her. He wanted her reply. She was tired fighting him, battling the emotions he evoked. She simply wanted to surrender, to believe, to love, to be in his arms. She gave a start. She should give a firm negative and he would leave and she would never see him again. But she found she could not utter a short word as 'no' that easily. It clogged at her throat and she swallowed, wanting to answer in the affirmative but too scared to affirm it. Where was her courage?

He stood calmly. 'I want my answer,' he paused, 'I want you.'

She heard the raw passion in his voice, persuading her, almost begging, and she slowly nodded, unsure if she was capable of any speech. She parted her lips, they were dry but before she could utter a sound, she found herself silenced by his. He pulled her to him roughly, his mouth coming down on hers. The shock of their hard pressure on hers gave way to a dizzying pleasure, the blood rushing to her head, deluging her in a quicksand of desire. Surprise gave way to pleasure and she responded Ravanously, kissing him back fervently, open mouthed and eager, thrusting her tongue deep inside his mouth, biting at his lip. He was taken aback, and whipped into a fervid arousal.

'My tigress,' he muttered thickly, grabbing her by her hair, pulling her face against his, one arm pinned strong at her waist. She pulled his head close, her fingers in his thick, curling hair, her other arm wildly moving down his broad shoulders, feeling the tautness of tension in his muscled back. He pushed her down on the bed, his lips still fastened on hers, parting her legs with his, his fingers unknotting her garment, slipping down. Soon, she lying bare and exposed to him. Her breasts rose and fell with her violent breathing. He was now sure she was giving herself to him to show him her power and her contempt of men and him in particular. Their passion was nothing but an explosion of physical violence. She could think no more. His touch inflaming her wildly, his hands crushing her breasts, moving over her body to her silken thighs, pressing the hardness of his against her soft voluptuousness. His breath, male and musky fanning over her face, her neck, her shoulders. His lips trailing from her moaning mouth down her bare neck to the pulse beating wildly at the base of her throat, inching further down to the swell of her throbbing breasts...

She did not hear the door of her chamber bursting open, she did not see the two angry figures rushing inside, she did not recognize her brothers pulling him away from her, leaving her singed from the heat of the fire that she was raging in.

'Get dressed!' she heard Ravan's curt voice over the haze which was fast thinning to make her understand what was happening. She blinked, pulling up her fallen silk uttariya closer to her, still trembling, more with a surge of fear than the consuming passion that had engulfed her. They had been caught—and in the most conspicuously and grossly unconventional position, she thought hazily. She heard a scuffle, Ravan's mighty fist driving into Vidyujiva's face, he being forced on his knees, his wrists manacled, Ravan's sword at his neck.

'No!!' she heard herself scream. 'Don't you dare hurt him!'

She rushed forward but was restrained by Kumbha's powerful hands. She tried to reach desperately for the dagger at Kumbha's waist, but he had anticipated her movement and immediately pushed her down, his grip almost breaking her wrists. She winced, ungovernable fear gripping her heart.

'No, please don't!' she beseeched, shocked herself at the pleading tone in her voice. She had never begged except to her father to not leave them. 'Don't kill him. I love him!' she cried.

The words were blurted out as a plea, not as a confession of love. But that one statement evoked diverse reactions in the deep, shattering silence. Vidyujiva's bloodied face eased into quick relief, breaking into a slight, twisted grin. Ravan looked at her in disgust. Kumbha, still grappling with her, threw her a despairing glance. But her eyes were locked on Vidyujiva's.

'Spare him, please,' she implored fearfully.

Ravan stood away, breathing heavily. She remained on her knees, her face bowed, turned away from him and she began to cry tears of fury and fear.

The silence was broken by the sound of vicious kicking by the guards, as Ravan prepared to strike with his sword.

'Take him away!' ordered Ravan after a painful pause, sheathing the sword back in its scabbard. 'Keep him in the dungeons. Shackled!' he showed his teeth in a savage snarl.

Vidyujiva was hauled to his feet and roughly pushed. He struggled and stopped to pause in front of Ravan as he was being led away.

'Don't punish her, Ravan. She is innocent. It is me who went into her room uninvited,' he said quietly. 'To get to know her feelings. I love your sister and want to marry her, but not without her consent or yours.'

Ravan's face suddenly relaxed and he gave his dry, wintry smile. 'You are an amusing rogue, Vidyujiva. There are times when I actually find myself liking you. But not today. Talking of consent, you seem to have cleverly managed her consent, you cowardly rascal. Too late for mine. You can rethink in the dungeons. And if you say she's innocent, then you were taking advantage of that innocence!' he spat. 'Your chieftains won't like it that you are my prisoner and were caught—not in the battlefield but in my sister's bedchamber!' He spoke evenly but his rage blazed through his flushed face and glittering eyes. They were murderous.

Her eyes desperately followed Vidyujiva's retreating back. He turned around to look back at her. His eyes looked bleak, dulled with pain, but strangely shining with an unsaid, indistinguishable emotion: triumph. He had won, he seemed to say to her. He had won her heart, but lost to his enemy. Her brother. Ravan. She sat motionless, wide-eyed, staring after him as he was dragged out of the room, out of sight, making her go out of her mind.

She remained on her knees, her eyes agonized, as the brothers stood watching her. Then slowly she got up, holding her wrist.

They faced each other, their eyes burning with sparks of fire.

'Don't hurt him to get back at what we did, I don't regret it!' she turned fiercely on Ravan. 'If he is guilty, so am I! How do you intend to punish me?' she jeered.

'Don't challenge me, I could well kill you with my bare hands right now,' breathed Ravan softly. 'But I won't kill either of you! It will be too easy a punishment. I shall bless him with a slow, protracted, painful death eventually but before that both of you can rot in the death of separation! I will keep him away from you, in chains and in misery in the dark dungeons and while you sleep here in your soft bed, you can imagine him below there in his dark, infested misery! Sleep well, sister!'

He turned on his heels, not sure of himself or his rage. He could have finished both of them now, but he reminded himself that Meenkashi was his sister, his flesh and blood, however silly or seriously in love she might be.

'There will be war if he is not allowed to go free and return to his kingdom. His people will retaliate!' she shouted after him, but a new fear was clawing at her. Ravan was ruthless and he could destroy Vidyujiva.

Ravan stopped to give her a malicious smile. 'And no, dear sister, no one can rescue him; his army won't dare to go to war with me, I have got their king,' he paused meaningfully. 'Only one person can rescue him and that's you—by marrying someone else whom I choose.' His thin lips moved into a grin, but there was no softness in his eyes.

'Who??' she said scornfully. 'You have been so busy with your women and your own wedding that you seem to have forgotten that you have a sister way past her marriageable age. Did it take a Vidyujiva to make you understand that your sister needs to be married off!?' she ranted, her eyes wild. 'As a brother you should have found a suitor for me. I decided to find my own but you disapprove, as seems to be your right. Why, because he is your rival?'

'So you well realize that and yet you went ahead!' ranted Ravan, his lips drawn back in a snarl.

'If not Vidyujiva, dear brother, which groom have you considered for me?' she taunted.

Ravan flushed a dull crimson. 'I shall marry you off to a beggar but not that bastard!'

Meenakshi trembled with rage and Kumbha quickly intervened, 'Losing your temper will not help, both of you!' he said sharply. 'Ravan, he is a powerful man, you cannot keep him a prisoner for long. And Meenu, you say you love him, but how well do you know him? He's an opportunist, I warned you before!'

Ravan frowned. 'You were aware of this dalliance, Kumbha?' he asked incredulously, watching Kumbha's obvious unease. 'And you didn't consider this significant enough to inform me! Had it not been for that watchful guard who spotted Vidyujiva entering Meenu's chamber, we would have been clueless! And mercifully, I was with you Kumbha, when the guard informed us or you would have hidden even this bit of information from me.'

Kumbha fidgeted, remaining silent.

'Now you know, so what are you going to do about it?' mocked Meenakshi, too chagrined to notice the knowing look shared suddenly between the brothers.

Ravan was quick to realize he would have to change tactic and handle the affair with care. For a brief moment, he wanted to tell his sister to obey or he would put her lover to death, but he hadn't the nerve. There was that frantic menace lurking in those feline eyes that warned Ravan that his sister could be pushed so far, and no further. If she had her way, she would have struck her small killer's hands on him.

'I am not doing this to hurt you, Meenu,' he started, with an effort, his tone placating. 'But to protect you. And us. Our family.

Our well-earned throne. Our empire. The devas took away our throne and had ousted us. The Kalkeyas too have been eyeing Lanka for long and Vidyujiva has almost succeeded in doing so, had I not overthrown Kuber. But that didn't deter him and he has waged wars with us, but each time I have defeated him. For the sake of peace, I invited him for my wedding. That was my mistake. I gave an inch and he has taken a mile; through you, Meenu. He is using you, can you not see through his sly ways? He is simply trying to wean his way into this family and kingdom through *you*.'

Meenakshi raised a brow. 'You don't believe that he can fall in love with me?' she asked bluntly. 'Or am I that stupid to be used as a puppet or a pawn?'

Ravan shook his head impatiently. 'You are smart, Meenu, but he is smarter, and he is sly. It is but a wicked game he's playing with you. He is a cad, he's a known womanizer and infamous for his roving eye...'

'So are you, brother, you are more famous for that than he is,' she replied spitefully.

Ravan gaped at her vicious irreverence.

Kumbha gave her a warning look. 'Mind what you say, Meenu! Ravan is our elder brother!! He is your guardian, he is there to protect you, listen to him! This Vidyujiva you intend to marry, how sure are you of him, his motives? Will he be faithful to you and our family? He is ambitious and power hungry, that's his sole test of loyalty, Meenu. He is a brute...'

'And my brother is a rapist, if I can live with that, why not another brute?' she scoffed, her eyes blazing

Kumbha's gentle eyes filled with horror. 'Meenu, that's enough! It's outrageous...'

'Outrageously true,' she said forcefully. 'How long will you shield your elder brother?'

Kumbha pursed his lips. Ravan looked speechless, too shocked. *He would not be shamed*, she thought wryly, *to respond*.

'You thought I didn't know?' she continued relentlessly. 'It happened once with Vedavati too...' she started softly, noticing

Kumbha's puzzled expression.

Ravan had gone unusually pale.

'You didn't know about it, did you, Kumbha? I suppose Ravan will explain to you later. And then there was Rambha,' she stated with a sneer. 'Ravan, don't go so righteous on me or Vidyujiva. We fell in love and intend to marry. But what about *you*?? During one of your raids of conquering the Heavens and throwing Kuber out from there as well, you raped Rambha—his daughter-in-law. She was your daughter-in-law as well, by relation,' she reminded scornfully. 'It did not poke your conscience. To avenge Kuber, you used Rambha to humiliate him, mindless that you molested a woman for your revenge and show your strength, you despicable coward!' she lashed, her eyes accusing.

'Silence!' roared Kumbha, making a move towards Meenakshi. She stood undeterred, glaring balefully at Ravan.

He was quiet, his eyes thoughtful but unashamed.

'These are political moves,' he said dismissively. 'After my win, Rambha would have been offered to me as a token of truce! She is an apsara, a temptress by profession...!"

'And that takes away her freedom to her body, her choice, her desires but gives you the privilege of over-riding her refusal and taking her by force?' she retorted furiously. 'Vidyujiva made love to me because *I* wanted him to, because I *allowed* him to...!!'

Ravan went white to the lips. 'Rambha was an apsara, you are not!' he repeated slowly. 'You are the princess of Lanka and your lover happens to be enamoured more over that fact! You are not going to be his queen, but a pawn in his game. You accuse me of low deeds, but he's playing a worse trick on you—he is attacking your innocence, your trust. And you are too naive to see through him, too much in love,' he added, derisively. 'Or lust.'

'Yes, I am and I want him,' she said savagely. 'You are a fine one to talk on lust, you with your whores all over the world!'

Ravan clenched his big fists. 'A whore, remember, dear, is a woman who can have more generosity of spirit than you will find in the people residing in palaces,' he said wryly. 'I have got more love and respect from them!'

'Your harem loves you, your family lauds you. But have you loved anyone except yourself, brother?' she scoffed, recalling Ravan's stricken face at Vedavati's death.

She saw him blench, his eyes hooded.

'You might have once but that unfortunate girl decided to end her life than be with you!' she said cruelly. 'And with Rambha you did not do it for lust but as a show of power! That's how morally reprehensible you are! By hiding this terrible truth, you think we shall all keep quiet. By this deed, you did silence our father forever, he hangs his head in shame. And that is why he did not attend the wedding! Not to open old wounds, as you claimed, Kumbha,' she gave a pointed glance at her other brother, '*You*, Ravan, are the one who should be ashamed, not me! Not Vidyujiva!'

'Don't you dare use that tone on me, Meenu,' snapped Ravan. 'Allowing our enemy into our home!' he spouted contemptuously. 'A lousy Kalkeya!'

Fury seeped into her face, flaring her eyes to molten gold. 'I was with the man I love! You, my brother, forced yourself on a woman. Is that more justifiable?' she grimaced, her lips curled in disdain. 'You, our enlightened emperor, am sure, are capable of more lofty achievements! You have no scruples, Ravan, not any more. For your greed and ego, you would stake your family! Your ego is your battlefield, your war, your violence—that is your enemy!' she said softly. 'You have no heart, just pride. And that mad urge to rule, be it over land, women or family, you tyrant!'

Ravan looked on dispassionately. 'If you think I am a cad, I am guilty as charged,' he said quietly. 'But I am trying to save you from another. Can't you *see* that? It is not a test of will, not my ego saying this, but a warning. I implore you, see sense, sister! I do not trust that man but I trust your good sense. I shall hold a swayamvar for you, but forget this man!' he said. Ravan never begged but he was now and for the shortest moment, she faltered. What did she know about this man Vidujiva but for her unreasonable passion for him? Ravan knew him better and more importantly, Ravan was her brother: he had promised to protect her, he loved her. *But so does Vidyujiva*, prompted a small voice. And she loved him too. What would she choose—Ravan's advice or Vidyujiva's love?

She stared at Ravan in wonderment, and broke into a short, laugh. 'Vidyujiva really must scare you for you to take such a drastic step—holding a swayamvar! Since when did asuras have swayamvars?' she jibed. 'And why the concern for my wedding— am I not a little old to be the blushing bride now? And who would marry me,' she paused deliberately. 'The sister of the mighty Ravan who can squash people like ants, maraud kingdoms like a conqueror, subjugate kings by dethroning them or decapitating them! Who would dare to marry me, brother?' she mocked. 'But for Vidyujiva.'

'I will not allow it,' said Ravan forcefully.

'And I will see to it that I marry him and no one else,' she retorted as crisply.

Kumbha looked from one sibling to another, facing each other, glowering in palpable hostility, one's will clashing with the other's ego, neither ready to submit. Surrender for them was not defeat, but death.

He started appealingly, 'Let's be more reasonable. Marriages are often made to consolidate power and settle feuds. This will be one such, Ravan. With Vidyujiva with us, we might be able to disarm him without shooting a single arrow. See it that way, we win!'

Meenakshi laughed hollowly. 'Aha, the win-win game! I knew I would have to pay one day for me being your sister!'

Kumbha continued, 'Ravan, give him the benefit of doubt. He might be genuinely in love with Meenu,' he suggested.

Ravan snorted in derision, riling his sister again.

'I shall wed Vidyujiva and only him, brother!' she defied openly.

'Over his dead body!' growled Ravan.

'You won't dare touch him,' she said fiercely. 'Nor will you stop me from marrying him. Like a good elder brother you will give us your blessings. Or,' she smiled faintly, 'soon everyone—

and that includes your naive, trusting bride Mandodari—will know about *your* wonderful deeds, not just mine!!'

She paused as she noticed the blood leak out from her brother's fair, handsome face. It was cold, white with fury. And the fear of possible humiliation that he would be exposed.

'I shall tell the world, I don't need to announce it, a mere rumour would be sufficient to shatter your grandiose image!' she said with devilish glee.

'Meenu, you cannot!' said Kumbha, his eyes beseeching. 'You can't hurt Mandodari in your fight! We are family!'

'So will Vidyujiva be, if Ravan allows,' she said softly, staring at Ravan with her bleak, snake's eyes.

Ravan stood still, absorbing her threat, her words which could destroy his respect, his status, his family.

'Don't doubt me, brother, but I shall go to your precious wife and tell her of your great deeds with Vedavati and Rambha, and your innumerable whores,' she articulated, each word soft and deliberate.

Ravan held on grimly. She saw him clenching and unclenching his fists helplessly. *That was all he can do now*, she gloated viciously. She had him now, and she would hold him powerless and gasping in her wrenching hold.

'I could, of course, supply all the relevant details for authentication. How would your doting bride react, I wonder,' she purred, a malicious gleam in her dilated eyes. She resembled a big cat of the jungle ready to spring on her prey. 'If I lose Vidyujiva because of you, I shall see to it that you lose Mandodari forever. I will see she hates you!!'

Ravan retracted as if she had hit him. But with an effort he restrained the unruly rage blazing in him. She had trounced him, overturning his decree and decision, by a small twist of words; the threat of the truth he dared not divulge to anyone, least of all, his wife, pregnant with their first child. His heir...

He felt himself strangely incapacitated, impotent in his helplessness. The flashing scene of Meenakshi hurtling herself at him as a child came flitted through his mind again. She was baring her claws again but this time attacking him without drawing a drop of blood. He knew it was not a hollow threat: she could carry it with spite and vengeance. As long as he allowed her what she wanted—her man and her marriage with him.

Ravan tiredly rubbed his hand over his face, then lifted his massive shoulders in a resigned shrug.

Kumbha gazed at his sister in stupefied amazement: she had arm-twisted Ravan with an open threat, exerting personal pressure and extorting his one weakness—Mandodari. She was never to know of Ravan's sexual-exploits; that was an unequivocal word of honour between the siblings. Meenakshi was about to shatter the peace of the family, knowing well the havoc if this truth be told. By showing the cunning, that ingenuity typical of her, she had prised control of the situation out from Ravan's hands. She had won her battle, she had won her love. But she did not know what she was going to lose.

'Kumbha, announce that there will be a double wedding now. Vibhishan's as well as Meenu's, on the same day,' muttered Ravan, his huge shoulders sagging in surrender.

'With Vidyujiva,' Meenakshi prompted with savage satisfaction, her eyes smiling victoriously.

In spite of the imperious tone, Kumbha had a sudden impression that Ravan was not just incensed but strangely anxious. There was a peculiar shake in his voice, and he seemed very breathless, a worried, tense expression on his handsome face.

'Why did you agree?' whispered Kumbha urgently.

Ravan said simply, 'Because she's our sister.'

Wedding

꧁

$\mathcal{I}$t was a perfect day and she was perfectly happy: it was her wedding day. She looked outside from her window, and even the sea was bright and cheerful, a frisky aquamarine merging with the blue, cloudless sky.

'How did Ravan agree to this marriage?' Kaikesi wondered aloud, as she stabbed the gem-studded hair comb in Meenakshi's thick bun.

Meenakshi winced at her mother's tone and action. The family had been expectedly shocked at the momentous decision, more so with Ravan's quiet sanction to it.

She breathed deeply and said, 'He loves his little sister more than he hates his enemy,' she replied with mock sweetness. 'Fasten the pin at a side, please, Ma!'

'It's your thick hair, how I envy it,' smiled Mandodari, quickly following the request, hovering brightly, despite the heavy swell of her pregnant belly. 'Better? As long as you are comfortable, you'll look the radiant bride!'

Meenakshi returned a stiff smile. Someone as beautiful as Mandodari paying her a compliment was embarrassing. But Meenakshi knew that they were genuine. Mandodari was a quiet but a frank person, her words rare but always honest.

Meenakshi felt a sharp twinge of guilt, recalling her ultimatum to Ravan. *But would I have had the courage to carry out the threat,* Meenakshi wondered, *and destroy this tender-hearted girl? Both my*

brothers knew I was capable of it. I knew it, but would I have had
hesitated speaking out the awful truth about Ravan to his pregnant
wife? She might not have: if not for Ravan, but for Mandodari's
sake. She was too good to be hurt by the wickedness of her
husband. She did not deserve it. In fact, Meenakshi pursed her
lips grimly, she did not deserve a cad like Ravan at all. And he
had the temerity to call Vidyujiva the same.

'Tsk, tsk, why that frown again?' gently admonished
Vajramala. 'Drive all those nervous thoughts away. It's your day,
dear, be happy and smile!'

Vajramala, looked elegant as always. Since the time she had
known her for the past ten months, Vajramala was the one person
whom Meenakshi had the deepest respect for. She had agreed to
marry a man who was hers only for six months of the year, the
remaining part she had to give him up to slumber and silence.
Kumbha was a good man, the best amongst them but his curse
hung heavily upon him. He had been fortunate to have a wise
wife in Vajramala, and she loved him unquestioningly. *Just like*
me. Kumbha had warned her, but she had dismissed it as words
of a distrusting brother. 'You are marrying your enemy,' Vibhishan
had cautioned.

'Please, could I talk to Ma before the rituals start?' she said
abruptly.

'But yes, a daughter needs her mother the most now,'
nodded Mandodari knowingly, a little disconcerted at the bride's
brusqueness. Vajramala was quick to pick up the cue and both
left the room.

'A daughter needs her mother most,' mimicked Meenakshi,
the moment the door closed behind the two departing girls.
'Really!' she snorted. 'I think I need my father more. He won't
be coming, will he?' she asked, with still a faint hope in her
heart. 'I thought he would, if not for me, but for Vibhishan...'
she added wistfully.

'Why don't you give up on him like he has on us?' asked
her mother wearily.

'He didn't give up on us, he gave up on Ravan,' she retorted.

'And you allowed it,' she added accusingly, her face set in determined malice.

Kaikesi gave a twist of a smile. 'It's easier blaming me or Ravan but harder for you to accept that your father left us, left you...'

'For the wife, for the son he had once forsaken for you, Ma,' she reminded her mother insolently.

Kaikesi's face darkened. 'That cruel tongue of yours, Surpanakha. You are as hard as your nails!!'

'But it's the truth,' said Meenakshi. 'You could not sustain father's love because you never loved him. You married him for a purpose, a function—that you wanted to get back your Lanka. You have it now, Ma, but you lost him. Not that you are very unhappy about it. Just as you are not happy about my husband either,' She clasped an urgent hand on her mother's. 'You are surprised a man wants me?' she asked bluntly. 'A good-looking man?'

Kaikesi said quietly, 'Does he want you or Lanka?'

'For once, Ma, why can't you be happy for me?' she said wistfully, more hurt than angry. 'You had everything—a man who adored you, a loving family. Let me be happy too. Let me have that chance of happiness.'

'Fine words coming from a daughter on her wedding day!!' sighed Kaikesi, looking every inch and gem the dignified Queen Mother. Kaikesi did not wish to argue further. 'Forget me, Meenu, forget all this bitterness, and be happy in your new lease of life. You are marrying the man you love. It's a privilege few have.'

I had to fight for it, thought Meenakshi viciously, *oh how I had to fight for him, for our lives, for us both*. Her mother had echoed the common sentiment running in her family—she had not approved of her choice either but not that Meenakshi cared for her opinion. Or her blessings, she shrugged mentally.

She gave her mother a long, searching look. She looked arresting in ivory and gold, her hair greying in streaks at her temple, her skin still dusky smooth and unlined. She dexterously folded the yards of the rich vermilion silk as she helped

Meenakshi drape it around her voluptuous curves. The flowing, fishtail antariya, the gold embroidered stanpatta and the shoulder shawl—the uttariya were all in red, as she had insisted, and not in contrasting colours as was the fashion.

'Talking about love and marriage, Ma, why is Vibhishan getting married to Sarama?' said Meenakshi interrogatively, slipping the thick diamond bangles on her wrists. She picked one ring, set with inconsiderable rubies and diamonds given to her by her grandmother. *Nani*, she sighed wistfully.

She reverted to her query. 'I was busy in the midst of my great love saga, but now it struck me. Wasn't Sarama singled out for Ravan once? But you decided to choose Mandodari over her, even though Sarama was supposed to be head-over-heels in love with Ravan. Both of you broke her heart, by turning down that proposal. So how did you agree or more importantly, why did she agree to marry Vibhishan? She loved Ravan, not him!!'

A wariness quickly descended on Kaikesi's expression. 'She agreed to marry Vibhishan instead,' she said tersely.

'You mean she comes from a powerful family you could not bear to let her go,' smirked Meenakshi. 'As the daughter of a powerful gandharva, it would be another marriage of convenience, would it not? Another political integration, a battle won without shooting a single arrow but just a garland round the lamb to the slaughter. Who is being sacrificed though I wonder— Vibhishan or Sarama?'

'Neither, both consented willingly,' her mother replied shortly. 'They love each other very much.'

'And what do you call love, Ma? An arranged marriage? A big wedding ? A large family of children?' she sneered. 'What you did? Or what Ravan and Kumbha and now Vibhishan is doing?'

'You mean unlike yours? But it is,' asserted Kaikesi. 'Human dignity matters, Meenu. A man for desire, takes a woman for the period of his lust, but when he has taken a woman for life, that is marriage,' she paused. 'Vidyujiva saw to it that he got to marry the sister of Ravan. Not that you'll be going away to Ashma,' continued her mother, thoughtfully. 'You will be here.

Convenient arrangement for both of you.'

Meenakshi could not ignore the bite in her words and wondered as to how Ravan and Vidhyujiva had come to this agreement without consulting her. She wanted to get away from Lanka, away from Ravan's sight and control, away from the unpleasant memories that followed her. She had been eager to start afresh at Ashma as the queen of the Kalakeyas. Not remain in Lanka as a sister of Emperor Ravan. Why had Vidyujiva agreed?

She voiced her doubt to the man himself on the night of their wedding itself. The rituals and feasts were over and they were welcomed into their bedecked bedchamber, festooned with flowers and laden with the fragrance of scented oil lamps and incense sticks. She was standing in the middle of the room, eager and shaking, feeling the desire for him raging through her. They waited for the door to close behind them, then he moved swiftly and slid his arms around her. She shivered as his hands moved down her back. She was only dimly aware of being carried to the huge bed. They were impatient lovers and did away with the preliminaries as swiftly as possible, ripping away at their garments, contorted with passion, in entwined limbs, tossing bodies, their rapid gasps of pleasure expanding to crescendo into orgastic, stifled screams. Still feeling him deep inside her, she gave herself up to his animal lust. They came together not too gently and when she moaned and tightened, he felt a sense of triumph. She tumbled away from him, damp and sweating, her pendulous breasts heaving in exhaustion.

'You *are* a tigress!' exhaled Vidyujiva, flat on his back, still panting, the sweat running down his swarthy face.

She stirred and looked up at him, her eyes glazed with a satisfaction she had never known before. She stretched her hand, running a slender, long-nailed forefinger over his damp, thudding chest, an angry scar on it, clearly visible beneath the black, curly hair. *One of his war wounds*, she smiled and pressed her breasts against him.

'Tired so soon, warrior?' she purred lazily. 'And what were you expecting—a blushing bride?'

She caressed the inside of his thigh and ran her lips down his neck.

'You were anything but the shy bride! Rather a tigress!' he grinned, snatching at her roving finger, his large body still atop her, his strong arms around her bare shoulders.'My back is still stinging from those nails! You clawed in bloody deep, my tigress!' he winced as he buried his face in the crook of her neck, tasting her bare flesh with a lascivious tongue. She shuddered.

It was bloody, she conceded, glancing down at his exposed back, the livid weal her nails had raked in those wild moments of passion. But a nagging thought subdued her arousal as quickly.

'Why aren't we returning to Ashma as we should?' she asked, pushing him away slightly and pulling the silk sheet over her as a shield to focus on the issue at hand.

Vidyujiva stiffened, raising his face from the fragrant hollow of her breasts, taking time to reply.

'I shall be staying here in Lanka,' he stated cautiously.

'We shall be staying back in Lanka,' she repeated, ardour evaporating to quick anger. 'But why? I don't want to stay here!'

'Because, my dear, your brother wishes so. And I agree with him too. It makes sense,' he reasoned, pulling away from her. She felt cold and strangely bereft.

'It makes sense being away from your kingdom?' she retorted. 'Makes sense not being king of your own land? Make sense being a vassal, owing allegiance and service to my brother, and staying in his palace and not yours?' She could not keep the tiny snap from her voice.

'My palace, Meena, is nothing like what you imagine,' he laughed shortly. 'It's not a palace, just a functional fortress. Where there are no servants, just warriors. Could you have lived in such a...heap?' he asked, throwing her a sly look before resting more comfortably on the pillows, his head flung back.

Meenakshi narrowed her eyes, the pupils in her eyes contracting into gold slivers, her eyes raking him, his nakedness not affecting her anymore. She had never been able to distinguish with certainty between his rough playfulness and his irony.

'It suits me better or you?' she asked sharply.

'Both,' he responded flatly, shrugging his great shoulders. 'Done that, I get to know Ravan and Lanka better. And you remain in your own beautiful home. That's sound reasoning.'

'But why would you want to know Ravan and Lanka better, when you are king of your own empire?' she persisted. 'We will live there, we will rule there. Let's go home,' she urged. 'I would like to meet your family,' she added as an afterthought.

Vidyujiva said impatiently, 'You met my family at the wedding,' he said shortly and she recalled the wariness with which they had welcomed her. She would have liked to know them better by living with them. 'Your family is my family. This is our home now, Meena!'

'No!!' it came out more forcefully than intended, but it displayed all her misgivings and her misapprehensions. 'Ashma is my new home.'

We would not be going away, after all, but will have to remain in Lanka, she thought with sinking dread.

He sat hunched but shrugged his broad shoulders again. 'Why, any girl would be happy to stay back in her home—especially as extravagant as this,' He swept an expressive arc of his arm over the opulent bedchamber. 'Meena, I, honestly, cannot give you the luxuries your brother showers on you...'

'I don't wish them! I have stayed in the forest all my life in all its frugality,' she interrupted hotly. 'These are but weak pretexts! You don't want to leave from here, don't you? You want to be in Lanka, be in Ravan's court!' she accused.

'Yes,' he admitted tersely, squeezing his thin lips. It made him look cruel.

'As his royal retainer?' she said condescendingly, sitting up straight, squaring her shoulders belligerently, thrusting her chest forward pointedly. He noticed the gesture, his eyes darkening.

'Why are we arguing?' he muttered, flushing a dull red. 'Your snarl is as vicious as your bite, tigress! I am his brother-in-law now, so my dear Meena, Ravan will have to treat me with more respect,' he remarked almost jauntily.

It annoyed her further.

'He would have more respect for you if you ruled your own kingdom well and not interfered with his!' she exclaimed. 'You forget you were his most persistent opponent. And the most powerful,' she added, hoping some flattery might make him gloat and change his mind.

'We are no longer enemies, Meena,' he was almost smirking. 'I married you and we are brothers by marriage now! Why live in war and violence when marriage is the better treaty of peace?'

'And better opportunity?' she asked caustically but her mind awakening to a refreshed fear. *Is he an opportunist after all, taking immediate and cunning advantage through their marriage? Is their wedding simply a planned circumstance of possible benefit, his expedient grab to power?*

He threw her a sharp look. 'That is practical, calm intelligence. Do you want war and bloodshed? Would you like me to war with Ravan and not broker peace? We can live here and I can be part of your brother's royal courtier, one of his trusted men, an enemy no longer.'

'Trusted??' she laughed mirthlessly. 'Ravan is not a trusting person. He trusts you like a snake. Don't ever forget that!'

'I know,' said Vidyujiva, his smile, slightly self-assertive. 'But I am no longer the enemy, I am related by blood now. Through you. He won't harm me.'

'A wedding changed the equation so beautifully and so quickly,' she commented, not without bitterness. The suspicion had resurfaced, she thought darkly, *had he ever loved me or had this been his ploy all along?*

He was quick to notice her unease. He tilted her chin and looked straight into her eyes. They were a turbid topaz, troubled and suspicious.

'You don't seem to realize that *I* don't want to be here!' she argued, her cheeks still flushed with disappointed frustration. 'Ravan dislikes you, you loathe him too, so why do you insist remaining here? You mention this palace as if its paradise for me, but it's a gilded prison. Take me away, Vidyujiva, please!'

she implored. 'We'll be happier away from Lanka!'

'If it makes you feel better and surer of me, then we shall leave Lanka,' he agreed quietly. 'I want *you* to be happy.'

'Then let's leave immediately?' she said with unsuppressed glee.

'But I still believe the best way for Ravan and me to get to know each better is to stay put,' he said silkily. 'Once we go, the age-old animosity will flare up. Don't you want a truce between me and him? Don't you want us to be a happy, united family without fight and friction, ending this feud once and for all? Give me a chance, Meena, to patch up.'

She lowered her lashes, hiding her confusion. What was she to make of him? It was an ideal situation: they staying back in Lanka, the seat of wealth and power with him better as an ally than an enemy. Their marriage had bonded new relationships, sealing a new friendship to cast away the age-old feud. Ravan had been forced to agree, would he extend a genuine hand of friendship? She was not too sure: more about her brother than her husband. She had hoped that by staying away from Ravan and Lanka, they would be distancing from their bloodied history. Would instead remaining in Lanka, under more cordial conditions, be a better option?

Taking her protracted silence as displeasure, prompted him into an explication.

'I was reluctant to the suggestion, which by the way, came from Kumbhakarna, and not Ravan. Ravan grudgingly agreed as did I,' explained Vidyujiva, running his fingers abstractedly through his full, curly hair.

'But why, when I am eager to leave from here?' she persuaded. 'Why compromise? Are you really welcome here?' she sighed. 'I would rather live with respect than wealth or power or false status. Ravan resents you and so does my family. You are after all, a Kalkeya and I dared to marry one. I want you to be respected, not looked at with suspicion...'

He turned to her, his eyes suddenly savage.

'That I married you to grab power? Usurp Ravan's throne?'

he asked bluntly.

She nodded, not meeting his eyes.

'I am frankly not bothered about the others,' he said. 'It's *you* who matters. I love *you*. And I married *you*, despite Ravan. How you managed to convince him, you can tell me some other day but I would rather have your trust than just love. Love cannot suffice alone. Just as hate cannot suffice the animosity between Ravan and I. We have to come to a truce because of *you*, but if you are unsure of me, then nothing holds. You got to trust me. As I trust Ravan. He won't harm us.'

Meenakshi looked wary, her watchful prudence crumbling slowly. Her open distrust was the only defence she had till now, sharpened over the years by her keen instinct for caution. She strangely placed blind faith in Vidyujiva, but did she trust Ravan to accept the situation as graciously?

'Will both of you get along? You have despised each other so long...' she said uncertainly.

'For you, he will have to compromise,' reassured Vidyujiva, with a triumphant smile. 'And so shall I,' he added hastily. 'For *you*. Neither of us dare upset the equation.'

Ravan would not dare, she thought grimly, recalling her threat. *He would not ruin the chance of his happiness over mine.*

His smile widened, 'You'll keep us on our toes, our swords intact, I promise!' he vowed. 'But I can't promise to not keep my roaming hands and lips off you!!' he grinned, kissing her nervous, fiddling fingers, his lips caressing each one with breath taking tenderness.

His attempt at humour and that treacherous touch eased the tense air, and she slowly smiled back at him, feeling slightly relieved. She leaned against him, relaxing against the strength of his warm chest and the steady rhythm of his beating heart. He was hers, she should never doubt that, not doubt him.

She felt him lower his head to her nape, sweeping away her thick mane, his lips on her bare shoulders, moving up her long, slim neck, his tongue flicking urgently behind the sensitive softness of her ear, his arms coming round her from behind, roughly pushing away the silken covers, kneading her breasts with violent insistence, his other hand trailing down, thrusting her smooth thighs apart. She heard herself moan. This was the perfect end to her perfect day.

Peace

'$\mathcal{H}$and me the baby, Meenu, your back must be hurting by now,' remarked Kaikesi, deftly shifting the sleeping infant from Meenakshi's stiff arms onto her lap.

They had named her son, who was born after twelve years Sambhukumar in a profusely lavish christening ceremony reserved for every new royal arrival born at the palace. But Meenakshi had already shortened it to Kumar.

She heaved a sigh of relief, tucking her angasvastra neatly across her breasts. They were pendulously enormous now while nursing, she grimaced. *Not that Vidyujiva minded*, as she recalled this morning with him. Semi-naked, semi-awake, she was sitting in the bed, nursing the baby. She had drowsily looked up to see him watching her.

'We are parents now!' he had exclaimed softly, his face flushed with adoration. 'But that does not make you less exciting!' he grinned before rolling off the bed to get dressed.

She had snorted at the compliment. She knew what she looked like—her eyes were drugged with sleep, her long black hair tousled, her breasts bare. She loathed letting him go. She watched him stand up and put on his clothes, then she closed her eyes as she heard him leave the chamber to join the waiting army waiting outside the citadel. He was going to war with Ravan. Again. These were the unhappy moments. Or those when he would return habitually drunk from the public house where he used to drink with his soldiers to be garrulous in bed.

'The leader has to mingle with his men. They are his mates,' he used to grumble. 'Not like your brothers with their superior airs.'

The smiling gurgle of Kumar got her mind back to the present. Kaikesi was beaming at the chortling baby and it suddenly struck Meenakshi that she had never seen her mother happier.

'You seem to be really enjoying being a grandmother, with the cavalry of grandchildren,' she remarked laughingly, watching Kaikesi surrounded by Ravan's eldest eleven-year-old son Meghnad; Kumbhakarna's chubby twins Kumbha and Nikumbha, all of a frisky four. Atikaya and Trishira followed their older brother Meghnad everywhere, although they were the sons of Ravan's second wife Dhanyamalini, whom he had married about a decade ago.

Kumar had been a recent, but much awaited addition to the boisterous brood. The only one missing was Trijata, Vibhishan's ten-year-old daughter whom Sarama refused to send to have meals with her cousins. *She does not hand her precious princess to anyone, not even her maids*, Meenakshi pursed her lips with exasperation.

Kaikesi's eyes brightened. 'The palace is now full of children and laughter! Like it was in my childhood, filled with cousins and chatter!'

'Not to mention the wailing and whining,' added Meenakshi good-humouredly. 'The nights are especially musical! The palace never sleeps!'

Nikumbha's bowl of rice had overturned, spilling the precious contents and he looked so dismayed that he was ready to burst into tears. Little Kumbha was helping himself hurriedly with the strewn rice on the floor.

'Just like your father, my darling gluttons!' said Meenakshi affectionately, picking up Nikumbha to clean him up. Kumbha continued filling his mouth with the fallen morsels. Meghnad looked at his younger cousin with open fascination, his plate of food, unattended.

'Ma, get the maid to help with these kids—one is over stuffing and the other is hardly eating!' sighed Meenakshi, prising the chubby Kumbha from the mess on the floor.

'That must be Meghnad!' said an amused voice. 'He has to be force-fed even now!'

Meenakshi turned to see Mandodari arrive with Vajramala, fair and lovely as always with the bulge of her belly prominent in the sixth month of her pregnancy with her third child.

'It is lunch time and the children insist on having food together with their Dadi,' griped Meenakshi without rancour. 'It's fun but quite a messy one,' she could not help smiling.

'Fifth,' commented Kaikesi.

'What?' asked Meenakshi puzzled. Her sisters-in-law burst out guffawing.

'The fifth time you smiled,' explained her mother, grinning. 'You smile at least a dozen times through the day since the dozen years you have been married! That's a welcome change from the sullen girl you were. And now with the baby just a fortnight old, you haven't been sunnier!'

Meenakshi had been married for twelve years and she could not have been happier. Vidyujiva had got along surprisingly well with all her brothers especially Ravan, who had come to value his advice. He was a favourite at Ravan's court now and after every war campaign, he was hailed the hero returning victoriously from the battlefield. He loved her and she adored him, even during the difficult time when she could not have a child for more than a decade. It had got them closer, though she knew Vidyujiva had been yearning for a child, irrespective of the gender.

'I want a child, son or daughter, does not matter. As long as I have someone, who is ours—yours and mine, that someone to whom I can give all what I have achieved,' he would say with a brief smile.

After years fraught with despair and disappointment, penance and meditation, spells and witchcraft, she had conceived and now with her son in her arms, she could not ask for more. She could barely recognize herself or her newly discovered bliss.

'It's good all of us are happy!' remarked Vajramala, scooping up the twins efficiently in her arms. 'I'll clean them up and feed them the rest of their meal and put them to bed. They love their siesta!'

Meenakshi was about to blurt aloud 'like father' again but stopped herself on time. Kumbha was deep in his six-month slumber and it pained Meenakshi each time he retired to the mountains to suffer his curse. How Vajramala could handle this with such elegant equanimity was beyond her.

Meenakshi settled down on the couch to feed Meghnad. He was a quiet, thin boy with angelic looks, a mop of curly hair and bright, intelligent golden eyes like his father's. For a boy so unusually quiet and even-tempered, his name was as ironic as was his nature, unassumingly mature for his age.

Meenakshi recalled the day the first grandson of Kaikesi, the son of Ravan was born. It was a wet, stormy night with lightning and thunder cracking the black sky with frightening ferocity. The baby was born, and it emitted a loud cry. It was not a cry, it was a boom, streaking the sky like thunder and shattering the rain, the storm and the lightening. Suddenly there was peace. The downpour miraculously evaporated and the storm lulled into a light breeze. A boy was born to the great Ravan. And the proud father named him Meghnad, one whose cry was like a cloudburst. Ravan had three more sons after him, but Meghnad was his favourite and everyone's including herself, Meenakshi admitted, patiently feeding him his kheer, which was all he gobbled with gutso. Kaikesi adored him: not because he was Ravan's first born; Meghnad was an exceptional child: intelligent, gentle and soft-spoken. But he was as stubborn and fearless as his father. And unlike his father, he was wise for his years—he had corrected his father several times and Ravan had been more amazed than angry at his temerity. *But you could not be angry with the little angel for long*, Meenakshi smiled, planting a kiss on his soft cheek.

He blushed shyly.

'You have finished your kheer, good boy, and so promptly,' she remarked.

'If you give me this kheer every meal, Meenuma, I promise I shall finish it as fast as Kumbha,' he said, his amber eyes serious.

He refused to call her by any other name—she was like a mother to him. 'You are my favrit mother!' he had lisped enchantingly as a two-year-old.

Mandodari laughed, 'Come away, Meenuma pampers you silly and gives a big boy like you, kheer instead of dal and rice and meat and fish. You didn't have your vegetables either today!' she reprimanded lightly. 'No meeting your Meenuma for a day—that's your punishment!'

Meghnad's big golden eyes were distraught. Meenakshi gave Mandodari a pleading look and she felt this thin arms hug her tightly. 'I won't let you go, so I can never not meet you!!' he whispered, burying his face in her lap.

'You are such a good boy. You are good in your studies and the bow and arrow but to make yourself strong you need to eat well too. Your mother is angry because you didn't have your lunch properly,' she said, loosening his clutching arms. 'You promise that you'll eat your dinner well and we can play again tomorrow with the baby. Done?'

'Promise!' he grinned, his serious face lighting up. He scampered off quickly before Mandodari changed her mind and issued more threats.

'He adores you!' said Mandodari softly, without envy.

Meenakshi glanced at her. 'He is adorable! He is my first nephew, the first baby I took care of,' she said, her eyes soft and shining with tenderness.

Especially during all those years when I could not have one, she winced. 'That's always a special bond, probably more strong than the one I have with Kumar. It's strange but true.'

'I know Meghnad is very special for you,' said Mandodari simply. 'I better go after him, he might disturb Trijata—he cannot do without her! '

'Sarama won't allow Meghnad to even enter her chamber,' she said tartly. 'Sarama and her lovely little world—with an obedient husband, her little princess and she!!'

'Now you sound like my Surpanakha!' laughed Kaikesi, 'baring her claws at last!!'

Mandodari smiled, refusing to comment leaving the chamber with the little boys trailing behind her.

'Mandodari is so good with Dhanyamalini's sons as well,' observed Meenakshi.

She saw her mother flush guiltily.

'Unlike me,' said Kaikesi shortly. 'I know you feel I should have been kinder to Kuber.'

And us as well, acknowledged Meenkashi silently.

'I was thinking about the goodness of Mandodari and not listing your faults, Ma,' she nodded. 'You did what you did to protect our interests. Ravan would not be what he is, if not for you.'

'You can guise a criticism for a compliment so well,' remarked Kaikesi dryly. 'You blame me, not credit me for Ravan's success.'

'Yes, his success,' repeated Meenakshi slowly. 'His success in relentlessly waging wars, winning them, crushing his enemies ruthlessly, parading his women...'

'Are you not proud of him? Do you never see his qualities?' interrupted Kaikesi.

'He's extraordinarily erudite and articulate. He has authored several books—from politics, medicine, linguistics to astronomy. He is a maestro on his veena,' she started enumerating. 'He is the best warrior, an archer and a swordsman. Then there's his unstinting generosity, his fierce family pride. But it somehow all comes to naught—his greed for more. It is all for himself, Ma, not for others,' she said quietly, without heat. 'He does it to feed his insatiable ego.'

Kaikesi insisted. 'Ravan is the best king Lanka has ever seen. No one is poor here, he is kind and just to his people, they love him...'

'But fear him more,' she reminded pointedly.

'A king has to be revered and feared,' said Kaikesi. 'That way there's no rebellion, free thought, free voice or public opinion.'

'He's a dictator, unconstrained by law or conscience,' Meenakshi said repressively.

'That he is a monster is more a rumour than fact,' retorted

her mother, annoyed.

Meenakshi sighed; it was futile arguing with her mother.

'I wish he was kinder to Mandodari,' she said instead. 'She has even graciously accommodated Dhanyamalini as his second wife and all his concubines!' she did not hesitate to add. 'Fortunately because of Rambha and her husband's curse, he cannot ravish an unwilling woman anymore!'

Kaikesi went still, her eyes narrowed. 'You know about Rambha?'

'Ma, the world knows but for our poor Mandodari. As they say, the wife is the last to know,' she jested, without humour.

She saw her mother open her mouth to retort but purse her lips instead.

'What is it?' she asked curiously.

It was unusual for her mother not to gibe in response.

Kaikesi nodded her head and slowly, 'Yes, the wife is the last to know and it's best Mandodari does not know about Rambha.'

'Or Vedavati,' emphasized Meenakshi.

'How do you know about that, Meenu?' asked Kaikesi sharply. 'Only Ravan and I know of it, not even Kumbha...' her voice trailed, her sentence unfinished as a thought struck her. 'Is that what you used against Ravan to make him agree to you marrying Vidyujiva?'

Meenakshi shrugged. 'As long as Mandodari does not get to know.'

'Knowing you, you will use it as a tool again,' said her mother uneasily. 'I am more wary of you than Sarama's sharp tongue!'

Meenakshi looked indignant. 'You never had much faith in me, anyway! Sarama is the most disagreeable and unpleasant person I have ever met! Rude and aloof, she makes it a point to not mingle with the family. She has poor Vibhishan under her pretty thumb and he follows every word she says. But then he is an uxorious man, foolishly fond of his wife! Unlike her, dear Ma, I have tried my best to help Vidyujiva blend with our family, made sure that he gets along well with Ravan especially. And he has been gracious enough to respect my wishes.'

An indecipherable emotion flickered on Kaikesi's face.

Meenakshi gave a slight frown. The couple were a contrast in both physical and mental description. My brother is one of those weak nondescript characters who always get imposed upon, Meenakshi thought irreverently, one who lived in perpetual nervous bewilderment, never quite sure if he is doing the right thing at the wrong moment or the wrong thing at the right moment. His wife Sarama is his opposite—extremely attractive, small and finely made with her clear-cut but somewhat cold features, her small, hard eyes and an aggressive chin which gave her loveliness a certain iciness. She is the person who exercised control over him and his opinions now. Anyone could see that.

'This is her way of hitting back,' continued Meenakshi, her face tight. 'She did not get Ravan and she is avenging that rejection. She dislikes all of us, even Vibhishan I suspect but she uses him beautifully. I shan't be surprised if she makes Vibhishan turn against us.'

'He won't ever go against Ravan,' said Kaikesi thoughtfully.

'You should have got her married to Ravan, Ma,' maintained Meenkashi. 'Instead of rejecting her for Mandodari, he should have wedded them both. Sarama would not have been slighted and turned vindictive. Anyway, he did marry Dhanyamalini later! And it's not that he would ever be a faithful husband or a one-woman man! What with his harem of gorgeous women, all too willing to please him!' she scoffed, eyeing her mother's discomfiture.

Though she disapproved of Ravan's ways, she camouflaged it by arguing that a harem was a royal preserve defining a king. 'It's likely that Sarama as Ravan's wife might have been a nicer person than she is as Vibhishan's!'

Kaikesi gave a weary shake of her head. 'Ideally, I wanted my sons to have one wife. Not like me,' she muttered. 'I know now what I did. I made your father marry me and be his second wife. I thought I had him, I shall have the world, but what did I achieve? I ruined two families instead—mine and Ilavida's, and turned brothers into rivals,'

Her mother looked pensive, her eyes darkening with sudden

sadness. 'That is why I did not want Ravan to have two wives. Which he did eventually,' she sighed, as if ceding her defeat. 'He doesn't listen to me anymore...' her voice faded, her dark eyes distant.

'He stopped listening to you a long, long time ago, Ma,' said Meenakshi, feeling almost sorry for her mother.

It was a new, unfamiliar feeling. Ravan treated her courteously, more a display of filial respect than polite sufferance. He had given her that one wish she had lived for—Lanka. She was the Queen Mother but somehow Kaikesi had come to realize, somewhere down the long way, that her son no longer needed her, heeded her.

She gave a wry smile. 'After Ravan, you seem to be grooming into an astute politician yourself, Meenu! Is your husband's political cunning rubbing on to you?'

Meenakshi was hurt to the quick.

'You still think Vidyujiva a self-seeker, trying to grab power?' she went swiftly belligerent, often unduly sensitive to criticism against Vidyujiva, challenging it whenever the occasion arose. 'How much more does he need to prove that he has our best interest at heart? That he is Ravan's loyal ally? He has won so many wars for him, sealed peace treaties, restructured the army and the country's economy, increased trade by introducing Ravan to all the foreign merchants he knew, and yet you do not trust him, Ma? All of you would rather fawn on Ravan than respect Vidyujiva!' she jeered, whipped up by an old, simmering resentment. 'He is the only one who can stand against Ravan, and Ravan knows it. But Vidyujiva won't, he promised me. But I am not too sure of Ravan, has he brooked for peace. Vajramala just mentioned that we are so happy. We are. But is Ravan? He is never satiated, he wants more—more wealth, more power, more knowledge, more women, more what else??' she demanded. 'What more does he wish for? He has it all. Lanka is flourishing—it's richer than the Heavens! But yet he drives himself and us, into his all-consuming conflicts and conquests...when will it end? Why cannot we live in peace?'

Kaikesi was taken aback at the sudden ferocity of her daughter's rant.

'You are rambling, Meenu, at some self-imagined slight to your husband!' she said, her tone even but sharp. 'I meant it lightly, but you are so humourless who cannot take a jest gracefully. I wasn't picking on him. He is your husband, not a child! Your husband knows how to look after himself!!'

Meenakshi flared. 'There you go again, you can't hide your contempt, can you? All those snide remarks...' she said harshly, the raw wound smarting again.

'Meenu, you twist a simple observation into a conspiracy!' said Kaikesi exasperatedly. 'No one is running down Vidyujiva. He has earned his respect and place in this house, in our hearts and in the royal court as well. He is family now, don't get so upset about some casual remarks!' she scolded, her tone had a lash to it, bringing Meenakshi to her senses. 'The baby's asleep. Put him in the cradle. It's a surprise how he doesn't wake up with you ranting five times a day!'

Meenakshi gave a sudden sigh, easing the tension immediately. 'Yes, I seriously wonder how I shall bring him up with my foul temper,' she grinned weakly. 'I guess if you could, so can I,' she said a little waspishly. 'But you are a better grandmother than you were a mother, I must say. You are marvellous in your new role!'

'Just as my mother was!' agreed Kaikesi. 'She was so good with you, but terrible with me. Grandmothers often are wiser and wizened mothers.'

Meenakshi smiled fondly, recalling her Nani. The void could not be filled, she thought, with a deep pang; she longed to see her. Nani would have been esctatic about the baby, indulging him with every attention, comfort and kindness just like she had been pampered.

'Can't we go and meet her some time, some way?' asked Meenakshi wistfully, filled with a strong urge to see her Nani in person. It had been ages...

Kaikesi did not reply. But there was a swift change in her expression: crumbling quickly to grief.

'Ma, are you all right?' asked Meenaskhi, surprised and suddenly uneasy. Her mother had gone pale, her dark eyes dull with remembered sorrow.

'I didn't tell you, because Kumar had been born that very day...' started Kaikesi, vainly clearing her clogged throat.

'Didn't tell me what, Ma?' asked Meenakshi, worry and fear making her voice unduly sharp.

'Your grandmother is dead. So is Subahu,' said Kaikesi tonelessly. 'They were killed in the Dandak forest...'

'And Uncle Mareech?' she asked, the question slipping involuntarily.

'He barely survived to tell the tale. He is still recuperating from his injuries...'

'He's here in this palace??' she asked incredulously.

'No, at Uncle Malyavan's home. He's being treated there.'

'Who killed Nani?' asked Meenakshi, the rasp in her voice as tearing as the pain in her heart. *No one could kill the powerful Taraka; she was invincible with her fearsome weaponry of magic.*

'Ram and Lakshman, the two princes of Kosala,' said Kaikesi, her voice breaking slightly. 'They were protecting Vishwamitra's yagna...' She could not hold her tears any longer, slipping quietly down her hollow cheeks, unchecked. 'Ma's woes all started with that Agastya. She lost Father and went mad with grief and worse, that curse, transformed her from a beautiful Yaksha into a hideous demon, disfiguring her beauty and her mind, turning her from a scholar to a demented woman, as ugly in heart as in appearance. Ma could never forgive him or the entire community of rishis for killing her husband and her father. As revenge, she started troubling them, disrupting their yagna, demolishing their huts, killing them, killing their cattle...she simply went beserk with sorrow and hate!' cried Kaikesi.

Meenakshi wanted to console her, hold the shuddering, shrunken figure in her arms, but she could find no words of comfort, no gesture of kindness; she was instead infused with anguished anger, obliterating other imperceptible emotions.

She heard her mother's painful voice speaking to her in spasmodic stillness.

'Subahu and Mareech helped her in her deeds, and the three,

as vengeance, were harassing the forests of Malaja and Karusha, near the River Ganga. It soon came to be known as the Forest of Taraka with she terrorizing the rishis and the public, and killing those who dared to set foot in that forest. The only one who confronted her was Vishwamitra, but he soon lost his patience and requested King Dashrath of Kosala to send his two older sons—Ram and Lakshman—to protect his ongoing yagna.'

'You knew about this and yet you did not send Ravan to protect Nani?' asked Meenakshi, not allowing herself to wallow in shock or sadness, more interested in the full facts. 'Ravan, who has conquered the world, could have easily defeated and killed Vishwamitra and those two princes!'

'Vishwamitra is a *brahmarishi*, he cannot be killed so easily!' said Kaikesi woodenly. 'Nor can these princes. They too are said to be extraordinary young men, and they cannot be defeated. They are his pupils and Vishwamitra is said to have exclusively blessed them with his secret knowledge of war and weapons. I confronted Mareech with the same question and asked why did he not inform us?' said Kaikesi. 'We could have saved them and Ma wouldn't have had to die such a horrible death...' she quavered. 'She must have been confident that she would be able to single-handedly destroy Vishwamitra and the princes—they were just teenaged boys after all!'

'Teenagers,' repeated Meenakshi dully. 'Those boys who killed Nani were mere kids?'

She could not keep out the shock from her voice, the crash of the distant sea waves in motion with her turbulent thought. *Who were these strange mortals?*

Kaikesi nodded despairingly. 'Mareech says Ram was hesitant to kill her as she was a woman and decided to maim her instead. He chopped off her hands to deter her from attacking him further. But using her magic, she changed form, disappeared and continued to attack them, unseen. It was only when Vishwamitra advised Rama, that as a prince, he had to carry out his duty regardless of his own personal reservations about killing a woman that Ram obeyed him, and killed her by piercing her heart with his arrows. Subahu was killed likewise and Mareech barely managed to escape from there. He reached Lanka, the day Kumar was born and we decided to save you the grief. You would have been devastated and moreover you were too weak after having the baby.'

She recalled that day. Kumar had been born after an excruciating sixteen-hour childbirth. She had to work hard to have him—first the severe penance and then the agony of those birth pangs. He was special—the fruit of all her patience and perseverance. As she heard her mother recount, all she could register in the daze of her misery, was that her son was born as violently as her grandmother had died. Had she come back to her? She caught her breath, holding him close to her thudding chest.

She felt her anguish ebb, love surging and filling her heart. But with the rush of emotion, she felt the bitter bile of hate in her mouth. *Ram and Lakshman*, she worded silently. *They killed my grandmother.*

Infidelity

❦

$\mathcal{S}$he had not seen Mandodari so agitated; not even when Ravan had got Dhanyamalini as his second bride ten years ago. Mandodari was friendly but there was an air of cold reserve; formality and propriety of manner was of utmost importance to her. She seldom broke away from her frigid taciturnity. Until she discerned, behind Mandodari's reserve and forced gaiety, a profound melancholy.

Meenakshi stumbled upon her distress by perchance. She had come into Mandodari's palace unannounced, searching for the boys. They were often together—even her two years old Kumar—as all of them looked up to Meghnad and loved him almost reverentially, even the shy Trijata, much to Sarama's chagrin. Meenakshi could not spot any of the children but for the sleeping infant Akshay Kumar, Ravan's youngest son, in his cradle, she found Mandodari sitting next to it, hunched, her shoulders shaking with violent sobs,

The sight turned her cold. *Had she had another argument with Ravan? They fought often; for all her deceptive demureness, Mandodari knew how to fight back, without giving an inch. Was it her mother's apsara blood or her father's wisdom, or her own stubborn individuality that I never saw her cower to Ravan's infamous bouts of mood and temper?*

Yet she was the only one who did not mince her opinions, voicing them with her usual calm straight forwardness. If Ravan was all impulse and desire, she was the anchor to his raging passions. If he was blinded to reason, she made him see it. 'That I go unheard and unheeded does not deter me,' she had once told Meenakshi. 'I have to let him know: it is unto him to become knowing...'

Mandodari reminded Meenakshi of a placid lake, deceptively calm but mysteriously deep. But watching her weep so brokenly, Meenakshi could not stop emitting an involuntary gasp of astonishment.

She had not meant to intrude, but the sound of the soft gasp made Mandodari look up at her, her face drenched in silent anguish.

At the sight of her, Mandodari quickly tried to compose her contorted features, wiping the tears hurriedly away. Meenakshi was the last person she wanted to face or confront at that moment. She wished she could tell her to leave. Meenakshi instead barged into the chamber, unheedful of circumspect consequences.

'What happened?' she demanded peremptorily.

Her offensively self-assured imperativeness, did not allow contradiction or refusal. Mandodari, in that defenceless moment, welcomed the brusque inquiry.

'Why are you here?' asked Mandodari instead.

'I had come to enquire about the boys,' replied Meenakshi, staring at the other woman's wan face.

'They are with Kumbha practising the mace,' was the subdued answer.

'What happened, Mandodari?' repeated Meenakshi, but her tone was gentler.

'You simply caught me in a low mood,' shrugged Mandodari. 'Just a quirky spell,' she added dismissively, forcing a small, brief smile.

Meenakshi was much too stubborn to be taken in by so spurious an argument.

'What is it?' she asked kindly, scrutinizing the tear-streaked face. Even tears could not mar Mandodari's loveliness.

Her kind tone strangely annoyed Mandodari. 'If I wished, I

would tell you,' she said coldly.

Meenakshi was more surprised than stung at Mandodari's sharp rebuff. Mandodari was extraordinarily upset.

'What has Ravan done now?' she guessed astutely.

Mandodari bit her lip.

'Is it because he has gone to Mithila for the swayamvar of King Janak's daughter?' persisted Meenakshi. 'What is her name?' she frowned. 'Yes, Sita.'

She saw Mandodari clenching her lips, her jaw tense. The reason seemed relatively trite and not unusual that Ravan would go for the swayamvar of pretty women. Sita was well admired for her transcendent beauty. And that he wanted to have her as his new bride was not surprising. Meenakshi was discreet enough not to voice her irreverent thoughts, more with respect to Mandodari's feelings.

She cast a reassuring smile. 'It must be Lord Shiva's bow and not Sita that must have prompted Ravan,' assured Meenakshi with false gaiety. 'He must be yearning to show the world that he's the only one who can string it. It is Lord Lord Shiva's famous bow, after all and Ravan prides himself of being his most ardent, faithful devotee. That bow is meant for him, and no one else.'

Mandodari shook her head. 'It won't happen. Ravan should avoid Sita,' she said in a whisper.

Meenakshi frowned, puzzled. 'Why? She is just another beautiful princess, a bride at her swayamvar,' she said. 'Not that it's much of a swayamvar where she gets to choose the groom. Rather it seems like she's a prize trophy to be won after winning a contest.'

'Exactly. And Ravan wants to win her,' nodded Mandodari, fretfully. 'If he wins...'

'That he will,' said Menakshi confidently. 'Is that why you are upset?'

Mandodari shook her head. 'He won't.'

Meenakshi looked at her incredulously. 'How do you know?'

'This bow—the Lord Shiva Dhanush or the Pinaka—has a history,' started Mandodari slowly. 'There is another one—the

Sharang, of Vishnu. Both were crafted by Vishwakarma. He presented the Sharang to Vishnu and the Pinaka to Lord Shiva. Once in a battle of wills, it was tested who was the better archer: Lord Shiva or Vishnu. Both came out with their mighty bows and there was a prolonged contest in which Vishnu was declared the winner. Enraged, Lord Shiva decided to do away with the Pinaka and handed it to King Devrath, an ancestor of King Janak of Mithila. Vishnu, mortified at his win, too gave away his bow for truce, presenting his Sharang to Rishi Richika, the grandfather of Rishi Parshuram.'

A frown creased Meenakshi's brow. 'Agreed it has an awe inspiring history, but what is the cause of your worry?'

'Sita,' said Mandodari and that single word was eloquent, yet mysterious. 'As a child, she is said to have moved the Pinaka easily while playing...'

Meenakshi burst out laughing. 'You are scared of that?? It must be a folklore, a fancy story to praise the princess. It's often done to inflate the egos of kings, princes and the royal family. We have stories here in Lanka about Kumbha who eats and sleeps. Or Ravan as the only scholar-king...'

'No that definition should suit King Janak, the rajrishi better,' corrected Mandodari. 'He is known to be a philosopher-king. He noticed how the little girl had been able to lift the immovable Pinaka, and he decided to use the bow to test who could win Sita's hand. The one who could lift it would be the best man in the kingdom deserving Sita.'

'Seems a difficult test if it takes a dozen people and a long cart to move it,' commented Meenakshi.

'It is an impossible feat!' cried Mandodari.

'Then why worry? If Ravan cannot string it as you insist, which I doubt, then he shan't be able to win Sita either. That should be good news for you.'

Mandodari still looked anxious. 'Ravan won't take the defeat so easily. He has set his eyes and his heart on both the Pinaka and Sita. Meenakshi, she is barely eighteen and your brother is in his mid-forties, old enough to be her father! How can he venture into her swayamvar? He will be ridiculed!'

'No one can dare ridicule Ravan,' retorted Meenakshi. 'They tremble in fear!'

'He hasn't been invited, yet he has gone to Mithila! I hope he does not start a war...' her voice trailed fearfully.

'Even if he does, he'll win,' she assured Mandodari. 'But a war is unlikely. No father likes his daughter's swayamvar to be reduced to a bloody battlefield. If you say King Janak is so wise, he shall not provoke Ravan in any manner.'

'If he does not get the bow or Sita, he won't take it silently. Ravan cannot taste defeat of any sort,' said Mandodari, her shoulders sagging wearily. 'I have lost him either way...'

Meenakshi held herself quiet, with effort. *Why was Sita a threat to Mandodari unlike all the other women Ravan had had?* She felt sorry for the woman standing forlornly in front of her. She was married to an insatiable man and his unbridled passion for women and war, his twin weaknesses, would surely lead to his downfall someday. *For women he would war; with war, he would take women:* She felt a flare of anger against her brother. *How much more could he hurt his wife? How much more would he devour than he could reasonably consume? Greed has turned the man into a monster, immoderately craving for all—wealth, will, wisdom and women.*

She almost reached out for Mandodari, her hands, sympathetic and stoical, but she stopped, reproaching herself. What could she console her with—hollow words and false assurances? She felt strangely resentful. Why did Mandodari suffer Ravan's dalliances? She did not reproach or complain, and saw Ravan for what he was and accepted it, with good natured tolerance and long forbearance. But was it honesty or dishonesty to oneself, wondered Meenakshi. Long sufferance was not strength; it was an affliction of the weak.

Mandodari seemed to read her thoughts. 'Why does our love never admit failure?' she asked painfully, in appeal. 'My marriage is a failure, but I don't give up. Why??'

Meenakshi said nothing, surprised at her question, watching

her sister-in-law closely, so lovely, yet so lost. Her eyes had a kind of wide, blank, broken look, frantic not to show the state she was in. As if she was caged in some permanent, controlled hysteria.

Meenakshi gave a shudder, she knew that feeling—it used to chase her before she met Vidyujiva. That is what this family, this golden palace did to you—make them prisoners on the extreme edge of themselves, controlling, holding, restraining, suppressing that frenzy of frustration, roiling in the patient endurance of pain and unhappiness. She had thought her tormented mind would unravel into madness; she had wanted to rush back to the sanctuary of the forest. But then, she had met Vidyujiva and her life changed forever.

'It would be better for us if we just gave up and accepted the failure, but we don't, never. We keep going through the cycle of hope, disappointment, love and disillusionment...' continued Mandodari, pushing her hair back absently. 'All for our men; we dress up for them, we keep house for them, we have their children, we carry on their lineage, we even suffer for them, and deal with their vanities and a lot else...why? Because we love them!' she said self-deprecatingly. 'Because I love *him!*'

It was as if she was talking to herself, realized Meenakshi.

'We bring up our children, we cope, we laugh, we make meals, make merry and make love. We can even live our life without our men, either at war or with other women. Or as widows. Ravan's women will lead to war one day, I know,' she breathed, her eyes shut. 'War and women—our two enemies,' she continued hollowly. 'But we take it, all the bad. And believe we are brave, and safe and good, but why don't we admit to this failure? It would do us a lot of good.'

Meenakshi threw her a look of bewilderment. *Why is Mandodari using the plural and uttering 'we' each time in her sentence? Why am I being included in her stream of incoherent thoughts and voice?* Mandodari seemed to be slipping, swaying obliquely in her chaotic mind, uncontrolled, her thoughts luxate. She did not seem to register what she was saying.

Mandodari clenched and unclenched her hands. 'I cannot

stop my husband from going to her swayamvar, can't stop him lusting after women, can't do anything but scream silently as he flaunts his lovers and his brood of illegitimate children in front of me. He was discreet earlier, I suppose out of some respect for me, but now...' she pursed her lips. 'And yet, fie, I can't stop loving him!!' she shouted, in despairing rage, her eyes glistening with shed tears and fury, hurt and betrayal. 'Why?? I should hate him. But I cannot,' she wept.

'Men are swines,' said Meenakshi, even though she did not agree with her own words thinking of her father. And Vidyujiva. 'Not all, I suppose,' she added weakly. 'All this is simply because of Ravan.'

'Yes, he'll be back soon and I'll pick up where he left off,' agreed Mandodari in a distracted tone. 'Undecided. Unsure. Afraid. Defeated.'

Meenakshi gave Mandodari's hand a tender squeeze, 'No, you are brave, Mandodari, to live and love a person like Ravan...' she said gently, forcing the safe tone back.

'Foolish,' refuted Mandodari dully, her eyes opaque with diffused pain. She gave a start, as a cry broke the stillness in the chamber. The baby had woken up; so had his mother as she was brought back to her harsh reality.

✑

Meenakshi could not let go of that picture of abject misery on Mandodari's stricken face, days after Ravan returned. She had been correct: Ravan had not been able to break the bow or win Sita, spurring him into one of his ugliest moods Meenakshi had ever witnessed. Everyone stayed away from him. He locked himself in his music hall, shedding all his weapons, shield and armour and took up his Rudra veena, stringing it for days on end. 'Music makes me forget all—and remember everything!' he had once told her.

While drying after a bath and thinking about her brother, she heard the Vidyujiva's footfalls in her room. Quickly she expertly lined her eyes with kohl, spent some more minutes fixing her hair, put a gold chain around her slim waist and surveyed herself. *Not bad*, she thought. She returned to the bedroom, walking slowly to the bed where he lay stretched, his eyes glazed as they drank her in. They looked at each other, her expression softened, and smiling, she moved towards me, that thing in her eyes.

She slipped beside him as he sprawled on the silken sheets. He smelt of wine.

'You are drinking too much,' she jabbed playfully.

He pulled her down to him. 'Just a swig with Kumbha,' he muttered thickly, his hands moving over her bare back. 'Had an argument with Ravan again!' he sighed.

'Ravan's gone mad!' she agreed. 'How can all of you bear it?'

She heard him give a short laugh.

'The court would not have functioned had it not been for you!' she continued. 'Funny set of brothers I have—one brutally violent, the second either in sweet slumber or doped drunk and the third engrossed in prayer and worship...'

He remained still, staring up at the engraved ceiling. 'They are your brothers,' he said absently. 'And I am but...'

'But my husband!' she said affectionately but she saw his jaw clench, his body stiffening in hostility. She moved closer provocatively, slipping her hands on his trim waist. 'Take a jest,' she murmured, her lips trailing along the rough bristle of his tense jawline. She rolled atop him, straddled him, feeling his interest in her body rapidly reviving.

He felt a white hot surge of desire go through him and he sunk his fingers deep into her loose hair at the back of her head and roughly pulled her hard towards his face, his lips descending hard on hers, crushing them, grinding them with rising fervour.

'Shut up, woman, don't talk about him! Isn't living with him through the day bad enough?' he snarled, pushing her down, his predatory lips gnawing and seizing, his bare legs trapping her, his hips thrust hard against hers. She felt a stab of sharp pleasure. They always made fierce love—quick, convulsive and ferocious. But this time she sensed a difference; his rage as it seared hot inside her, deep and strong and livid, pushing forcefully, expelling all his fury and frustration into her. She could feel it in his savage thrusts, the marauding lips on her bare flesh, pillaging and plundering, his sweat glistening on his face, his eyes glittering feral. He gasped, his groans escalating into a shout—it was raw desire curdled into a cry of unleashed rage. She felt his fevered breath on her damp skin, his red, flushed face, buried in the thick fragrance of her hair, shuddering with the last spasms, spent and drained. He rolled over on his back, his head flung back, his arms outstretched but his fingers still touching hers, not breaking contact.

'My tigress, as always,' he breathed, panting, still watching her.

Meenakshi smiled, hoping his anger was spent. She did not pursue the matter. The ensuing silence was long and drawn, punctuated by their heavy breathing as they lay sapped of strength.

She broke the silence, hoping he had calmed down. She touched his cheek lightly.

'So who won Sita eventually, if not our peeved Ravan?' she asked, more to change the mood and the moment.

Vidyujiva frowned. 'A prince from Ayodhya—Ram. That's what little I got from your brother's rant.'

Ram. The name stilled her breath for a second. *Ram, the one who had killed her Nani and her uncle.*

She straightened up quickly, sitting upright, her ears keen.

'Ram,' she repeated slowly.

Vidyujiva looked surprised. 'You know him?'

'I know of him,' she said stiltedly. 'He killed Nani.'

Quick realization dawned on his face, his eyes narrowing. 'That young lad! 'Yes, he and his brother Lakshman was with him as well at Mithila,' he supplied, his thick brows furrowed in thought.

The two brothers, the two killers was all what her stunned mind could assimilate. *But they were exceptional boys*, her instinct warned her. *They had vanquished and destroyed Taraka, in spite of her invincible arsenal of magic and sorcery. They were clearly immune to spells and conjuration, seeing through the impossible even the dark powers of the supernatural. And now Ram broke the Pinaka, another great feat. Almost like divine intervention. Who was he, this mere mortal prince?*

She felt a cold shiver crawl up her spine. It was not fear, it was a cold sense of premonition. The same which Mandodari had experienced about Sita, haunting her with an ambiguous terror. *Sita and Ram; both strange and powerful. Who were they?*

'From what I have heard, Mithila is celebrating not just the wedding of Sita with Ram but Lakshman's with her sister Urmila,' he announced blandly. 'Their cousins will be marrying the remaining two brothers...'

'All in the family. You seem exceptionally well informed,' she raised her brows.

'Ravan wants me to keep him duly accounted of all what's happening in Mithila and Ayodhya—he's reduced me to a messenger boy!' he disclosed with a tired shrug. 'He is obsessed with Sita. And Ram.'

'Ram defeated him,' she murmured faintly and she could well imagine Ravan's rage at suffering a public humiliation. 'Not only did he not get Sita, he was also trounced by a young boy almost half his age and experience. And it happened in the view of everyone. That is what's killing him—the disgrace, the loss of his self-respect, pride and damned ego,' she added, with a shake of her bejeweled head.

'Good,' said Vidyujiva feelingly. 'Possibly he'll know now what it feels to be thwarted, to stew in disappointment! Seems like he finally might have met his match,' he said heartily.

She sighed histrionically and gazed at him, her eyes a warm honey gold. 'You were a match for him too, had you not taken a step back,' she smiled.

'Step down,' he corrected, clenching his jaw.

She touched his arm. He flinched.

'It hurts...' she said, trying to soothe him, but cleaving open a throbbing scar.

It was a statement, a fact, both rarely spoke about. They

made an effort to avoid discussing Ravan; it was a topic often difficult to handle and it required immense tact to balance sanity of thought and emotion. Today was an exception and Meenakshi could see that Vidyujiva was still troubled, his body taut with tension, his mind in visible turmoil.

'Ravan won't allow anyone to share his glory,' he said grimly. 'Rather he won't credit you with the glory you deserve.'

'What did he do?' she asked precipitously.

'Same old story,' he said tiredly, stroking his short beard. 'I won the campaigns against the Yakshas, but he prefers to boast that it was he who vanquished Kuber and his folks forever. The Yakshas won't dare strike again, I saw to that!' he said, a pulse beating his temple, his mood procellous.

'Ravan can't get over Kuber,' she explained exasperatedly. 'He threw him out of his kingdom, took his crown, chased him to Indralok, publicly humiliated him there, raped his daughter-in-law Rambha, what more does he wish for?'

Vidyujiva nodded. 'He will stoop to any level to hit back. And he will not give up. Ravan does not believe in making peace. Just war. Now I am to lead another attack on Indra, Agni and the devas. Ravan wants to take Meghnad too for his debut foray into our brave, bloody world of war!!'

'Meghnad?' she was startled. 'He is a child of sixteen!'

'Exactly, I tried telling him the same. Ravan turns around and says I don't need to get insecure by a child!' He was on the verge of exploding out of the bed, Meenakshi could feel his thighs tense and quiver with rage.

'Meghnad is his weakness, he adores him!' she commented. 'And he was born to be the perfect warrior, Ravan saw to that!'

Ravan hoping his son would be born invincible and that no one in the world could defeat him, had called on a priest for the perfect auspicious time: all planets so aligned in ideal position to augur the birth of a highly knowledgeable and brave warrior. That was how Meghnad was born. Mandodari, of course, was affronted and was dead against Ravan playing around with natural forces and the Nav Grahas but Ravan as usual, didn't listen to her.

Vidyujiva heard her story with a cynical smile.

'Our son is special too,' he said eventually. 'I don't want Kumar to grow to be a mere lackey of Meghnad or any of your brothers' sons. He is a Kalkeya prince. He deserves more but he won't get it in Lanka...'

Meenakshi felt a frisson of fear. She pressed her fingers tenderly over his throbbing pulse at the temple, trying to draw fire. Making love was always wonderful: it made him less sullen, she was thinking, and each time was better than the last.

She succeeded. He turned his hard body towards her, leaning his arm, his exposed neck, his tanned, angry face towards her. She kissed him slowly, biting his lower lip, trying to wean out the fury within. He pulled away, tearing his lips from hers, grabbing her by the shoulders, his fingers sinking into the soft flesh of her upper arm.

'That's not the solution, not now, never was,' he said gruffly. 'It's not about us, but him!'

'What do you intend to do?' she asked quickly, rubbing her arm delicately but not able to rub off the bruising fear. She turned to look at him and her heart contracted to see that sullen dark look back on his face again.

'What is it?'

'Just thinking...can't a man think, for God's sake?' She flinched at the harsh note in his voice but she had guessed what he was brooding about.

'Don't fight Ravan!' she pleaded frantically.

His eyes grew dull in their bleakness, immediately sorry for his harsh words. Why did she love him so much? Was it because he was the man created by her imagination, whom she had been eagerly seeking all her life? She had so much fear of the past—he could tell that from the way she never spoke of it. It was one of his reasons for marrying her, to prove she would never have to return to her family for love. He would give it to her. He took exaggerated care of her like a bungling man entrusted with the fragile, forever scared of losing her.

She remained still, waiting and watching his hard face and

the way his eyes shifted, reminding her of an animal in a cage.

'You don't want me to fight Ravan, you hadn't wanted us to stay in Lanka...!!' he muttered. 'That's what you have been insisting all these years and I didn't listen to you—but for you, for our sake, for the sake of peace and sanity. But I can't bear it any longer—Ravan is getting worse by the day!' he expostulated. 'He is a tyrant! He is now openly insulting me, trying to cut me to size every time,' he said restlessly.

'Do you wish to return to Ashma?' she asked shortly, trying to hide her mounting alarm.

He nodded his head, sinking it dejectedly into his large hands. 'Yes, if it comes to that. I would still like to stay here but it's hard. You had warned me about him and I tried...'

He swallowed convulsively. He was gulping down his pride, his ambition, his hopes: Meenakshi could palpably feel it. She nodded.

'It won't be easy for either of us at Ashma,' he warned, a note of impatience in his voice. 'Especially for you. You are used to wealth and luxury.'

'While you have always been obsessed with money,' she retorted. 'Aren't you?'

'Frankly no, because in my country we don't have much money, so we don't get the chance to put a value on it,' he shrugged. 'But I guess too much wealth does the same. Ravan despite having everything, all possible wealth, values nothing!' he grimaced. 'I can't take this anymore. I have decided what I have to do. And I want you to agree with me...' he paused, staring at her with his liquid black eyes.

She shivered. The deadly quietness of his voice was much more effective than if he had shouted at her. She knew how to deal with shouting and screaming, but not the quite, firm voice.

They would be leaving Lanka. She should have been elated. But she was not unhappy either. Instead she was riddled with a strange fear, permeating from her soul, its clawing tentacles pervading into every thought and emotion.

Death

'*Indrajit! Indrajit!! Indrajit!!!*'

Meenakshi heard the jubilant cries ringing in the streets below. 'Who is Indrajit?' she asked in frank wonderment.

'They are hailing Meghnad,' smiled Mandodari. 'Lord Brahma renamed him Indrajit—the conqueror of Indra—after he defeated Indra during Devasura Sangram, the battle between the devas and the asuras where he tied him up to his chariot. Lord Brahma intervened and requested him to free Indra. Meghnad agreed and pleased at his humility, Brahma granted him a rare boon...' she broke off, her face radiant. 'They are all heading home. Victorious as always,' she exclaimed, her soft eyes gleaming with a new light. It was not just the glow of bearing Akshay, now a toddler of three, but unbridled pride for her oldest son. Mandodari could not have looked happier.

Ravan had correctly surmised his son's extraordinary capabilities and taken him for this war despite Vidhujiva's misgivings, and he had returned home like a true warrior, crowned a hero. *Like his father had once been. He was a better person than his father though*, pondered Meenakshi, feeling pleased for both mother and son. Meghnad deserved his title. He had been an excellent student, the favourite of Shukracharya, the guru of the asuras who had trained Meghnad to obtain divine celestial weapons; the *Pashupatastra*, *Brahmastra* and *Vaishnavastra* at such a young age. He had acquired them effortlessly.

'Get the tray of pooja, Mrunalini,' she ordered her handmaid. 'My nephew deserves a hero's welcome!'

And with her usual flourish and a roll of her hips, Meenakshi proceeded towards the royal women waiting for the victors to come home. And then they arrived: first the hailed hero, Meghnad, followed by Kumbha and Vibhishan. Ravan and Vidyujiva were not to be seen. She frowned, her heart piling furiously against her ribs.

Meghnad was climbing the steps. Tall and lithe, he had broad shoulders, a narrow, deeply tanned face, piercing, large hazel eyes and a thin hard mouth. He was the perfect combination of his parents, inheriting their good looks, but he exuded that authoritative air and personality that defied his tender age. Seeing her, instead of his beaming smile, he put up his hand to stop his mother from performing the customary welcome *aarti*. Ignoring Mandodari's shocked face, he brushed past her.

Meenakshi caught his arm. 'That's rude, Meghnad. It's your moment of glory,' she said. 'She wants to give her blessings. We all want to celebrate.'

He turned to face her, his anguish painted clearly all over. The look took Meenakshi's breath away, injecting the first prick of fear.

'There is nothing to celebrate!!' he said laconically. 'We are in mourning!'

She was thoroughly alarmed now.

Kumbha placed a hand on his heaving shoulder.

Meghand turned his face away, as if he could not face her anymore. Meenakshi felt the dread getting heavier, plummeting her heart, dragging it down. She had the horrible feeling of things crumbling and suddenly knew what was going to be told to her before the words were spoken by Kumbha.

'Vidyujiva is dead, Meenu,' he muttered huskily, with all the courage and propriety he could muster. 'He was killed in the war in Asmanagara while conquering the netherworld.'

The frightening silence that greeted her stampeded her into panic. The words wrenched out her breath, her heart, her soul.

There was a roar in her mind. She saw the tray tremble in her hands. She clutched at it frantically, her nails scrapping hard against the polished gold. She felt it being removed gently by Kumbha, as he enveloped her softly in his embrace. But the warmth couldn't reach her; she felt cold, icy as the blood stopped flowing in her veins. She held herself stiff, rigidly formal, holding on to the last vestige of her senses.

No, she moved her lips silently, the whisper dying in her throat. *He could not be killed so easily. He could not die...*

Through a thinning haze, she saw the bulky figure of Ravan. She stretched out a quavering hand towards him, she did not know why. Was it of help, succour or accusation?

He flushed red, as deep as his war-weary, bloodshot eyes. She felt a chill uncurling from the pit of her stomach.

'How??' she whispered.

Kumbha looked uneasy, his eyes averted. 'He died in war...' he mumbled.

She glanced back at Ravan, as he stood grim. Meenakshi looked from one brother to another, the grief replaced by quivers of suspicion.

'Tell me,' she ordered. 'Say it! I want to know how he died!'

His eyes opaque, Ravan spoke featurelessly.

'He did not die a warrior's death in the battlefield,' he paused. 'He was killed by his own soldier after the war.'

She stared, the words slowly percolating.

'By a traitor?' she murmured .

'No, one of our men...'

'Stop it, Ravan, please,' pleaded Kumbha. 'Don't say it!!'

His fingers were digging into her arms. She shrugged away from Kumbha's hold, her face damp, her eyes wild. 'What is it that I should not be told?'

'That it was a vengeful husband who killed the lover of his wife!' said Ravan. 'Not an enemy on a battlefield.'

She shrank from the enormity of the words. Her husband had been someone else's lover...

'You are lying!' she shouted her cry gurgling in her throat

as she saw his eyes trail to the maid standing behind her.

Meenakshi heard a sharp intake of breath.

She whirled around to the white-faced, terror-stricken face of Mrunalini, her mouth open in soundless horror but it screamed of guilt, an open confession for all to see.

Meenakshi found her hand rising in misty fury, striking the beautiful face, her nails hooking deep and savagely raking it— from the smooth forehead down to her open, wide eyes down that pert nose, her full lips to her shapely chin.

Mrunalini screamed in agony, her face to her bloodied face, falling in an undignified heap, her body writhing. 'My eyes, my eyes!! I can't see!!' she whimpered, her cry choking in her own vomit of blood. The guards quickly took her away.

Meenakshi turned on Ravan, her eyes feverish, gleaming bright. 'You allowed a mere soldier to murder your general?'

Ravan remained still and stolid, his fists clenched.

Logic seemed to urge her to believe him, yet something deep, stubbornly inside her, refused to register his words.

She took a step closer to Ravan. Though a head shorter, she projected the power of a wronged widow, of the fury of a grieving wife, of an embittered but powerful woman, a sister questioning her brother's point to prove, with the full might of wrath and hate behind her.

'Is it so easy to kill a general?' she whispered and paused, drawing her lips off her teeth. 'Who was he? Did you have him killed? Was it on your orders?'

The hoarse whisper hung in the air, chilling the room into a sudden stillness.

She saw Kumbha shake his head, colour rising to his face, the fleshy hands ball into fists, clenching and unclenching his fingers.

Ravan remained impassive.

'You did!' she confirmed, seeing the truth flash through in his golden eyes, dilating in unregretful ratification.

'Did you not have the courage to admit it to take refuge in some weak lie? Can you not tell the truth, that you are a murderer?' she lashed.

Kumbha held her arm, restraining her, afraid she would claw Ravan's eyes out too.

Ravan, stood unmoved, his face twitching. He drew in his breath. 'You want to hear the truth, dear sister?' he started, dangerously soft. 'But do you have the courage to listen to it? See it, accept it? You, Meenu, you are the one who takes refuge in a lie you believe to be true. But that does not make it the truth. Your husband was a bastard, who tricked you in love, in marriage, and who dared to attempt usurping my throne. He had already usurped you, sister, you besotted fool! He was...'

'Ravan, please don't..!' whispered Mandodari.

Meenakshi swivelled her head, confused. *Everyone seems to be knowing something but not telling.*

'No, let her hear the truth,' he said. 'Yes, I killed Vidyujiva with my sword, I drove it into his chest,' he said.

He had imagined himself imparting the news gently, for her to absorb the shock. He had not visualized her looking up at him in unbridled hate and snarling. 'You did what you had wanted to do from the very first time you got to know about us—you wanted to kill him and you did!'

Kumbha interrupted, 'He was a traitor, Meenu! He always was, he was planning a coup. We found out, have rounded up the ministers who were supporting him...'

'Brothers in crime!' she spat, her voice shrill. 'You expect me to believe that, believe you?'

'Exactly! You won't, you never have,' said Kaikesi helplessly, yielding her tone to go soft, pleading. 'That's why we could never let you know!'

Meenakshi felt cold all over. Her mother knew as well. *Was this a plan, a subterfuge to misrepresent their roles in the dastardly crime...*

'What other truth did I not have the courage to tell you? That he was a scoundrel who spared no woman in the palace,' continued Ravan relentlessly. 'Let you know he was whoring with all the women in Lanka, and he whored himself to you too so that he could gain power and crown! Let you know that he was always the wretch I knew he was, an enemy in our midst, our family, dreaming of taking the throne someday. Let you know that he planned to have us all killed; let you know that he intended to do all this under your very nose!!' he continued, between his teeth. 'He was waiting for the opportune time when Kumbha would slip into his slumber next month, so that is one brother less to fight. He had it all planned, but what he did not know was that we knew about it. I had kept watch on him always. He could fool you, never me!'

She shuddered, putting her hands to her face. 'For which he had to be killed?' she gasped, her face slack with shock and fury. 'How do I know it to be true? You never gave him a chance to live and to explain...'

'A traitor is like a mad dog, he has to be put down,' retorted Ravan, his shadowed eyes on his sister, his stare intense and unnerving. 'I killed him as the last resort, on that battlefield. He deserved no explanation, and he had none to give. He died as he lived—ignominiously!' Ravan muttered through clenched teeth, his voice low, a muscle in his jaw twitching. 'Nor do I deserve your hate, sister. But I am ready to take it, take on the slur of having murdered my brother-in-law...'

She flinched, her face a sickly waxen pallor. 'You did not deign him worthy of a respectable death. You saw that he came to an ignoble end!'

'But it was a common foot soldier who did not allow Ravan to take the blame,' intervened Kumbha quietly. 'After watching Ravan kill him, the soldier ran to him, and wept at his feet, "Sir, you did what I was going to anyway—kill the scoundrel. He is my wife's lover. She works at the palace as your sister's personal maid and all I could do was watch helplessly and hear stories about them. I intended to kill him but you have done the deed. You have killed brave kings and unconquerable devas, don't tarnish your noble name by being known as the killer of this lowly cad. Let me be held responsible for this act, you don't deserve to carry his nasty blood on your hands!"'

Kumbha fell silent.

'But I am ready to be branded your husband's murderer, Meenu,' said Ravan, his voice steady as his eyes. 'I am that brother who made his sister a widow. By killing him, I saved my family...'

'Yourself,' she corrected. 'Your throne, your power, your position.'

'I had to. He would have destroyed all of us. I have no pretexts, no pretences,' confessed Ravan.

Their eyes locked: hers glittering fire and his a clear, calm amber, with flecks of gold. He remained silent, no more further words of justification. The stretched silence, was deathly still, carrying the stench of blood and hate, lies and hurt, love and longing, family and fortune...

'You confess about the deed by making it sound noble. But all of you are lying about him,' she said tonelessly, her mouth dry. She had that same look of wary defiance of being perpetually suspicious and angry, as if bracing to take the next knock life was going to throw her.

'We are not, Meenu,' said Kaikesi, her voice no longer beseeching. 'We just did not tell you earlier, we did not have the heart to let you about him. He was a rascal, all of us could see that but for you. You were besotted with him! He had a mesmeric spell over you, and you could think of no ill. You used to cling to him as if he had saved you from us! You went crazy at the smallest criticism, how could we dare to tell you the terrible truth? You treated him with possessiveness and devotion. You would not have understood, not then, not now.'

She stretched her hands eloquently, hoping her daughter would follow the depth of her distress. Meenakshi threw her a venomous glare, making her cringe at its intensity.

Meenakshi felt Mandodari's soft hands on her shoulder, as if she was reaching for her, daring to do what the others were so fearful of: touching her lest she attacked violently.

'It's true, cruelly true!' she said. 'We hoped you would discover it on your own but you never did. You loved him, trusted him too much to ever suspect him.'

And suddenly a light exploded in her mind, recognizing

the crucial flaws she had missed: her mother's often abrupt statements, Vajramala's discreet comments, Mandodari's discomfiting sympathy, Sarama's unwarranted sarcasm, Kumbha's hapless face, Vibhishan's avoidance and Ravan's stony, watchful stare. It all made sense now: they were hiding a lie they thought was the truth. Meenkashi saw in a flash why Mandodari, in her dazed, painful rant was speaking in the plural and including her in her story of disillusionment. Meenakshi and Mandodari were suffering the same pain, that same unfaithfulness.

'I don't get it, Meenu. All of us are telling you the same thing—he had to be killed to save ourselves. Do you love him that much to hate us so?' Kumbha added, after a short pause. 'Why? We love you, Meenu, we are family. Then why don't you trust us? By killing him, Ravan has saved not just the crown, Lanka and us but you too. Don't you see? This is your chance too. You are free from that evil man—he used you, he fooled you, he betrayed you, yet you insist he is true and we are evil. Why do you keep siding with him? Why do women do that, give up their family so easily for their lover?!' he asked in angry exasperation.

In that question, Meenakshi got her answer, crediting a sliver of veracity at her brother's desperate appeal. Women, she knew, were reduced to the elemental, their most vulnerable when they were facing love and family. They became cleansed by their capacity to give love. But what Kumbha did not know that they could hate in all its unadulterated purity as well. Her family had destroyed her. Her love. Her husband. Her own small family. She hated all of them just now. She had been unwanted in her family, and it was Vidyujiva who had saved her from them. He had given her the love that none of them could offer, that warmth, that peace, that sense of being wanted, the belongingness. Not her mother, not her brothers.

She heard Kumbha's imploring voice cutting through her heaving emotions. 'You are our sister, why would we brothers harm you in any way?' he entreated. 'What have we done for you to be so suspicious of us? Ravan curses himself every single day that he was not there to save you from Kuber. He swore he would protect you. And he has. He avenged Kuber because of you, Meenu. You know that. He warned you against Vidyujiva but you fought him, coercing him into getting you married to his most hated enemy. He could have got him killed there and then but he listened to you, not because he feared your threats, Meenu. He would have gladly taken Mandodari's hate for your love, your welfare. But he saw how madly you were in love with him and he did not want to hurt you. He agreed to your terms and suffered each day watching his enemy living in his home, basking in the new wealth and power, betraying his trust, and worse, betraying you by sleeping with all the women he wanted. It was almost like cocking a snook at all of us—he dared to get away with anything because we dared not hurt you. Yet...'

'Yet you killed him!' she grated in a hoarse whisper. 'You killed all my hopes, my future...'

They believed that I had naively fallen in love with Vidyujiva; it was not love, they thought, but my hopeless foolishness. And now they were giving me proof of my stupidity, by listing his crimes and reasoning their self-decided punishment. Vidyujiva's transgressions were evidence to not just his wickedness but my gullibility.

But it was irrelevant to her: she did not believe them, she could never trust them. She trusted her love for him, she could never doubt that. *But did I trust his love,* a small voice taunted. No, my family had never loved me, never liked him loving me. They assumed a sensible person like me could not be foolish in love. That by falling in love with him, a new, silly Meenakshi was born. By making her fall for him, he had eliminated the suspicious, wary, Meenakshi, wiping out her intelligence, and shrouding her with naivety. He had seduced the gullible girl into willing collusion, surrendering to him in her mad love, in ignorance and in faith. But my family in their own distrust of him, had destroyed him, had destroyed the love, and destroyed me too.

'It was a plot you had long conspired in the pretext of going for war,' she rasped, her eyes chips of cold gold. 'How did it happen? Did the three brothers surround him and struck him each with a swing of his sword?!!'

Vibhishan gasped, looking haggard. She had the impression that he wanted to tell her more and waited perceptively, her eyes contemptuous. He was a weakling, ready to jump opportunity and situation. His stroke must have been the most feeble.

'Ravan did not want us to bloody our hands with the dirty deed. He said he would take the onus,' he admitted, his expression torn, looking into her hollow eyes.

She wanted to laugh out aloud. She did: shrill and long. 'Aha! The ever noble brother—Ravan, our great benefactor!' she jeered. 'All of you, in the guise of looking up to him, are nothing but his sycophants. Your fawning obsequiousness was always disgusting but today it shows the depths to which all of you can fall! You lie for him, you pretend for him, you kill for him!!' She unclenched her fists, flexing her long, slim fingers, the nails glinting.

'And worse, you tarnish my husband's good name!' she spewed venomously and stopped short.

'He wasn't in love with her or any other woman...' she said it so quietly none could scarcely hear her. 'I know it! He wouldn't have done a thing like that. He wouldn't have taken another woman into my home. He wasn't that type.'

She stopped, looked quickly away, her hand going to her face.

Kaikesi wrenched her hand away, holding them hard at the wrists. 'Your love for Vidyujiva has made you crazy. He is dead, he had to die, he would have got all of us killed, you fool!' shouted Kaikesi. 'Blaming Ravan or us is not going to help you. We have already done that by removing him from our life, your life. We are helping you!'

'You have undone me,' screamed Meenakshi in demented despair. 'You killed whatever I had. And it is because of only one man—Ravan. Ravan hated him, Ravan dreaded him, Ravan was threatened by him and what does Ravan do to anyone who challenges him?' she hissed, venom gushing out. 'He removes them like he did with Father. He finishes them like he murdered my husband! Which brother makes his sister a widow for his own ambition, his fears?' she cried, livid tears coursing down her ravaged face.

Kaikesi was aghast, struck with consternation and dread for her daughter.

'Oh my dear, no, you would have been killed by your husband sooner or later the moment you were inconvenient!' gasped Kaikesi, folding her hands together in desperate entreaty. 'Why don't you believe us? Go and talk to those who conspired with him, hear what they have confessed to...'

'By the fear of Ravan?' she scoffed, her lips curling. 'Like he did with that soldier and Mrunalini? How much did he bribe them with to confess what they were forced to say? Ma, you will do anything to protect your precious son. He is your lifeline, you will cling onto him, till your last breath. He is your hope, your aspiration. But all you did was create a maniacal monster whom you cannot recognize or prefer not to recognize, but keep covering up for him. He threw out his own father from his home, he plundered, he raped Vedavati, he raped Rambha, but you turned a blind eye...'

She was cut short by a soft whimper. Mandodari, white as marble, her eyes hard as granite, turned to her. 'Stop it, Meenakshi, don't let your grief and anger hurt the family that it kills every ounce of love and respect,' she said, trembling, her face now a picture of dread.

Meenakshi gave a brittle laugh. 'Another advocate of my dear brother! Or should I say a blind fool?' she sneered. 'All of you claim I am a besotted fool, but here stands another— Ravan's wife, fawning, faithful, foolish!! You think I am being spiteful, Mandodari? I am being truthful, and hope to open your eyes, your mind and your love and see Ravan for what he is. He raped Vedavati and she killed herself. He raped Rambha and he got cursed, which is why all the other women are saved!' she said ferociously, tearing into the shocked silence. 'That is our biggest family secret, Mandodari, which, not just you but none know about! Why? Because no one dares utter a word against the mighty king, our beloved Ravan. And now he murders my husband in cold blood but on the pretext of protection of family. It is preserving his honour, his throne, his ego!'

Burning in murderous frenzy, Meenakshi watched each member inflicted by the violence of her words. Gloating and victorious, she knew she had won nothing, lost everything. But that knowledge gave her momentary solace, a secret satisfaction she gleaned from their horrified, hurt faces. She had struck at them, the shiver of glee reinforced by the nasty smirk that disfigured her darkly attractive face.

Mandodari wanted to rush to her rescue but Meenakshi seemed beyond help; she now reminded her of a wild, wounded cat, snarling and baring her claws, roaring and prowling in untamed fury facing Ravan who stood stiff and still, his face a mask of cold impassivity.

Kaikesi made a small, convulsive movement. And in the elderly lady's face, Mandodari saw a flicker of rage and revulsion contaminating the look of kindness Kaikesi had been trying to reserve for her daughter.

Kaikesi breathed heavily, her words laboured. 'Meenu, you were always ugly, not merely in your looks but your ugly, twisted mind—mean, vindictive and....oh, so unlovable! You are Surpanakha, not my daughter but a monster. We tried to save you from one, but we forgot you are one yourself! Both of you deserved each other, one's mercifully dead and you, I know, will make life hell for us!'

Meenakshi trilled again, her eyes dancing wildly. It was an appalled, envious, victorious laughter ringing hollow and harsh, divested of the last vestige of innocence and joy and trust. She flounced from the room, a graceful, feline figure in gold silk; diamonds sparkling in her hair; fear and fury in her heart. She paused to look up at Ravan, her eyes blazing into his.

This was her moment of truth. She wanted to see him dead.

Surpanakha

I am like the jungle's tigress, Surpanakha thought, her keen, topaz eyes, dilating. The tigress would run if it could, just as she wanted to right now—flee from Lanka, away from her family. But when trapped, it becomes one of the most dangerous and vicious of all jungle beasts. She was like that tigress. If she saw a way out, she would have run, but she was trapped in her grief, churning into fury. *My revenge would be my respite. Ravan has to die for this murder.* But she knew it was a special person who would have to kill him—her son. She would train Kumar to kill Ravan. But she had to make her plans. Her immediate one was to leave Lanka. She would now have to pretend to allow all to believe with the intent to deceive. Her deception was her sole self-preservation.

It had been a quick month since Vidyujiva's death. She was walking out of the palace as her father once walked out. The only words echoing in her ears were her mother's, *'You'll make life hell for us!'*

And I will, she promised herself, *for each one of them. From today I would be the Surpanakha*, she reflected, as she passed the row of members of her family, some stupefied, the others bewildered. They had left her with nothing, except with a vicious determination to seek solace through vengeance. She was not frightened. She had been purged of fear once she knew for certain that Ravan had decided Vidyujiva should die and had killed him.

Vidyujiva, his memory ripped through her tortured mind, bleeding her weeping heart. The glowing embers of him lived and from time to time he seemed to visit her in her dreams with his crooked smile but the beautiful face got bloody, fresh blood frothing out from an open wound in his head, dripping, then gushing down, bubbling out...till she screamed and screamed only to wake up to a silent night, her screams dying in her throat. She had been dreaming; she had to wake up to a new reality—her vengeance.

She was strangely aloof about their reaction—her brothers had implored her not to leave unlike her mother, who had stoically agreed with her decision. Ravan had been expectedly furious, when she had announced after Vidyujiva's grand funeral, that she wanted to leave the palace to settle in the Dandak forest where Mareech had retired.

'What is this new madness, Meenu?' he asked in open exasperation, throwing her a worried look.

'I *was* mad, brother, when I heard the news of Vidyujiva's death, not now,' she confessed, in a low, unsteady voice. 'And I apologize for the terrible words I uttered. To all of you, especially you, Ravan,' she said slowly, her voice low and contrite. 'I guess what I could not handle was Vidyujiva's deception rather than his sudden death,' she swallowed, forcing the bile down her mouth. 'And I could find no one else to vent out my fury to but you! It's awful all what I said. It is unforgivable,' she said abruptly.

'There is nothing to forgive, Meenu,' said Ravan gently. 'It was hard on you and you were bound to be upset. I am relieved that you realized later, if not sooner, what the reality was...' he stopped discreetly. 'I did what I had to do for all of us, even if it meant being branded a common murderer.'

That you are, she thought viciously, *and you shall pay for it dearly—with your life. And your precious Lanka too*, she observed the gold high columned corridor of the chamber. *I shall bring all this and your beautiful world down, besides your ego*. But she kept a straight face and nodded. 'You are our saviour, you have always thought of family first. It took me a long, painful time to realize that,' she murmured, her voice desolate.

She sat down quietly. She knew her brother was powerful and no one could kill him—no deva or asura. But for one. Her son: he was like her Nani, indomitable, unconquerable. She would take Kumar away from his uncles and Lanka and groom him to kill Ravan. She would seek Mareech's help, though he had to be kept in the darkness. Mareech would teach him the magic of witchcraft and sorcery, the only way Ravan could be killed.

She knew no one could help her fight against her brother, no one but herself. If Ravan believed that he had got her, he was colossally wrong. Her happy days were over, courtesy her brother. There wasn't going to be a husband into whose arms she could rush. There wasn't going to be any more mornings when he taught his son to master horse-riding. There was not going to be any more of anything. Instead, it would be Ravan who would be with her until he died. Her heart first and then her brain had lurched ludicrously. 'Until he died.' And the words kept ricocheting in her triumphant mind. She had her purpose in life—she would kill Ravan through Kumar.

Sitting in his grand music room, she looked at Ravan thoughtfully, playing the veena so passionately: he always strung it more beautifully when he was stressed. His eyes shut, oblivious to her plans, oblivious to the future she was going to snatch away. Just as he had of hers. One against two. One life making two lives unhappy. It did not add up. It was unfair: he had killed her happiness and he was sitting there blissfully, happy again with the world. He would have to go. She felt no compunction, no guilt, no hesitation. For there was no other way out. She would have to kill her brother.

She said, 'I want to leave Lanka. It has too many bad memories for me now.'

Ravan put aside his veena and stared at her, astonished. 'Where would you go?' he asked, almost stupidly.

'I have thought it all out,' she explained, her voice hard and clear. 'I shall go to Mareech at the Dandak forest. I have always loved the jungle, preferred it to the palace, in fact,' she smiled wistfully. 'I would like to live the remaining years of my life there with Kumar.'

'Remaining years, nonsense!' he exclaimed. 'You are young, you can remarry!'

It was a tactless remark, but Ravan, she saw was overcome with emotion.

She laughed shortly, 'No, not now, not so soon. But at Dandak, I'll have the entire forest for myself!' she forced a chuckle. 'And I won't need your permission, I hope?' she narrowed her eyes, waiting expectantly for his answer.

'No, no, it's all yours!' assured Ravan hastily. 'I give Dandak to you—and everything with it—its animals, forest and people, the men in particular!' he grinned raucously, masking his nervousness. 'Anyway, our cousins Khara and Dushan are already placed there with their army. You shall be safe and protected,' he added, more to reassure himself than her.

He still found it odd his sister living alone in the forest with her little son, relinquishing the luxury of the palace. That episode of Vidyujiva's death had been particularly violent and he wished no more of such incidents in the palace. Secretly, he was relieved to see her go. He could not stem the guilt that gushed through him each time he saw her. He had made her a widow and her presence was a daily reminder of his crime.

He would have been appalled of what his sister was thinking. *Ravan was wasting my time with this ribald talk*, she thought impatiently. She wanted to leave Lanka immediately. Right away. Somehow she wanted to get away from this wretched place, go to Dandak, train Kumar and make him kill the man who had murdered his father. She wished Kumar could grow up quickly. He was just five. It would take at least another ten years for him to be a young boy who avenged his father's death. And then, he would kill him.

'I leave early tomorrow morning,' she announced flatly. 'I came here to tell you this and have your blessing. And of course, to apologize again for my horrendous behaviour that day...' she said uncertainly. She shut her eyes, to hide her pain, the hate shining in them.

'Please don't leave. This is your home...' he pleaded for the last time.

She began to look dejected, but she was acting all the while, her mind screaming her agony. She walked slowly to the window as if to admire the gardens for the last time. *They will burn*, she vowed. *Your cherished Ashok garden will be reduced to ashes. Just like your life.* Beyond the tall trees of the garden, she could glimpse the sea, its monotonous hollow sound rising up viciously from below, the waves throwing angrily against the cold, bare rocks, as if unaffected by its foaming wrath. Like Ravan and she. She and Ravan...

She gave a quick smile and turned to him. He still sat on the ostentatious couch, watching her. She stopped at the other end of the couch and rested her hands on the top, making her lips droop at the corner, to give an air of utter misery.

'I shall return whenever I want, dear brother. I know I shall always be welcome here. But right now, this palace, however beautiful, has a lot of ugly memories. I want to wish it away. Help me please, brother, to forget it. Let me go. I shall come back one day,' she promised, her smile thin.

And that is how she had left the golden walls of Lanka, looking back at the receding fortress as the chariot took her away from it, the sound of the sea deadened in the waning distance. She was staring back vacantly as if she expected to see Vidyujiva emerge from the calm blue water. He would not. Her face looked as if it was carved out of ebony. She looked down at her five-year-old Kumar, whose hand she held firmly in her grasp, careful her nails not hurting him. From henceforth she was Surpanakha: she was shrugging off the cloak of Meenakshi forever as she left the shores of Lanka.

'Grow up fast, my son. We have to return to Lanka soon.'

Kumar

✿

*E*ach time she looked at Kumar, Surpanakha was painfully
reminded of Vidyujiva. As she watched the tall, eighteen-year-old
strapping boy chop down the branches of the tree, his swarthy
face glistening in the hot sun, she thought that he was much
like his father...

Months had turned into years, many summers had set
and gone, winters had chilled her bones, yet her memories of
Vidyujiva glowed vividly in her hopeless heart. When in the
evening stillness she heard from her hut the voices of distant
animals, preparing to sleep or when she saw a splash of wild
flowers or the storm howled in the forest, suddenly everything
would rise up in her mind: how she had met him on the terrace
at Ravan's wedding, his late night visit into her bedchamber,
the early mornings when he used to make love to her with the
mist on the mountains of Lanka or him returning battle-weary
yet eager to hold her tight, their passion as tempestuous as the
roaring sea and those long, hard kisses...

She would wander aimlessly in the woods, remembering it
all and smiling; she remembered every moment spent with him
as fresh as that day. She would feel as if he was still with her,
beside her. She could never forget Vidyujiva: Kumar did not let
her forget him even for a single moment. Free of those family
cords, she had seen to it that Kumar had been thoroughly trained
by his grand-uncles Mareech, Khara and Dushan to master all the

celebstial and occult weaponry, yet the boy yearned for more. He wanted the blessings of Lord Shiva, just as Ravan had obtained. And he would go into penance soon.

'I have cut the wood to last you the next season, Ma,' the low tenor voice of Kumar interrupted her thoughts. 'I will take your leave now.'

She was not formal with Kumar, and as he bent to touch her feet for her blessings, she hugged him fervently. 'Go, son. Achieve the impossible and fulfil your responsibility,' she muttered, but her eyes flashed a different emotion. Each time Kumar looked in them, he saw either tender love for him or the simmering visceral hate she reserved for her brother and the revenge she thirsted for. He knew he was her sole hope, her salvation.

She kissed him on the forehead, and without a backward glance, she saw him trudging down the barren tract of the forest, his lithe frame soon disappearing from view, the thick foliage closing behind him. She felt the sharp sting of tears. Her tears were for her son and his lost childhood, and the curse of being a father-less child. *But not defenceless*, she reminded herself fiercely. She had to let him go and it broke her heart. Loneliness, as she knew from experience, was a worse thing to suffer.

☙

For six months, Surpanakha awaited his return. She had never been a patient person but enduring trying circumstances had tempered her down to develop an even forbearance for the sake of seeking her revenge. She was bidding her time: vengeance was hers. It was just a matter of time.

Meanwhile, she found solace in her unhappiness in Janasthan. It was the most treacherous portion of the Dandak forest. People feared to tread there, and so did the animals. There was a strange story behind such a reputation.

Once upon a good time, Janasthan was a flourishing province ruled by King Danda, who was fond of hunting. At one such hunt, he raped Aruja, the daughter of Rishi Shukracharya in the forest. When he came to know of what had befallen his daughter, he cursed the king and the land, damning both to unending hell. 'This is for both who cannot distinguish and respect the boundaries of behaviour of man and animal, and to such let this land too become a jungle!'

He cursed and whipped up a dust-storm so violent that it destroyed a thriving kingdom to a fearsome overgrowth of thorny bramble. This was the Dandak forest, and it was here that she had discovered the freedom she had yearned for, to employ the power to act, speak or think without externally imposed restraints. Shukracharya had been right—in a forest there are no boundaries, no social impositions. Man makes rules and breaks them, to trespas and trounce them; but in the jungle, he has to follow a different law. Animals, free and untamed, were more true to their nature, Surpanakha believed, than Man, who had turned against his. Treacherous to his own kind. Man was the most cruel, revelling in his mindless violence. *Like her brother.* The forest was the great battlefield: confronting Man with the beast. But what about his inner beast, she wondered, again thinking of Ravan.

In the wilderness called a jungle, Man could not rule here through his power: he had to survive with the animals. It was a war for all: battling every day for personal survival. And in such a place did she live now. And she loved it, finding beauty in the ravaged wilderness. Unlike Lanka, where there had been ugliness in that magnificent palace. In Dandak, existed a natural discipline of the wild, where all feared but respected the other, be it animal or sapling, manav or danav. The forest was everyone's to have but none's to possess. That is how all lived here: freely, yet restrained with reverence for all. This was her Dandak, her Janasthan, the place where she had been reborn from Meenakshi to Surpanakha.

A daughter's rape had spurred her vengeful father to run a happy kingdom to wasteland. Ravan had raped too—women and land, robbed and plundered yet he prowled free in his abode. But for how long? *She* would punish him. Would the sins of its king, reduce Lanka from glory to gore? *Yes, I would. I would burn Lanka to another Dandak,* she pledged, her eyes brooding bleakly.

The rushing figure of Khara interrupted her reverie. She straightened up to greet her cousin but noticed the expression on his face. He was openly weeping, his massive face screwed in grief. She stood there feeling cold chills running through her, a sick feeling gathering inside, churning into a tight knot.

'Kumar! Kumar!!' he wailed, the tears flowing down with the sweat. 'He's dead! Someone killed him!! I...I...found him lying in a pool of his own blood, his head cut off...'

She thought she let out a soundless bloodcurdling cry but it was the sound of her heart exploding. She tried to fool herself: I am dreaming, this is a nightmare. Cold terror coursed through her body, as she curled her fingers into her palm, the nails scraping her skin, burying slowly into the soft flesh. Her knees gave out, crumpling to a heap. She felt a fire flare in her yet she was sweating ice and she heard herself mutter out loud, 'Don't let him be dead...don't let him die...please, God...don't let him be dead!!'

Khara took her cold hands, uncurling her fingers. They were bleeding. 'I'll take you to him,' he said his tone sober. 'You need to see him.'

No, she screamed in her mind, but felt her body being propelled to the waiting horse and being helped to sit on it. She found herself been taken through thick woodland, over dales and hills, over parched wasteland and uninhabited wilderness, till she reached a low-lying wet-land of bamboo forest.

She climbed down the horse slowly, afraid of treading a step further as it got her closer to her son. Scared and sick, her reluctant feet refusing to move, she told herself that she would have to go and look. She had to go down there and see where Kumar was. She paused, the rush of the bloody memory of Vidyujiva's mutilated body swimming before her eyes. Even in death, Vidyujiva had looked hard and suspicious. His glazed eyes had been fixed in an angry, terrified stare and the livid gash on his open chest still glistened in her tortured mind. He had been bare, and a gaping blood-encrusted hole just below his last rib, had told her how horribly he had died.

She trembled, pushing the image away and to force herself

to witness a fresh horror—her son, dead and decapitated. She saw him, his head flung a foot away from the trunk, his body unbruised, not a cut to blemish its beauty. Her heart swelled, an agonizing pain tearing from within, slowly bringing down her dreading eyes down to the bed of grass he lay in. She felt the cold trickle of sweat running down her back.

There was a large red stain on his headless neck, half submerged in a thick puddle of brackish blood. She could see the body with his feet splayed and hands, neatly by his side. His face was young and smooth. His eyes were shut as if in deep, beatific meditation.

She leant against the swaying bamboo, and as unsteady and simply gazed in pounding horror. Then the burden of her legacy of hate suddenly crashed down on her. She began to hate herself, Ravan and his wife and her mother and Kumbha and Vibhishan and the whole horrific, bloody trail of revenge she had started. She wanted to get close to them all and get her hands on them, raking them with her nails, gouging their eyes and brains out with her bare, bloody hands. She wanted to hurt and kill them all because of what they had done to her. She no longer cared what would happen to her. She just wanted to even things up, she screamed savagely, but she knew that she was just fooling herself, because if she did kill them all it would not help her. It would not bring him back. Nor would Vidyujiva ever return. She would not surrender to the dark tide of her ineluctable destiny. This had been her madness. She had lost her husband and it was because of her demented lust for revenge, she now had lost her son too. She could never take off the taunting image she had of her son facing what he had faced alone: the small smile on his serene face when Death had struck him, cruel and unexpected.

She gently laid her angavastra on his serene, dead face with an unsteady hand.

The ground seemed to rise up under her and she felt Khara grab at her arm. They both stood staring.

'Who killed him??' she asked.

'We don't yet know,' he said contritely.

'It seems like the deed was done with a smooth swing of a sword,' said Surpanakha, her eyes stark, her voice raving. She turned on him, distraught with misery and hysteria. 'And only a warrior can do that. Search for him!' she ordered viciously. 'Whoever he is, he cannot escape from Dandak! I want him found, I want him alive so that I can kill him myself!' she screamed, the words resonating ferociously through the dry forest, rustling the dead leaves from a long stupor.

Two Brothers

$\mathcal{S}$urpanakha stared unseeingly at the dense thorny bushland outside her hut. It was six weeks since Kumar's body had been found, but the assailant had yet not been traced. Khara's army was scouring every nook of the Dandak, every pond, every village. It had not been a villager, or a common man who had killed her son. The stroke had been that of a warrior. *But who was he? And why had he killed Kumar when he was meditating, seated peacefully under a tree? Even amongst the lowest thief and bandit, there was an unsaid code of honour that one does not kill a defenceless man, especially when he is praying. For a warrior, this is a sacrosanct vow which cannot be breached. Who was then this coward who had committed this lowest act of dastardliness? Or was it a show of stark brutality? Had it been Ravan? Had he suspected what I was up to and removed the very weapon I was intending to use against him?* But she brushed aside the idea as quickly as it had surfaced. *No one, not even Mareech has hazarded the intention roiling in my heart and mind.* But Kumar was dead. Her shoulders slumped in abject defeat. Ravan had won: she would not be able to kill him after all. She had lost her all. Her husband. And her son.

A loud rustle of feet disturbed the eerie silence of the jungle. Khara was back. And from the expression in his eyes, he had news to disclose.

'There are two young men and a woman roaming the Dandak forest. They are the princes of Ayodhya, Ram with his wife Sita and brother Lakshman...'

'No!' Mareech gave a strangled cry. 'What are *they* doing here??'

Surpanakha was startled.

'They have been exiled and visiting this forest. They were first seen at Chitrakut and have just arrived at Janasthan. I saw them building a hut,' supplied Khara. 'I was going to attack them but Dushan warned me against it,' he added.

'You cannot kill Ram and Lakshman!' retorted Mareech, naked fear in his eyes. 'They are too powerful...'

Khara gave an irreverent snort.

'I forbid it,' ordered Mareech quietly, the grizzled eyebrows lifted. 'I don't wish for any violence with those princes! They are dangerous and best avoided. They must be passing by, leave them alone!' he repeated warningly.

Khara made a grimace, but nodded grudgingly. 'As long as you know how to explain it to Ravan,' he shrugged.

'I shall do the needful,' replied Mareech curtly.

He stood, not unlike a guarding eagle, watchful and alert despite his thin, frail frame and advancing age. Every inch of him had been dedicated to a life in the service of Ravan and his family. Probably he would not survive his wounds after all; they had weakened him considerably and he had retired to a life of quiet and meditation. But the rheumy grey eyes were still keen and clear, and what he lacked in speed he made up in experienced efficiency; he was a family loyalist, almost too genuine to be true, too good to deserve Ravan.

Ram and Lakshman, the names stirred an unpleasant memory. *They were the two young princes who had killed Nani and Subahu and fatally wounded Mareech*, she recalled with a jolt. *No wonder, Mareech had reacted with such perceptible horror.*

Surpanakha knew that Mareech would not take any aggressive action against these strangers. Besides, Ravan trusted Mareech and had given him and her complete independence to govern the forests. Ravan was a generous king, shrewdly investing enough political power onto his vassals , granting them immunity from any arbitrary exercise of authority, even if it was his.

'They killed your mother, Uncle,' she reminded quietly, but her eyes were smouldering.

The bent old back stiffen but the yellow wrinkled face showed nothing: more a parchment of old age.

'Exactly, that is why it's not time for action or reaction, but discretion. I know their strength. They are invincible. It is best we keep away from them!' he rasped, collapsing into a convulsive fit of dry cough. 'I had barely managed to escape then!' he gasped.

She handed him a tumbler of water. The old man drank it carefully to avoid another paroxysm.

'It is possible that they, or one of them, killed Kumar,' she said tightly, her jaw clenched. 'They fit the description of warrior we are looking for.'

Mareech violently shook his head. 'They are too honourable, bound by the code of kshatriyas. They would never kill a defenceless man, especially a man in meditation.'

'They would kill an asura,' she argued.

'No, be it anyone, they would not harm an unarmed opponent,' said Mareech stubbornly.

'For one who had been ingloriously defeated and almost killed, you seem to have a good word for them,' she observed with a rueful twist of her lips.

'It is good sense!' he coughed. 'And don't get carried away by the stupid aggressiveness of Khara! We need some sound, practical judgement too or we will start a war here in Dandak!'

Khara scowled but remained silent, throwing Surpanakha a questioning look. She nodded slowly, the word war whetting dormant emotions in her. She kept a straight face but her mind was seething with a rush of excitement, her brain triggered with an explosive sequential reaction, lighting a scheme, that she knew with certainty would lead to war and the eventual destruction of Ravan and Lanka.

In a blink, she saw her aborted plan unfolding in slow resuscitation. *Ram and Lakshman.* Through them, she now again had the means and method to bring her brother down. All she needed were these two brothers to fight her war. *But how?* They would have to challenge him into war. With them here in her forest, she would have to make better use of them than they in an inconsequential skirmish with the bloodthirsty Khara. She wanted them onto a larger battle, an unprecedented war—with Ravan. That is what she wanted: a deliberated, planned one where she masterminded the campaign, without anyone knowing it, neither an unsuspecting Ravan nor the brothers to be her pawns in this game...

Ravan had to be viscerally provoked enough to wage a war with these two princes: a small, irregular clash at Dandak would not arouse him into grabbing his weapons. But again, *how?* And she got the answer instantly: Sita. She was here too, the woman whom Ravan had lost to Ram ignominiously when he had failed the test of stringing the Pinaka. *He had not even been able to move it,* recalled Surpanakha, with a cold gleam in her eyes. *He had lost his dignity, his pride, his prestige—and the princess, in that one inglorious moment.* She recalled his rage, his despondence, his utter sense of defeat when Ravan had returned to Lanka, suitably vanquished. *Sita—he would do anything to get her. Once he knew, she was here, he **would** take her. And Ram and Lakshman would try to stop him and in the battle, they would kill Ravan.* She felt a quenching sense of calm as the thoughts blistered through her mind, raising hope and victory all over again.

Her son was dead: she had no time to grieve or avenge his loss. That loss again because of Ravan: Kumar had died because of her brother, unrequited in his ambition to avenge his father's death. This trail of blood would have not begun had Ravan not killed Vidyujiva...

Now it was a larger succor she sought: the death of Ravan, preferably an ignominious one on the battlefield, mauled and mangled, his carcass eaten by scavengers...

But there was yet something amiss in her burgeoning scheme. Ravan would not come charging down to Dandak to war with Ram for Sita. He was a shrewd man, more prone to slyness than wisdom. He needed a pretext to seize Sita away. If not his dubious sense of honour, the fear of Nalkuber's curse hung heavily on him that he could not force himself on an unwilling woman like he had done with Rambha. Ravan would need an honourable reason to hide his dishonourable intentions, he would try to woo Sita, not wield force. And to have Sita, he needed a lofty, honourable pretext; she would give him that. And in a flash, she knew what she had to do.

'Where did you see them?' she asked Khara, abruptly, ignoring Mareech's warning glance.

'Here at Janasthan, some distance away, deeper in the woods,' he supplied promptly, his eyes lighting up with the prospect of some violence about to break.

'I am simply enquiring as a precaution,' she smiled with feigned assurance. 'But Khara, do keep a watch on them. Or better still, I shall do it,' she hastened to add. 'You are quite likely to make your presence felt sooner and more obvious than needed!' she said eyeing pointedly at the stocky, bulky figure of her cousin. His face was round and fat, and covered with a web of fine veins. His eyes were deep-set and cold, his straggly moustache hid a mouth, thin and unpleasant. He looked what he was: an angry asura, who thwarted and threw out the unwanted in the forest, more often with his strength than sword.

Mareech laughed, nodding his silver crowned head. 'Better you than him! Stay hidden, Meenu, you have learnt all the tricks and spells so you can watch them even while being invisible!'

'Meanwhile you can keep track of who killed Kumar, Khara!' she reminded him sharply. 'I have to know, who and why.' She stared up at him, her eyes hard in the harsh sunlight.

She watched him plod back to his horse, then paused to scowl at her. 'You want me to inform Ravan?' he growled.

Both she and Mareech were unanimous in their quick reply. 'No!! We shall let him know when the need be. He need not be riled with petty things. And anyway, he's away at war, fighting the Kalkeyas again.'

But he won't be killed in the war. Ravan needed a Ram to kill him. Only a mortal could accomplish the deed, she recalled Brahma's boon to Ravan. Her son, though the son of a mortal, had not been able to finish the deed.

The new plan surfaced slowly, deadly and dark, born out of the agony of hate. Her brother did not know what it felt to be small and weak at the face of brutality, would never understand what it is to be powerless in anger and hate. She would make him endure that same feeling of helplessness. She would not kill him so easily: death would be a quick release. She would make him suffer the tragedy of loss, make him writhe in that anguish of the death of a loved one, even if it meant the loss of innocent lives, that of her family, her brothers, her nephews...

She saw the risks, the tragedy plainly spread beneath her, like the roaring waves of the sea crashing against the cliffs of Lanka, the water receding calmly thereafter. She was like that angry wave. She needed to hurtle the cliffs to retreat in peace thereafter...

But before that, she needed to stir a war, which will annihilate Ravan, his city, his kingdom. And Sita would be that cause, that reason and she, Surpanakha, would be that culprit to precipitate the mayhem. The thought made her smile, a small, determined grimace that contorted her face into a hideous smirk.

The plan was simple. She would approach the princes and befriend them, getting to know their intention for coming to the forest. She would return to Lanka, wailing to an enraged Ravan how she had been assaulted by them to which a prickly Ravan would be sure to retaliate. She knew how her brother's mind worked: he always declared war for a lofty purpose. For this war, she would be the purpose but Sita will be the goal. She would be the dishonoured sister and Ravan would be the righteously furious brother who would avenge his sister's disgrace. She knew that he would respond to salvage his lost honour, shame Ram not just by war, but by also snatching away his Sita.

One of Ravan's strength was his family. He was proud and protective: he loved and owned them with ferocious possessiveness. That is why he had despised his father because he could not defend his family, especially when Kuber had tried to abduct her. And from that incident onwards, Ravan had never been the same. His strength became his weakness. No one dared to even utter a word against his family or cast an irreverent glance.

He had been particular about her—his only sister—and he had loathed Vidyujiva for this one reason that the King of Kalkeya had used his sister to eye his throne. And that is how Ravan had justified to the world that he had killed Vidyujiva—for his sister.

She would make him kill again for her, she vowed. She would bring Ravan down to his knees, in humiliation and horror, forcing him to wage war with her supposed violators and strike back.

It did not take her much time to detect the two exiled princes. One fading evening, she saw the three of them sitting near their cottage. It had been neatly built with a stout fence, to ward off wild animals. *But what about wild women and watching asuras*, Surpanakha snorted, as she inched forward to take a closer look.

Her eyes were drawn immediately to the one standing. He was tall and lithe, his face set in a strange serene amicability. He must be Ram. From what she had got to know, the citizens of Ayodhaya had wept when he had left for his exile, following him till the banks of the River Sharayu, wailing and beseeching him to return. *He must be an extraordinary person to evoke such loyalty and open adoration from the public*. She gazed at him longer, liking him more every passing moment. He was tightening the string of the bow, his muscles rippling hard under the tanned skin, his face intent on the work. Her hands turned into fists as she felt a surge of hot blood rush in.

Surpanakha swallowed, her throat suddenly dry, her face flushed. A wave of raw, gnawing lust swamped her after a long time. She closed her eyes to shut the sight of him, trembling with the ferocity of her reawakened emotions. She tore her eyes away from him to glance at the other young man. He was sitting hunched, sharpening the sword on a whetstone. He was scowling at the brandished sword yet she again she felt washed away in a white hot wave. *This one must be Lakshman and he is quite magnificent*, she thought. He had sharp features from what she could see from a distance—a square–shaped face; small, close-set eyes and a sharp, hooked nose that dominated his face, giving it a certain cruelty that was absent in the face of his brother. But he had an immediate boyish charm, which shone through once he smiled. He had stopped scowling and right now he was grinning at his brother as if they were sharing a joke.

She did not know what fascinated her more: him or the sword. She was mesmerized by the rushing motion of the sword, reminding her of how her son had been killed. Was this man the mystery swordsman who had killed Kumar or was she wildly over-imagining things? The swish of the sword on the stone, made her grind her teeth, the sound taunting her, draining her of the desire she had felt for this young man. He was now bending low over the moving sword, his bronzed hand gripping the sword tight, his body taut, drawn tense, the muscles bunching each time he moved the sword. Again she felt hot blood move through her.

She expelled a deep breath. Things were not happening as she had planned. She had intended to seduce these two young men and she had been confident they would be easy prey like most men, humiliatingly susceptible to her sexual allure. She had not accounted for her raging lust for the brothers that left her weak and trembling with unfulfilled desire. She wanted them, badly, madly. She wondered what it would be like to have him and her body grew hot, moist and yielding at the thought. He certainly seemed to be a skilled, intense lover, but she would control him. Her heart began to hammer as she imagined the moment when he would take her roughly in his arms. She made a move to approach him, and then stopped. Although she was now convinced that she wanted him, she was suddenly frightened of the possible result. The urge to rush forward and expose herself to them was nagging, but she stopped herself on time, her knees sagging as she sank slowly to sit.

Angry with herself, she looked down at her body—parched, pinched skin, thickening waist, and sagging breasts, which she once used to flaunt. At her age, what did it matter? Her age? She paused to look in the reflection in the pond. How old was she? Why bother about her years? She looked at herself critically—

her heavy figure, the coarse face with its high cheek bones, the dull yellow coloured eyes, the short, sharp nose. She might have looked older, she had not cared or bothered till now.

She stopped. She could not run away from herself, from her desires. She had not had a man since Vidyujiva's death, and slept with loneliness as her only companion.

Her son and her husband, she pondered, her mind drifted back into her past: something she caught herself doing as she grew older. Who had been there for her but her son whom she had given her all, whom she had groomed to kill. But it had been he who had been killed. She had lost them both and suddenly they seemed like dark, ambiguous shadows.

Because of her brother's position and his wealth and power, no one had ever thought she might need help. She had but herself, lonely and ugly, undesirable yet desiring...

She got up for a brisk walk: another antidote to that sweeping loneliness, a habit she had acquired to kill that darkness smothering her. Her mind lingered still in the past. Help? Who had helped her ever? Not her father or her mother nor her brothers. Had she been alive, her grandmother would have but she had been killed by the very two men she was lusting for.

She shut her eyes in shame and grief. Is that what she had got reduced to: what lust did to your feelings about your own body? To find yourself reduced to a lump of meat—however unattractive—to get aroused and hoped to be made love to? Was it not a simple, untamed urge coming out of spontaneous desire, essential for satisfaction. Is that not what her Nani had taught her: that there was no shame in desiring a man, that a self-assured woman be comfortable with her flowing urges and desires?

When she thought of what she had almost been about to do, she flamed with a wave of hot shame, an anger she had never felt at herself before. She had acted like a lonely, desperate woman—which she was, a voice mocked her in a constant echo—trying to find solace in lust and look feverishly for some man to fill in the lonely hours.

But a spurt of anger prompted her to ask, *why be ashamed?*

She had reasoned with herself, the desires she felt. She had done nothing to make herself feel ashamed. In fact, she told herself without much conviction, that she wanted it. She wanted those two men just as she had wanted Vidyujiva. She wanted to share something, to blot out this awful loneliness... That was the kind of help she wanted and yet how few could or would give her that? In solitude, one welcomes any living thing. In complete loneliness even a certain tenderness can be born.

She continued watching them, admiring the breadth of their shoulders, the huge hands and their innate masculine aura. She couldn't deny she was drawn to them: her plan would have to be changed slightly. She would have them first. And *maybe just this once I can indulge in the attraction*, she shivered with delight. *We can have today and tonight, all of tomorrow and tomorrow night together. And maybe a few more nights...before I use them against Ravan.*

She knew she could not sit around in the woods, waiting for the hours to pass while she had them within her sight. *Surely, they would feel the same way once they met me.* She again looked down at herself. She could not appear in front of them looking like a hag; she was too grizzled, tired and gaunt for them.

She sat lost in thought. This time she had a plan she would not allow to crumble.

Dishonour

$\mathcal{S}$he approached them, with a suggestive sway of her flaring hips, walking with confidence and purported friendliness. She saw them quickly straightening themselves up, fully aware that the two men were eyeing her, their eyes taking in her appearance: the angavastra draped casually over her slim, bare shoulders, revealing the top of her cleavage; the thick hair hanging loose till her slender waist and the sari knotted seductively low at the generous hips. She saw that their eyes appraised what they looked at, but she wanted more than the casual appraisal. As she approached them, they quickly shifted their eyes.

She was thankful she had changed into her younger self again. Being the dark, voluptuous, slim, young Meenakshi gave her more confidence than appearing before them as she was—a jaded, unsightly Surpanakha.

They appraised each other, each wary: Ram greeted her with a ready smile, but Lakshman glanced at her suspiciously, frowning.

'Good day, lady, I am Ram, the prince of Ayodhya,' said Ram amiably, bowing slightly. 'This is my brother Lakshman,' he explained, waving to the sullen faced young man. She threw him a quick look. *He would be more difficult to persuade*, she decided.

'We are a little surprised to see a woman walking all alone in the forest,' continued Ram, a boyish, embarrassed grin lighting up his face. 'Is this forest not dangerous?' he said. 'Though admittedly, it's beautiful too!'

'As dangerous and beautiful as me?' she laughed huskily. 'No, Panchavati is not dangerous, it is idyllic, the greenest part of the Dandak, which I happen to own.'

She noticed the surprised look on Ram's face, Lakshman was listening to her keenly, his face impassive.

She continued with a little chuckle, 'In this forest, no one dares harm me, not even the animals! Even they know I am Surpanakha, the sister of formidable brothers like King Ravan of Lanka, the powerful Kumbhkarna and the virtuous Vibhishan. I assume you have heard of them?' she asked suggestively, to make them in awe of the huge power she portended. 'You mentioned you were a prince but you are dressed in bark, the clothes of rishis. What are you princes doing in the forest?'

From the corner of her eyes, she saw Lakshman make an impatient movement. Ram was courteous, his eyes full on her, the smile still fixed on his face. They were like two rocks in a rushing stream. Now close to him, she could feel the heat.

His smile widened. 'Well, lady, you're the first friendly asura I've seen since coming to Dandak!' he said. His voice, was soft, and he added, 'Most have attacked us!'

'I am no danger!' she laughed back throatily. 'See? I am not carrying any weapons,' she smiled, raising her arms high, pushing her breasts up against the thin fabric, outlining every curve on her body. *Invited to look, both the men are struggling to maintain eye contact*, she thought with some amusement. 'You still have not told me why you are here.'

'I have been exiled from my kingdom and I have come to the forest with my brother...and my wife,' added Ram specifically.

Surpanakha clenched her jaw, mentally noting the emphasis.

'We have decided to stay here for the remaining last year of the exile,' Ram continued. 'I hope we are not bothering you.' He grinned at her—a warm, friendly smile that made her feel good.

'No, you're not bothering me. I am free to do what I want, what I like...' she chuckled. 'You are *my* guests, you are welcome to the forest.'

'We are honoured, we appreciate it.' He leaned forward,

looking directly at her. 'I want you to know, madam, I really appreciate this.'

Suddenly, after a long time she felt good. The smile was so warm that she found herself thinking that Ram was a really nice person.

She said, 'Curiosity wasn't the only reason why I stopped to talk.' She paused, and asked bluntly, 'I like you, I liked what I saw. I hope you like me too.'

He looked taken aback at her bluntness.

'Who wouldn't? You are our host, the lady of this forest.' The conviction in his voice made her heartbeat quicken.

'Oh, that is good then,' she purred, moving close to him so that she could smell the musky scent of him. 'How about getting to know each other better?' she smiled, casually moving her hands to reach for his, their bodies treacherously close.

He almost took a step back, the smile freezing on his face, not reaching his eyes. He looked wary, a little amazed, more amused.

'I would have been honoured! But I am a married man, and I have my wife here as well, let me introduce her...' he said smoothly.

'Sita!' he called out, the smile back in his voice, and a moment later a tall, slim, fair girl appeared from the hut, wiping her hands with her angavastra.

Surpanakha took a deep breath. She was ethereally beautiful, her oval face marked by delicate features—soft, warm eyes, a tiny sharp nose and a small rosebud mouth, a blushing red against her porcelain white skin. *It's no wonder Ravan is so smitten with her*, she thought viciously. Strangely Sita reminded Surpanakha of Mandodari: both had a distinct gossamer fragility which was deceptive. Mandodari had always displayed a subtle, indomitable strength in her and Surpanakha suspected so did Sita. It showed in her steady, firm eyes.

Sita smiled softly, clearly happy to see a guest. 'Please come inside,' she invited.

Surpanakha was flummoxed; she knew how to deal with the men but not this exquisite, soft-spoken creature. She ignored her, turning to Ram again.

'What would it take to be yours?' she murmured.

Sita's eyes widened in surprise and Surpanakha noticed Ram slip a possessive arm around his wife's waist. She felt a flare of jealous fury; he was amply letting her know he was not keen.

He smiled, 'My wife is here with me, so I cannot oblige your wishes and desires, lady. I cannot have two wives.'

'That is irrelevant, your wife cannot hamper us,' she insisted, refusing to give up.

Ram shook his head good-naturedly and smiled that set her blood on fire.

'But my brother here is a free man—he is single and available unlike me,' he said silkily, but there was a glint of sudden amusement in his eyes.

She eyed Lakshman; he looked surprised, almost annoyed, his broad shoulders leaning against a tree. He was beautiful, virile and wonderfully male. She licked her dry lips, her hands turned into fists as she felt a surge of a heated wave wash over her. She found herself walking towards him.

But his face was dark as thunder, unamused being dragged into the conversation he did not wish to be a part of.

He looked at her coldly, his tone polite, 'Dear lady, I heard what my brother said. I am single but I am also a married man. I have a wife waiting for me at Ayodhya...'

He had a voice that would send an immediate prickle up most women's spines.

'Again the wife-reason!' she gave a forced smile, stemming her exasperation. 'She is in Ayodhya, which like her is far, far away! But I am here, right here, so close to you...' she breathed, her breath hot on him.

There was a pause while he looked down at her, his eyes frank, and she looked searchingly at him, her eyes hopeful.

'But my Mila's right here, in my heart,' he said intensely.

It was like a slap on her face but he said it with such emotion, that Surpanakha was momentarily taken aback. He sounded besotted with his faraway wife, whoever she was.

He was saying, 'I could not bring her as I am my brother's servant, at his service all the while. And that is the same reason, I cannot be yours, lady,' he said stiffly, glaring not at her but his brother, a disapproving frown on his handsome face.

They are rejecting me! But why, she thought wildly. *I am young and beautiful and desirable. Why did they not like me? Am I not enticing enough?*

Lakshman's brow suddenly cleared, and said gently, 'I am but a slave. Do you wish to be a slave's slave or the master's? You deserve someone better, madam, and that person is Ram as you had rightly chosen before!' After a pause, he said teasingly, 'He is trying to fool you. You can be his second wife! Go to him, is he not better looking than me? He will make a better husband too, dear lady.'

She was confused, looking from one brother to the other: there was a certain tension in the air and suddenly Surpanakha realized that both of them were laughing at her, reeling her to and fro like a toy, like a mere means of amusement.

She stood in the middle watching the two brothers, handsome and cruel, grinning surreptitiously, sharing a secret jest. She was that jest. Sita had moved closer to Ram, gauging the changing mood of the situation. She was clearly let in on the joke too.

Surpanakha felt a flare of ungovernable fury. Were she and her emotions so frivolous so as to be played with and to be sniggered at so openly?

She glanced at Sita, her eyes cold and flat. *She* was the reason why Ram had rejected her. She was the one whom Ravan was still pining for her. She was the one who had come between her and both the men, snatching them away from her. She had ruined her entire plan: she could not seduce these men, nor cry foul to accuse them of molesting her, and start the intended war. This one woman who was meant to start a war had turned her dream to dust. The unruly rage made her tremble, the chuckling faces of the two men taunting her of her folly.

She took a step forward, her face livid, 'You wretch!' she snarled in frustration, lunging at the petrified Sita.

Ram seemed to have anticipated her intention for he stepped forward, thrusting Sita aside with his arm to protect Sita. The good-natured face had turned white with cold anger. 'I shall have none of this!' he said icily. 'Lakshman, take care of this unvirtuous, ruttish rakshasi and teach her a lesson she will never forget!'

She barely registered his words as she rushed quickly towards Sita, when suddenly she saw Lakshman step towards her, grabbing her by the hair, his fingers tugging hard, his sword swinging in his other hand. She froze in shock.

He would not dare kill her, she thought savagely, as she wrenched away and whirled at him, her eyes blazing, her arms outstretched to lash out her claws.

Lakshman ducked, and tried to grab her arms. She came down on him, her hands clawing at his throat. She hooked her fingers and slashed at his face as her left hand wrenched at the sword, forcing him to drop it. He looked stunned, holding her wrists, but she was surprisingly strong, the sharp nails yet aiming at his eyes and throat. His sword had fallen and she put more weight on him, hoping to break his grip, kicking his legs viciously. She was getting her way, as she could feel his hold slacken. But he quickly swung her over, getting her arm in a lock and slamming her over on her face. She could feel his weight on the small of her back and he put a little pressure on her arm. She gave a loud yelp and he eased up.

'You don't dare hurt me!' she screamed hoarsely, her voice suddenly taking on a harsh note, fear uncurling fast. 'My brother will kill all of you!'

Her bruised face was set and her yellow eyes glittered with the viciousness of a cornered tigress. Her eyes were wild, her long black hair hung over her face making her look demented. In the tussle, she reverted to her original self, her dark face contorted with frustrated fury.

'She is a shape-shifting asura' said Lakshman victoriously, pinning her down hard.

Ram's clear voice had a sharp lash to it. 'Don't kill her!' he ordered tersely.

'Why because I am a woman?' she taunted. 'But you killed Taraka, remember?'

She had the satisfaction of seeing Ram's face go white. Lakshman yanked her hair. He whispered in her ear. 'Evil has no gender, lady, and in war too, the enemy has no gender. It has to be destroyed, be it a man or a woman, manav or danav! You are no exception, you are our opponent, you dare attack my sister-in-law and you *will* be punished!'

'Don't kill her please!' beseeched Sita.

Lakshman looked at his brother.

'Maim her,' said Ram. 'She will remember her dishonourable crime and not attack a helpless woman again.'

But her retort died in her throat. *Maim her, what weird barbarity was this and for what*, she thought panicking. *For displaying desire for these two handsome men? How could someone so beautiful be so ugly and cruel? What were they furious about—me attacking Sita or me assaulting their chastity, their moral righteousness? Was it their apprehension for my uninhibited behaviour, assuming it to be an overt vulgarity, an open display of unleashed carnal anarchy? Was that why they had laughed at me, ridiculing me in their contempt and amazement, their arrogant condescendence condemning me for my feminine profanities?* Thoughts tumbled in her brain, seized by waves of terror and drowning the fury.

Lakshman released her suddenly and she gasped for breath. *What was he going to do to me? Molest me as I had planned to accuse them of?* Fear grabbed her throat...*No, he would not!* The brutality of that very act she had intended to use as a weapon against them, made her quail.

She caught a glint of the blade of his sword. Her silent scream froze in her throat as the sword came down treacherously upon her. *He was going to kill me after all*, and she closed her eyes. She heard three, quick swishes of the sword before she felt a sharp pain on her face and felt the gush of warm blood on her skin. What had he done? Her face exploded in pain, throbbing violently, a thousand shooting pain pulsating in a charged wave, drowning her in unspeakable agony. She couldn't move her face, each movement an excruciating torture yet she looked around wildly, moving solely her eyes. And then she saw it: her eyes falling to a sickening sight. Three odd bloody pieces of flesh and cartilage strewn carelessly in the dust. She stared at it confused and befuddled, the pain coursing through her, not allowing her to think. She touched her face again: it felt odd, her hands slipping off the wetness of her blood. She had no nose! She gasped in frenzied horror. Her frantic hands moved further over her ruined face...she felt no ear where it should be. Nor the other, her frightened mind whispered to her. She looked down comprehendingly. It was the straggly remains of her ears and her nose that were lying at her feet. It was then she screamed, her wail sailing through the still air.

She clutched her hands over her chest, on her knees, begging, sobbing for mercy, the blood and tears dripping off her bowed, mutilated face.

Lakshman let go of her suddenly, the disgust stark on his face as if her wretched face sickened him. Her anxious terror had aged her.

'Go, woman, go! But as a woman, I ask, how can you harm another?' he snapped viciously, a sudden flash jumped into his eyes. He looked terrifying. 'For whom, us, we men? You fight for us??'

She saw him shake his handsome head, his lips curl in contempt, his eyes glittering with loathing. She could never forget his face, imprinted in her frightened panicked mind, tasting her tears mixed with her blood. The terror on her face was grotesque to see. Her wide open mouth, as it formed a continuous scream, was an ugly hole in her face. She was pressing her body against the tree like an animal trying to get back into its burrow, and from her finger nails came a nerve jarring sound of scratching as she clawed at the rough trunk, in a futile, panic-stricken quest for escape.

She turned and ran, forcing her feet to flee, in a fire of agony, her fingers splayed over her bloodied face, hoping to cover the pain and the shame.

Homecoming

$\mathcal{T}$he flickering evil in her washed-out hazel eyes warned her of the gutted pain ripping through her. Yet she was surprised at her calmness and how evenly her heart was beating. She had absorbed her trauma swiftly and her self-made medication had slowly healed the raw wound of her torn face. The physical pain had subsided substantially; but not the ache in her heart or that pulsating throb in her mind, taunting her relentlessly. She had manoeuvred herself into a folly that had almost cost her her life, and now, she had to consider what she was to do.

She had two new enemies to deal with now—Ram and Lakshman. Her hideous disfigurement mocked her every moment. She was going crazy with the need to take revenge, but her brother had to pay first. First she lost Kumar, and then, this mutilation—both had hampered the plan she had nursed for all these years. *The two beautiful princes who had made me ugly will do the deed for me*, she grimaced at the thought. She winced, her face still throbbed. *And then the two princes will pay the price of humiliating me*, she pledged, dangerous fury boiling up inside her. Her hands balled into fists, as she recalled every drawn out, excruciating moment, rekindling the burning embers, the licking flames incinerating her: she would hurt them, even kill them. *Someday, but not now. Their time would come too*, she swore grimly, *but first I have to use them against my brother*.

She was in Lanka now, strolling again through those high-ceilinged, columned halls after all these years. She had thought she would come back with her son. She had lost him, she had lost her husband, her dignity, her honour, but not her will. *Never my will*, she promised herself. She was here to meet Ravan not anyone else, not even her mother. Kaikesi did not come out to greet her. Not that Surpanakha had expected it. All she could recall about her mother were those harsh words screamed at her years ago as a child—'*Be a woman, Meenu, not a self-absorbed snivelling urchin. I can't bear self-pity. You should be ashamed! Ashamed!!*' The word rang like the knell for all hope. She owed none of her family anything but ashes in their mouth.

Surpanakha pulled the veil closer to hide her face, entering his court, bemused at the rapid, active commotion her unexpected arrival seem to have triggered, her presence almost seemed unwanted, unwelcome.

Ravan sat bejewelled and resplendent in his royal finery, the heavy gem-encrusted gold crown on his head. Seeing him, she could not but ponder a little waspishly, that age never helps anyone. Fifteen years ago, Ravan had been one of the handsomest men. Now his thick, wavy hair was thinning and receding. He had put on too much weight, his trim waist now thickened into a visible paunch. Standing over six feet, powerfully and heavily built, he still managed to be an impressive though a fleshy figure. He looked astonished, golden eyes focused on her, his mouth sunken between raddled cheeks. He had the stillness and the probing stare of power. As she walked slowly to the grand gold throne, the beady eyes examined her.

'Why are you covering your face?' he asked, looking surprised.

'When did our women start wearing veils for sex segregation??' he laughed and the court joined in perfunctorily, in a raucous chorus. 'We have nothing to hide, even our virtues!' he roared.

Surpanakha contained herself with an effort. She regarded him, he was still shaking with silent laughter. Watching his face turn red and his paunch jerking as he laughed, she felt cold despair grip her. She had a frightening feeling that she might give in to her anger and ruin a plan for which she has already suffered many losses.

She wordlessly removed the veil to reveal her face.

There was an audible gasp of horror, some out of fear, some out of repugnance, their revulsion stark on their shocked faces. All found her face grossly offensive at sight.

Ravan had gone a blotchy white, a muscle beating at the jowly jaw. He was shaken at what he saw.

His heavy face darkened. 'Who did this?' his voice husky, but loud enough to echo menacingly through the silent hall.

She swallowed convulsively. 'The same two men who killed cousin Khara when he retaliated for this mutilation with his fourteen thousand men army,' she said, surprised how steady her voice sounded. 'Ram and Lakshman, they killed them all.'

She saw him give a slight start. She continued. 'The same two men who mutilated and killed our grandmother, our uncle Subahu and crippled Mareech mama years ago. Before Ram got married to Sita,' she added slyly. 'The two princes of Ayodhya.'

Ravan's expression changed from jovial to glacial within a moment. His face was paralysed with shock, the initial resilience absorbing the horror and then raw rage gripped him, the rushing blood to his face mottled it purple, making the veins in his neck throb and giving his face an expression of vicious rage.

'*They* are here in my kingdom??' he spat out.

And she told him the story exactly the way she had intended. 'Yes, they are in Dandak. I came upon them at Panchavati. Ram is in exile to live fourteen years in the forest. He is accompanied by his brother Lakshman...and his wife Sita,' she stated innocuously.

She saw Ravan go still. She ignored it but she knew she had caught his interest and he had caught the bait.

'When I questioned who they were, they revealed that they intend to live the last year of their banishment in the forest to eradicate it of all the asuras. They had killed Viradha, the cursed gandharva Tumburu in a demon form and they were celebrating. I was intrigued—they looked jubilant and powerful and Sita so beautiful!' she paused, piquing his interest further. 'I introduced myself as the sister of Ravan, the asura king. They were unimpressed, shrugging how you had lost Sita's hand at her swayamvar,' she said softly.

Ravan's fleshy face had lost colour.

'But why did they attack you? What did you do?' he asked sharply.

Surpanakha had been expecting this query, his suspicious mind would never permit to believe hearsay. She knew Ravan was a cautious king, after all, he had planned so long and deviously to kill Vidyujiva. He would not rush into a war blindly, without gleaning more facts. But he had two flaws—unfettered ego and his unflagging lust for women—and she intended to twist both for her purpose.

'It was because of Sita,' she replied, her tone truculent. 'She was so lovely that I remembered how you once wanted her and here she was in our forest...!'

Ravan's eyes narrowed.

'I can well imagine why you went for her swayamvar,' she hesitated, then plunged on, 'Her beauty is sublime! She is more beautiful than Menaka or any other apsara. She is the loveliest!' said Surpanakha, praising enthusiastically, her eyes gleaming with admiration. 'And I thought she deserved you, like you were destined for her! Or else why would she be in your forest, brother? And when I saw Sita with them, I thought that this was the chance to snatch her away for you! I know you had lost her and this would be the best opportunity to have her back,' she nodded, looking at him knowingly. 'I made a move to carry her off for you but Lakshman was quicker. He attacked me, and disfigured me to teach me a lesson!' she whimpered. 'A lesson? I was doing this for you, brother, and see what they did to me!!' she wailed. 'You sit on your throne in all your power and finery, but see what those two brothers did to your sister in your own territory!' she demurred strongly. 'They attacked me while that lovely wife of Ram looked on, clinging on to him, playing the wife in distress!' she snivelled cunningly, watching his jaw tense.

He sat still.

'Ram ordered Lakshman to punish me for my crime. The

brother obeyed and dragged me by my hair, to throw me out. I tried in vain to defend myself, but I had no weapons, I was unarmed and that did not make him hesitate. I clawed him, I struggled and I screamed but was soon overpowered. Lakshman was stronger and held my hands,' she whispered, her voice hoarse, choking.

No one dared interrupt her, the room silent, stilled with the screams of the violence soundlessly reverberating.

Taking a deep breath, she continued, 'Ram pronounced that I be maimed so that it would be a reminder to me and for you as well brother that whoever even glanced at his wife would be punished!!!' she inhaled deeply in a long pause. 'Lakshman nodded and drew out his sword. I begged and I screamed but...' she stopped, shuddering, her shoulders shaking. 'He sliced off my ears and nose...I had blood dripping from my face, on my hands, blood everywhere!' she whimpered, her voice scaling low. 'They threw me out with the warning—to let you know that the mutilation was to be a sign of dishonour to the clan of asuras and the royal house of Ravan. By disfiguring and not by killing me, he was sending a message across: not to challenge them. Or Sita,' she paused. 'I was sent as a messenger to you, the great Ravan, and to let you know what all they can do.'

Ravan sat impassively, his eyes receding in distant thoughts. *He must be recalling that humiliating moment when he lost to Ram that day at Mithila, so many years ago*, guessed Surpanakha instantly. *He must have seen Ram and Lakshman, if not met them. But he would soon meet them on the battlefield to meet his death, if I played it right.*

'They chased me out like an errant dog from my own jungle,' she continued, her lips quavering, her eyes filled with unshed tears. 'And as a show of strength and superiority, the two of them together killed Khara, and the commanders Dusan and Trisiras and our entire standing army at Janasthan. I was the only survivor as was meant to deliver the news. I rushed to Lanka,' she was sobbing quietly now, the tears flowing freely.

The silence was only broken with her sobs, no one uttering

a word, shocked into speechlessness. Ravan got up from his throne and approached her, his eyes filled with an undecipherable emotion. It was soft and soulful. It was love. For the shortest moment, she felt a twinge of guilt: what was she doing? She wanted to kill this man, who stood tall and mighty, yet humble and helpless in his love for his sister, grief dulling his eyes, his face stricken. She was orchestrating her brother's death right now, and she could still stop it, halt this madness. Save him, save her family, save herself... But the image of her husband's mangled body brought into this very room flashed before her, the dastardly way they had murdered him. She trembled; she could not forgive, never forget. She buried her face in her hands and wept.

Ravan could not bear it any more. 'Stop dear sister, you have suffered enough. They shall pay for what they did to you,' he faltered, choking on the words.

She raised her wet face. 'Now I shall have to live with this face as a constant reminder of my humiliation, *our* humiliation, brother!' she corrected cleverly.

She wiped her tears, her thick lashes hiding her triumph; she was going to milk his guilt to drain him.

'Brother, don't rush into any untoward decision. Let us all think it over,' suggested Vibhishan, breaking the tender moment.

Her grand-uncle nodded sagely. So did a few other courtiers. Surpanakha was frantic, quelling the panic, were they going to dissuade Ravan? Where was Kumbha, she frowned. His absence in court could mean that he was deep in his six months slumber which made her subterfuge easier. Kumbha would have been more difficult to convince.

She sighed. 'Yes, don't go to war, brother. Stay silent and simmer in your open insult. I was a fool to come here!' she said brokenly, making a move to turn away.

'No, stop, Meenu,' pleaded Ravan, the imperative tone absent from his voice. 'Don't go. I will not fail you...'

She shook her head, eyes filled with fresh tears. 'No, dear brothers, live in peace here. Let me suffer my pain in private but I have one question before I leave—while you live in this golden palace with all your great wealth, power and impunity, I was made to suffer, brother! For what? For being the sister of the mighty emperor Ravan? They attacked me, they killed our cousin, your finest commanders and an army of fourteen thousand strong people. How do they get away with their crime and the invincible Ravan who bows to none, does not wish to retaliate?'

Vibhishan made a movement. 'We cannot rush into war...'

Ravan raised one arm, palm outwards to silence his younger brother. 'They attacked your sister and you prefer to remain quiet?' he demanded.

'But she tried to abduct his wife! Any husband would have but retaliated!' argued Vibhishan. 'Our sister has been harmed but she is not innocent...'

'I did it for Ravan!' cried Surpanakha plaintively.

Vibhishan interrupted. 'But you knew Sita is married to Ram, how could you even think of it?' he asked angrily. 'Would you have liked if Vidyujiva had got another woman?'

Inwardly she flinched, gripping her hands so hard her nails turned white.

'And how could you think of bringing Sita here, Meenu, as a gift to our brother? Would you not be unfair to our sister-in-law Mandodari?' he persisted. 'Being a woman, how can you make another woman suffer so?'

Before she could reply, Ravan cut in curtly. 'That's another matter not to be discussed here,' he grimaced. 'Your sister is the victim here, not a culprit to be interrogated!'

Surpanakha's eyes glimmered in satisfaction. She had Ravan's full attention and sympathy.

Ravan turned to her kindly, his tone soft but determined, 'Your suffering shall be vindicated.'

'All I am saying is let's take it more calmly,' said Vibhishan quietly. 'We have already lost our army at Janasthan. Let's wait and see...'

'Wait for what? I wish Ram would have killed me rather than

make me suffer this ignominy!' she spat furiously, the brutality of those long minutes washing over her again, swamping her in agony. She pulled at his arm roughly. 'What sort of a brother are you that you are not moved by your sister's plight?' she cried, raising her voice. She wanted to scream at him to rot in hell, but she bit that back. 'Is this what I deserve? Ram called me a *rakshasi*, who merited to be handed the most heinous punishment—mutilation!! They did it to our grandmother too before they killed her, don't forget that!' she said venomously, shivering with rage.

Ravan winced. Vibhishan shrugged her hand away, staring stonily at her. She glared back. He had always been spineless, never standing up for family or owned a speck of familial pride. Her contempt was palpable. His cowardice increased her courage.

She walked up to Ravan with beseeching eyes. 'I thought Sita was worthy to be your wife, I was wrong. I should have let her be with Ram—happy and smiling as she is right now with him—while I stand here in front of you, disfigured, your cousins killed and your army vanquished. How do we matter? But it should matter to you, *your* name is at stake. This is an affront to you, not just as a brother but as a king, an emperor, the most powerful in the world whose sister was attacked in his own territory!' she taunted cruelly. 'What would people say that the famous Ravan could not defend his sister, his clan, his race... his honour?' she paused, allowing the words to pierce his ego. 'After all that transpired, those two wretches continue to roam carefree in our forest, the brave Ram with his beautiful Sita in Panchavati, right under your nose, in your very kingdom!'

There was a deafening silence, then Ravan asked quietly, 'They are still at Panchavati?'

There was this deadly note in his voice she had heard before—when he had confronted Vidyujiva in her bedchamber.

'Yes, they are enjoying their victory over us!' she rued fiercely. 'Enjoying in Panchavati, revelling in its beauty and sanctuary for the remaining months of his exile before Ram goes back to Ayodhya. With Sita to be his queen,' she said.

Her heart was racing as Ravan's amber eyes flared a fiery gold. She had caught him, he had nowhere to go. He would now think only about getting Sita.

'What will you do now, brother?' she prompted him shrewdly. 'I had come to you, not to seek shelter in this palace. You are not my refuge, you are my last resort to seek justice!'

'You mean revenge!' retorted Vibhishan.

Her eyes cold and contemptuous, she replied, 'If that is how you want to word it, if that is what you deem so, o righteous Vibhishan, then so be it; revenge is my way of getting justice. I shan't get what I lost but neither shall I meekly accept it. I want justice, I want my revenge. I ask not as a sister of the king, but as a citizen who had been attacked by an enemy!'

'You provoked them!' said Vibhishan angrily. 'In your fight, don't involve the king and the state!' He turned towards Ravan, 'Please, don't allow emotions to decide. It is dangerous...'

'So what do we do?' snapped Ravan. 'Sit quiet? They have entered my kingdom, attacked my sister, annihilated my army, killed my commander-in-chiefs and what do I do?'

'Don't wage a war against them!' implored Vibhishan. 'These two exiled princes together wipe out our army—without any help or army of their own. It's an impossible feat but they did it. All's quiet now. Don't send in more troops, it'll break the uneasy peace.'

'Peace!' shrieked Surpanakha, arresting the shifting sands of the conversation. 'Vibhishan, Ravan is an emperor—he either surrenders or accepts defeat, these are the two options you are giving him. The choices of a coward,' she said derisively. 'But he has a third, which you don't offer him. Declare war!'

Vibhishan's protests were silenced by the imperious wave of Ravan's hand.

'There is a fourth,' stated Ravan softly but he could be heard in the farthest corner of the long hall. 'They attacked my sister, a woman. Now I shall take their woman too!' he said tonelessly. 'I shall take Sita.'

I have done it, she shouted silently in victory. She had

pushed him into his well of hell. Vibhishan looked too stunned to respond.

Malyavan who had been silent all this long, interceded, his hoary head shaking in disagreement. 'Ravan, you are a warrior. Either declare war on Ram like an honourable warrior as retaliation or stay quiet. But don't use a woman as a means or an end.'

Ravan flushed an ugly red, as if he had been caught in a lie. The old man had shrewdly realized the reason behind Ravan's decision: his reawakened desire for Sita which she had cleverly tapped. Surpanakha, as sharp-sighted as a cat, was swift to grab the situation and the opportunity before it keeled over.

She smiled, a small, thin smile. 'This happened because of a woman, Nana, don't forget. Through Sita, I can get my justice without shedding a drop of blood. Or it would be a bloody war between two warriors. She is Ram's weakness. She is his chink in the armour.'

Malyavan's face looked suddenly more aged and anguished. 'Seizing Sita would be the end of us, of all that we stand for! Abducting a woman will start a war, a dishonourable war. It is shameful and unworthy. A wife cannot be punished to teach a husband a lesson. Who should know that better than you, Meenu?'

She went cold, her eyes frosty. 'That is *why* I am saying it. If it can avoid bloodshed, snatching Sita away from Ram, would put him tight in his place,' she threw Ravan a quick look. Ram is so besotted with Sita that its likely that he would be too broken-hearted to fight back. And who would help him? He has only his brother and no army...'

'The two killed an army of fourteen thousand,' Malyavan reminded evenly. 'And a powerful sorceress Taraka and rakshas Subahu so many years ago. Don't dismiss these boys, they seem to be exceptional.'

'Stop it! We are wasting time and effort arguing,' Ravan shouted impatiently. 'It is decided, and I want no further debate on this,' he added curtly, eyeing his brother and grand-uncle. 'I need to think how to go about it. But I shall take away Sita and teach Ram a crushing lesson for having done what he did to my sister!'

Surpanakha bit her lip to stop smiling. *Again that noble pretext of saving his sister's honour when it was Sita whom he was after.* She was closer to the savage promise she had made to herself: to see him dead...*I shall have him killed, even if it meant annihilation of my family, this palace, this kingdom, my race. He and they and all have made me suffer as I had never thought it was possible to suffer.* Her heart was slamming against her ribs. *I would do it, I would,* she told herself.

Mandodari

$\mathcal{S}$ita had arrived in Lanka. Surpanakha got to know immediately hearing the commotion outside at the gold domed porch. Ravan was standing on the wide marbled stairs with a struggling Sita in tow. *Just as I had struggled with Lakshman's iron grip, trussed and helpless*, she thought with vicarious delight.

Mandodari stood in front of Ravan, defiant and aggressive, her usually calm eyes sparkling with fury.

'You will not get her inside this palace!' she said evenly. 'This is my home for my family. *She* is not family!' she reminded him quietly, flashing the mutinous Sita an inert glance.

'I have no wish to be part of this family!' retorted Sita contumaciously, through angry tears. 'Lady, if you can see, I have been abducted by your husband and have not come here on my free will. I demand to go back to my husband!' she ordered regally. 'As a woman, I hope you respect my wishes and as a wife, lead your straying husband to the right path!'

Mandodari, was not offended at the stinging rebuff but regarded Sita with a searching gaze, a glimmer of admiration in her eyes.

She shook her head, speaking to Ravan, who was about to stride past her, dragging Sita with him.

'*Stop*! I shall not allow you to enter our home with this woman!' she repeated, not raising her voice, but there was an odd sternness in her sharp voice. 'Ravan, can you not see her?

She is crying, clearly she does not want to be here but you have seized her against her wishes. I will not have any woman enter this house against her will.'

Ravan shrugged his large shoulders, 'She will come around. Give her a palace to stay...' He was speaking to Mandodari but he could not take his eyes off Sita. She looked so lovely that she took his breath away. He had to make a considerable effort not to gaze at her, staring at her all the while, drinking in the sight of her. *It was the look of a thirsty man*, Surpanakha decided with an inward smile.

He found Sita's presence disturbing, and from his impatience, his determination to behave was wilting.

'No, I don't want her here!!' said Mandodari forcefully. 'No weeping woman stays in my home. It is bad luck, it is a bad omen, Ravan! Take her back!'

Ravan glowered. 'She stays here, Mandodari,' he said calmly, but his mouth tightened and there was a sudden flash of anger in his eyes. 'I am the King of Lanka...'

'And I am the Queen!' she said furiously. 'I am your wife and I demand that a tearful woman will not be allowed into my house, who has been snatched away from her husband! She is not like your other women,' she said disdainfully. 'Those women, though married, are willingly and happily staying in this palace. You wooed them, didn't you?' she mocked. 'Woo this weeping woman too, before she is allowed here. You are this great, handsome charmer whom women cannot resist. I am sure, you can use some of your charisma to win her...'

'What sort of a wife are you, who allows a husband to take another woman?' questioned Sita.

Mandodari flicked her an odd look but did not bother to reply, turning again to Ravan. 'I challenge you, Ravan, I shall only allow her into my house as your willing woman...'

'Never!' interjected Sita fiercely.

'You underestimate my husband's charm,' said Mandodari grimly, but Surpanakha knew she was mocking her husband, with subtle aplomb.

'He is evil! And not the brave, great king he boasts to be. He killed the old, feeble Jatayu!' lashed Sita.

Sita was clearly referring to her abduction. It had been an elaborate plan, involving just two people—Ravan and Mareech. Ravan had rushed to Dandak to meet Mareech, clearly to seek his help. How Ravan had managed to convince their reluctant uncle to agree with the scheme, she could merely guess. Ravan must have probably threatened the poor old man with whatever remained of his short and tattered life. Mareech, as instructed, had changed his form into a golden deer. The plan was deviously simple: Mareech as the frisky deer hovered around Sita's ashram and attracted her attention, immediately bewitching her. She pleaded for it with Ram. Mareech rushed away from the ashram, forcing Ram to chase it, leaving Sita alone with Lakshman, one opponent less for Ravan to tackle. But, Mareech screamed in Ram's dying voice, calling out for Lakshman for help. A frantic Lakshman rushed to his brother's aid. Then, Ravan, in the guise of a roaming mendicant, begged for alms and the moment Sita had proffered it, he had seized her by the hands and rushed her to the waiting Pushpak Viman to fly to Lanka. On the way though, he had been attacked by Jatayu, an old, formidable eagle who had given him a tough resistance until Ravan had grievously injured him by cutting off both his wings. *He must have plunged from the sky and must be dead or dying*, guessed Surpanakha. *Like Mareech*, she thought. Ram must have killed her uncle, she was sure. He had been dying anyway and surviving a slow, painful death each day. He must have sought deliverance at his hands. He was the first victim in the string of deaths which would soon take place—a bloodbath, she reckoned unemotionally. As had been Vidyujiva and Kumar.

The image of her dead son roused Surpanakha from a familiar, unforgotten anguish. She suddenly felt restless, grief mingling with self-anger. She still had not been able to trace the identity of his murderer...

Mandodari's derisive tone pulled her back to the present, to the place behind the filigreed screen of the window, from where she was watching the scene of Sita's arrival at the palace.

'She calls you a coward, my lord,' said Mandodari scornfully to Ravan, whose face was coldly impassive, a pulse twitching at his temple, his big hands in a fist. 'Won't you prove otherwise and court her instead?' she suggested, softly, surely. 'The day she agrees, I shall allow her in this house. I give you a year.'

Surpanakha caught a glimpse of the vicious twist of the mouth and the half mad expression of contained rage on Ravan's face. There was a sharp note of determination in his wife's voice he had never heard before. Mandodari faced him, her dark eyes unhappy and angry. She had cornered him with her wise words as always and the prick of conscience made him angry too.

'Agreed,' he snapped coldly and tense, his huge hands on his hips, his jaw moving. 'Till then escort her to the Ashok garden,' he said, nodding to Trijata. 'She will be kept guarded there.'

Trijata, who could not boast of her father Vibhishan's amiableness nor her mother's beauty or flippancy, looked distinctly uncomfortable, and it showed on her ordinary, dull face. But she obliged with a low bow and led Sita away.

Sita cast Ravan a departing look of defiance, her voice dangerously soft but ominous. 'A year is a long time. To free me, Ram will come here to Lanka and kill you!'

Ravan smiled, a thin, tight smile. He stood there, breathing unevenly and quickly, watching her until he lost sight of her and turned on his heel with all his regal hauteur.

But Surpanakha did not miss the shadow of fear which had fallen on Mandodari's lovely face.

The moment everyone had left, Surpanakha came out from the filigreed shadows of the ornate windows, corbeled from the wall.

Mandodari gave a start, composing her bemused expression and thoughts.

'All those taunts...it was not a challenge for Ravan, was it? It was your way of protecting Sita from him,' observed Surpanakha. 'And protecting Ravan as well. Subtle but smart. Both did not realize it.'

Mandodari face was glacial. 'You always know all. Who can

fool you?'

Surpanakha ignored the jibe. 'But Sita does not need to be protected, Mandodari. Ravan is too unnerved by that curse. It haunts him! He dare not touch another unwilling woman for he knows that would be his last day!'

'I imagine.' Mandodari's voice was bitter. 'But his arrogance might permit him to think otherwise. He believes himself to be immortal and if I can protect Sita or any other woman in any way, I shall,' she pursed her lips, a mettle in her voice. 'But the same cannot be said about you. You planned this, you instigated Ravan!' she accused, her eyes steady but suffused with anger. 'How could you? How dare you get her *here*...!?'

'I did it for my brother!' cried Surpanakha in all earnestness. 'He has been pining for her for years and you have been so accommodating about his other women all these years, so why not Sita?'

'Because Sita is Ram's wife! He will come to Lanka to get her back. You heard Sita just now, did you not, you foolish woman? Then why did you needle Ravan to get the poor girl here?' cried Mandodari. 'Was he not supposed to have killed her so that you can have those two men?' she asked shrewdly. 'That was not a cheap deal between brother and sister but a blatant lie reserved for me. Knowing that, yet he got her here in Lanka?'

Surpanakha shrugged her shoulders helplessly. 'He did it for *me*, Mandodari!' she insisted, pretending to shield her brother. 'To teach Ram a lesson for what he did to me,' she said sweetly, thrusting her face forward, a hateful, contorting grin twisting her carved face. 'To take revenge on his sister.'

'No, not for you but to have Sita!' fumed Mandodari. 'He has never got over her or that he lost her to Ram. This is just a pretext to even up. Sita is his weakness and he will never give her up!'

So is his ego his weakness, Surpanakha shouted silently, *besides that disgusting lust for women. Both will bring his downfall: I shall bring his downfall!* Another thought struck Surpanakha, *Sita happens to be Ram's weakness as well. He would give his all for her, recalling the look he reserved for his wife. Both these men's weakness would be my strength.*

'You need not fear Sita, Mandodari,' she hastened to assure her livid sister-in-law. 'He can never touch her unless she acquiesces. Which she never shall. Sita hates Ravan as much as she loves and above all, respects Ram. Ravan will not be able to win either—her love or her respect.'

'You knew this and yet you provoked him to get her here!' accused Mandodari.

'I wanted my revenge and I did it for Ravan too!' she pretended to confess meekly. 'Once she was here, he would be satisfied and his life's yearning would be quenched at last. Though I have nothing against Sita,' she shrugged. 'She is but a pawn to pay what her husband and his brother did to me!'

'You dragged a woman into a men's war!' seethed Mandodari. 'You used your brother to take your revenge against those two princes through Sita!'

Wrong, so, wrong, gloated Surpanakha. *I shall use the two princes to take revenge on my brother. Through Sita.*

'Sita was but a bait,' she admitted, unrepentantly.

'You silly woman, do you realize what you have done?' smouldered Mandodari, with all the anger she could muster.

Yes, and this is just the start of your hellish nightmare, smirked Surpanakha, her face wooden.

'What did I do, Mandodari, but suffer the pain of humiliation?' Surpanakha wore an offended frown. 'I laid it straight to my brother whether he could help me or not? I have lost all—my husband, my son—all I had was my dignity, and that too was stripped by these two princes from Ayodhya. Who else could I turn to? He is my brother, Mandodari,' she pleaded with just the right catch in her voice. 'Who could help me salvage my tattered honour, my battered face but Ravan?'

'It was not for you, you fool, but for Sita he is fighting!' snapped Mandodari.

Surpankaha smiled inwardly, *yes, I know.* 'No, no, Ravan loves me!' she cried in feigned indignance. 'He has always protected me, has he not? Even from Vidyujiva,' she could not help saying.

Mandodari looked immediately guilty, missing the sarcasm.

'Ravan loves only himself!' she said under her breath.

So now you agree, smiled Surpanakha silently.

'I don't know what to fear more—the presence of Sita here or the soon ensuing war with Ram,' said Mandodari, her face so pale she looked ill. 'Oh, why did you come back, Meenu, to lead your brother to bloodshed?!'

'Bloodshed?' queried Surpanakha innocently. 'It's a bloodless revenge. Sita has been abducted, there is no need for war. Ram will realize the hard way what it is to harm the sister of the King of Lanka.'

'Of course there will be war, how can you deny that possibility, Meenu?' asked Mandodari agitatedly.

'But even if Ram does challenge Ravan to war, Ravan will not shy away. He loves war!' said Surpanakha, knowing she was sounding stupid.

'Exactly! That's what I dread! Ram will not remain quiet, nor shall Ravan!'

'You mean to say,' said Surpanakha slowly, frowning. 'That Ravan is having this war for Sita and not to defend my honour?'

Surpankaha hoped she had an injured look on her face.

'Did you not get that?' lashed Mandodari scornfully. 'In your ignorance, you encouraged him to start this war!' she accused shakily.

Surpanakha's heart skipped a swift beat. Had Mandodari seen through her? She had not, Surpanakha was sure. She would have to continue with this charade.

Her hands flew to her scarred face. 'No, what have I done?' she murmured in mock horror. 'I came back to seek his help, not his doom as you accuse me of, Mandodari. Why do you and Ma keep blaming me?' she lamented in fake pain.

Her mother, thought Surpanakha bitterly, had none been too pleased at her return to Lanka and voiced it amply.

'It happened because you came back...' said Mandodari flatly.

Surpanakha flashed her a look of extreme annoyance.

'Instead, can you not be honest enough to put it on Ravan?' she snorted. 'Who can arrest his lust for war and women, can you, Mandodari, could Ma? This lust of his is the venom, poisoning him of his values and respect, his sanity, his peace of mind...'

And eventually his life itself, she concluded wordlessly.

'Ravan will surely be killed if he goes for this war!' cried Mandodari despairingly.

'Why will he be killed, he's immortal! It not because of me or Sita that he wants to war, but because he loves it. Are you saying it is his folly,' she mocked innocently. 'He is the most learned man, why would he not learn to listen to others? He knows he wins each time, so will he now. He is always so sure of himself!'

Mandodari nodded, wretchedly, believing her to be concerned. 'He is highly educated but not enlightened. He is a brilliant scholar, but that does not necessarily make him a good man,' she sighed. 'Because of the lack of scruples, a scholar like him has turned into a rakshas!'

Just like I did, agreed Surpanakha grimly. *But it was all of you, my family, who turned Meenakshi to become a Surpanakha bent on destroying everyone and everything.*

'But probably Ravan does not realize that his mind is being slowly corrupted by his lust, greed and desire for power,' she said, nodding slowly. 'You are right, Mandodari, you know it so well but hate to admit it.'

'Yes, I guess I am to blame too. I cannot blame only you for what Ravan is doing,' said Mandodari sadly. 'First his mother and then I allowed him his way too often, too easily! He should know better that to win the heart of women, you need humility and honesty not just lust! If he has gone to war for the sake of a woman, he is arrogant and ignorant, making Sita a subject of dispute as if she is a piece of land to be acquired! It is he who is going to start this war and even now, though he can prevent it, he won't!'

'Make him, dear Mandodari, before it is too late!' cried Surpanakha, in pretended terror.

'He won't...' repeated Mandodari, her voice hoarse and

shaking with disbelief, her stark, blanched, lovely face damp with cold sweat. 'I shan't allow it, I can't have this war, and I can't have this woman here!'

'Can you stop Ravan? Has anyone ever been able to?' asked Surpanakha helplessly and Mandodari, whose back was towards her, could not see the vicious expression on her face: her lips drawn in a snarl, making her marred face more grotesque.

'What do I do...?' cried Mandodari, staring at her blindly, muttering through bloodless lips. 'But watch my husband go to his death?'

That, sneered Surpanakha triumphantly, will be my justice.

Vibhishan

$\mathcal{T}$he war was yet to begin but Lanka was burning, a screaming conflagration. And so were parts of the palace, its famed beauty curling into wisps of soot in the licking flames. Surpanakha watched the city burn, the reflection of the blaze flaring in her vivid eyes.

Hanuman, the monkey-man, Ram's unusual looking messenger, had been sent to Ravan's court, requesting to free his wife to be sent back with honour. Ravan had refused and got the envoy arrested instead, shackled in ignominious iron chains. Hanuman had retaliated in a manner Ravan would have never expected: he flexed his muscles, breaking free from his chains, lighted his tail and brandished it around, torching the palace and the garden. 'Ram shall come to this city, to Lanka's shores to free Sita' were his parting warning words, before he sprang out, creating havoc in the city wherever he went.

She could hear the wails echoing from the burning citadel but the loudest one had been for Ravan's youngest son, Akshay Kumar, who had been the first to be killed in the skirmish. *That tender fourteen year old boy, a little younger than Kumar, with the golden eyes of his father.* Surpanakha shrugged, *he was paying for his father's sins.*

No, a voice taunted her, *you killed him. Just as you got your son killed...*

It is not me, it is him, she shouted to herself. Ravan was the harbinger of evil in this house, he *was* evil. Watching him weep, over the slight figure of his dead son had filled her with a momentary sense of calm, like sprinkling water on a raging fire. But the embers were still burning in her. To kill him, there would have to be more deaths—a pile of them—all in the very family she had been born into.

Ravan was not what he was. The death of Akshay and the destruction of his beloved city had shaken him. A wise man would have retracted, as Vibhishan pleadingly advised, but Ravan remained unrepentant, the sight of Sita flaring in him an obdurate hope, and persistence. The burning flames of the city had been extinguished but not the flicker of egotist fury, raging within him. Surpanakha could see it in his eyes and in that madness, he threw Vibhishan out of his court, this palace and the kingdom, for having dared to speak against him. Vibhishan had implored then argued heatedly to return Sita to Ram. Ravan flew into a rage, accusing him of being a traitor who would rather side with the enemy than his brother when things went wrong. In a full court attended by generals and nobles—like Prahasta, the commander-in-chief and young royals like Indrajit and Nikumbha, the young son of Kumbha—Vibhishan had been the only one who had dissuaded Ravan from going to war against Ram. The others had agreed, some concertedly, some grudgingly. None had questioned his decision but for Vibhishan who had staunchly maintained the only way to avoid the war was to return Sita to Ram. Surpanakha had to concede reluctantly that she had underestimated Vibhishan: her younger brother had more moral courage than anyone else in the court. His defiance had cost him heavily. He had been banished from Lanka.

Vibhishan had left quietly, amongst rumours that he had met up with Ram and his army of the vanars, the monkey army under King Sugriv of Kishkinda. That was not surprising, his undeserved reputation as a pacifist coward notwithstanding.

Like never before, Kaikesi had gone against Ravan, refuting Ravan's decision about his brother's exile. Ravan had remained implacable, curtly telling his mother to leave the room; she should be fortunate he had not had her thrown out of the palace. He would have, Surpanakha smiled with silent glee, had he known Kaikesi had met with Vibhishan and it had been she who had advised him to go to Ram, from the last snatch of conversation she had overheard.

Surpanakha had caught her coming out of her son's chamber. Kaikesi's face had lost colour with the fear that she might have overheard the last part of the exchange. Surpanakha had nodded reassuringly. Only a relaxation of the muscles around the stern and unbeaten mouth of Kaikesi appeared to her like an expression of courtesy. They looked at each other: there was no love lost.

Surpanakha decided it was terrible what time can do to a beautiful woman. Often, in our memories, those we no longer see, age gracefully but looking at her shrivelled form, and the heavy pouches below her dulled eyes, Surpanakha recognized a vision fading—an old, defeated woman with eye pouches of grief. She too knew the outcome of this war. She had been crying: she had been inordinately fond of Akshay, his death the first blow in the coming days. Surpanakha searched her memory, and the last time she could still remember her mother at her most vulnerable was when Kaikesi had wept brokenly in her chamber as she had recounted how Nani had been killed.

Their eyes met in mutual acknowledgement: hers a calm hazel clashed with the brightness of unshed tears of her mother's tired eyes. The tears enhanced the brilliance of her dark eyes. Those same eyes looked away, but not before casting a glance of searing accusation at her, as they always did. Kaikesi walked away without uttering a word to her daughter. Surpanakha looked at the slouched, retreating figure of her mother and the thought which had always troubled her, resurfaced irreverently. Had her mother ever felt any love for her father or her, or had she loved just one person in her life—Ravan?

Surpanakha squared her shoulders and entered Vibhishan's room with her strategy well chalked out.

'You know Ravan is in a foul mood,' started Surpanakha watching his perplexed face closely. 'He did not mean what he said. Stay in the court...'

'...and get insulted again!' cried Vibhishan, his pallid face working to a furious red. 'He openly accused me of betraying him, saying I was like a bee who moves from one flower to another, searching for the sweetest nectar. That I was nothing but an opportunist who was leaving him for personal gain. What do I gain but his wrath each time I try to give him some counsel? A true friend and a brother is who warns when he is going wrong, doing wrong. The others are adulators, busy flattering, preferring to please than to guide,' he rued, his eyes bitter. 'Ravan has been openly insulting to me for years and I have tolerated it, in spite of Sarama cautioning me otherwise...'

Sarama, thought Surpanakha, *the perpetual instigator*. She might as well facilitate her in turning Vibhishan against Ravan.

'But this time, Ravan has overstepped his conduct,' said Vibhishan soberly. 'How can he abduct a married woman and keep her here against her wishes? Ram, like a fair warrior, did not challenge Ravan to a battle but sent across a messenger to send her back. But Ravan in his mindless arrogance, had the envoy chained like a common prisoner! That's not done!' he exclaimed, recalling the horror of the day. 'Hanuman was a messenger to be treated with a certain civility as is the conduct expected from kings. But Ravan behaved like a boor, in flagrant disrespect. Hanuman burned down his city, his son got killed, and this is just the beginning of the unmitigated tragedy he has brought on himself!'

'And when you told him this, he threw you out!' she said, her voice sympathetic. 'Like a common culprit.'

His face sagged. 'I am not common, nor am I a culprit. I too am the son of Rishi Vishravas and Kaikesi. I am as learned as Ravan if not more, then why do I suffer his daily disdain?' his voice trembled in pain. 'Because he is my brother and I love him. I can see he is beckoning his own destruction and I tried to stop him, but he turned against me instead!'

He was still worrying about Ravan, not himself, the silly man, Surpanakha looked at him with silent astonishment.

'What are you going to do now?' she asked with feigned anxiety.

Vibhishan wearily rubbed his jaw. 'I don't know,' he said helplessly, lifting his plump shoulders. 'Where do I go? Ma advised me to go to Ram...' his voice trailed uncertainly. She had overheard that part of their chat, but she feigned ignorance. Inadvertently her mother had made it easier for her, preluding her plan into action.

He sighed. 'But I was wondering if I should go to Father's ashram and retire from this play of power and politics. They never did interest me...' he threw up his shoulders in despair.

'Vibhishan, you are good at it. You are the best advisor any king would be proud to have, you counsels are respected by all here, except, of course, Ravan. But he's too foolishly conceited to recognize your wisdom. Had Kumbha been here, he would have said the same,' she assured him.

'Kumbha is sleeping away his six months,' he reminded her almost angrily. 'He is lucky, he can get away from this mess every half year!'

'Exactly, all hope and reason rest with you,' she cajoled, her voice entreating. 'If you give up, what will happen to Lanka, this throne? The war Ravan is thirsting for is sure to end with only defeat and death....

Vibhishan flinched, his eyes distressed. 'That is what I had hoped to avoid.'

'You cannot. Ravan will not listen to you or anyone else. Even the death of Akshay has not made him realize his folly. Who is there but you after Ravan? Kumbha is in his blissful sleep, who will look after the kingdom? You, Vibhishan,' she said, her tone silkily persuasive. 'You now have a responsibility. You cannot abdicate it by running away to Father's ashram. You could be king too,' she paused. 'You are good, kind, wise and brave. You care for the public and you are not foolish to wage unnecessary wars to salvage your ego. Don't you see?'

'Yes, Sarama keeps insisting the same!' he muttered, running his hands agitatedly through his scant hair.

Surpanakha continued, pressing her hands in his. 'Kumbha is not entitled simply as he is handicapped because of that curse of his. It is not that you are usurping the throne, you are protecting it! Kumbha cannot help you, so, it is you who needs to look after the crown, Lanka, the people...' she sighed, patting his shoulder. 'Don't wash your hands off so soon.'

There was a long hesitation. Surpanakha allowed him to think, resting his chin on his folded hands. She knew she had triggered the wheel of thoughts in the mind of her brother, to churn out new hopes, new aspirations, a fresh, new ambition—he could be king.

'But who will agree with me?' he said, pondering for long. 'No one, not even grandfather, has the courage to go against him. Ravan represents the asuras, he is our king, the emperor. No king or noble will go against him and take my side. Vidyujiva tried and see what he got!'

His face went scarlet as the statement slipped off easily from his tongue. Surpanakha went stiff then cold, her heart contracting. With an effort, she swallowed and nodded her head. 'Yes, I know, I agree,' she whispered, licking her dry lips. 'That is why you need to seek help.'

'But who?' he asked in anxious exasperation. 'I have no one! Ma mentioned Ram but...'

'Whom is Ravan fighting right now?' asked Surpanakha, slyly.

'Ram.'

'With whom?'

'His brother, Lakshman. They are a formidable pair.'

'But even Ram realizes that to vanquish Ravan, he needs an army. Whom does he have?'

'The vanars under Sugriv,' answered Vibhishan, a little stupidly.

'And what does that mean?' she prompted, a small smile touching her lips.

Bewildered at her many, direct questions, it slowly dawned on Vibhishan where they were leading.

'That Ram with Lakshman and Sugriv have a standing army,

waiting to attack Lanka!'

Her eyes were very intent as she nodded again. 'Kumbha cannot help you nor can Grandfather. And none of our cousins. All owe allegiance to Ravan, they are too weak and scared to break off from him,' she said primly. 'So who can help you?' she paused. 'Or rather whom could you help with your advice and information?'

His brow cleared. 'You mean the best option I have is go to Ram?' he said slowly. 'As Ma too suggested...' he paused to contemplate.

'Do you have any other alternative you can think of??' she questioned.

Vibhishan shook his head, his dull eyes, suddenly bright with anticipation and expectations. 'Yes, I can go to Ram and help him fight his war against Ravan!' he announced excitedly, filled with quick conviction. 'I will help Ram in defeating Ravan!'

Not defeat him, you fool, he needs to be killed, fumed Surpanakha.

'But will Ram take me?' he said, his eyes clouding with hesitation and doubt. 'Why would Ram trust me—a brother of his enemy?'

Surpanakha waved her hand dismissively. '...who was forced to part company because his brother the king, would not listen to good counsel from you,' smiled Surpanakha. 'That's what you tell him. Ram will see the goodness and the fairness in you, Vibhishan. How you have suffered under Ravan and that not just you, but the kingdom needs to be freed from such a dictator. Ram knows it's not a silly skirmish to win his wife back. It is fight between right and wrong. Is Ravan right or Ram?'

He nodded but threw her a long, searching look, she found disconcerting. 'Surpanakha, you suggested this war so now why are you helping me...?' he began slowly, his words unsure. He threw her an appraising stare. 'It was because of *you* that Ravan went after Ram. Because the two brothers had disfigured you,' he said, hesitantly, his earnestness dwindling. 'He abducted Sita for you! The war is for you!'

'Is it?' she said with a little sneer. 'Or was it for himself? In the pretext of avenging my mutilation, Ravan found a way for his own lust. And is it about me anymore, Vibhishan?' she asked quietly. 'Yes I prompted him, I wanted my justice, my revenge. But is it for me that Ravan seized Sita or was it because he had been thwarted by her once? If it were for me, he could have attacked the two brothers at Dandak itself and fought a righteous war of honour as Grandfather had suggested. But did he? He chose instead to abduct Ram's wife, a woman he wanted to marry a long time ago. He saw an opportunity to win her. It is for her that he is fighting Ram, not for me. He wants to confront Ram, not for me but for Sita. And you know that too, that's why you opposed him on moral grounds.'

Vibhishan still looked uncertain, his eyes shifting uneasily. 'But you were the one who started it! You tried to abduct Sita for Ravan. That was preposterous and for which you had to suffer the ignominy of a cut nose!'

'Yes, I was a fool,' she lied frantically. 'And have I not been punished enough?!'

Vibhishan was thinking too much, too hard, too correct.

He was looking at her keenly. 'Ravan has always helped you, then why are you telling me to go against him?' he asked astutely. 'Why are you against Ravan?'

She lifted her hands helplessly. 'I am not against him, I am thinking of you!! You are not like me—I have no hope for myself, dear brother, I have lost everything,' she sighed, staring at him, her dull yellow, dark ringed eyes alight with pain. 'My husband, my son, my looks, my pride. What do I have but to live a life at the mercy of Ravan? I have no choice. You have. Ravan looks after me well and I am grateful for his kindness. He loves me...'

'But do you?' Vibhishan's eyes were searching hers.

'I do, he is family,' she lied easily, her eyes steady. 'Or would he have been the first person I turned to when I was attacked by Lakshman? He has always been a kind brother to me but for that one incident when he killed my pet goat!' she laughed shortly. 'Both of you don't get along. Its best you part ways, isn't it? But when I see what he does to you, I do feel bad. You are my brother too, a brother whom the other has thrown out unceremoniously. What can you do? I am torn between two brothers and I was trying to help you, not instigate you against Ravan. I can't help him, the situation is beyond that now, thanks to Ravan's stubborn ego. But it is up to you. But where can you go but to Ram?' she added artfully.

There was a wild, look of incomprehension in Vibhshan's usually calm eyes, his face a greenish-grey, sick with fear and uncertainty.

'But am I a traitor by not being with my brother in his hour of need?' he whispered, a tormented look haunting his face. 'Is that not what I shall be if I leave Ravan for Ram? A brother going against his own brother for the enemy?' he buried his face, swamped by sudden guilt.

She would have to do her best and be quick to wean him out of his bout of remorse. She touched his heaving shoulder lightly.

'It is he who has thrown you out, you have not left him, you had no choice,' she stated. 'You have betrayed none—neither your brother nor your country. You are the rightful son, the rightful brother who tried to show his brother, the king, the right path. He banished you instead. But you are still the prince of Lanka, you have a right over it as well,' she started, speaking slowly and distinctly, keeping her face straight. 'You respect Ram, he is the epitome of goodness and wisdom. He is the leader whom you would have wanted Ravan to be like, he is the leader you want to follow. You are a learned man, wise and enlightened. Does your conscience, your beliefs tell you to heed a brother like Ravan who usurped an unwilling woman?' she drew in a long, slow breath. 'Or a righteous enemy like Ram who is fighting for his wife's honour?'

He clasped his hands, frowning. He had to answer it for himself, she did not wish to prompt his thoughts anymore. Again there was a long pause, then Vibhishan crushed his fingers in a tight fist and looked at her, his eyes narrowed.

'I shall meet Ram,' he said, unhesitatingly. 'But I shall go alone. I cannot take Sarama or Trijata with me. I shall send them to Sarama's parents.'

'No,' she refuted quickly. 'That would look suspicious and guilty! Besides, you need someone to let you know of what is happening here.'

'But they will be the first ones to face the ire of Ravan once he gets to know I have...defected,' he argued, panic in his voice and eyes. 'He will imprison or kill them!'

'No, never,' she shook her head. 'For Ravan, family is most precious. They are his brothers' wife and daughter. He would not ever harm them.'

Vibhishan violently shook his head. 'They would be held for treason!'

'Calm down, brother,' she pacified him. 'Trijata has been assigned to look after Sita. Ravan needs her and Sarama to mediate between him and Sita. He cannot ask Mandodari. Vajramala would flatly refuse, she is too close to Mandodari. Let me assure you again, he won't hurt your wife and daughter. Whatever his flaws, Ravan would not harm his family.'

'But he did. He killed Vidyujiva,' his words trailed, fear choking him. 'He was his sister's husband.'

It took all her effort, not to scream back at him and tell him he had been part of the conspiracy too. Where had been his ideals, his conscience when he had allowed his brother to murder her husband in cold blood? He had not raised his voice then.

For a moment, Surpanakha wondered if she was letting off Vibhishan too easily. If he went to Ram, as she had suggested—he was sure to provide them with all the inside information essential for them to win the war and kill Ravan. Kumbha would be sleeping away in deep ignorance and when he woke up, he would find his younger brother crowned the King of Lanka. Kumbha was a simple, straightforward man, and though he would be devastated at the death of his beloved Ravan, he would not hesitate to help Vibhishan rule Lanka as devotedly.

But did Vibhishan deserve the crown in this war? His face had changed: from a courteous, mild spoken man who spoke his mind courageously, who was braver than he appeared. His piousness made him irresolute at times, and right now he looked worried; torn between family and fortune and his future. He had a strong-willed wife to steer him fortunately as he quietly left Lanka, keeping her and their daughter at Lanka.

Ravan, she knew, would not harm them. He was too wise and too watchful of his image. Ravan would not risk shattering his image of a devoted family man and be termed a butcher who killed two innocent women, his family members. He had done it once but had been forgiven quickly. Vidyujiva, after all, had not been family, but an outsider who had committed treason.

Now she would betray Ravan, her brother, her king. But even in his last dying moments, as life sapped out of him, Ravan would never know that it was she who had been the traitor...his sister.

Sita

 avan was a disturbed man; if not about Vibhishan, Sita occupied his mind and attention. Every day he went to meet her and each day she refused him with a stinging rebuttal. It was almost comic—the powerful hulk of a man beseeching to the slight, frail woman. She was stronger than he believed her to be and he was arrogantly sure that she would succumb to him one day. But each passing day, Surpanakha saw him becoming increasingly restless: something he had been experiencing in a milder degree since the day Sita had arrived. Fear and frustration made him furious. His love, his liberty, he told her and perhaps even his life, seemed to lie hopelessly in the hands of Sita.

Surpanakha was his new confidante, as he had no one to share his woes with. She heard it with a strange fascination, how he admitted that the sight of Sita had touched off a spark inside him which no woman had up to now succeeded to do. Watching Sita, gave him a sense of satisfied pleasure but he wanted more. He had lost his sleep, and would lay sweating in the semi-darkness, as his mind saw only Sita in the garden, not far from him. That was the thing that kept him from sleeping—the picture of her lifting her thick, chestnut coloured hair off her white shoulders, the shape of her, sitting under the tree, the young, fresh beauty of her, and the realization that she was not his but Ram's wife, piercing him with fury and frustration. The war did not scare him, but that she would leave him, assailed him with agony.

Why had she married Ram he kept asking himself. A princess wedded to a prince who was now a pauper, a wanderer who had dragged the poor girl with him. How she must have suffered, but yet she had eyes and heart only for him, seethed Ravan, torn and tormented.

Surpanakha watched his wretchedness and tried to snap him out of this mood, as Ram had touched the sandy shores of Lanka, with his army. The war had begun. Kumbha's twin sons and Prahasta were the first martyrs in the first battle. Sufficiently jolted, Ravan had promised her he would do his best to stop thinking about Sita and focus on the war. His granduncle warned him repeatedly that she was another man's wife and therefore sacrosanct. She wasn't for him. She couldn't possibly be for him—ever. And the idea drove Ravan more crazy, frenzied in his frustration. He was crazy to think of her the way he was thinking of her, but it didn't help, he confessed to Surpanakha. He just couldn't get her out of his mind. He tried to be cordial but Sita refused to listen to him, to talk to him. He went down on his knees and promised her she would be his Chief Queen, unseating Mandodari, but Sita simply turned her lovely face away, hard and unrelenting. Ravan sat on his heels, his face pale, his eyes burning, slightly mad. He sat still for a long time and Surpanakha almost felt sorry for him; he cut a pitiable figure. He got heavily to his feet, his face now getting back some colour and walked out of the garden and to the palace. He was shaking with frustrated rage.

Surpanakha turned to Sita,

'How more do you want to be convinced?' she said. 'He has done everything he can for you—from writing poems, giving you gifts to grovelling at your feet. He loves you, he really does.'

Sita shook her head, 'He only wants to possess me. It is his ego, not his love speaking. A true man in love looks after the happiness of the woman he loves and my happiness is with Ram.'

'I have met Ram,' smiled Surpanakha grimly. 'But I must admit, Ravan is more flamboyant and charming. Ravan has it all—good looks, wealth, power and knowledge. He is a scholar in the Vedas, Upanishads, the Tantras, astrology and even the occult sciences and dance and music. He is a man none can refuse.'

'He may be knowledgeable but he has no wisdom, he has power but he has no pity, he has pride but knows no humility,' stated Sita, her face unperturbed. 'He knows only to own, not to prevail. For him, all are things or pets to possess, to subdue and to make them obey to him. My Ram has nothing, but just his love, thoughts and humility. That suffices for me, I am the wealthiest wife in the world.'

Sita never ceased to amaze Surpanakha. Her serene complacency was disconcerting. Surpanakha still had not yet had an opportunity to gloat and this day would be it. She wanted this girl to feel the same terror which had gripped her when Lakshman had held her arms and brought down his merciless sword on her. To instil that little hint of fear, to wipe out the calm composure off Sita's face.

She smiled maliciously. 'Ravan can always force himself on you,' she purred, the menace thick in her voice.

'The body, you mean,' Sita shrugged her slim, fair shoulders. 'I am more than just a body. He cannot possess my heart, my mind, my soul. They all belong to Ram.'

Surpanakha did not know what was more astonishing: the girl's immeasurable love or her immense faith. Both were her shield, they were her conviction that none could break. 'You keep talking about Ram, dear girl but what has *he* ever done for *you*?' asked Surpanakha equably. 'He broke Shiva's bow to prove he was the best; he gave up his crown for his brother; he went on exile for his father. But what has he done for you? You gave up a lot for him—your trust, your home, the luxury of the palace; I don't doubt your love,' she stated, with a purr in her voice. 'But love is measured, if not judged, in selflessness, not bravado. Ravan has given his all for you—his pride, his crown, his family, his honour, his reputation, and even his precious Lanka! So, who loves you more—Ram or Ravan?' She asked.

Sita stared back wordlessly but the defiance had dimmed.

Surpanakha shrugged. 'You may realize it a little late...'

'Ram is here in Lanka, that is why Ravan is so agitated,' she said slyly. *If not fear, let Sita writhe in hope,* she thought viciously.

'I know my Ram will come here for me. And kill Ravan. But Ravan will not come to his senses till it is too late,' said Sita.

Surpanakha flushed, Sita's confidence was annoying,

'You are fortunate that you have the hospitality of the Ashok garden, how appropriately wooded with the Trees of Lust, dedicated to Kama,' she sneered. 'They are bursting with the flowers of love, still intact and not reduced to ashes in the fire like the city,' she said tightly. 'The city which burned because of *you*.'

Sita smiled, 'But who got me here? Ravan? Or you? All will blame me for Lanka burning, I can see it in every accusing eye. But will they blame Ravan for his senseless ego? Or you for your unfettered passion? It all started because of that incident at the forest, did it not?'

Sita was staring at her mauled face, still livid in its grotesqueness.

Surpankaha stared at her coldly and thought, *Sita had the temerity to remind me of that day.*

'The brother is the protector of a sister's honour even in our society,' said Surpanakha, through clenched teeth. 'And a sister's honour means family honour as well. Your husband and brother-in-law violated it and shall get their due.'

'Punishment for what, for spurning your advances?' reminded Sita softly.

She would have struck the smiling face, clawed her eyes out but Surpanakha, trembling with suppressed rage, stopped herself just in time. One false move now and all would get undone. Ravan would be saved of a certain death she planned for him.

She clenched her fists instead, her nails buried in her palms, breaking her skin but tightening her resolve.

'Aha the fair, chivalrous Ram, the great protector of women and the weak!' she leered. 'Yet he ordered Lakshman to maim me. Does my mutilation fit in with your image of your precious Ram as the pious one, the dharmic man that he is supposed to be?'

Sita's face softened. 'He did it to protect me,' she said. 'He assumed you were going to attack me, and he was right. You were going to hurt me.'

'Is that your defence for him??' Surpanakha asked stiltedly. 'Or is it your not-so-subtle suggestion that I, the immodest woman, an adulteress, deserved what I got?'

'As I said, it wasn't for your advances,' said Sita, her face flushing, 'but for the fact that you were going to attack me. To prevent...'

'To prevent or to punish' mocked Surpanakha, an ugly smile on her lips. 'Or was the motive for my mutilation not only punishment but deterrence? And what had I done wrong that I deserved this punishment? Tell me.'

Sita was silent, she did not have it in her to hurt the feelings of the wounded woman any more than what she must be suffering.

Surpankaha misconstrued her silence as guilt. 'Could they not handle a woman prepositioning them? Did they have to laugh and ridicule and make a filthy joke of my desires? I am still laughing!' she gave a hard, barking laugh. 'They grinned, they teased, they goaded me into a temper and I could vent it only on you, the silent spectator watching in amused silence!' she spat, her breathing laboured. 'If they found me so crass and crude and unwelcome, could they have not just politely refused me like the chivalrous warriors they claim themselves to be? You claim the immediate reason for my disfigurement is my attempt to attack you. But is it, Sita? I think, however, the implied reason is my attempt at adultery. Yet, how proper was Ram's jest? If he is so upright as you claim, and had refusal in his mind all along, why, then, did he send me—a woman who has openly come to him—to his younger brother knowing he was married too and very much in love with his wife? Could he not have refused me directly? Both the brothers thought it was a game and tossed me to and fro like a playing ball between them! Give me an answer, Sita, or are you making an effort to evade the question of their behaviour?'

Sita bit her lip. She lost her poise and looked uneasily at Surpanakha. She had no words of defence. How could she explain to Surpanakha that in the world she lived, there was a deep suspicion of women's power and desirability flaunted so openly and when unchecked by male control. Surpanakha's overt sexuality had taken the men by surprise, amused them greatly and they had played along till the amusement had gone awry. Surpanakha had been the predator and they the prey, but in a swift stroke of the sword, from an aggressor, Surpanakha had become the victim.

Sita could not aspire to complete objectivity or be squeamish about it either. Though she felt sympathy for Surpanakha's plight as the woman blinded by infatuation and desire, she could not refrain from admiring Surpanakha for her forthright independence. Sita admitted to herself that she was as uncomfortable with Surpanakha's boldness as was she with Ram's violence. Both made her distinctly uncomfortable, both were far from her definition of the normative. She felt a need to explain them to Surpanakha but found she could not. Looking at the monstrous and scarred Surpanakha's face, Sita did not have the heart to translate her thoughts into words. They would be harsh, their ethical implication ambiguous. Whatever she said, would not be able to ease the pain or that humiliation.

Sita's cool, unafraid gaze disconcerted Surpanakha. Incensed by her silence, Surpankaha continued, wanting to hurt the girl irreparably, 'You have no answer? Or is it because, for the shortest moment, there is a possibility that he was attracted and tempted?' she paused deliberately for the significance to sink in, her lips smiling, her eyes not. 'Is it that guilt that spurred the usually pacific Ram to turn violent?' she finished venomously, her eyes flashing a brilliant gold, the pupils dilated.

Colour rushed into Sita's wan face and drained as fast, taking her breath away. She stood motionless, her hand against her slow thumping heart, white-faced and trembling, registering the ugliness of the words hurtled at her. She did not believe them, she would never consider it. It was absurd yet she did not want to hurt the wounded woman standing in front of her with all her bitter belligerence. More calm now, Sita could recognize the malice in them but also the agony. She saw Surpanakha fondling her long talons: she was nothing but a pitiable, vicious animal who was mauling her mind as her face had been.

Sita forced an uneasy smile.

'I cannot answer for either of them,' she said blandly. 'But to not see me hurt, Ram hurt you. Lakshman was more honest— he rebuffed you outright, confessing he was married and loved his wife, who also happens to be my younger sister. He does and I shall tell you how much. You are not the first one to be attracted to him...'

Surpanakha sat there staring at her, feeling the blood burning her face, but Sita continued, 'Some months ago, an apsara tried to seduce him. He refused stoutly and spurned her overtures. Angry at his rejection, but unknown to him, she cleverly left a strand of her hair on his shoulder to incriminate him in the eyes of Ram and me. The moment I saw the strand, I jumped to the wrong conclusion and confronted him. Aghast, he made a huge fire and said, "If my love for Urmila is not true, let me burn in this fire and Hell afterwards!" Saying so, he jumped into the fire! I was too shocked to react. Lakshman stood there, unscathed, with not a burn or a bruise. He stepped out, bowed and said, "Do you need more validation?" He walked away but Ram warned me never to treat his love for Urmila so lightly.'

'He is mad!!' whispered a visibly shocked Surpanakha.

'Yes he is. About Urmila!' smiled Sita fondly.

Surpanakha was shaken by the story and the depth of Lakshman's emotion. *His Mila*, she recalled. *Urmila, his wife, his sole weakness. As Sita was to Ram, Urmila is to Lakshman. Now she knew how to hurt him*, swore Surpanakha, her stare flinty.

But that would be for another day...

Kumbhakarna

###

$\mathcal{R}$avan had not fought a single war without Kumbhakarna. At the sight of the growing pile of his dead soldiers he came to a momentous decision—he would have to wake up his sleeping brother. He was the brute force of his army, the commander while Indrajit was the mastermind of all the military strategies. *The brawn and the brain*, mused Surpankha, assailed by a wave of trepidation at the news. Kumbha was going to be woken up after just month into his insensate slumber.

But waking him up had not been part of her plan. The fact that he was in his coma had been a boon; not just because his absence would weaken Ravan's fighting strength but because she did not want to lose him in this war. *I do not want him dead*, she thought frantically with a fast sinking heart. She had managed to keep Vibhishan away from bloodshed and possible death by weaning him away from Ravan, something Kumbha would have never agreed to. He would be at Ravan's side, loyal till his last breath.

Ravan's unexpected announcement had sent the first tingle of fear in her. Kumbha was sure to die in the battlefield by the hands of Ram or Lakshman and she, his sister, would be solely accountable for his death of that brother whom she still loved. The one who had been there for her always, all the while right since childhood shielding her from a domineering Ravan to her mother's barbs till the grim days after Vidyujiva's death. He had been the only one who visited her regularly at the Dandak.

Her face turned to stone, her heart freezing. She could do nothing but watch impotently as dozens of rakshsas desperately tried to wake him up with trumpeting elephants, blowing conches and beating drums. After two days of hard labour, he was roused. Provided immediately with a hearty meal, he was soon summoned by an anxious Ravan. He would be sent to the battlefield and Kumbha would willingly do it for his beloved brother: Kumbha was destined to die in this war she had orchestrated. She sat there, helpless in her room, watching and waiting, so tense that she could scarcely breathe. She didn't have to wait long.

'Is this what you wanted all along?' asked a voice, soft and wretched.

She spun around, her face pale, her eyes alarmed. Kumbha was in her chamber, big and bulky, his face grey as the grey in his wild hair. He had aged badly as well, his face dissipated from over-drinking. She had always suspected he drank for the same reason she rebelled—to escape the darkness of his own spirit. But right now as he gave a long look, there was something about his manner that made her uneasy.

'Ravan told me everything...' he began.

'And you agreed to go to war for him,' she retorted.

'I did let him know the only reason for this tragedy is his imprudent love for that man's wife. As long as she is here, Lanka and all of us will be annihilated. Her release will be our salvation. But Ravan is adamant; he wants Sita and he wants Ram dead.'

'And you agreed?' she had wistfully, hoping for once in his lifetime, Kumbha would go against his brother. But she knew it was futile.

'I told him he should have fought Ram first and then taken Sita if he wanted, but Ravan was so enraged that he almost threw me out of the room...'

'Then do that!' she begged. 'Go back to your sleep and forget about him...'

Kumbha shook his massive head. 'I told him I shall obey him 'not just because he is my king, but also a brother.' But as a friend, I cannot agree with what he is doing,' he said bleakly.

Surpanakha looked at him desolately, his next words tearing her apart. 'I shall be going to war today!'

'You shall die, just as your sons did!' she cried. 'Did you mourn for them? Did anyone grieve for them? Were they meant to die so young for their selfish uncle? For their *king*?? And what about Vajramala, think of her!?' she asked desperately, hoping he would give up his resolve in the pall of grief and love.

'She knows. She is a wise one. And strong,' he muttered hoarsely. 'What about you??' he asked suddenly. 'Ravan recounted me all what happened—your disfigurement, Sita's abduction, all of it. But I know that is not the whole truth, Meenu.'

He paused waiting for her to answer. She stared wordlessly. 'He does not know what you have planned for him. That his sister whom he adores, wants to kill him,' he enunciated each word with cold finality. 'He never shall know, I'll spare him that heartbreak. I know it but I want to hear it from your lips. I want to hear how you planned to have him, your brothers and family killed in cold blood!' he said harshly.

In spite of her control, she felt the blood draining out of her face. Kumbha was the only one who had guessed her scheme. She knew she would never be able to fool him; she never could. He had always been too perspicacious for his good. He knew her too well.

She shook her head violently as if to deny the wicked fact.

'You fooled Ravan into a mindless war which he has lost even before it began, it is just that he doesn't realize it! You are pushing him to a certain death —and all of us too,' he raged, his voice suppressed. 'To wish him dead, you are willing to sacrifice other innocent lives at the altar of your senseless revenge...'

'Senseless?' she choked. 'My revenge is as senseless as Vidyujiva's murder!'

'Stop it, Meenu,' cried Kumbha, holding her by her shoulders. 'You will kill us all in your mad lust to avenge that one death. We have lost Khara, Dushan, that little boy Akshay, our cousins, my sons...how many more of our family do you want dead to keep Vidyujiva's memory and murder alive?'

Surpankaha shook his hands away, getting to her feet. Her face was white and her eyes were glittering.

'Don't place the blame of the war on me, Kumbha. You know better. It is Ravan and his mad obsession for women and war and acquisition that this war is on us.'

'You stoked that fire...' accused Kumbha.

'Yes!! I thought he would be man enough to face Ram on the very first day of war and get killed!! Instead, he is dragging his entire family into death and destruction because of some misplaced sense of loyalty! All of you are ready to die for him!'

'Is that what has always riled you?' Kumbha barked impatiently. 'That he was loved and adulated and doted upon? I knew you were jealous of him, some sort of a sibling rivalry the two of you shared, but just that you would take it to this level is plain evil!' he said, the disbelief resonating in his voice.

There was a new emotion seeping into his florid face: dislike. 'Ravan adores you, wicked woman, and he will do anything to protect you. And what do you do—conspire to kill him through this war? He killed your husband to save you!'

'To save his throne!' she spat venomously.

'Vidyujiva would have lost interest in you once he was the king, don't you realize that even now? He used you to ingratiate himself to Ravan, he used you to protect himself from Ravan, and he used you to get back at Ravan and overthrow him...'

She drew in a long, slow, breath, trying to control her rising fury. 'We have been through this before, you cannot make me believe me. You, Kumbha, will believe what Ravan says and does. All of you have always covered up for Ravan, refusing to see for what he is! He loves only himself and he will remove anyone who comes his way—first our father, then Vidyujiva and Vibhishan. He will get what he wants, and it is Sita this time! His weakness has always been women! He abducted her for himself, not to avenge my humiliation!'

'You led him into that trap!' accused Kumbha. 'If I were there, I would have never allowed it. I see through you too,

Meenu. You have always been manipulative, artfully skilful in influencing and controlling anyone to your own advantage. But this is no childish manipulative techniques. This is cold-blooded, pre-meditated death of your brother, your entire family! And for whom? For that one worthless husband of yours?'

Her lips moved into a stiff smile. 'You admit to it too, at last! You were part of it!' she shuddered. 'He was the only one who loved me for what I was. And I loved him for what he was. You may not want to believe it but he was always good to me. I want you to know about this. I believe I was the only person in the world whom he treated decently,' she said, swallowing convulsively. 'I do know he had a rotten streak in him. There was nothing I could do about that. I loved him—I don't know if it was wrong or right, I just loved him! It was my bad luck that I loved him. Just as it is my bad luck I am Ravan's sister.'

Her voice faltered but quickly hardened. 'And don't speak to me about family, Kumbha. I was never a part of it. I was barely tolerated...'

'Is that what you wish to believe to justify your sense of wrong?' asked Kumbha, his dark eyes infinitely sad. 'You are our youngest sister, the child in our house. All of us in our own way, were protective about you to the point of being almost possessive and even custodial!! You took that as our disapproval. 'Agreed Ma was often over-critical but she was to all of us except Ravan...'

'Exactly!' she snapped, a bite in her voice.

'But is that a reason enough to drive you to hate us?' he asked incredulously. 'Why, Meenu, why did you always consider us your enemy? How easy was it for you to dismiss our love and claim you were unloved! Do I not love you? Yes, even when I know you are going to have all of us killed in cold blood! As my sons died...' he said hollowly. 'If I can forgive and love you inspite of that, why can't you forgive Ravan? Why can *you* not??' he shouted in pain.

There was a deathly pause and she could hear him breathing heavily.

He shuddered. There was something so clinical and cold, and

sinister and evil about his sister. She was beginning to frighten him, and yet, she was his sister...

'Because all of you destroyed my one chance, my one moment of happiness,' she seethed, her eyes a wild, leaping fire. 'I know he was crude, brutal and dangerous, but he did have his decent side. He meant the world to me. He was the father of my child. I was crazy about him, you all knew that yet you went ahead. Are you not guilty of killing my husband?'

'Yes!!!' bellowed Kumbha in admission.

Surpanakha choked, her grief curdling in her dry throat.

'But how much more are you going to punish us for it?' he cried.

There was an edge to his voice: an edge which told her that he was getting jaded with the burden of his guilt as well as the disgust of her deeds.

'To kill Ravan, you do not hesitate to stake the whole family, the city, the people, the entire asura race. Do you know how many soldiers have already died fighting your vengeful drama?'

'It is Ravan leading his men and family to death, not me!' she screamed, her voice shrill. 'You tell him, not me. Tell him to go pick his weapons and fight on the battlefield with Ram instead of hiding in his palace and throwing every member of his family to death! See if he will stop a war for the sake of a woman, for his huge ego, for his mad urge to see Ram defeated!'

Kumbha moved away from her. 'You are now using Ram just as you used your son, Meenu,' said Kumbha bleakly. 'You were training Kumar to kill Ravan. I see it now. Both of you hid it so well each time I visited you. You poisoned his ears, his mind, indoctrinating him with hate and revenge against his uncle. But for what, Meenu? Kumar died too. I didn't know whether to feel sorry or sad for you. You resented Ma for using Ravan to retrieve Lanka and her past glory. She did it for us, she didn't want her kids rotting in hell like she had once. But you went a step worse—you did not spare your son either! You used your son as a weapon for your war! *You* killed him!!'

Her face had lost colour, her pallor a sick grey. 'I did *not* kill my son!!'

'You did! You are responsible for his death just as you will be for the death of this family,' he reiterated harshly. 'Meenu, in your demented cry for revenge, your so-called justice, did you ever have time or emotion left in you to mourn Vidyujiva? To grieve for Kumar? Did you ever feel sorrow and sadness or was it only hate and fury and recrimination?!!'

His words swirled around her, misting a miasma of anguish in her dry, tearless eyes. 'You devil!' she said, her voice a vicious whisper. 'You stupid, blundering devil! How dare you talk about my pain, my loss when you too were responsible for all my misfortune! Did you stop Ravan ever? Your blind love for him did not permit you to see any wrong, your blind loyalty stopped you from restraining him. Like you are doing now; you are going to fight a lost battle, you are fighting for a lost cause. If you are so righteous, why do you not return Sita to Ram when you can and stop this war once and for all? But you would rather die than disobey him. I might be wicked, but you are a fool!'

'I would rather die as a loyal fool than a treacherous brother,' he said hollowly.

Surpanakha winced. Kumbha was a simple man, not as intelligent as his brothers but much wiser. Right now he was a torn man, caught between his love for his brother and his bleeding conscience. And so close to a violent death. Perhaps Kumbha had never even thought of death before, as they had been invincible for so long. It was a situation in which such a man either succumbs to fear or he grows in stature. Kumbha was fearless and by his last gesture of remaining by Ravan's side, he had proved he was brave as he was loyal—even at the cost of his death. The thought tore through her, shaking her with a frustrated, helpless fury that she could not help him, she could not stop him.

Sweat was glistening on her face, her eyes fevered yet imploring. 'Ravan deserves the death he has brought on himself,' she said savagely. '...and on the family he so proudly claims to be a benefactor and lord over. But he is the one who will force each one of you into war and get you killed. Ravan is his own nemesis and the nemesis of our family!' she blurted, tears streaming down her haggard face, her lips quivering with choked anger.

There was a long, dull moment of silence, then she said, 'Say I am wrong!'

Her voice was off-key and strident.

She sat down abruptly, staring at him, her eyes pleading, face drenched with flowing tears. 'Don't. Please don't go, Kumbha!' she whispered, choking on rising tears in her throat. 'You know it's futile. It is death for you as it was for your sons!'

'I know,' he said simply. 'But I cannot leave him when he needs me most.'

'Why can you not make him see reason? Why?' she cried in impotent anger and anguish. 'Why could you or Ma not stop him ever? The two of you were the only ones who could. You have that power over him. He loves you, won't he listen to you?' she cried.

'You know he won't. And that's how you wanted it to be,' said Kumbha woodenly. 'You started a war, Meenu, but you don't have the power to stop it. You want to see Ravan's end but that also means the end of all of us!'

'No, I can't send *you* to your death!!' she beseeched, holding his arm. She drew in a shuddering sob. 'I am sorry, Kumbha, but I can't see you die! I love you!!'

'Ravan is your brother too,' he reminded her gently. 'Can you not save him?'

She regarded him as if he were a stranger.

'None of us can,' she said, her voice brittle.

'Nor can you save yourself, Meenu,' replied Kumbha tiredly. 'I hope Ravan's death and this annihilation will give you the succour you hope for. You'll lose all, love and family, but I do hope you get some peace. It's only compassion that heals suffering, remember that. Find your compassion. That is my last blessing for you.'

She shook her head violently. 'Don't pity me, please! Save yourself. Don't go!!'

'I worry, Meenu. What will happen to you after all of us

are gone? For that one man, you lost everything!' said Kumbha, sorrowfully. 'Even your son!'

Surpankaha face crumpled. 'Don't!! Don't bring up Kumar again...'

'I have to. I have information about him.'

She regarded him, her body suddenly tense. 'What do you mean? What do you know of Kumar?' she croaked hoarsely. Her eyes opened wide as hope flickered. Her heart began to pound.

'That he was said to be killed by a faceless assailant. One whom you still have not been able to trace. That is what I came here to tell you. My spy at Dandak, Akampan, was one of the few survivors of the war at Janashthan. He informed me just now who killed Kumar.'

The moment seemed to drag, pulling with it a rush of memories, her young son decapitated, his head rolled away from his body, his eyes shut in serene, everlasting slumber.

'Who?' she moved her lips in a soundless whisper.

'Lakshman,' said Kumbha quietly. 'It was an accident. He did not see Kumar, hidden in the grove while he was thrashing the long grass. He struck Kumar dead instead. It wasn't what you thought, it wasn't an act of malice or a deliberate attack. It was a mistake, and a tragic one at that.'

Her hands, her heart, her mind, still steady, she heard every word, studying her brother's face, keeping her expression under control although she felt as if she had been knifed over and over again. She looked closely at him and she felt as if an icy draught had brushed over her, leaving her cold.

'But how? How did your man know?' she trembled.

'A rishi witnessed it. Fearing your wrath, he had kept silent but Akampan got it out of him. I repeat, Meenu, it was an accidental death. It was not murder. Don't vent your vengeance on Lakshman now. Please don't, for your sake.'

For a long moment, she stood staring at her brother, aware only of the faint sound of the sea pounding afar and the violent beating of her heart. During that moment, her mind was paralysed by shock, then her resilience absorbed the shock, and fury gripped her, sending blood to her face, making the veins in her neck throb and giving her face an expression of vicious rage. *Lakshman, who had forced me to my knees, grabbed my hands, and sliced off me nose and ears. He had killed my son.*

'Lakshman,' she murmured, the tears dried and caked on her anguished face.

Kumbha flinched. There was this deadly note in her voice he had heard before. He knew she would not heed his words. She would seek her revenge on that man, some day, some seasons later. But she would.

Meghnad

❧

$\mathcal{S}$urpanakha thought the day would never end: each minute was like an hour. Kumbha was killed by Ram just before dusk; the bravest warrior, he confessed, he had ever fought. Ram and Kumbha fought long and late. Kumbha was a master archer but as the day wore on, he could not withstand Ram's arrows and fatally succumbed just as the sky got cloaked in the orange glow of dusk. Assaulted from all sides by frenetic vanars, spears and arrows, the wounded Kumbha got both his arms torn from his massive body till he crashed onto the battlefield, vicious and valiant till his last breath, the earth trembling taking in the weight of his last act of loyal bravery.

Ravan could not believe his ears. His brother had been unconquerable. As he was. He raged. He ranted. He roared in grief. They had been inseparable, he wept openly. Strangely Kumbha's death seemed a prelude to his. Ravan seemed to realize that.

'But *I* cannot die,' he kept muttering. 'No one can kill *me*.'

'Except for a man,' reminded Malyavan, his aged eyes weary. 'Ram is no deva or aditya, gandharva or daitya. He is a mortal! Ravan, end this before it is too late for you. You have lost your cousins, the twins, all your sons but for Indrajit. Now Kumbha. Who else? You'll end your family, our dynasty!'

Ravan grunted. 'Vibhishan is alive, and he will be king after me and carry on!' he scowled. 'That is what he wanted—to be king, sit on the throne! But he won't rule, Indrajit is there and his son...'

Surpanakha saw Malyavan heave a weary sigh, too fatigued to argue with his grandson. Ravan was getting abnormally edgy by the hour, obsessing over rituals and grand yagnas when he should be in the battlefield.

'I agree with Dada,' intervened Indrajit, the gash on his chest still livid. The previous day he had fatally injured Lakshman with his mighty Shakti. Surpanakha had thought she had lost her opportunity to seek vengeance against the man who had killed her son. But Lakshman had been spared miraculously. *Ánd I would never spare him,* she vowed.

'Ram is no ordinary mortal, Father,' remarked Indrajit, his voice suppressed. 'Neither is Lakshman. He recovered from his wounds by the Sanjeevani, the wonder herb brought by Hanuman from the cold, distant Himalayas. He should have died by this dawn. I have defeated both the brothers twice in the battlefield. I have been fighting them for three days now and have seen them at it, Father. They are like gods! I think we should make peace.'

Ravan felt a rush of blood to his head. He drew his lips drawn back in a snarl. 'Are you too scared to fight them, Indrajit? Or should I revert to your original name, Meghnad?' he growled. 'All thunder but no courage?'

It was a cruel, unfair taunt to a man who had single-handedly wiped out Ram's army. Indrajit's Nagpash was as deadly as the Brahmastra and would have been successful in killing both the brothers with his special serpents which had bound the two princes, their fangs killing them slowly.

Married to Sulochana, the daughter of Anant-Sesh, the Serpent King, Indrajit had weaned the deepest, deadliest secret of the warfare of the Nagas. Ram and Lakshman would have died had it not been for the surprise rescue by Garud, Vishnu's eagle who had pecked and killed all of Indrajit's snakes.

Indrajit flushed, his calm eyes glittering. 'You know I am not a coward, Father. I would rather die than be one. I am telling you what I have seen on the battlefield. All of my brothers have been killed and so has been my dear uncle, and they were all unusual warriors,' he said evenly, his handsome face darkened with a cold fury. 'I am not afraid of dying but if my death can save you a defeat, then so be it. I will die for you!' he said through stiff lips, his voice charged.

Indrajit's outrage was not a display of his hurt and humiliation but the sinking realization that he was fighting a lost war.

Ravan looked visibly shaken, shocked at his son's unexpected outburst; Indrajit had never raised his voice at anyone. But in the assimilated shock, Surpanakha recognized fear lurking in his golden eyes. He was scared what his son was claiming was true and as that fear battled with pride, arrogance won. Ravan refused a truce. This meant the war would go on, more would die on the battlefield...

Surpankaha's heart contracted. Meghnad was her favourite nephew; he was her baby before Kumar was born. As a wailing infant, she had cradled him in her arms for hours till he went to sleep. She had fed him his meals patiently till her back ached and neck stiffened. She had recounted stories to the long-lashed, curly-haired little boy with all her persuasive charm. She had raised him like her own son right till the day she had left Lanka for Dandak. She had lavished all her love and affection on him which she had invariably denied to Kumar. She had been his second mother; he had been her first son.

And today, it was not only Ravan, but she as well, who was pushing the young man to his premature death. She glanced at Ravan; *how could he do it? I didn't want Kumbha to die or his young twin sons to, I don't want my Meghnad killed as well. It had been Ravan alone who was supposed to die on the battlefield. But he would be the last to die. Before him, all those whom I had once loved would be sacrificed.*

But Surpanakha was hopeful. Meghnad indeed was Indrajit; he was said to be invincible in battle, not because he was the only warrior ever to own the three ultimate weapons of the Trimurti—the Brahmandastra, Vaishnavastra, and Pashupatastra. But also because he performed a special yajna before every battle.

He would be performing one at dawn in a cave temple outside the city.

It was a boon given to him by Brahma besides the title of Indrajit. Meghanad had asked for immortality, but Brahma had replied that absolute immortality was impossible as it was against the law of the nature. Instead, he granted the young boy another boon that he would never be defeated in any battle, if he completed his yagna of the goddess Prathyangira. On the completion of the yagna, a celestial chariot would transport an invisible Indrajit to any battle. He had used this trick as well as the samadhi mantra Lord Shiva had granted him, to escape Ram's and Lakshman's fatal arrows till then.

She met him outside his palace as he was leaving for the temple to perform this puja at Nikhumbila. She found that she was ill at ease in his presence; perhaps she was plagued by primitive sensations of guilt; perhaps she was upset by the complacency of Ravan or his arrogance that he would not lose his beloved son.

'Be careful, Meghnad,' she beseeched. She was the only one who called him by that name. He would always be her little Meghnad, shy and gentle yet fierce and ruthless on the battlefield. 'Don't let Ravan's words affect you. You are un-vanquishable, never doubt that.

'But my time has come, Meenuma,' he said unexpectedly. He confessed it with such stark poignancy that Surpanakha's blood ran cold.

'Don't be silly, you are indestructible! You are allowing Ravan's words to get to you...'

Something in his tawny eyes stopped her.

'It is Lakshman,' he said quietly. 'I saw him. He survived my poisonous Naga arrows, my venomous fumes, the Nagpash, all the tricks and magic I had in my possession. I have exhausted all of my supreme magical powers you had taught me once, Meenuma. I darted across the clouds and skies like a bolt of lightning, mixing skills of sorcery and deceptive warfare, vanishing and reappearing behind Lakshman's back, trying to catch him off-guard. He rebuffed me each time. I defeated Indra but I cannot defeat him. As a last resort, I used my fiercest and deadliest weapon, Shakti, on him yet he lived,' he paused, breathing heavily. 'He lived, because he is destined to kill me.'

Listening to his words, she felt the cold fear clamping her heart again. Meghnad did not look fearful. In his eyes was a certain calmness: desolate, yet a determined serenity, as if he knew he was going to die.

'You are tired, Meghnad, you need rest...'

He cut her short, with a firm shake of his beautiful head. 'Was it a curse or a boon, I don't know but I am meant to be killed by an extraordinary man—a celibate with unusual powers, he who has not succumbed to any woman's charms for fourteen years. And in Lakshman I recognized that man. I see my death in his eyes. He will kill me.'

That name again, that man again. Surpanakha cringed at her nephew's ominous words. A sworn celibate untouched by a woman in the last fourteen years: an impossibility but Lakshman was credited with it. A mix of memories, those of humiliation, violence and desire brought the colour rushing to her face. Who should know better than she, she thought bitterly.

She turned sharply to Meghnad. 'You leave for your yagna early tomorrow morning, Meghnad. No one will dare touch you. You shall come back victorious as always!'

Meghnad's handsome face twisted into a forced smile. 'I shall meet Ma and Sulochana,' he said laconically, but there was a note of finality in his voice. 'Look after Sulochana once I am gone, Meenuma.'

Before she could retort, he had swiftly turned away to stride down the long corridor. He had gone to bid his mother and young wife farewell. Surpanakha blinked, the weight of what she had done too heavy for her to bear. She dragged herself to her bedchamber and lay on the bed, thinking of Vajramala, Kumbha, the dead twins and Meghnad. She could not sleep, peace evaded her. She lay there, her mind tormented, then after a while, she began to weep, the tears streaming down her face, wetting the pillows, drenching her soul. Finally just before dawn, she shut her eyes, heavy with pain and guilt. Sleep was her antidote to loneliness, her sole solace from grief.

She woke up to the cries of wails. She got up startled, taking a moment to register, pushing sleep from her bleary eyes. She remained motionless, her mind crawling with alarm.

'What is the commotion about?' she asked a frightened maid.

'Prince Indrajit is dead!' she stammered, her scared eyes flooding with tears.

She felt suddenly cold and a little sick. 'But it's still early morning. The war cannot start before sunrise!' she found herself saying but she was trying to reassure herself.

'He was killed by deceit!' cried the maid. 'The Crown Prince was at his usual pre-dawn puja in the cave when Lakshman and Lord Vibhishan attacked him...'

Surpanakha did not wait to hear more, her rushing steps leading her to Ravan's palace. She guessed instinctively what must have happened. Vibhishan knew Indrajit was vulnerable if he never finished performing the yagna and the man who would destroy this yagna, had the power to also kill him. Vibhishan had told Lakshman of this secret, the dirty rascal. She should have never spared him, she raged, cursing herself. Behind all his piousness lay treachery and deceit. He had fooled her too.

The sight that met her eyes in the palace hall stilled her heart. Ravan was sitting slumped, his face in his hands, his eyes staring bleakly at the cold, marble floor, his lips a thin, hard line. Mandodari was staring sightlessly at her husband, her face haggard, a mask of cold misery as she held on to a dry-eyed Kaikesi. The young widow, Sulochana sat in silent despair, her eyes vacant, her hands listless in her lap, absently patting her little son's curly head: a replica of the young Meghnad. Her eyes trailed up to the boy's mother; Sulochana's young, lovely face were lined years of anguish and heartbreak she had been made to suffer these last few days. Not to dismiss the trying time she had since she had come to Lanka as a bride, thought Surpanakha with a twist of her lips.

Meghnad had won his wife through controversy and conflict.

She was the daughter of Sheshnag, Vishnu's invaluable aide, who had wanted her to marry Indra. She refused, expressing her desire to marry Indrajit instead, the one who had defeated Indra, choosing the winner over the vanquished. Her father had been furious but Indrajit on getting to know her love for him, had confronted Indra yet again and it had been Vishnu, over Sheshnag's protests, who had got the two married. Love had won but Lanka had not been an easy place for her to live. Ravan had denied her the right to worship Vishnu. She was a torn woman, forced to choose between her love for her husband and her devotion to Vishnu, unable to betray either. But Indrajit had promised her that he would never come between her and her faith. A wise Indrajit respecting his wife, loved her more for the unusual woman she was, a girl who had defied her powerful father and Indra and who had dared to unhesitatingly love and marry him. Today she had lost him forever.

'Indrajit was killed by treachery, Ravan,' Malyavan was saying. The grand old man looked defeated, supplying tragic news every day. It was as if life was sapping from him, without a single wound being inflicted on his body.

He continued, his voice breaking, 'Or he could never have been vanquished. Lakshman and Vibhishan went to the yagna-agaar, knowing full well that Indrajit could not use any weapons while praying. Indrajit is supposed to have fought Lakshman with the utensils of the yagna, he even managed to escape from there!'

'Vibhishan!!' muttered Ravan, shutting his eyes to cut off the grief.

Grief gave way to fury as she heard Vibhishan had been solely responsible for Meghnad's death. Lakshman might have dealt the blow but it was the hand of the uncle that killed his young nephew.

Surpanakha walked into the chamber, approaching her mother. She stared at Kaikesi, and there was an expression in her eyes that turned her mother to look away.

'Ma, you advised Vibhishan to go to Ram,' said Surpanakha, slowly and distinctly. 'Lakshman and Vibhishan attacked Meghnad before sunrise before the time of battle, when he was defenceless, when he was praying! It was betrayal, it was disloyalty, it was treason, it was a murder!! That is how low your son has stooped! See what you made him do!'

There was a stunned silence in the room, broken by the quick gasp of Kaikesi. Ravan gave his mother a bewildered, searching glance, the blood receding from his face, shocked beyond words. Kaikesi looked up at her daughter strangely. She returned Ravan's accusing gaze with a slight nod of her grey-haired head, still beautiful and regal, lifting her frail shoulders helplessly.

'Yes, I did...'

'What a family I have, full of traitors!' he said in a low growl, leaning forward, his face set and his eyes frightening. His face suddenly crumpled.

'My son, oh my son...!!' he buried his face in his hands.

'I am not a traitor, Ravan!' cried Kaikesi strongly. 'I am the mother of three sons. One is dead. The other exiled. You threw him out! Yes, Vibhishan, before leaving Lanka mentioned to me he was thinking of meeting Ram. I agreed. Would he have listened to me? Have *you* listened to me? I told you not to abduct Sita. Mandodari pleaded the same. But you did what you wanted. You got Sita here. I warned you Sita might be that Vedavati...' she whispered in growing horror. 'That was the beginning of the end. You knew Ram would retaliate, you wanted to confront him. I protested again but you flew into your usual rage. Probably being your mother you could not throw me out as well!' she shook her head sadly. 'My entire life I aspired for one dream—to have Lanka back and I did all I could to retrieve it. I got it but at what cost? I lost my parents, my brothers and I shall lose all—my sons, my grandsons...was I destined to see this day??' She broke off, the words ending in a strangled cry.

Ravan pushed his jaw at her, his face turning a dusty red. 'After what I have heard, I don't need to see you anymore!!' he declared, his eyes murderous. 'I can never forgive you, Ma...no, you are my mother no longer!!'

Kaikesi recoiled as if Ravan had slapped her, pressing

trembling hands to her gaunt face.

'No!! Please no!' she cried, the tears now flowing unchecked down her raddled cheeks.

His eyes were now glaring, frosty and cold. He turned his back.

Surpanakha felt a swift glow of succour in her hour of anguish. She had turned son against mother at last.

'Stop it, all of you!' Mandodari's tremulous cry thrust the room in sudden stillness. 'I have lost all my sons. And all because of *you*,' she turned her tortured eyes on Ravan. 'You sent them all to their death, each more ghastly than the other. Today it was Indrajit's turn. They all died young and tender. For whom? *You!*' she said, her voice flat and vicious. 'Why? To appease their father's obstinate ego, his desire for a married woman! Is that the legacy, those blessings that you gave your sons—death and disgrace? It was a curse for them to be born as your sons!' she hissed through bloodless lips. 'Shame on *you*! You live at the cost of their lives!'

Ravan made a desperate movement towards her. She halted him, raising one shaking arm. 'You disowned your mother just now for not listening to you. But when have you ever heeded our words, our pleadings, our requests? Should we not have disowned you too a long time ago? Instead, each one of us—your brother, your cousins, your uncles, your young nephews, your sons have died for you—while we women suffer a living death as your wife, your mother, your sister, your daughter-in-law! Have you ever thought of *us*? What you did to us and what will happen to us once all's over? Men die their glorious deaths on battlefield but is it glory or grief for us? With what face can you confront Vajramala or Sulochana, or me?' she paused, staring at him with glazed eyes. 'O my lord, we did not want your gold and glitter and what did you give us but grief?'

She collapsed in her chair, trembling hands covering her weeping face, her soft sobs screaming of her churning anguish in the silent room.

Malayan reluctantly broke the silence of the sobs, 'I think

you need to know the full details of what happened, Ravan. You are the only one left now. What Meenu says is true. It was treachery. After his yagna was destroyed by Lakshman, Indrajit decided to fight him alone. But seeing Vibhishan at Lakshman's side, he directed his arrows at the uncle whom he had vowed to kill for his treason. He let loose the Yamashatra but Lakshman intervened and countered the deadly weapon...'

'How could he do that, how did he know?' interrupted Surpanakha sharply.

'Kuber helped him,' said the old man, his head sunk in dejection. Ravan's heavy face darkened. 'He gave Lakshman his astra to counter Indrajit's.'

'He got an opportunity to get his revenge at last!!' she breathed, her face white with fury. 'First Vibhishan, then Kuber!'

It had been a heavy price to pay for Lanka. Kuber and Vibhishan—both brothers, both responsible for his son's death. Surpanakha was swamped by the same helplessness when she had beseeched Kumbha; she thought she would be untouched by the tragedy of loss, but it lashed her cruelly each time, the welts red and livid. Kumbha and now her Meghnad, killed by the treachery of his uncles. Fury mingled with grief, but hate prevailed, as she felt the sharp prick of unshed tears. They were dry tears of defeat and death. Enemies did not deserve a second chance. Ravan had been magnanimous, he should have had them killed when he could. As he had Vidyujiva. Where was his ruthlessness where his brethren was concerned? His blood had turned against his.

'Someone will have to go to the battlefield to get back his body or it will be mauled through the day,' said Malyavan quietly. 'It was the bloodiest, longest battle that has ever been witnessed in the three worlds. Lakshman directly confronted Indrajit and they fought face to face through the day and it is believed that the gods, and all elements of Nature and the celestial protected Lakshman from Indrajit's deadly shafts. Eventually, it was Lakshman's Indrastra that killed Indrajit. His death is their biggest triumph, they claim. The vanars were dancing on his body in victory. Ram's army is rejoicing as if they have won the war already!'

She winced. *There was no respect in death, no dignity for the fallen. There was no hero in battle, just corpses. Honour meant nothing once dead: honour was a merit for the living. The Gods had protected Lakshman but who had been there for Meghnad? He had been protecting Ravan instead. He died because he was fighting for the wrong, for a sinner, for his father. My Meghnad, lying like a broken, discarded toy in the battlefield.* She choked on a sob. But there was no one to retrieve his mangled body but Ravan himself, the sole surviving asura.

She got up, trembling.

'I shall go,' she said. 'Meghnad deserves better. He was the best. Mightier than my brother here, Nana, and that is why they are celebrating. I shall bring him back.'

'No, I shall,' requested Sulochana, but there was a firm resolve in her voice. 'I'll beseech them to give it back. I have to see him one last time,' she said steadily. 'I am a warrior's wife.'

Those words again. Vajramala had uttered the same at Kumbha's funeral.

'I am a warrior's wife, a mother of two martyrs. There are many more like me, widows and mourning mothers of young soldiers. They need me. I have to leave now. I cannot afford tears, anger or hate,' she had said, patting Surpanakha gently on her shoulder and departed for the soldiers' tents. 'I don't seek revenge, just rest and peace.'

The mildness of her tone had put Surpanakha to shame. She had been overwhelmed, for the first time feeling a twinge of mortification. She was afflicted with that same coursing emotion now.

Surpanakha gave the girl a look of respect. Dignity had overruled grief.

'Lakshman beheaded him with the Indrastra,' warned Malyavan. 'It won't be a pleasant sight.'

She nodded and left the room, elegant even in sorrow. Ravan suddenly stood up and rushed out of the room. All were taken by surprise. But Mandodari lifted her face from her hands, stifling her sobs, and quick to realize where he was heading. She ran after him. Surpankaha was puzzled and went to the window to watch from above. Ravan had reached the Ashok garden, the naked sword, his Chandrahas, glinting in the sunlight, his stride purposeful. Her heart skipped a beat. *He is going to kill Sita!* Trijata who guarded Sita fiercely, was not to be seen. That was fortunate for the girl for Ravan would have surely killed her in his present, demonic fury. It was the unexpected figure of Mandodari who interceded and stopped him, coming between him and Sita, grabbing his raised hand, her fingers clamped firmly on his thick wrist. Surpanakha could not follow the conversation but from what she could glimpse, the distraught Mandodari was the only one to have the power to halt a grief-stricken Ravan from murdering Sita. She saw him sinking to his knees, his arms clutching at her waist as if to save him from drowning in depair, burying his face in the folds of Mandodari's sari, his massive shoulders shaking, weeping unabashedly with long shuddering sobs. She saw Mandodari gently place her hands on his bent head, holding him, both weeping for their dead son.

Surpanakha felt herself go cold, then warm with the flare of frustrated rage, the heat fanning her face. The sight had moved her: but it did not stop her hating him. She hated him more at this very moment; more than ever before: a hot, livid hatred. Why was he so broken, so frenzied in grief now when he could have stopped it? Just a few hours ago, he had taunted his son to lay down his life for him. Meghnad had.

Ravan does not deserve such a worthy son. He deserves no one, nothing but a shameful death. Why could he not just die and spare the others? If he had stepped on the battlefield the very first day and confronted Ram as I had hoped, the others need not have died. He had allowed his brother, his nephews, his cousins and all his seven sons to die for him. What was in him that inspired such loyalty and love?

Kaikesi

They—the women of the palace—had been sitting together all day but the afternoon seemed interminably drawn out, as the great war came close to end. It was as though, sitting there for hours in silence, no birds chirruped, no elephants trumpeted, no horses neighed. Even the crickets had ceased to sing, and rain drops on the heated earth just prolonged the wait. Somewhere far off there was a storm, and it was approaching across the sea into their country, Lanka. The storm tossed the sea, the waves tall and furious but the moment they reached the beach of Lanka, they fizzled into a quiet, soft foam, their energy, their vitality spent, the anger drained, strangely speaking of the peace coming from the violence. Like the eternal sleep awaiting us, mused Surpanakha.

With the stillness after the squall, amidst the rising heat, at dusk, came the news. She got what she waited for so many years. Ravan was dead!!

She allowed the news to sink in, to savour it, to live that one small moment of utter bliss. She had waited long for it. She wanted to hear the minutest, the most lurid details as the news poured in. And yet, she was strangely assailed by fitful images of the long-forgotten memories of the past—Ravan helping her swing the sword as she practiced, his roar of hearty laughter, the quick jerk of his head as he spoke.

She remembered him as he was last evening: eerily at ease

and prepared during his last night of his life as he prepared for the final day of the war. It had seemed that this was the first time she had seen Ravan so relaxed. Or was it his quiet acceptance of defeat? Ravan had played the veena for some time, stringing a melancholy raag that tugged at her frozen heart strings. It was like a peace offering to all who had died for him—his brothers, his sons, his family, his soldiers. He continued late in the night till Mandodari begged him to stop. He relented and instead picked up the Ravan Samhita, his book on astrology, but to her, watching him closely, he seemed to be reading with unnatural slowness. He had fastened his eyes on one passage and he kept them there a long time before he turned the leaf. Was he seeing his life, his lost future and that of his family, doomed because of him in those pages? His lips moved a little. He might have been praying: they were all about to die. Had he, as the situation grew darker, lost the sense of responsibility, like a lost warrior who abandons his chariot and no longer bothers to watch the oncoming spear or the swinging sword?

Surpanakha could see him in the battlefield. He would have been less of a man of action and more of a philosopher most at his ease, waiting passively for the end.

But she would not allow these intrusions of nostalgia blunt her moment of joy. Hate was bitter but revenge was always sweet. When she had sensed his hour approached near she had shut her eyes and watched him die: saw him gasping for his last breath, the last shudder of life in his body, a final relaxation of the muscles around the hard unbeaten mouth, before those amber eyes closed on the immense weariness of existence...

Killed by Ram as she had planned. But more than the proof of his death, it was that strange sense of fulfilment that he had died a lost, broken, defeated man. It filled her with exaltation. Ravan had died a hundred deaths before he was killed by Ram's single arrow penetrating the navel which carried his nectar of immortality. She could see him as he lay in the battlefield, his arrogance spent, his power and knowledge come to nought, lying in a pool of his blood, dripping into the hard ground of the battlefield, the glory and pride ripped away like one of his mangled limbs strewn beside his corpse. Surpanakha rejoiced. It was over. She was at last rid of him. Lanka was rid of him.

But Lanka would survive without its old king. It was time for a new king. Vibhishan, in his pious pomposity was getting ready for the coronation to be held tomorrow. All would be in full attendance including the victorious Ram with Lakshman, Sugriv and Hanuman, who would be flying out to Ayodhya, the same day on the pushpak viman, Vibhishan had so graciously offered as the swiftest means of transport.

She heard a movement behind her. The women had returned from the funeral. It had been a sober affair, lacking the grandeur befitting a flamboyant king like Ravan. Mandodari and her mother, both leaning against the other, together in their grief, sharing the loss of the one man they had both loved unconditionally. Mandodari slipped into her chamber quietly but not without surveying her with a deliberately impassive manner.

Kaikesi walked slowly towards her daughter, her dusky face aged and lined, creased and crumpled and ancient in its intense sorrow. Her skin was like a translucent parchment, the wrinkles a fine web on her still beautiful face.

Kaikesi waited until she was close, then she slapped Surpanakha hard. Surpanakha was stunned, not prepared for her mother's violence. Her head jerked to one side. Then her mother slapped her again.

Her honey-toned eyes widened, flaring. She stepped back, her hands going to her flaming cheeks, staring at Kaikesi, bewildered. But suddenly she calmed down, allowing herself a small, secretive smile.

'We now share something, Ma. That same, tearing grief, of seeing our sons die before us!'

'Get out!' said Kaikesi tonelessly. 'Before I hit you again!'

Kaikesi looked down at her with the inflamed eyes of a mother who defends a dying son.

Surpanakha raised her blotchy face, defiantly.

'That is all you could do, Ma, hit and scream!' she said

unpleasantly, her voice even, her eyes steady. 'I have not forgotten anything!'

'What do you want, you devil?' hissed Kaikesi. 'I have not forgotten anything either. What a wretch you were from the day you were born! How we have resented each other. How I hate you just like you hate me...*Why*?' she cried. 'I was your mother and you were my child but yet...' her voice sounded baffled. 'What did I hate more; your ugly face or your ugly nature? Those sweet manipulations of yours, turning brother against brother, wife against husband, mother against daughter. You snatched my mother away from me too! You think I never saw through you?'

'No, you didn't,' said Surpanakha with a long sigh, a crooked smile on her cracked lips. 'Never. You would not have guessed what I had in mind all along.'

Kaikesi gave her searching, incomprehensible look.

Surpanakha returned the look, watching her mother, motionless like a tigress about to spring on her prey, her eyes alert and unblinking. But she was not going to let this tall, white-faced, haunted-eyed old woman off her hook, nor let her shift her responsibilities nor let her salve her conscience so easily.

'I killed Ravan. I trumped this war to have him killed on the battlefield by Ram. Just as he had killed my Vidyujiva. I suppose I gave him a more dignified death though.'

Kaikesi shook her head. 'I always knew you would harm my Ravan some day,' she said listlessly. 'That's why I wanted you to stay away from him, away from Lanka the moment Vidyujiva was killed. I know you planned it all the moment you exposed me in front of Ravan,' said Kaikesi. 'You snatched him away from me then, you made him hate me...!' her voice broke. 'How I loathe you!'

Surpanakha smiled, watching her mother work herself into a state of frenzied grief.

Kaikesi continued, 'You were always a little hellion. You deliberately set out to be difficult, making all those violent scenes trying to gain attention of your beloved father, tearing us apart, breaking the family, pushing us to fight and quarrel, yelling and screaming if you didn't get her own way! You did it to everyone, tantrums and tears and rage and rants. When you were older, you became insufferable! You were the one who weaned my husband from me. Which daughter does that?? You were a little fiend!'

Kaikesi began to move around the big room, beating her fists together. 'You were determined to ruin us! Why did I have to produce such a child! I just couldn't stand it any longer. God! It was a relief to get you out of my hair when you got married and I thought you would leave us forever, away from this palace, from us, from Lanka!'

Kaikesi's cold, hard eyes fixed hers, the rasp in her mother's voice brought ugly memories rushing into the darkest crevice of her mind. She looked at her mother, ranting. Her thin, wan face had that savage expression she had often seen when she had been incensed. It was there now but magnified in its growing madness.

'But Ravan loved you too much and was adamant of keeping that rascal husband of yours under his eye and you stayed put here! Again you tried to create problems with Sarama and Mandodari, Ravan and Vibhishan. They did drift apart; you got what you wanted! But then, mercifully, you left when that wretched husband of yours died...I was so relieved!'

Her eyes a glacial gold, she contemplated her mother.

Kaikesi gave a mirthless cackle. 'Of course I accept some of the blame for what went wrong with us. I've behaved selfishly—living my dreams through my sons; you could never be a part of it. You just did not fit in with our way of life nor we with yours. You were always an aberration. When you finally did leave Lanka, I thought it best to let you make your own life at Dandak. I was ready to give you your share of wealth and kingdom, but you never asked for it.'

'Why would I need gold coins in the wild jungles?' said Surpanakha. 'I was happier in the forest than in the palace. Be it at father's ashram or Dandak...'

'Aha! Your beloved father!' scoffed Kaikesi. 'He left you just as he left me! He never loved you know, you just liked to believe he did. It comforted you, giving you some sense of false security.

Or to pit him against me.'

Surpanakha said thoughtfully. 'Forget father, Ma. You never came to visit me. Not once. Not even when Kumar died.'

'Was I mad to meet you? It would have started all over again, those fights, those blame-game!' she made a savage little movement with her hands. 'You have no idea the peace I had once you had gone! We were so happy, laughing and merry... but then, *you* came back!'

Kaikesi looked strangely at her. Her eyes were remote. Surpanakha remained silent, allowing her mother to vent her venom. She had lost Ravan. Her grief had opened up all her emotions, the bloodiness of the tragedy splattering her very being, driving her slowly out of her mind.

'Yes, I came back,' Surpanakha gave a smile that did not touch her bleak eyes, dilated and large, like a snake about to strike. 'I got what I came for.'

Kaikesi leaned forward, her eyes glittering. 'Well, what did you come back for?' she demanded. 'Ravan and I, we have fought hard to come this far. We got back Lanka, we got back our glory, we got back our wealth, our happiness. But you, you undid everything! I was destined to have it all because of Ravan and lose it all because of you! Why did you come and sour our ambitions and make our lives a living Hell?' she paused, her breath coming fast. 'Because I have been unlucky enough to have spawned this hateful, spiteful animal! You! Each of my son was born to fulfil my dream of Lanka but I always suspected you were born a monster, born to ruin my family, my Lanka, the whole asura race!!' Kaikesi raised a shaking hand to her sweating face. 'You started the war and I had to watch everything burn before my eyes. A war your brother fought for you and died for you!' said Kaikesi shrilly, her eyes wild. 'A brother died protecting his sister's honour! You killed Ravan! I lost my Ravan because of you...he's gone!!!' her cry gurgled into a sob, her slight shoulders shaking in racking grief. She suddenly pounded her clenched fists at her. 'Why did my Ravan have to die? God! I wish it was you who had died a long time ago to spare us all this pain, you wicked little devil!!'

Surpanakha's smile died, replaced by a look of unamused incredulity. *How my mother hated me; probably as much as I hated her*, she thought dryly. Her mother's abnegation of reliving those painful memories made her yet believe in the goodness and glory of her dead son. Just like she blamed her. She lived through the make believe, the lies, the enactment of a life-long pretence.

Kaikesi clutched at her arm, 'Was it you or was it that Sita who made my Ravan die?' she screeched, her lips quivering. 'He was not to die, he was immortal. But for that one woman, that Vedavati... she had cursed him that she would bring about his death...but then who is Vedavati? Not you,' she pushed Surpanakha away, her puckered face twitching. 'Was it Sita? Was Sita-Vedavati? Or was Vedavati-Sita?' she burst out in a giggle, trilling long but soon it gurgled into a whimper. 'She killed my son! Sita killed Ravan!! And you wretch, brought her here to Lanka!!'

Kaikesi lunged at Surpankaha again but the younger woman stepped back adroitly, grabbing her mother by her wrists.

Kaikesi's raised, off-key cry had brought Mandodari rushing to the chamber.

'Why do you excite her?' she snapped, losing her composure.

Mandodari motioned a handmaid to take Kaikesi away. The old woman allowed herself to be led away, frail and meek, but suddenly swung round to again stare at her daughter through glazed eyes for a mad, chilling moment, then turned and went from the room.

'Can you not see she has lost her wits?'

'Perfectly,' retorted Surpanakha. 'It's obvious.'

Mandodari flicked her a look of contempt. 'Children have a way of paying back old scores, don't they?' she said mildly. 'Meenu, what more do you want from that poor, deranged woman? Is it because she is your mother and for the way she treated you in the past? Will you stop at nothing!? Leave her, Meenu, leave us. Let us be.'

Surpanakha grinned maliciously. 'I shall. I have no intention of staying here. Not even for Vibhishan's coronation. Or your second wedding,' she added spitefully. 'Quick celebrations after the mourning!!'

Mandodari's pale face flushed, the blood rushing into her lovely face. 'I have to do it, Meenu,' she said quietly. 'Not for my sake, for Indrajit's son. I am protecting his rights.'

'Politics of power, I could never understand the game,' laughed Surpanakha shortly. 'You play it well though. You suffered my brother all your life, never steering him from his wrongs. Were you weak, Mandodari or you were just not bothered? I always wondered!'

Mandodari regarded Surpanakha, her face expressionless, her manner distant.

'I was in love,' she said simply. 'I loved him, I don't know if it was right or wrong—I just loved him, despite all just as you loved Vidyujiva, Meenu,' she added sadly. 'Despite everything.'

Surpanakha's lips tightened. 'Aha, the favourite defence—Vidyujiva!' she paused looking straight into her sister-in-law's mocking eyes. 'You never cease to fling his name on my face. But he was not like Ravan, Mandodari. He forsook everything for me. He left his kingdom for me. He lived here in indignity, dismissively identified as my husband, as the "poor brother-in-law of the rich Ravan" not respected as the king of Kalkeyas, as he rightfully was. He suffered the humiliation, he endured my brother's taunts every single day. He did it for me. What did Ravan do for you, Mandodari? Heap you with the same indignity he reserved for Vidyujiva? Flaunting his women, parading his machismo?' she rasped. 'If you say Vidyujiva did the same, which I still refuse to consider, he had enough respect for me and my status as his wife, to be discreet about it. Or was it the heap of gems that was more enticing for you as the Queen of Lanka? Did the wealth and the position compensate for the daily humiliation? Difficult to give that up, is it not?'

Mandodari stared wordlessly at her, her eyes bleak.

Surpanakha continued, 'My husband did that for me. You might have regaled yourself as being a Queen, but you were definitely never your husband's Queen of Hearts!' she finished brutally.

Mandodari could not contain her contempt any more. 'But I was his strength,' she replied quietly. 'You will never understand.'

Surpanakha scoffed. 'Strength?? Was it strength or weakness? You were just too weak or more politely put, too mild for a forceful person like him. But yes, to endure him too needs a certain amount of strength.'

She glimpsed a strange emotion flit in Mandodari's calm, dark eyes.

'You have taken my all, Meenu—my husband and all my sons. I should hate you too, should I not? And exact revenge as you did? And so should Sulochana and Vajramala and Dhanamalini if all of us go by your mindless logic. We should despise you, seek our retribution. But I cannot detest you as your mother does. I can only pity you...'

'Mandodari, I don't need your pity. Or your hate. It does not matter. I got my justice,' smiled Surpanakha.

'Did you? Has the pain ended? Have you got your salvation?' questioned Mandodari, a tiny sneer in her voice. 'What do you have? Nothing. I have my grandson, my family...'

'A mad mother-in-law!' prompted Surpanakha irreverently.

Mandodari winced. 'You are heartless!! If she has gone mad, so have you, and a long time ago! Or who would destroy one's family, your blood, your son in your senseless war. You killed him too!'

'Kumar was killed by Lakshman, your new husband's new ally,' lashed Surpanakha. 'The same man who killed *your* son through deceit with the kind help of your future husband. Go, welcome them with open arms!!'

'I accept both Ram and Lakshman,' said Mandodari. 'I want peace. The war is over. But is it for you? I have a kingdom to be given as a legacy. What is your legacy? Hate and revenge? What will it give you now? Ravan is dead. He was a kind man and he allowed you here but where will you go? Vibhishan won't permit you to stay anymore. You started this war, you ended it the way you wanted it to end. You used all of us in your wicked little game. But, frankly, it was not the war that destroyed us. It was you. Ram, Sita or Lakshman were never our enemies. It was *you*! You, my family, a sister I thought I had,' she firmed her voice, her intention. 'And I don't want you here anymore. You are evil. You are Surpanakha.'

When Mandodari looked at the eyes of Surpanakha, they were like twin fire gleaming. It seemed to her that evil itself was looking at her—that unknown force that had torn her family, her love and all what she cared for

Surpanakha gave a short, brittle laugh. 'So many questions, and you seem to have all my answers!' she chuckled mirthlessly. 'I don't want to stay in Lanka. I would not like to live in a land where a king rules with a queen whose husband and son he killed.'

She had the pleasure to see Mandodari flinch. 'Is pious a new word for politics?' she asked pleasantly. 'You may gilt it, my dear, but the truth shows its ugly face, like mine. And you have no choice but to live with it—to live with the man who was responsible for killing Ravan and Meghnad. You hate me, admit it but will you hate him less?' she said in a conspiratorial whisper. 'And what about that sharp-tongued Sarama, will she spare you? You think she'll take this marriage of politics too kindly?'

Surpanakha saw Mandodari go pale, and just for a moment she felt a sudden, strange compassion for her. She did not deserve any of this, not even the fire of her revenge. Mandodari was the one who was left burning in that fire alone, the one amongst them, who had lost the most, and all for her faithful love for Ravan.

She sighed, and for some time, she sat staring out of the window, observing the sun rising from the sea, heralding a new day. The sea was quietly smiling, as the cool breeze whiffed through the open windows, the tide ebbing out softly, the previous day's work done and lazily stretching out to start another new day again. Her face was flinty, only the glitter in her eyes hinted at the turmoil that was going on in her mind.

A thin smile lit up her stone-like face. 'Be in your new hell, Mandodari. I am leaving Lanka. My work is done here.'

Ayodhya

*S*he would never look back. Ravan and Lanka were far behind, far away, but as Surpanakha strolled the streets of Ayodhya, she knew the shadow of both would fall on this city and its king and queen. She would see to that as Chandra, her new form. She had come to Ayodhya for them—Ram and Lakshman. *The righteous King Ram,* her lips curled in derision, *how hard he had tried to prove his wife as 'pure and pious' in a trial by fire at Lanka those many months ago. What a gift for Sita when he had finally freed her. Had he given her freedom or humiliation? Was it his defence or means of her protection?* Surpanakaha knew why Ram had done it, even earning contempt and censure for doing so. He had done it to shield Sita, to save her from public suspicion. The wise king that he was, he knew the fickle, doubting public would always wonder aloud and raise questions about those months of her captivity with a womanizer like Ravan at Lanka. The agnipariksha performed by his wife would prove to the world that Sita was innocent, pure and untouched so that no one would ever dare point fingers at his wife, the future queen of Kosala.

But she, Surpankaha, would play the same game; she would see to it those fingers remain pointed at her, at him, questioning both, with the shadow of Ravan between them. *I would keep the spirit of my brother alive,* she smiled viciously.

Pious. Virtuous. The words which defined the royalty of Ayodhya. That same king had called her unvirtuous. *'Lakshman,*

*take care of this unvirtuous, ruttish raksasi and teach her a lesson
she will never forget!'*

His words still burned, lighting up the glowing embers. That
fire would consume her someday but before that, she would
reduce their lives to ashes as well. She would see to it those
same words he had flung at her would be used to describe his
wife. His queen. His Sita.

All she had to do was start and circulate a rumour. And
soon, not just Ayodhya, but Ram's entire kingdom would be
discussing ugly gossip, this vicious mixture of truth and untruth
passed around by word of mouth and loose tongues. She had
just done that now while talking to the trinket seller, insidiously
implying the fate of their unfortunate queen in the hands of that
ogre Ravan. The woman had nodded. Surpanakha was sure she
would repeat it to her friends. That's how the word would spread.
Tomorrow she would come to the market again and insidiously
sidle the same innuendo into another gullible citizen of Ayodhya.
Soon it would be idle whispers, screaming aloud as scandal. She
had to simply wait and watch...

She hurried back to the palace of Ayodhya. She had managed
to get herself work here as a handmaiden for the finicky Mandavi,
Bharat's glacial-looking wife. She had been careful not to seek
employment either with Sita or Urmila. She might have changed
her form but she knew Lakshman was sharp and he would see
through her guise the moment he set eyes on her.

Lakshman, the name tore at her heart. She had reserved the
most brutal revenge for him—a life where he would beg for death
and death would be a release from the suffering she had planned
for him. But right now, she had to deal with Ram and Sita.

'Where had you gone, Chandra?' asked Anupriya curiously.
She was the chief handmaid of Urmila.

'To buy some trinkets for myself. The ones here are so pretty!'
smiled Surpanakha. 'Not like the heavy ones we have in Lanka.'

Anupriya brightened. 'You wear trinkets in Lanka? I thought
everyone was decked in gold and silver, the city is so rich that
there is not a single poor person there. Is that true?'

'Yes, it is a land of plenty, a land of golden dreams,' said Surpankha wistfully, surprised she missed Lanka.

'Then why did you leave such a bountiful country and come here to Ayodhya?'

'Because of my father. He is a small time trader,' she said shortly, wary of revealing more information than necessary. She had to deflect her curiosity. 'As I said, the trinkets here are more delicate and fine.'

But Anupriya refused to be distracted. 'Tell me about Lanka. All of us what to know more about it. After all our king defeated yours, the famous Ravan of Lanka!'

'And our queen was captured by him and kept in captivity,' piped a voice snidely. It was Ruta, the kitchen maid. 'Did you know what happened? Did you ever see the king?'

Several of the other girls nodded their heads vigorously. The older maids looked at Surpankaha expectantly. This was her opportunity.

'Of course, I saw our King. He was the most handsome man— tall, fair, with golden eyes which used to shine as bright as his crown...but yes, your Queen would know,' she smiled. 'She was with him for almost a year! She would certainly know better!!'

Some girls giggled, a few women frowned.

'Can you draw him?' asked Ruta.

Surpanakha grunted in feigned horror. 'Draw? I am no artist! Scribble would be a better word!'

The girls laughed loudly.

'What are you girls giggling about?' asked a soft, sweet voice.

Surpanakha's blood ran cold. It was Sita. *What was she doing in the kitchen? Which queen visited the royal cook house*, she fumed, a wave of panic smothering her.

'Welcome, my lady,' smiled Anupriya. 'We are done with the lunch as you had instructed. More ghee even in the rice because our king likes it so. The lentils and vegetables have been simmered in ghee as well.'

Sita progressed into the kitchen, smiling and stirring the pot to check the consistency of the dal.

Surpanakha kept staring at her.

'Stop gazing, you fool,' reprimanded Ruta. 'It's disrespectful. Keep your eyes downcast!' she hissed.

'What is she doing here?' she hissed back.

'Our queen loves to cook. She is involved in every meal right from collecting the herbs to laying the table!' whispered the maid. 'Especially now since she is pregnant.'

Surpanakha's eyes narrowed into gold slits; she had arrived at the right time.

'So what was the joke about?' asked Sita again. 'I heard a lot of laughter. '

There was an awkward pause.

'Yes?' prompted Sita encouragingly.

'We were talking about the King of Lanka,' said Anupriya hesitantly. 'How he was defeated by our King,' she added hastily watching Sita's face go pale. 'We were praising King Ram.'

'But then our Chandra claimed that King Ravan was a very handsome man, as she is from Lanka,' interrupted Ruta slyly. 'She said you would know better!'

Sita's eyes had gone bleak but she forced a smile. 'Who is this Chandra?' she asked instead.

Surpanakha found herself being pushed right in front of Sita. She kept her face lowered. Not that she would have been recognized; she was a slim, young, girl of sixteen now. No one would be able to guess her to be the dreaded Surpanakha.

'You are from Lanka?'

She nodded, her eyes still downcast. 'I am sorry, my lady. I was missing my country and I was talking about our King and how happy the people were in Lanka. They asked me about him and I described him and they were teasing me if I could draw him. I cannot eke a steady line,' she explained. 'But we have all heard you can draw very well. Could you draw him instead please?'

Sita looked a little startled.

'Please, my lady, we want to know how that monster whom our dear king killed looked like,' pleaded Ruta, insistently.

'Please!' It was a chorus now and Sita reluctantly obliged with a quick, uncertain smile. She took some rice flour and swiftly drew some lines, a rough, incomplete sketch and stopped abruptly.

'I am no good at this!' she sighed. 'Urmila is the artist in our family.'

And she stood up decisively, leaving the kitchen hurriedly.

There was a short silence at her abrupt departure.

'She sure looked troubled!' observed Ruta.

'She would be! He was her captor!' defended Anupriya angrily. 'It was silly of you to ask her to draw him! How insensitive could you be Chandra?'

While they were talking amongst themselves, Surpanakha had swiftly completed the unfinished portrait.

'Yes, I was impudent,' she agreed. 'But see how beautiful she has made him! She was being modest when she said she was not an artist, she has brought him alive in this picture...look!!'

And so it was. Ravan looked so life like that he seemed eerily real, almost like a presence in the room. They looked at the portrait in open fascination. He was indeed a handsome man.

'He is better looking than even our king!' said the irrepressible Ruta.

'Hush, this is outrageous. If the King comes to know, he'll throw us all out!' exclaimed the old cook.

'Why should he?' flared Ruta. 'If the Queen could be with this man for so long why can we not look at his picture?'

'Impudent child, mind your tongue!' shouted the cook. 'And wipe off that image immediately. I want no further talk on this!!'

But the image refused to be scrubbed off. All the maids tried it, all the retainers, the servants, the footmen and the lackeys. None could wipe the picture from the floor of Ram's palace and that was how the rumour first started milling around within the palace walls.

The old cook ordered the mason to change the flooring of the kitchen but the damage had been done. From the palace, the whispered talk wafted through the walls to the city outside, to the countryside and spreading swiftly and surely, from a rumour to a raging scandal.

'She drew the picture with all her love that was why it did not get wiped off...'

'She was with that rake the whole of the monsoons, how could he not have laid a finger on her?'

'Our king killed the enemy but the he could not kill the ugly rumours...'

'It's strange she is pregnant now after all these years...our king is a fool!'

And as the stories got more vicious, Surpanakha realized she had done the needful—she had smeared the good name. As opposed to her something said, she now waited for something done. It took an angry washerman who threw out his wife because she took shelter at a boatman during one stormy night to bring matters to the king's court.

'Our king can accept it. I will not. Get out!!' the washerman had said.

Ram reacted in the manner Surpanakha had expected him to. Torn between being husband and king, the king in him took over to perform his duty even if it meant letting go of the woman he loved. That she was pregnant did not deter him. He told Lakshman to leave Sita in the forest. Lakshman did as he was ordered but from what Surpanakha could gauge from the palace talks, Lakshman did not take it too kindly. For the first time he questioned his brother, his idol, his king. He could never forgive either himself or his brother for the deed done. Surpankaha was surprised as she had not expected Lakshman ever to rebel against Ram. He did it this once for Sita. Urmila was more voluble than her husband though.

'Does public opinion matter to you more than your wife?' she charged Ram openly, her face tight. Surpanakha saw she was fighting for her sister, for her tarnished reputation and for the relationship that had got swayed and shattered so easily. By the whiff of a mere rumour.

Urmila was relentless in her censure. 'When you left for your exile, I recall the people of Ayodhya begged you not to go. They followed you till the River Sharayu, imploring you all the way.

If what they say matters to you, why did you not listen to them then?' she raged. 'You should have stayed back at Ayodhya and obeyed them, not your father. How is it that the voice of the same people becomes a verdict for you now against my sister? Why do you lend your ear to their ugly allegations, some loose talk that will die its own death? Why is their word the last word? And why should Sita suffer for their crime? She was presumed guilty when she gave her trial by fire. She was exonerated then, was she not? That agnipariksha was a test for the people, for society as well—to think twice before casting aspersions on others. So now why did she again have to face the test of your people? You did it so that none could criticize the future queen of Ayodhya. But could you stop those malicious tongue? Where is the famous justice this Raghuvansh family, this dynasty of the Ikshavakus are known for? I demand it for my sister!' she cried.

But no one heard Urmila. Her pleas, her fury, fell on deaf ears, blind eyes and hard hearts. Surpankaha was reminded of herself—she begging for her husband, shouting for justice but none had heard her as well. Not Ravan nor any of her brothers or her mother. Urmila too was screaming at a heartless man, a heartless family.

Surpanakha realized with a start that too much good was bad. Being good could be bad. It had done Sita no good, it had done Ram no good either. Seeing the family being torn by this single decision of Ram suffused her with an odd sense of satisfaction. It was but a small part of the retribution she had desired and designed for them. But that she could witness it first hand, right in front of her eyes made the pleasure she so derived, more meaningful. It was like when Ram, Lakshman and Sita had witnessed her humiliation and disfigurement. They had damaged her face; she had damaged their family and reputation beyond repair. Her nose had been chopped off: she had severed the ties between husband and wife: now dishonoured, disgraced and shamed. It was what each of them—Ram and Sita and Lakshman— were enduring now, she revelled in grim contentment.

Urmila threatened to leave the palace and join her sister. So did the other two cousins, creating an immediate crisis in the family. It was an open revolt by the women. Lakshman took control of the situation. It was only when he implored his wife, almost grovelling at her feet that Urmila stopped herself from leaving him and Ayodhya. *They loved each other truly*, Surpanakha decided with bitter graciousness. She had hoped her ruse would be able to tear both the couples away. She had succeeded with Ram and Sita but with Lakshman, she had not. Urmila had saved him; she loved him too much. In fact, the tribulations had brought the two closer as never before.

But Surpanakha would not be so considerate; she had a different plan for Lakshman.

Lakshman

*I*t was an evening which, brought back the memories of her childhood—the dimming lights and the wafting smell of sandalwood. She remembered her father standing in the palace, she tugging at his hand desperately, his voice filling her with pretended hope. The hope had exhausted for a long time since then. So many years ago...

Surpanakha blinked; she was in Urmila's chamber, looking down at the sleeping baby, a small smile of contentment on his pink, puckered lips. Her breath caught in her throat. Like her Meghnad. And her Kumar. The serenity on the infant's tiny face threw Surpankaha into a whirl of vivid memories: Kumar and Meghnad as toddlers, waddling into her open arms, their smiles wide, toothless and trusting. Dead, but so long ago that she had almost forgotten how they looked....was that how time healed wounds? How deceptively facile. But she would not allow herself to forget anything. She could not, she would not. She had come here to kill Lakshman's son, Prince Angad. All she had to do was smother him with a pillow. No one would know, or maybe few would guess. But her stiff fingers could not close on the small cushion. It mocked her. A warrior-princess about to kill an infant. Was that how brave an asura she was? Was she as wicked? Has she stooped so abysmally low? Had her vengeance made her such a hideous monster? Her mother had been right after all...she was a monster.

Left alone in the chamber with those gushing memories while gazing at the sleeping baby's face, Surpanakha listened to the echoes of rushing memories: Kumar crying, Meghnad's last words to her, Vidyujiva's whispering in her ear, Ravan's hearty laugh, Kumba's warning words lingering in the stillness of the falling dusk. And she thought, musing, that this was another episode in her life, almost drawing to an end, and nothing was left of it but a memory, flickering bravely like a flame in a storm, the past mingling with what was to come. Her heart contracted, feeling strangely moved and sad, and conscious of a slight remorse...

'Who are you, what are you doing here?' asked a voice sternly.

Surpanakha stiffened, touching the cushion lightly and turned to face the suspicious eyes of Urmila. Each time she looked at Lakshman's wife, Surpanakha was struck by the serene intelligence that shone from her face. It was a face of more intellect than beauty. And Lakshman loved this face. And she planned to strip it of its beauty as he once had hers. That was why she was carrying out the plan she had reserved for Lakshman. Kill the baby and rip his wife's face.

Lakshman had killed her son, and she would do the same. But she had had to wait till Urmila had given birth to Angad, now fast asleep in his cradle, oblivious of the murderous danger he and his mother were about to face.

Surpanakha stirred.

'I had come to return your combs, my lady Mandavi had borrowed,' said Surpanakha easily. Urmila's fascinating comb collection was the talk amongst the maids. One had giggled how she had seen Lakshman tenderly removing it from his wife's hair, freeing her thick mane from the constraints of the comb. Surpanakha looked at it before handing it to Urmila. *Another symbol of their love*, she thought bitterly.

'You may leave now,' said Urmila abruptly.

Surpanakha made no motion to leave. She stood still, her fists clenched, struck by an unexpected chilling numbness. She found herself immobile again—in action and thought—afflicted by that same paralytic pang of conscience. Her will and wit betrayed her, as she could not bring herself to attack. She could not assault and kill a harmless baby. Or his innocent mother. She was shocked with the helpless feeling that she felt herself go cold with fear. What was wrong with her, why could she not kill the two people whom Lakshman loved most dearly? That had how she wanted him to suffer, that had been her plan for revenge: murder the son and disfigure his wife's beautiful face. She trembled, not in frustration, but the fear of the act, the dastardly brutality of her intention. She was nothing but a lowly, heartless, cold-blooded murderer. Her hand touched her face in mortification.

'You are Chandra, aren't you?' said Urmila suddenly. 'Mandavi's handmaiden.'

Surpanakha nodded mechanically and forced her feet to move. With a resigned horror, she had to admit that she could not harm either of them. *Why?* she thought desperately, *why am I feeling so incapacitated? Was my shame and conscientiousness stronger than anger?* She was confused, scared, unfamiliar feelings coursing into her frozen veins. She would have to leave the chamber before she gave herself away. She dragged her feet and tried to move away, wanting to suddenly flee and slowly started inching backwards.

'Wait!' Urmila's sharp order stopped her in her tracks.

She glanced back and her face turned pale. Lakshman was standing behind his wife, tall and menacing. She had avoided meeting him the entire year she had been in the palace, not trusting her reactions to him and the gnawing fear that he would recognize her. She felt a shiver run through her as she saw him so near, for the first time since she had come to Ayodhya. *Was it fear or fury? Or the reaction to the memory of brutality of his violence? And what was he doing here; he was not supposed to be here in Ayodhya, but at Anga to visit his sister Shanta who was unwell.* She had planned it such: to do the needful in his absence.

'I need your help with my hair as well,' said Urmila, flashing a wide, warm smile. 'Since you are here, could you do it, please?'

Surpanakha swallowed. She could not trust herself to speak. Not with Lakshman casting her that long, probing stare. His frown deepened, marred his handsome features, his full lips thinned in displeasure, his smouldering eyes narrowed in mounting suspicion. His face hardened visibly and his hand crept to the hilt to his sword.

'She is not what she claims to be, Mila,' he said softly, coming to stand between her and his wife. 'Take Angad and leave the room. Call the guards.'

Urmila was quick to realize what he was implying but Surpanakha was faster. She was standing closer to the cradle. She snatched up the pillow, hovering it close on the baby's sleeping face.

Urmila's hand went to her mouth, her face waxen, her mouth opened in a wordless cry.

'How long have you been here, Surpanakha?' said Lakshman quietly, a nerve beating at his temple, naked contempt flicked in his dark eyes.

Surpanakha choked back an angry sob. That cool, indifferent look he had given her told her as no words could his opinion of her. What really hurt her was that she knew his opinion of her was the same as her own.

'Long enough to get what I wanted—infliction of the same injury, that same insult in return for one that you made me suffer,' she hissed, the cushion precariously close to the baby's cheek. 'I saw to it that Sita got dishonoured as Ram had disgraced me once, divested of her status as you divested me of my beauty. It just took a rumour started by me to spread the fire...'

Lakshman took a step closer, his face white with cold fury. Urmila grasped his arm, but her eyes were on her, clouding with sudden anger.

'It was you! You schemed all this! It was because of you that Sita was banished!' whispered Urmila hoarsely.

Surpanakha marvelled at her loyalty. Even in her moment of personal danger, Urmila could think only of Sita.

Surpanakha smiled mirthlessly. 'Sita is gone. Just a tiny rumour drove her out of this palace, out of Ayodhya, out of the kingdom, no more a queen but a vagabond in some forest!' she smiled, her lips twisted in open scorn. 'You can start thinking about yourself and your child, my lady. Your husband might kill me right now but before I die, I shall do what I have come here for!'

'You are the devil!! I should have killed you when I had the chance!' swore Lakshman, his eyes glittered in anguished rage. 'But instead I listened to Ram and sliced off your nose. I should have beheaded you!'

'I would have preferred death to what you inflicted on me, Lakshman!' she cried. 'You made me suffer so much for so long. You disfigured my face, how would you like to see your precious wife's mangled as well? I don't need a sword to cut off the nose, my nails will do the needful!!'

She had the satisfaction of seeing his face go bone white, his dark eyes filled with fleeting terror, to be swiftly replaced by an exploding fury. 'You dare touch my wife and child, I shall make you die a death so terrible that you had wished you had never met me!' he rasped through clenched teeth. 'Don't make me kill a woman!'

She turned on him viciously. 'How does it feel to be trapped?' she spat. 'I know I will not get out of this chamber alive. But I won't kill you, Lakshman or your wife. Death would be too easy on you. I want you to live looking at her with that ugly, scarred face for the remaining days of your life, hating yourself, reminding yourself what you did to me, I did to her!'

She saw him tightening his hold on the sword. He had beheaded her Meghnad, her Kumar with that same sword, killing them both treacherously. She was swept by a fresh wave of sorrow. Grief led to rage and hate: she was caught in the whirl again.

'Living in dread already?' she smirked. 'How does it feel to watch the agony of the person you love? To see your Mila with her beautiful face torn?' she paused, watching the stillness in his eyes. He really must love her, she thought wildly, the fear in his eyes spoke vividly. She should have attacked her when she had the chance. And smothered the baby. 'Or to know what it means to hold the dead body of your child in your arms?' she continued, choking, her amber eyes smudged with glistening grief.

Her words seem to unarm Lakshman, a faintly puzzled look on his lean face. 'What has my son got to do with this?' his frown deepening, his one arm still protectively hovering over his wife.

He was moving closer to her, his sword still in his other hand.

'You killed my son!' she cried. 'Or are you a filthy liar too, noble prince of the Ikshvakus?'

'I didn't!' he breathed, a hot flush on his face, his eyes blazing. 'If I killed him in the battlefield, I did not know of his identity. In war, you kill the enemy, not a person.'

'You killed my hapless son when he was meditating, you heartless coward! In Dandak, remember?' she choked. 'Why, *why* did you have to kill him??' she sobbed in futile fury.

Lakshman looked stunned at her ravaged, grief-stricken face. He suddenly froze, struck by a thought. His eyes widened in quick comprehension.

'That boy...he was your son?' he said disbelievingly, so softly that his words came out as a harsh, soundless whisper.

She continued to stare at him, her eyes unblinking, giving a slight nod. 'Do you deny it still, you wretched soul??'

'No!!' His hard face crumpled, his hand loosening the grip on his sword, his eyes confused, a haunted glint in them.

Surpanakha found she had the opportunity to strike at Urmila with her one free hand, her nails bared, but watching him distracted, his face contorted in an undecipherable emotion, she stood rooted to the floor.

It was a terrible sight, like a man gasping for breath, hope sapping away, smothering in despair. He stood uneasily still like a tree about to be felled and it was on Urmila's gentle touch on his shoulder that he moved. He stared at Surpanakha and never had she seen such tortured eyes, smouldering with charged emotions flitting on his anguished face: remorse and repentance, guilt and penitence. To witness that rush of those emotion was like a watching a dying man, his heart ripped open and bleeding, baring his soul. It unnerved her, like a long, gushing wound with the gurgle of blood spurting out. She almost stepped back, flinching.

She had been expecting wrath and loathing in his eyes, like she was used to. Instead, what she saw left her floundering. In the background, she could vaguely see Urmila's pale face, her wide eyes, agonized, restraining Lakshman's arm yet protecting him, steadying him as he swayed slightly.

He stepped towards her unsteadily. Surpanakha braced herself, ready for his attack, holding the cushion closer. He was holding his sword in a tight grip, his knuckles white. And what he did next was entirely unexpected. He sank to his knees, trembling, but his eyes were steady and so were his stretched arms, holding out the sword at her. It was a gesture of abject surrender, the prisoner before the king, guilty as accused.

'I did not realize that it was your son I had killed,' he started slowly. 'All I knew that it was a young, innocent boy who had died under my reckless sword,' his voice faded, throbbing with emotion. 'But it was not a mistake, it was a crime, a dastardly one I could never own up. It was a crime I have never forgiven myself, haunting me each day and night for the past years,' he shut his eyes briefly. 'Today I know whom I murdered. It was me, Surpanakha, who killed your son and I accept any punishment you give me,' he said unwaveringly, handing her his sword and bowing his head slowly to expose his bare nape, where when struck the head would be decapitated from his body. Like he had Meghnad's, she flinched. And her son's.

She took his sword in her nerveless fingers, staring at the bare expanse of his neck. All she had to do now was to raise the sword and strike precisely at the base. From what Malyavan had taught her, it was not easy and it needed tremendous strength. But she was sure her pent up rage and vengeance would give her enough strength to kill him in one stroke. But she found to her growing horror that she simply could not. She barely managing to grip the sword and gauge its weight. She could not kill him! She did not have the courage in her to draw even a trickle of blood, she thought hopelessly, her hands falling at her side.

And in that moment she realized why she stopped: it was not shock. It was compassion. In Lakshman she saw her dead

Vidyujiva, in Urmila she saw herself and in the tiny Angad she saw her Kumar. She could not hurt any of them. Not him, his baby or his wife. It would be history repeating and in her hands lay the power to repeat another tragedy. She had wanted this for so long, she had yearned to see Lakshman suffer and live through his pain, his last days spent in agony over a lost child and a hideously scarred wife, reminding him of his transgressions. She had wanted him to suffer what she suffered. Not just the physical pain but that heart wrench of rejection, of having none to love. But she could do neither. Conscience or compassion, what stopped her? She faintly recalled Kumbha's last words to her, '*Compassion heals suffering...*'

Compassion. It was a new, raw feeling, coursing through her, strangely draining yet filling her with fresh, buoyant emotions.

She let go of the sword, hearing it fall down with a heavy clatter. She glanced at Angad. He had slept through the crisis, even the crash of his father's sword had not woken him up. Either he was born lucky or lazy, she rued with dark humour.

Lakshman's bowed head snapped up and he gazed at her in anguished incredulity. His sword lay at his feet. She stood standing over the baby's cradle, her face lowered in abject misery. She was no longer Chandra but the Surpanakha he had maimed in violent anger. He could have grabbed the sword and killed her right there, but something in Surpanakha's dead, hazel eyes, her slouched shoulders and the stoop of her slight frame displayed defeat. He saw Urmila gently picking up the fallen sword and handing it back to him. He could not take it, he kept staring at the wounded woman.

'I was not planning to kill you anyway, Lakshman' confessed Surpanakha with a weak grimace. 'The punishment for you was to make you suffer through your wife and son,' she looked vaguely at him. 'But I found I can't kill a child or harm a woman. I always knew we asuras were proud people without sentiments but now...' she shrugged wearily. 'Are you going to kill me? It would be a release!'

'I cannot kill a defenceless person,' he said quietly.

'I am not vulnerable, I have my nails,' she said listlessly.

'You are defenceless, with no further motive to goad you,' he said. His dark eyes smouldered. 'How could you forgive me for killing your son? I have not, I can't forgive myself!' he muttered savagely, under his breath.

'Possibly that was your punishment—to suffer in guilt,' she said hollowly. 'I was not meant to give it.'

'But you meted it to Ram and Sita,' he whispered, he looked up, his eyes twin pools of despair. 'They were innocent unlike me. Why spare me and not them? Could you not have been as kind to them?'

'Kind!' she laughed. 'I am not kind to you, Lakshman. The sword which you gave me to behead you, might kill you one day,' she warned ominously. 'It's your future I can see. You disfigured me at the insistence of your brother. You heeded him blindly when you were ordered to leave Sita in the forest,' She saw his jaw clench. 'It is this blind love for your brother will kill you one day!'

'I shall accept it,' he said bleakly.

His words, Surpanakha oddly reminded her of Kumbha's unswerving loyalty to Ravan. He had died for his brother.

'And what about you, Surpanakha?' intervened Urmila softly. 'What future do you see for yourself?'

'None,' she said simply. 'I have nothing to live for anymore. My stubborn faith in a future which somehow will be better than today has long gone. I lived all these years on that single urge for vengeance. I got it, partly through Ravan's death, through Sita's disgrace, and through Ram's anguish. The last part I had reserved for Lakshman.'

Urmila nodded. 'But you did not get it because you did not do it,' she reminded her. 'You were a victim too. Of your wrath. Not just Ravan and us.'

Had it been a helpless baby which had killed the fire and the fury? Or was it her shame? Or had it been repentant Lakshman at her feet, offering his life for the life he had brutally snatched from her? Or was it that swift look of empathy he had shared with her in a moment of grief and not seen her as the terrible woman that she was? Was it that one glance of acknowledgement that she had wanted from him, without the condemning contempt that had doused the humiliation of rejection?

She had to get away from here. She had lost her purpose but won some sanity, she thought wretchedly. Urmila's next words stopped her.

'Surpanakha, your revenge had become your friend. You had gotten so attached to it that you could not let it go,' said Urmila. 'I have lived through that too: I made grief my companion, tried to make it a part of me when Lakshman was away those fourteen years, killing me slowly. But then, I wanted to live for my Lakshman and that's when I discarded grief. I wanted to be happy, I wanted to live!' cried Urmila, throwing her an appealing glance. 'You have to allow yourself to be happy but not without letting go of pain and anger. Or you start believing that unhappiness is your destined happiness. In your sorrow, you consider yourself a victim and every victim prefers to believe they were innocently persecuted. But few realize that they are their own tormentors. You tormented yourself with your refusal to submit to a larger truth.'

'And what is that??' taunted Surpanakha. 'In those black moments, one usually has no faith, I had no faith at all.'

'Your search for peace, your anger of not being loved. Your rejection,' replied Urmila gently. 'For that, how many times were you going to take your revenge over and over again? All have suffered for their actions, can you not see that? There is no reason for your reprisal, each had to answer for their action. Even Sita,' she sighed. 'She wanted her magic deer, that illusion of happiness when she already had it! Ram had to learn what virtuosity truly means, he has to live it like a man going to the gallows, suffering and awaiting his final moment, his final justice. And Lakshman, shall forever remain the tormented man, tortured in his loyalty, suffocating in his guilt. That he killed your son. And that as her protector, he could not save Sita from disgrace and banishment. None of us can escape it.'

Lakshman threw his wife an appealing look, before burying his face in his hands.

Surpanakha glanced at both of them and saw Urmila for what she was; she was not just his wife. She was his soul, his conscience and she would always be with him, for him.

'None of us are innocent, all of us are guilty of our actions,' said Urmila. 'But we have to take onus for those actions, should we not? You cannot blame it on others or on fate to have created our fortunes and our misfortunes. It is us, Surpanakha, we have none to blame, or absolve, but us. There is no escaping our responsibility.'

Surpanakha shook her head. 'Urmila, you have a soul of a saint or is it a scholar? You try to correct my morals, and yet I didn't do much that's wrong, not really wrong, did I?' she said self-deprecatingly. 'I killed my brother, my family, ruined Ram and Sita and make Lakshman endure a worse fate. That is the story of my life.'

'If it is any solace to you, all of them never stopped suffering since that fateful day,' said Urmila. 'Things were never the same again. How much more will you punish them? Worse, how much more will you punish yourself

'Your baby exhausted my thirst for that punishment,' stated Surpanakha a distant look on her face. 'He doesn't deserve for what his father did. Nor do I want him to be an orphan like mine was...it was all because of *me* and now let me end it, once and for all.'

It was said very simply without rancour or rage or reprisal: all seem exhausted. A person's conscience is not simple, Surpanakha had thought she had no conscience, that she was a simple asura woman, who could not unravel what motives, what temptations and self-delusions she had. She stared at her hands, the talons long and sharp. 'My mother was right, I am a wicked person.'

'You are an angry person,' corrected Urmila.

The older woman's face trembled, her lips quavered, screwing up her eyes, then suddenly put her hands to her head and broke into sobs. *What despair, what grief was in the older woman's face!*

Urmila thought. It seemed she could not make out the reason of the tears, and she had a guilty, agitated, despairing expression, as though she had omitted something very important, had left something undone.

'You are angry with the world,' continued Urmila gently. 'You did not feed on violence and revenge, you yearned for your lost world.'

Urmila's perspicacity was too gracious: it allowed her wickedness to be treated with undeserved kindness.

'Is that how you see it?' sighed Surpanakha. 'I don't want forgiveness; it cannot undo what I have done. No one can forgive me. Memories can make monsters too. It seems an odd thing for a sister to become a murderer, but I suppose I'll have to pay for my transgressions; I was too busy making others pays for theirs. I do not want to shift the guilt,' she said with great seriousness. 'I shan't blame it on faith or fate. I suppose you think I ought to find some way to forgive. Even my brother. And Ram and Lakshman. Perhaps even my mother. She wasn't such a bad person after all. Children hate too easily,' she sighed. 'I didn't want you to suffer my fate. Or your child.'

'Because of Lakshman?' said Urmila softly, as always acutely sapient and gently discerning. Those eyes were a complete give away—something she could not conceal. They were the unhappy, puzzled eyes of a person who was suddenly not sure of herself, who knew she was going the wrong way, and not strong enough to do anything about it.

Surpanakha felt her hear skip a beat. Urmila asked too many questions. The only questions of importance were those which a person asks himself. Why could she not get over what Lakshman had done to her? Because he had rejected her. Because he had not reciprocated his feelings which she nursed for him.

She regarded Lakshman. He looked a stricken man—suffering and defeated. In the innumerable lines of premature age which crisscrossed the handsome face, she thought she could detect a wrestle of agonies, like a wrestling of fighting demons. Urmila was correct; he was not the man she had met at Dandak. The pride had been broken, the anger doused and in its place was guilt, raw and corrosive. It was eating into him. The guilt that he killed an innocent boy, the bigger guilt that he could not stop Ram from banishing Sita and that it was he who had left her in the forest. He had got his punishment, she realized wearily. *Would he have been able to take more of it,* she wondered, *if I had killed his child and deformed his wife?*

She cannot hurt him any further. She gripped her hands together, struck cold by the dawning fact. A few minutes before there had been a moment of closeness, of sympathy, even of friendship between them, but that moment had passed. She and him, they were each alone. It had never been hate, but her fury of rejection. She had yearned for him and his acceptance of her and she was still searching, still yearning for that acceptance: searching, stumbling and falling. But now she was too weary to get up and fight.

She was tired. Tired of it all.

She got up, dragging her feet, walking slowly out of the chamber almost unnoticed. She wondered with a sense of resignation, even of relief, whether this was going to be the climax of vengeance. She stopped at the doorway and glanced back.

Urmila was holding Lakshman, his head buried in her neck, his tall frame racked with slight shudders. Their love flowed between them. She paused, moved by the poignancy of the sight, the image she would reserve till the last breath in her body. She was reminded of a sobbing Ravan with Mandodari. The men needed their women, and often they did not know it. Love, trust, respect were words to utter, emotions to experience but what about need? That ambiguous void that is necessary to be filled yet oddly lacking? That need to have someone with you, to live with all your life...

She walked away from them, away from the palace, away from Ayodhya, far, far away. She realized she was still walking; she had been walking for days and weeks now; she did not know where. Lanka? Dandak? Or some random shelter in this kingdom? Or her father's ashram? She was not aware even if her father was alive. But she was sure she would not be welcomed at either places. It did not matter anymore, nothing mattered any more. All was over, she had nothing left in her.

Was regret considered a matter of choice? She had lost all those she had once loved: Vidyujiva, Kumar, Kumbha, Meghnad. For whom could she go on? A fleeting image of Meghnad's little son swept before her dulled eyes. Her heart contracted. He was at Lanka, her Meghnad's heir, who had the same shy smile, large, amber eyes with those incredibly long lashes like his father's. He was the hope of Lanka—that golden city that glowed in its quiet resplendence even when fallen and bruised by war. And she had been the princess of that land: Lanka's Princess.

Lanka, she whispered to herself, and she found herself drawn towards it...she could smell the sea, hear the same monotonous, hollow echo of the crashing waves. She took a step, and then another and another: she was walking deep into the ocean, the waves lapping high at her ankles, rising up from below, echoing of a strange peace of eternal sleep.

She closed her eyes shutting off the sight of the rising waves, hearing instead the sound of the sea she had always loved. And in the rushing sound of the water, she heard a constancy, a complete indifference to life and death. But within its churning waves, she listened to the hidden sounds of silence, the peace of eternal salvation, of the unceasing movement of life upon earth, of unceasing hate towards forgiveness, of violence towards peace, and that peace towards perfection...

That perfection, that happiness of sitting beside a young Vidyujiva who in the dawn seemed so beautiful, and they together so soothed and spellbound in the magical surrounding, she cradling a baby, the soft cheek warm against hers: was it Kumar or Meghnad? Then through her closed eyes she again saw the ocean, the cool mountains, the sinking clouds thinning to a hazy mist, the open sky...Surpanakha thought *how really everything is so beautiful in this world if one makes the effort to see it; everything except us, ourselves. What we think and what we do, when we forget our human dignity and the higher grace of our existence. I had lived a dead life, would I die a better death?*

Take me to Lanka, she begged to the foaming waves. She kept walking, ignoring the sinking sand, the crashing waves, and soon she felt the sifting ground under her feet giving way to a bottomless, dark abyss and the sea gently closing over her. She smiled as she again shut her golden, staring eyes to the eternal peace of that swirling darkness.

Epilogue: Phulwati

'Surpanakha forgave Lakshman,' said Kubja quietly, tears rilling down her lovely face. 'Did that forgiveness wash away all her hate and revenge, anger and anguish?'

Krishna nodded. 'It is all about acceptance. And rejection. Hate turns to love, despair to hope, grief to happiness, life to death. Her lust for revenge turned to repentance the moment she accepted him and herself.'

'But could she ever forgive herself?' asked Kubja. 'She got almost all of her family killed. She couldn't live with that yet in her last moments she wanted to be with them...'

'Her body was found on the shores of Lanka,' said Krishna soberly. 'She was cremated with full honour. As the princess of Lanka.'

'Is that why I was born a hunchback, to live my life of misery and humiliation—to pay back for all what I did?' she whimpered. 'To live without family, love or respect? Is that the retribution? But then, I wasn't accepted in this life too...' her lips quavered.

'But I have, dear, I have accepted you,' he said softly.

Krishna smiled and in his smile he could see a certain future, one which the unsuspecting woman beside him could not see but who would have to live it once more...

That in her final quest for Lakshman's acceptance, Surpanakha would be reborn, many centuries later, as Phulwati, the fiesty daughter of a local chieftain, in love Pabuji, the hero of war and the fiercest warrior of their clan and the reincarnation of Lakshman. They will decide to marry, but on the day of the wedding, he will be called to war, leaving his seven pheras unfinished and his bride alone, to never return, dying on the battlefield. It was like before, Krishna decided—Lakshman the eternal celibate warrior refusing to accept Surpanakha, and she, eternally unrequited in his rejection.